Hal Porter was born in Melbourne in 1911. While writing, he worked in country Victoria as a school teacher and librarian. His published works include three novels, th… f poetry, seven volumes … biographical works incl… *Balcony* (1965). These *Se*… 1971. Hal Porter died in 19…

IMPRINT CLASSICS

SELECTED STORIES

HAL PORTER

INTRODUCED BY
FAY ZWICKY

ANGUS & ROBERTSON

An imprint of HarperCollins*Publishers*

AN ANGUS & ROBERTSON BOOK
An imprint of HarperCollinsPublishers

First published in Australia in 1971
by Angus & Robertson Publishers.
First paperback edition in 1972.
Reprinted as an A&R Classic in 1975.
Reprinted 1977, 1982.

This Imprint Classics edition published in 1991 by
CollinsAngus&Robertson Publishers Pty Limited (ACN 009 913 517)
A division of HarperCollinsPublishers (Australia) Pty Limited
Unit 4, Eden Park, 31 Waterloo Road, North Ryde
NSW 2113, Australia

William Collins Publishers Ltd
31 View Road, Glenfield, Auckland 10, New Zealand

HarperCollinsPublishers Limited
77-85 Fulham Palace Road, London W6 8JB, United Kingdom

National Library of Australia
Cataloguing-in-Publication data:

Porter, Hal, 1911–1984
Selected Stories.

ISBN 0 207 16158 5.

I. Title.

A823.3

Cover: Country Street Scene, *1959*
Sali Herman born 1898 Australian
Oil on canvas, 44.2 x 75.8 cm
Purchased by the National Gallery Society, 1959
Courtesy National Gallery of Victoria, Melbourne.
Printed at Griffin Press Limited, Netley, South Australia.
5 4 3 2 1
95 94 93 92 91

INTRODUCTION

Audacious romantic invention was hardly the name of the literary game in Australia of the 1930s. Words pressed into fictional service in that barely articulate culture aimed for naturalistic accuracy, and adhered to the bleak truths of intellectual and emotional deprivation in depressed rural and urban settings. So, when a 'word-haunted ephebe' began publishing baroque, uncategorisable prose-poems called, for convention's sake, stories, earlier readers may have been understandably surprised, irritated and bemused. Fifty years down the track, I suspect that today's responses will be little different, the irritation possibly intensi-fied by changing social ideologies.

'Après mot, le déluge' was James Joyce's jokey assessment of his role as linguistic catalyst: it could just as well have been Porter's in the Australian context:

> Leather land! Old man land! No animal, no one, trod the mottlings of unendurable browns except outrider dust mopping and mowing, spiralling on feckless feet, willy-willy dodging emptiness in emptiness.
>
> 'The Daughter of the Late Bishop'

Australia, evoked by a poet with obsessive, headlong energy, rhythmic cascades of sound, impressionistic spurts of colour; a poet at the mercy of mood and memory. Above all, an artist who wore language like a life-support system the better to survive and bear witness to the ruins of childhood Eden.

The progress of the life is inseparable from the growth of the artist's imagination. The perception of the self as a separate being occurred very early in Porter's development but, paradoxically, was linked to a very close involvement with his mother:

> One's mother is the inescapable first being one senses in detail. For years all the others are blanker surfaces. It is impossible to realize that others have flaws one knows she has, that her sins and graces are, greater or weaker, also theirs. Her firstness is her power; from her: early good, early evil, but, oh, early reality.
>
> 'Act One, Scene One'

This early reality is, of necessity, a skewed affair of intense love and hate. It will colour his fiction from the beginning to the end of his writing life: its premises will remain immutable. Behind the sensitive child, all senses on full alert, caught in familial miasma, stands the other self, the alienated hero-observer of Porter's autobiographical *The Watcher on the Cast-Iron Balcony* watching himself watching life:

> I seem to be often watching, now and again with Mother a shape behind my shoulder, but most often alone. This watching, this down-gazing, this far-away staring, is an exercise in solitude and non-involvement.
>
> *The Watcher on the Cast-Iron Balcony*

That clinical detachment sits naturally with the self-generated objectivity of the monkish, Flaubertian artist. It will remain with him long after he has left that childhood balcony, both prop and bolster to the essential narcissism of the artist-as-child. It will not save him from the pain of living or from the need to craft those masks of personality we call the writer's 'characters': 'I have watched myself watching the small suburban creature, the uninnocent good boy,' says the narrator of *The Watcher on the Cast-Iron Balcony*, and we know the life ahead will make for uncomfortable fiction.

We meet this self-conscious boy observed with the colder adult eye in the opening story, 'Revenge'. He is stuck in a railway compartment with a woman of theatrical dimensions 'like a great vase gusting out scent'. Gust and disgust run neck and neck. He misses nothing, forgives nothing:

> He flicked one glance at her flung-open fur coat, the dress that was a fluid screen of huge poppies, the operatic spray of boronia, the gorgeous *maquillage*. One glance placed her. He went on reading.
>
> 'Revenge'

This thirteen-year-old has *read,* indeed. Omnivorously and precociously as only lonely country children can. On this occasion it's de Maupassant's *Boule de Suif,* its chilly cynicism appropriated to shield the boy's puritan squeamishness in the face of extravagant female carnality:

> He knew what he was reading. It passed inexorably through the mincer of his mind: no gristle of bestial behaviour disconcerted that machine.
>
> 'Revenge'

The brutal metaphor points the way to later images of women described with an equal blend of fascination and horror, the detail sometimes verging on the hysterical in the intensity of its moral recoil.

Mothers and maiden aunts have left potent legacies to Australian artists of both sexes, larger-than-life visions of corrup-tion and purity cast in the idealistic crucible of childhood. Mothers first, then. Perhaps because our daily lives have been long on masculine stoicism, but short on histrionics, dramatic colour and animation, the jackdaw paraphernalia of hetero-sexual femininity has been grasped at by both writers and painters as a life-giving imaginative stimulus and a handle on the absurd. Taken to his mother's room, Porter produces one of the many talismanic catalogues summoned to keep him moored to her stagey, chaotic reality:

> There: half-open drawers voiding camisoles, stays and petti-coats; there: hat-pins, hand-bags, ring-trees, curling-tongs, bangles, hair-rats and -switches and -nets, atomizers, dyes, tangles of amber beads, fur necklets with mean noses and

eyes, spirals of dusty hair wound off tortoise-shell combs, fuzz snipped from her armpits, toenail cuttings . . .

'Act One, Scene One'

The mother, mistrusting her own feelings as woman and mother, confronting failed conjugal reciprocity, hoards her props, spreads her social energies in the theatrical entertainment of strangers, assuming the role of aesthetic arbiter, mouthpiece of conventional conscience, and factotum of misrule:

> She was curdled, perverted, unintelligent, silly as a bantam. I loved her passionately . . . She listened, eyes enlarged with stupidity and belladonna, to *her* son, her production, making prim sentences, performing monkey-tricks from her scroll of small-town middle class duplicity.
>
> 'Act One, Scene One'

The readiness to settle for vicarious fulfilment through her male offspring has a familiar Lawrentian ring, as does the son's savage resentment. Such mothers ignited the creative fire in their sons, fed it with their own unsatisfied needs, fracturing their sexual identity between heterosexual and homosexual strains. Patrick White's mother was portrayed more abstractly in his autobiographical memoir, but the star-turn is as capricious as her son is acidulous:

> Ruth, the titular mother, bound us to her by a series of surprises such as changes of dress, presents, tantrums, powers of organization, and bursts of general knowledge. But she wasn't always there, what with committees, the fittings, the luncheon and dinner parties, or else she was lying down with a headache or falling arches.
>
> *Flaws in the Glass*

We're close to Sunset Boulevard with these unpredictable predators, forerunners of megastar Dame Edna: high camp sharpened by pantomime and vaudeville, armpit fuzz and falling arches the nails in illusion's coffin.

It's interesting to find that in the year Porter published 'Revenge' (1937), the robust sardonic swirl of William Dobell's brush was bringing Mrs South Kensington's thrusting nose, scornful mouth and censorious eyes to garish life. During the Second World War, the theme of female coarsening and vulgarity deepened its acid tracks in Dobell's 'Tattooed Lady' and in Albert Tucker's savage 'Victory Girls' with their dangling parodic breasts and macabre vermilion grins. The iron cage of Australian provincialism has housed some rare, ambivalent birds in its time, the songs their mothers taught them far from ideologically pure.

I have referred to some of Porter's artistic contemporaries not only to catch a whiff of the historical ambience, but also because I anticipate hostile reaction on the part of some readers to Porter's surges of misogyny. What, for example, are we to make of the following sentence from 'Vulgar's the Word'?

> Women are most harmful when their bodies think they are at rest and they think they are thinking.

Rooted in an ethic of male superiority, his unregenerate aesthetic may repel an audience purged by post-War feminism. I don't like it myself. However, it would be a pity if this kind of lapse (and there are many) were allowed to deter readers from appreciating other remarkable aspects of Porter's art.

Maiden aunts are another story altogether, as we have learnt from Patrick White. Their sexless, ancient wisdom and survival strategies represent a stay against change and decay, and Porter gives a moving account of the young adolescent's yearning back towards the untainted certainties of early childhood in the haven of his aunt's 'old-time immobility'. Nurtured by 'apples, raspberry vinegar, brown eggs, butter pats, lemon cheese, quinces' (Porter's catalogues are never random, each item an exuberantly precise token in a broad associative stream), the devout eye moves on to 'red-and-white-beaded milk jug covers, bentwood Vienna rockers, biscuit barrels crammed with rock cakes, the chromo-lithograph of Queen Alexandra' ('At Aunt Sophia's'). His sense of place is matchless, the feverish accumulation of detail catching the spirit of the age with stunning particularity.

The train journey to his aunt's house is a magical promise of paradise:

> Already, trees are drinking and grazing along one, two, three sunny rivers. The train chants through the green ball-room of autumn where the nude gums, the half-burnt magpied gums, circular-waltz in vast arcs to the rear. Swagmen logs are prone among sheep; dove-coloured smoke flees past windows.
>
> 'At Aunt Sophia's'

The Arcadian glamour of the natural world interacts with the boy's buoyant romanticism in a lyrical flight as heady and hypnotic as Dylan Thomas's 'Fern Hill'. Colour, image, fantasy transmute the historical facts, creating a shimmering web of illusion that, for luminous beauty, is unrivalled in our prose canon. Afloat on words, intoxicated by their physicality, Porter's vision is nonetheless precisely grounded in the mundane, his insatiable passion for its engorgement and possession suggesting a deep need for anchorage in the ordinary as a means towards self-definition: these exist, therefore I am.

The very concreteness acts as a safeguard against the charge of self-indulgent 'poeticism' and romantic effulgence of the swoon variety which mars so many exercises in nostalgia. Given Porter's idiosyncratic syntactical inversions, compound words, onomatopoeia and alliteration (often confused by readers with poetry), he sails close to the rocks but, miraculously, seldom founders.

At his least effective, Porter can be mannered, affected, and cruel, particularly when dealing with women and foreigners. At his best, the true lyric voice infuses individual patterns of emotional recollection of place, freeing us from those fixed linguistic codes engendered by preconceived naming and classification.

The aunt's garden 'where a little boy once found skylarks' nests and snake-skins', where 'magpies gargle ecstatically', and where 'house and beehives dodge out from the mulberry trees', epitomizes prelapsarian bliss. The aunt herself is imagined in a mist of tremulous, near-maudlin aestheticism that assigns her the status of a minor deity without apparent irony, the icy perception focused on the mother noticeably absent:

> He closes his eyes. Dressed in black, yet, yet, what is the colour? It is unique, a mirage; through its gleam the flower-stem fibres of her kindliness, the blue of her love, all the subtle and overlapping shades of her stubbornness, eager searchings, knowledge, superstitions and, sometimes, unpredictably, the opalescence of a smile so exquisite that her withered lips and false teeth are only the paper on which a deathless sonnet has been engraved.
>
> 'At Aunt Sophia's'

By contrast, there are sharp, spunky aunts observed with earthier admiration. In 'Great-Aunt Fanny's Picnic', for example, a plethora of aunts assemble for a photograph, disclosing their conjurer's marvellous comic flair:

> With their tweedy aunts, with wavering aunts, champagne-bottle-legged golfing aunts, tittuping aunts and Burne-Jones aunts, they advanced towards and grouped themselves below Uncle Eustace who had mounted, civic-statue-like, the top of the vault . . .
>
> 'Great-Aunt Fanny's Picnic'

Idealization of the past often goes together with an excessive sensitivity to corruption and decay which Porter saw as characteristic of the world into which he was born. He also knew, with a poet's insight, that without art the human spirit disintegrates into the anonymous statistics of history. If writers have a part in defining and preserving the sense of a culture, the lyric poet has a stake in reminding us how it *feels* to be a repository of ancestral memory. He not only brings to the task the singular associations of sights, sounds, sense impressions that constitute a distinctive identity, but also records communal observances and pieties which are the manifestations of his origins and moral heritage. These, in turn, help us to sustain an inner life in a country which has shown cavalier indifference both to the preservation of the past and the resources of a living language.

Porter's best stories are, in a sense, elegies for lost innocence, a theme which, in 'Country Town', is expanded into a rich, poignant lament for the death of old maiden aunt Australia. The town's past is juxtaposed with its present reality in the mind of an observer who has never stopped looking and listening. His 'nostalgic, just tearless eye' recaptures and recreates a loved world, loved unsentimentally 'as one might inescapably love a hypocrite uncle as boring as immortality and with the points of view of a blowfly'. Porter's Melbourne of the 1930s is so irresistibly evocative of my own childhood that every detail sent seismic shocks of memory along the spine:

> Gone cabby, rabbit-oh and fish-oh, John Chinaman greengrocer, the dago ice-cream cart and its bell, the Hindu old-iron man, the scissors-grinder, the Afghan pedlar, and all their clockwork nags which wore in midsummer their earholed equine millinery above wowserish William S. Hart faces; gone the mediaeval pageantry of hearse-horses, Black Prince plumes, the top-hatted undertakers in cutaway coats. Gone what was called the night-cart though it came, two-horsed, also in daylight . . .
>
> 'Country Town'

The writer is fleshed out with the substance of what he sees and hears. He devours time impersonally, breaking out of his dislocated anonymity as the watcher from time to time with a confessional burst rather like Whitman in 'Song of Myself':'I knew lies, carnality, happiness, despair, even viciousness and *ennui.*' Like Whitman, too, the surreal inclusiveness of his catalogues seems to encompass many of the deepest complexities and paradoxes of the human condition:

> Do the sleepless, the wide-awake dying, the woman in labour, the telephone girl on night-duty, the late reader, the insomniac debtor, the youth entangled in prayer, the adulterers under the river-bank horse-chestnuts, the High School teacher correcting algebra, the saxophone player limping homewards, do they all really know, when they hear the whistle that bores the night like an enchanted gimlet . . .
>
> 'Country Town'

Back on maiden aunt territory, even the town pianos are metamorphosed into Chekhovian spinsters:

> I heard only the melancholy of old-maid uprights behind fringed holland blinds. Fingers of unseen pale hands tinkling '. . . *I loved beside the Shalimar* . . .' where, indeed, are you now?
>
> 'Country Town'

The *now* is total dislocation, bitterly regretted, 'an Ionesco stage-set, a province without memories, or memories only of the day before yesterday', the haunt of displaced foreigners, the 'New Australians walking in the very heart now of our barbarians' luxury'. Sicilians, Albanians, Greeks, Latvians, Dutch, Germans, Hungarians, and the truly dispossessed — 'drunken aborigines under the Wy Yung Bridge, the voice crying, "You bloody dago bastard, you!" the male tears and threatening knife in the shadow of the tannery.'

Porter, born in Melbourne in 1911, grew up in Gippsland but left the country as a cub reporter in his teens. He eventually taught school in the city, going on to teach in Adelaide, Hobart, London, and to spend a year in Japan with the occupation forces. His last appointment took him back to Gippsland as a librarian, more specifically to his home town, Bairnsdale, on which the story 'Country Town' was based.

His stories reflect this migratory process, not just literally but metaphorically. His characters and the elusive narrating 'I' are always on the move, haunting and haunted figures in a world in flux. The seedy boarding-houses, bars, hotels of the adult world are substantial enough and yet, like the human inhabitants flitting like grotesque dream figments in and out of each other's lives, seem about to vanish into the wide sky. Arrivals, departures, loss and transience are Porter's main preoccu-pations exposed with varying degrees of charity through the sharpest eyes and ears in Australian fiction. In a spectrum ranging from farcical satire to tender lyricism, his achievement remains unique.

As a postscript, I think it should be noted that I did not choose the stories in this collection. They were chosen by Professor Leonie Kramer for an earlier edition for which she wrote a succinctly comprehensive introduction. Invited to write a new introduction twenty years later, I don't think that mine improves on my predecessor's. In fact, I was so symbiotically affected by the stylistic density of Porter's stories that I found myself ankle-deep in despised adverbs and adjectives for which, as a teacher, I'd once have prescribed severe pruning. Such is the effect of a brief association with a 'word-haunted ephebe'!

Those stories I have focused on give some idea of which aspects of Porter's work have interested me most as a poet. Had I made my own selection, it would possibly have included a few different pieces and omitted those whose impact has be-come more dated, more tasteless, or both. However, given the range and variety of Professor Kramer's choice, I am pleased to have had the opportunity to further explore the complexities of Porter's multi-dimensional, chimeric genius, warts and all. I hope new readers will find the venture equally worthwhile.

FAY ZWICKY
Perth 1991

CONTENTS

Revenge

The woman (expanded, velvety, a dahlia) and the boy (unexpanded, formal, a cold bud), each with a reserved seat, were the only two in that compartment of the country train.

He knew who she was.

She had not the faintest idea, my love, who the little brat could *possibly* be.

When she dramatically and vividly slid open the door from the carriage-corridor, there he disappointingly was. Outside—the organized hurly-burly of the city station, beyond that the ranting city itself. Inside—the waxwork boy already set square in his place, rug over knees, school-cap pulled straight, dead-straight, above his horn-rimmed spectacles.

He flicked one glance at her flung-open fur coat, the dress that was a fluid screen of huge poppies, the operatic spray of boronia, the gorgeous *maquillage*. One glance placed her. He went on reading.

She had scarcely arranged herself like a great vase gusting out scent, before the train started, feverishly coursed away from the city.

In an hour, the sooty girders, the clay cuttings armed with agave and yucca, the hoardings decoying with Brobdingnagian bottles of invalid port and miraculous soaps, the suburban stations of salmon brick and glaucous tiles, were all well behind. Behind, too, were the outrider housing schemes with their mustard-yellow doors, verandaless and treeless and uneasy. Now they were in the country the houses had verandas, vines and barge-boards; it was five o'clock; shadows swam out from old pines across the old green Gippsland paddocks in which stared the clown-white faces of Noah's Ark Herefords.

During this hour the boy did not move except to turn the pages of his book in an old-fashioned way, finically, but as though they were not weighted with lusts, despairs and anguishes, as though his spotless fingers and steady eyes were not in contact with distracted and venal lives, as though he were reading *The Boer and His Horse* or *Grace Darling*.

He knew, however, what he was reading. It passed inexorably through the mincer of his mind: no gristle of bestial behaviour disconcerted that machine.

While thus reading and mincing he had also filed what he knew about her. *One*: on holiday from boarding-school, he had seen her in *The Mikado* at the Mechanics' Institute Hall; the scenery had been restless, rain on the corrugated iron roof had obscured—professional Nature outdoing amateur artifice—much of the performance, but not the vicar's too strenuous Nanki-Poo nor her too fruity and voluptuous Yum-Yum. *Two*: he had heard her in the greengrocer's ringingly vilifying. It was something about tomatoes. "I am just not used to this sort of treatment," she had declaimed under the fly-specked witch-balls. *Three*: he had seen her several times in her small crimson car, leaning from it, always yackata-yackata-yackata. *One*, *Two*, *Three*—filed!

He knew her conspicuous and mockable, and that he had never seen her at any of his mother's cocktail parties. To him, that was all. That was not all to her.

She was engorged with loose affections, brimming with sentimental foolishness, loved talking on and on, imagined that children found her charming. The first time he raised his head from his book she was ready, hurled her smile like a hoopla ring; cigarette smoke flowed across her gold-shot teeth; with exaggerated graciousness, in the scented and fluting voice she used for men, she said:

"How far are you travelling?"

Was he staring at her? She could not tell because the near-setting sun had struck his spectacles to discs of brass like the lit lens-eyes of a robot. Meticulously, frigidly, he intoned an unnecessarily complete sentence:

"I am travelling from the city right through to the ter-min-us."

"Ah-ha!" she said, and executed a pink, kindly and silly laugh. "Right through, eh? To the terminus, eh?"

He made no reply. She could not see his eyes. His face was alabaster.

"That's a long journey," she said. She poured more syrup:

"That's a long, *long* journey for a little boy, isn't it now?"

The brass discs flared in her direction; the face continued immobile, but some subtle subsurface convulsion told her that she had over-melodiously sung the wrong bar.

"I am thirteen years and two months old," said an edged voice. "I am small for my age."

Then, with princelike patience, as though she would not understand but he must get everything absolutely straight, with a distaste and weariness suggesting that this had had to happen before: "However, heredity will rectify that. At thirteen, my father was very like me. He is now over six feet tall, and weighed one hundred and ninety-four pounds last holidays. Time will tell."

The point of a tongue delicately moistened his lips. "As well, I do not find the journey long. I make it six times a year, and this is my fifth year as a boarder. I relish reading in trains."

Finished.

He lowered his head, the light slid from his spectacles, his eyelids dropped, he was reading. Piqued at finality after an explanation frosted with reprimand, her screen of poppies stirring and smouldering, she could not restrain:

"What are you reading?"

"*Boule de Suif*," he said curtly, not raising his eyes. "By Guy de Maupassant."

His accent was flawless but she had no idea what he was saying—Barbara Cartland was her literary Everest.

Silence.

A little later, still without looking up, for he had seen already her gaudy bookstall magazines, *noblesse oblige*, he explained, "Maupassant is a French author. Nineteenth century."

Now he lifted his eyes to her. They were unflickering, unequivocal, disdainful:

"His themes are realistic and awesome. This volume is a translation. Naturally, because. . . ." He paused. He made a point. ". . . because I am only thirteen."

The intention of his last words, a reproof more oblique than she could understand, but an unqualified reproof, made her flush: she immured the gold of her teeth behind painted lips, she puffed defensively at her cigarette, as his eyes went back to the book she flashed, "You apparently like school more than ordinary boys."

When, after careful delay, he revealed his eyes they assessed her as though she were lunatic; she felt icy vermin race in her sheaf of flesh; her scent cheapened; her dress-poppies rusted; her fur coat, she remembered, was torn at the arm-pit. Thank God! she thought stupidly, I have on my new undies.

Implacably his wry voice decried her: "I enjoy certain aspects of school and certain subjects. The Head is awesome. The food is vile, although Heppingstone *secundus* abides it. Heppingstone is *mon ami* and, at the moment, we both hero-worship the tennis coach. We are passing through an unhealthy phase, but Heppingstone avers we'll outgrow it. I *think* Matron told him that. Matron is not awesome; she is unbearable."

His manner said *All women are unbearable* and *You are unbearable* and *Is that all, for God's sake?*

His voice said, "Forgive me if I go on reading. I am engrossed."

He read, and the train screamed in . . . approval? surprise? horror?

She butted her cigarette, screwing it to destruction, noticing that it was only half-smoked. She lit another, began petulantly to read her twopenny-coloured lies, and the train flung itself olympically through sunset and twilight into night, deeper and deeper into the country, while the obtuse and petal-shedding woman skimmed a no-world of sick charm, and he coolly trod among provincial bigotries, rivalries and lusts.

Now and again, clashing like a chain-gang and windily yawning, the train stopped at small stations; each time it did so its loneliness, unhomeliness and difference from the fixed and natural became more marked: out there and out there, thrilling voices were fired towards the stars and seemed to call "Home!" or "Love!" or "Life!" Girdling the horizon were tea-time lights in windows; she imagined table-chatter, a singing kettle, a cat asleep by the stove, a wireless playing *Ah, sweet mystery of life*! In this compartment there was nothing to sustain her, no one to exchange smiles, gossip and magazines with, no one for whom to unroll the velveteen bale of her femininity. Just as the train bared its flaring breast to the disregarding airs, so she must, as it were, uselessly bare hers to neuter immaturity, the sliding-door meantime squeaking like mice and trembling as though desire tenderly but resolutely tried it. From another part of the train she could hear Italians singing with fervent drunkenness; she jetted smoke from her nostrils, and felt like slapping the cap from the controlled head opposite. Little pip-squeak! she thought, stuck-up little cissy!

The train began to chant more slowly and throatily; its steeplechasing across the plain was over; it was climbing the foothills.

The boy closed his book: some foreseen moment had turned up. He folded back the rug, stood up, put the book in the rack. Noticing his tender grooved nape, her dislike faltered; faltered more when he took off his spectacles, and snapped them into their case. How much less canny and excluding he now appeared! He—the stern unblinking—mildly blinked, pressed his thumb and forefinger on his lids, rolled his eyes, blinked rapidly; finally, removed his cap and put it also in the rack. Curls! He had curls!

Amazingly, he blinked in her direction, spoke, addressed her!

He said, "Please excuse me if I lie down. I always slumber when the train reaches the Haunted Hills. Not that I believe what they say. Nor Heppingstone. But it's awesome, so I snatch a little slumber."

The woman said nothing, but she smiled; the freckles of gold in her teeth were like the freckles of gold in her brainless, expansive nature. Thus blessed, he decorously folded his compactness and certainty, eyes, nape and curls into his rug and stretched out, face covered, as the train laboured into the Haunted Hills.

Since pioneer times tales had been handed on that no bird sang in these hills, that cattle would not stay there after sunset; there were legends of hell-deep caves and spectre bushrangers. As the train fagged among them, no longer exulting and fanning wings of fire and loveliness on the night, the hills despaired, moaned, reverberated; the train now and then shouted passionately. The boy breathed toward sleep.

And presently the lover with whom the woman had spent several city hotel-room-nights peered through the transom-window, saw her lonely in her fleshy flowery beauty, slid open the door, closed it like a burglar, came to her.

"Darling!"

Through a sustained kiss the known bodies ratified past fulfilment, recommended and endorsed future experiences. Then the man, unplugging his mouth, indicated and questioned about with his eye-brows the rug-parcelled body.

Unmaliciously, heedlessly, the woman whispered, "Only a kid. Asleep. A little cissy", and donated herself again—overblown fragrance, an armful of panting summer—ah! The drunken Italians were whining *Santa Lucia*, one tenor wail skiting above the others.

Asleep?

No.

The opening and closing door had nudged the boy from half-asleep to fully-awake. Unable to see, he had heard everything: through the train's drudging in the hills, through the bleak echoes and the complaints of lust in worsted enfolding lust in fur and flowers, he had heard the silence of the kiss. Next he heard, "Only a kid. Asleep. A little cissy."

Rage shocked him. *Little* was a vicious swipe, *cissy* was a vicious swipe—one to each cheek of his heart. The cheeks of his face reproduced these assaults; he felt the aggrieved and blazing flesh.

Therefore, moveless, patient, he waited until he was sure the colour had waned, until his heart had faded cool and stringent again. Then, even while the train exhaled terror, and groaned in the spook-riddled hills, he silently sat up.

When the snap of the spectacle-case struck apart the two bodies, he was sitting erect, curls lidded down under the cap, rug across knees, face untenanted. He was polishing his spectacles.

"Oh!" cried the woman, as though someone had spat on her.

The man, surprised, glanced at her before aping a grin—too palsy-walsy—at the boy. He was the sort of man who would wear a ready-made bow-tie, and he wore one. It was speckled, and matched his twirp's socks. The boy polished on; the train clambered more desperately.

Confused, dismayed, the woman heard the man: "Well! A

spot of the old shut-eye, eh! And how far are you travelling, Buster?"

This time, she had no doubt about the revealed, the naked eyes; they condemned intrusion; the voice replied with callous politeness:

"I am travelling right through to the ter-min-us."

Her veins crinkled with horror; this scene had been rehearsed; a nightmare was being dreamed twice.

"Well!" said the man, and he touched his little bow with poise, with great poise. "Well, well! Right to the terminus."

Stop, stop, she suffered. *Stop! Say no more*. Yet she said nothing, sat with her sap stagnant, heard the dangerous sentence through to its end:

"Well, now! Long trip, eh? Long trip for a little codger!"

The boy replaced the polishing-handkerchief in his pocket before he said, with the chilly boredom of a priest weary of exegesis and embittered by its futility:

"I am thirteen years and. . . ."

"Please, dear," the woman said—quickly—placing her dimpled hand—how heavily! how mutton-chop!—on the man's sleeve. Oh, the man was shrewd, very. Though astonished at her, he caught on:

"Thirteen!" he roared. "Imagine me! Wow! I thought you were fifteen at least."

The boy: marble. Could statue eyes sneer? And what *could* he say?

"Well!" said the man. "Well, I'd best be toddling; I'll be saying toodle-oo." He pressed down on his worsted hams, pushed himself upright, said, "Nighty-night!" This was to the woman; regret, intimations of fun-to-come and I'll-get-in-touch informed it. He slid the door open, flicked a man-to-man grin at the boy and " 'Night, Buster."

The boy had on his spectacles now; he stood and reached to the rack for his book; his back to them, he said with saxophone clarity:

"Good night, Mr Paget."

At that moment the train reached the crest of the hills, and screamed long and exultantly. Behind it lay the songless slopes and unplumbed caverns, the city, the locked hotel room, consummation and contraceptives. The train, ripping open its jewelled breast, continued to crow while the transfixed woman and man eyed each other.

The machine's jubilation ceased; it began to hasten downhill; the man, stuck at the doorway with his pussy-cat bow, said to the boy reading the book:

"Well! So you know me!"

"Certainly, Mr Paget. I've seen you at your Moderne Emporium."

"Well, fancy that, now." The man was vaguely flattered.

The woman, her gestures over-sure and prolonged, lit a cigarette. The boy read.

Inspired—his head was screwed on—the man tipped her a wink meaning *Watch this, hon'*.

"Well, old man—" he began. The boy regarded him with dispassion.

"I wonder if you'd do me a favour. I'm playing cards in another compartment. You seem an intelligent type. How about keeping an eye on Mrs Paget here for me, eh? Can't leave the weaker sex untended, eh? And look here. . . ."

He knew he had the situation in hand, always had it in hand—how else build up Moderne Emporiums, own a motor-launch called *Whoopee* and a snappy eighteen-footer? He opened his wallet, fingered, displayed a ten-shilling note.

"Look here, as bloke to bloke, you won't be offended by some expression of gratitude, a little something to buy a . . ."

"Book! A nice French book. Nineteenth century," said the woman, recklessly presenting her golden fangs.

"This Maupassant cost thirteen shillings," said the boy.

Squinting slightly, the man replaced the ten-shilling note, and handed over a pound.

"I am very grateful, Mr Paget," said the boy. "I shall buy a Chekhov."

He did not smile, nor did he look at the man again, and, by the time he had folded the note and put it in a small purse and the purse in an inner pocket, the door was closed, the amused man had gone, the woman lolled smoking. The Italians were now quarrelling; the train, bold again, roared and flaunted as it hurtled downhill through the night. The boy was plunged in his pages of ardours and stupidities, and spoke four times in the next two hours, courteously, ritualistically, duty at five shillings a time:

"Are you quite all right?"

In answer the woman showed her gold-measled teeth offhandedly, for she could see now that the purchased boy was nothing more than a harmless, tinpot little mug, a lah-di-dah sook.

So, at peace, they reached the terminus, they descended from the appeasedly hissing train.

The woman went along the platform to the luggage-van but, "*Dolling*!" and "Dolling, daddy's getting your luggage, dolling," sang the boy's mother sprinkling his face with expensive lipstick and gin-sweet kisses. She was gay, gay; the platform astir with her exhilarated friends. "We're in the midst of a lovely *party*, dolling. Aren't we in the midst of a *lovely* party?" she cried to everyone. "Maxie's come to meet you, and Roddie, and Mary, and dear Auntie Lal . . . where *is* Lal, Bobsie? Oh, it's wonderful to have my enormous son home again!"

"Don't be awesome, mummy," he said, because that was what boys said, but he smiled around in a way he knew seemed shy and engaging at the same time.

His mother was as restless as a diamond: "I *wish* daddy would hurry with your things. Be a sweet, Maxie, and see what he's *doing*. He's *utterly* tipsy." Then she said, dazzling, to the boy, "Did you have a nice trip? You weren't . . ." her voice paled and abated, ". . . you weren't in the same compartment as those. . . ." She meant the Italians, squat men reeling by in striped suits of crumpled shoddy—unsinging, sullen in a nimbus of garlic.

"*No*, mummy. I travelled with that Miss Morrison. You *know*. She's awesome. She said I was. . . ."

"Morrison, dolling? Morrison? *Not* our village Melba!" And she laughed, and all the others laughed. "How wonderful!" they all cried. "How *wonderful*!"

"She's awesome, though. She had the nerve to say I was. . . ."

"Hist!" said someone. "For Gawd's syke!—the Morrison draws nigh."

As the woman, the flowery one, the dulcified and velvety, approached, the revellers were very occupied with gaiety.

There was much din. She saw the boy standing neatly in front, and she smiled her gold-stained smile at him, and the din seemed to increase. He cut it to the ground, reaped its jingling stalks to silence with his soaring, faultless voice.

"Good night, Mrs Paget," he cried from his Calvinistic face; and higher and more clearly in the silence, "Goodnight, Mrs Pag-et."

(1937)

Miss Rodda

It was wet today. A vast voice poured in above the cataracting sea, over the sullied beach, over the streaming esplanade. Tamarisks tormented themselves in the immeasurable monologue. My back to the sea, I lifted my head and saw the mansion in which Miss Rodda lives.

Designed by her architect father, the folly is narrow and lofty fantasy, a left-over from pantomime. It might aptly have displayed a *siste-viator* to buffoons in hooded cloaks with paint cracking on their grimaces, to masked dwarves, to Harlequin on a plum-duff horse with a mane like Neptune's. I expected the rain to dissolve the almond paste which must be the mortar of its gladiolus-coloured bricks, or a woman with a plush rose to appear and rest her bosom on the edge of one of the wrought-iron balconies.

Even downpour could not tarnish the gaudiness, nor the grey raving of the sea outnoise boulevardian airs from *Carmen* that seemed to be being played by a velvet-collared quintette with dirty finger-nails and Pernod breaths. Neither could my knowledge of the house's interior and occupants kill that aura of mawkish romance. Perhaps, inside, a word-haunted ephebe wrote on cards sometimes found in corridors or trinket-boxes . . . *Xanthophyll*, *Quince*, *Chinchilla*, *Eau de Lavande*, *Crocodilo* . . . words like signatures of Middle-European tenors. Or, maybe, among gossip-chairs of ormolu velveted by a primrose dust, faded some forgotten actress so frail, a weed-woman, that she must ever recline, posed for no claque.

My eyes climbed the windows hunting the white-leaded face and restless old mouth of this actress.

I found a face.

High at one corner of the house is an impurely romantic tower, red-tiled, with a circular window. At this was a doughy blob, the face of Miss Rodda which I had not seen for ten years. Then, it was not askew like the head of a hanged bird nor had it a lopsided smirk. Remembering, for the first time in years, my last encounter with Miss Rodda, I became embarrassed and was about to move off when it seemed that—despite the distance between us of space and time—her eyes turned and looked into mine meaningly as though we were centimetres apart and intimate. My embarrassment increased; I felt guilty, author of a crime too abnormal to be mentioned, forgiven or recalled. My cowardly eyes, eschewing her deadly stare, swung down and saw again the gate I had last entered when fifteen . . . ten years ago. . . .

It is Thursday. It rains. A vast voice hurls in above the careering waters. Tamarisks agonize in the immeasurable oration; my raincoat smacks like a fish.

My claws, senseless and violet, slip on the handle of amber glass. The gate lurches violently in, dragging my skinny body with it. I fight the gate shut.

Weak now that there is no wind to strive against, I almost fall on the asphalt separating house from fence. There are middle-class shrubs, infragrant, dirtily wet.

I do not go to the front door extravagant as a cathedral's. Miss Rodda, not looking at me, has said tonelessly, "You will not come to the front door. You will use one of the side doors. I shall show you which one." It is a small door that is entered from a long veranda partially glassed-in and having a floor of tiles with a blue sweat on them. To myself I call this place a conservatory. Indeed, as soles strike tiles, I whisper, from habit, "Conservatory!"

Inspired by this I imagine I hear my meagre quick aunt: "I've had a talk with Miss Rodda. Do you hear me? She's willing to give you music lessons; three guineas a quarter. That's really very cheap. But you mustn't say anything to anybody—do you hear me? She's giving lessons only to you. A favour. Something to occupy her time. *She* doesn't need the money, and she's not actually a teacher. However, she's studied under the best people—do you hear me?—at the Conservatorium."

Conservatorium . . . conservatory . . . a rabble of invalid ferns and begonias in green-painted tins with cut and curled edges. Stepping among these frizzed receptacles I hear the piano being played. Miss Rodda is playing. It is unbelievable that she can play such music—chill, fleet, sprinkling. I am tempted to look in corners, behind the tins, for a naked urchin of bronze hugging a bronze trout, a fountain.

I knock on the door.

The music, the fountain, goes.

I hear no footsteps. The door makes no sound in opening yet is open, and Miss Rodda stands there. She is dressed, as always, darkly. She wears, as always, her necklace of mud-green beads.

"You are late." These words have no intonation of reproach. Her lips scarcely move; the exterior of her face is so still with the stillness of something pendulent that it seems a sullen fruit blanched in gloom. It is as though not only the mechanism of voice and emotions is worn-out, but that some cardinal inner spring is broken, permitting the subtle outlines of face, coiffure, shoulders, breasts and hips to sag. Her feet should be large with down-drawn, unused blood. They are not. They are small; they take her swiftly into the house into which, by legerdemain, she shuts the air as one would a sick brute.

I follow her, distressed that she will suddenly fuse into the twilight within, will vanish and leave me vagrant in this cave of many rooms, many openings, many greenish windows behind which grope shadows. The house is stupefied, under-sea. Wind and rain have delivered up tone and potency; amorphous shapes, blundering shapes of drowned men, dangle sluggishly across the panes.

We reach the music room where, because of candle-light and a fist of fire and two pianos in which the three candles and the fire are reflected and re-reflected, there is more an atmosphere of warmth, of sharp edges and definite planes. The fire, however, does not warm me as I pass it; the Wedgwood plaques and caskets, the Sheraton barometer, the piecrust table, the congested marble of the chimney-piece, oppress me with their lifeless substance; here, too, bloated formlessness flounder against the panes.

Fronting the mean fire is an armchair, on it a plaid rug, body-rumpled. That is his, I think, that is Mr Rodda's; he has been sitting by the fire. I have never seen him, but imagine him: tiny, dribbling from a pleated mauve face, creeping away from rug and flame at my knock. He is tottering and shivering now in one of the rooms with all its doors and windows. There can be, I am certain, nowhere for him to sit: the absurd notion has months ago become mine that there are only two chairs in the house—the armchair and a neo-classical chair, lyre-backed, which sits before one of the pianos. Two chairs, one for him to occupy gnawing his old Mandarin-coloured finger-nails, one for her to use as she plays eternally and disinterestedly watery curves and sprayings of music, while purposelessly enclosing them in all directions are rooms of ponderous treasures, coffin air, aquarium green and nameless enervating emotions.

I take off my raincoat.

I wind my hands together furtively and painfully to warm them. It is useless.

I sit. The top edge of the lyre sticks into my back. I am forced, reluctantly, to use my voice which does not sound like my voice: "What shall I play first, Miss Rodda?"

"Your new scales"—as though she does not care whether I play or not. She touches her beads without being aware that she moves. I direct my hands onto the ice-bound keys of a piano unwilling to give up its noises. I press down my right thumb and my left little finger. There is a brief sound; immediately after this I am startled to hear Miss Rodda speak again:

"How is your aunt?" Her voice is tintless, but her unusual question and its unusual place disconcert me.

I lift my fingers and begin to weave them together: "She is very well, thank you, Miss Rodda."

She says nothing. In the silence I think, "She does not care if my aunt. . . ." The candle-blades do not move; the green wind gulps soundlessly at the windows. Once more, her voice from the dead of her face: "I told you to play your new scales."

Confused, hurt, I re-arrange my hands at the keys. I play. My fingers scrabble foolishly as crabs among the cold whites, the cold blacks. I make discords, begin again and again and again.

Is she listening?

She is not watching. At last, desperate, I rattle octaves down and up, marring triumph by merely one discord. I can do no better. I stop. She stirs, wavers like something water-sodden moves. She touches my shoulder. I stand. She sits. She plops her hands carelessly into the sneer of the piano. She plays octaves down and up, down and up, down and up. It is to continue thus for ever: she embroiders at some tasteless thought; she has forgotten me.

And then—horror!—she makes a discord, my discord. There is no sign that she notices this except an imperceptible pause, after which, as I stand squeezing hands together and expecting an unimaginable happening, she begins to play icily and easily the music of the fountain. While the fountain criss-crosses jets and arcs of frosty drops her eyes turn with incredible slowness towards me, and I hear her voice:

"How is your aunt?"

"She's—she's very well, thank you, Miss Rodda."

"She is very well? That is very nice. That is *very* nice." Her fingers glitter malicious water from the instrument. Then, frightening me, her voice takes on stinging colours:

"You have been coming to me for a year?"

"Yes, Miss Rodda."

"You—your aunt owes me for your lessons."

"I. . . ."

"Your aunt owes me twelve guineas."

"I—I suppose so, Miss Rodda."

"You *suppose* so! You—! Has your aunt any intention of paying me?"

I am appalled, humiliated. I do not know what to answer. I recall that my aunt has said, "It's a wonder Miss Rodda hasn't sent her account. You might say something about it to her—do you hear me?"

How am I to explain this? I try to speak, am ultimately able to squawk, "I think my aunt was waiting for your account."

The result of this makes me call out. Miss Rodda's hands flash from the keys; she springs up, knocking over the chair, and begins to speak close to my face in a rapid, flaming voice: "Account! Account! Account! Your wretched aunt had every right to send the money. Long ago. To send it to me." Her voice ceases in a tangle of unseemly sound. She is panting.

She almost runs to the chimney-piece and strikes her palm venomously on the marble. Swiftly she hurtles back to where

I stand like a gawk. Her eyes are open, the lids strained back from the slippery balls. I see how passionate and mobile her face really is; she is handsome—straight nose, black eyebrows. Colour gushes to her cheekbones, into her lips. Her teeth are white, white.

I am too ashamed and terrified to say anything. Indeed, the one explanation I have is too involved to be impartible. I can only witlessly watch emotions hacking after each other upon her face—outrage, despair, anger, hatred. Incapable of movement, I must see this last distortion intensify: her face thins, becomes mottled; her gums show; her eyes are again half-hidden by heavy lids.

She grabs my wrist; clips in her fingernails, and squalls hoarsely, "I must have the money—must—*must!* Go and get it! Bring it here immediately! Your wretched aunt—send an account!—she knows perfectly well I wouldn't."

She fiercely pushes at me; she is thrusting me out of the room, out of the house. Her necklace of beads snaps, disappears with a thick cry, leaving her sinister and more horrifying than before, unrelievedly impure and frantic. I stumble before her, dodging through a confusion of doors, beneath towering pedestals on which gesticulate monsters of metal. I feel that I am plunging through windows, the house shuffling apart about me; there seems a muffled clamour of seas and drunken winds through which Miss Rodda's voice flares like a knout, "Go! Go! I must have it! Bring it tonight! Go!"

I stutter, I babble, and as I flee for a great length of time my babblings and stutterings seem always behind me. "Yes, Miss Rodda, tonight. Yes, Miss Rodda, tonight. I'll bring it tonight, Miss Rodda. Yes, Miss Rodda, tonight."

At last, through the last of doors, the wind, rain-weaponed, bounds at me. A living gate with its inimical glass handle resists me. God! God! *God*!

I am catapulted, trembling, on to the beach. I walk, automatically, for days, years. I have left my raincoat behind and become saturated. I am horrified at what has happened; cannot conceive myself telling my aunt all those immoral, impossible things. At the same time I am inexplicably distressed for Miss Rodda; the wind rips from my mouth the endless tickets: "She *must* have it. She *must* have it. She *must* have it."

I arrive shivering, about to collapse. My aunt pounces like a jay: "Where on earth have you been? Late for dinner. Where's your coat? Where's your coat? Do you hear me?"

"I left it at Miss Rodda's."

"You what—? How on earth could you forget your coat?" I do not reply.

"Speak, child! How could you forget on a day like today? You'll have pneumonia. And what was that idiot of a woman thinking of to let you go without it? Pneumonia, that's what. She must be mad. Go and change—do you hear me?"

It is impossible to explain to my aunt, even to speak to her. I blame her anger for my silence although realizing that, had she not been angry, I should still not have had courage to mention either the twelve guineas or Miss Rodda's attack.

Thursday night rains by, wails by wind-whipped, creeps by with its tail between its legs.

I use Friday for the engrossing and subtle occupation of soothing my aunt.

On Saturday I begin to fret her with elaborate reasons for taking money to Miss Rodda. I disgustedly listen to myself saying such things as, "No, she hasn't mentioned it. But she's been looking at me queerly: it spoils my playing. Anyway, I've got to collect my raincoat—I'll pay then." I hear myself saying thus too many times.

On Sunday I am entirely devoted to my nagging; nauseated by the knowledge that my aunt will be ultimately influenced by her own common sense rather than my cock-and-bull rigmaroles.

On Monday, exasperated, my aunt peevishly scratches a cheque into existence. She vilifies Miss Rodda and threatens me with castor oil; she is sure I'm sickening for something—do I hear her?

I run, actually run, to the gate with the glass handle. I knock exultantly on the side door; I shake with excitement, my throat dry as a statue's. My knock touches off an engine of silence in the mansion. Behind this newly-started silence I uneasily realize another silence—the solid, infrangible silence that succeeds a cataclysm, the silence of utter cessation.

Suddenly, the lesser silence is patterned with footsteps. The deeper silence remains untouched. I listen dubiously to this silence and to the footsteps that make inexorably through wall after wall towards the door. They are not Miss Rodda's. They are too heavy—I am sure of it—to be her father's.

Ultimately I hold my breath to watch the door opening for a long time. When it is completely open, and not until then, I see a very tall, broad, flaccid shape. Strangeness, like a biblical pillar of smoke, blurs it and its great face. I know it is staring down at me as though I am striped pebble.

"Is Miss Rodda in? Please."

"No." Its voice is wide and profound; the sole word, reverberating back into the colossal husk, seems a paragraph. Gulliver in Lilliput, the shape awaits me.

"I have brought her money, the money for the music lessons."

A mass, a huge hairy hand, advances from the obscurity and with astonishing delicacy removes the cheque from between my thumb and finger.

Silence.

What shall I say now?

What shall I do?

I attempt to see clearly the shape before me. There is a buried roar and then: "I am Mr Rodda." The voice dustily drums through dark abbey tunnels in the Giant Despair body. "My daughter, for whom you have so kindly personally brought this acceptable cheque, is not at this moment in. No. My daughter is now a patient in the public hospital. She is, they tell me, seriously unwell. She cut her throat early this morning." I am so hypnotized by the sonorous echoing, by the soothing and involved modulation of the voice, that I scarcely comprehend the meaning of the words. Gradually the echoes breathe away within him. Scarcely has this happened when the voice begins again. This time it opens strongly; a blast of anger makes the timbre brazen rather than resonant and, while the voice remains turned inward, it *tells* me the censurable fact: "She used my *good* razor."

I seem to see Miss Rodda's face, and infringing on it more and more quickly like transparent shadows of windmill sails expressions of outrage, despair, anger, hatred and—terror. Then there is stillness, the silence she has left in the house, the silence of cessation.

As I retreat backwards, blinded by silence, prepared by

polite habit to say good-bye to the gigantic structure into which the cheque has vanished like white bat into midnight, I squeak, "I am too late!" Mr Rodda displays by no gesture, no comment, no slightest movement, that he hears anything.

"I am too late!"

What do I mean? For what am I too late?

Today, with head awry, face an unravellable knot of grimace and silence, Miss Rodda looked down from the tower window. She looked, through rain and time, into my eyes. Or did she?

It was absurd to imagine her eyes deliberately accusing from her aerie by the sea above which a cold, immense voice ranted of some nebulous but desirable freedom, a voice that, immured in her tower of tiles and lath, in the tower of her own havocked body, in the tower of her esoteric sorrows, she could not hear and will never answer now even should she hear.

It was absurd of me to think unhappily, as I looked up, of calling out, "I'm sorry, Miss Rodda. I'm so sorry. But I did bring the money as soon as I could."

(1937)

At Aunt Sophia's

Actually the journey begins while Gregory and everybody watch from edges of eyes two svelte horses fastidiously tipping the asphalt with the fore-rims of hoofs as a man wearing a confetti of chaff on his serge entices them—the archduke steed in robe and visor of rose, the haughty czarina in blue plaid and mask, the eyes black-rimmed with *ennui*—into the train to pastures, parklands, the country. The man fondly closes doors, pink nose quivering tragically under cap-peak. Immediately he is trampled underfoot by all who have already forgotten his beatification.

A bell and voice begin, "All aboard! Passengers to Gippsland—all aboard!" Crikey, where is the bag of bananas, the Tobler chocolate? The train simmers diligently under late-Victorian cast-iron archings. "Ta-ta! Ta-ta! Ta-ta! Ta-ta!" Gregory cannot trace the creature chirping thus as girders, black hats and ostrich feathers slither backwards. Someone agonizes, "Oh, get to a window and wave to them!" The agony remains in the carriage corridor when the corridor is empty except for a juiceless glove too frightened to stir or whimper.

Already, trees are drinking and grazing along one, two, three sunny rivers. The train chants through the green ballroom of autumn where the nude gums, the half-burnt magpied gums, circular-waltz in vast arcs to the rear. Swagmen logs are prone among sheep; dove-coloured smoke flees past windows. The Albanian crouches opposite, under the ventilator cord—swaying, swaying—a noose. He sneers at it. For the seventh time the huge flowering baby throws its bunny-bunny to the floor.

Spokes of the world revolve serenely—maize, mangel-wurzel, sugar-beet—in that world satin horses pose by dams brimmed by milky-weak tea, at the whitewashed gates of dairy farms, near haystacks with cake-slices cut from them. One horse, the one that did this last year and every year, rocking-horses up, down and off, to circle back more terror-stricken from a Dominican inquisition of pines. Telegraph crucifixes flip by. Mushrooms. Wild hop. Prickly Moses. Dogwood. A cage of maize-cobs. Last year Gregory knew which was wild cherry, which she-oak. But this year, now, which is which? The bunny-bunny springs into the spittoon.

The noose above the Albanian and his stained cigarette and hidden dagger prophetically vibrates. Trees and trees, and trees with charcoal cupboards burned in, yearn broken-armed towards hills. At gravel-and-geranium halts mongrels brace legs and bark, magpies gargle ecstatically. All this is excitement crusted over beauty, and means something. Soon, in a few moments, Gregory will pierce the crust and know what it all means, but hardly having begun, everything is over for Gregory and everyone; the train screams, is wrecked, sinks hissing, is abandoned. The Albanian escapes the noose, and leers away with his knife through a surf of faces that open and shut in the noisy sunshine.

Aunt Sophia, brittle as burnt biscuit, blatant in her smallness, is a stake driven into the shore; women exasperatedly side-step her old-time immobility and odour of menthol. Miles off, mad among crates and dress-baskets and Gladstone bags, the raw-nosed man, reborn from underfoot, terrified at what he might find, desperately unbars archduke and fatigued czarina. Somebody or a bird whistles *Everybody's doing it, doing it, doing it. . . .* Gregory sways on the carriage step, unable to move until Aunt Sophia sees him, until her cheek twitches—pricked by an invisible insect. She sees him. It twitches. He moves.

Instantly a net seems to fall; he and his schoolboy portmanteaux struggle in its glinting and heavy mesh as he advances, blind, to accept Aunt Sophia's kiss. Again, where his re-paying kiss lights, occurs a tic as though not he but some insect . . . the insect of happiness. . . . Happiness, love, and yet, in the waters of her colourless eyes he sees what he expected, a startled gleam. He blushes. Cruelly it cannot be hidden that this is first of all the years he must bend *down* to Aunt Sophia, the first of all the years she does not take one of his portmanteaux, first of all the years he is fourteen. A scalding mercury rises in the almost interminable cylinder of his throat to congeal at his celluloid collar; his body becomes grotesque and unoiled; the day turns its face aside.

He is in the buggy, and it out of Main Street, out of town so swiftly that he still fossicks in his wonderful waistcoat for the ticket, and is amazed to find it gone, to realize that he only must somehow have given it up.

"Yes, aunt."

Upright, her black-gloved hands much too small to control the masculine mare she easily controls, she asks the same questions she has always asked, the same questions in the same voice. He gives, as always, visit after visit, the same answers. They are certainly the same but seem not to be. His extra knowledge gives unintended intonations; obscenities miscolour respectable words.

Aunt Sophia is all in black. Or is she? Even if he dare scrutinize her in a glass case labelled *Australian Aunt (Provincial), 1912 A.D.*, Gregory could not be perfectly sure. If he close his eyes. . . . He closes his eyes. Dressed in black, yet, yet, what is the colour? It is unique, a mirage; through it gleam the flower-stem fibres of her kindliness, the blue of her love, all the subtle and overlapping shades of her stubbornness, eager searchings, knowledge, superstitions and, sometimes, unpredictably, the opalescence of a smile so exquisite that her withered lips and false teeth are only as the paper on which a deathless sonnet has been engraved.

". . . and all the rain after the drought has caused such a fancy to-do, Gregory. Fruit blossom in autumn . . . look!"

Thereupon, to illustrate, a hobbledehoy tree arranges itself nearby in a paddock; a tree tagged with green leaves and fever leaves and small mottled apples decorates itself also with sprigs of bride's blossom. Gregory almost says, "Ah!" Ah! I wonder if that tree. . . . If the buggy will stop for an hour or two . . . but the landscape, with his mind in it and his distress, flutters forlornly past, past the train, past the buggy, past. Everything is too significant and intangible, as though he Paul-Pried through father's shagreen-covered telescope the fragmentary goings-on at Camelot.

"Yes, aunt." What?

". . . dark shadows under your eyes."

"Yes, aunt."

Dark shadows of vast rotating wheels stuttering across the stubble of life: *down* to kiss, a startled gleam, dark nights of impurity and. . . . *Aunt Sophia did not give me a menthol jube!*

He is so astounded and hurt that he scarcely feels the buggy turn the corner to the cemetery glittering and quiet as salt, past the brick-yard, to the walnut trees, peppercorns and barns of Aunt Sophia's.

Near the gate, Young Alec, who has been dead or packed away for a year, slices sulkily at the boxthorn hedge with a bill-hook. He is smaller and less fascinating and years younger. He gapes a "Hullo, Greg!" and is lost in the sound of the tissue-paper bag of menthol jubes which rustles of its own accord from its niche in Aunt Sophia's person.

If Gregory could scent a solution instead of nothing under the blue umbrella of sky!

The dog comes bouncing and laughing at the flickering wheels; house and beehives dodge out from the mulberry-trees; at this instant Gregory knows that the day will be more and more crippled, will hobble its melancholy race against nothing; he knows that the bird on the pump-handle is the first of the robins, too early, and that rouge on its breast this year is not of paint but of blood.

Hung from the passage ceiling the Japanese wind-bells jingle from the slices of glass a melody that no more satisfactorily supports last year's libretto. The odour of the house is less satisfying though unaltered, is poignant though distilled from the same mildest things: Northern Spy apples, raspberry vinegar, brown eggs, butter pats, lemon cheese, quinces, red-and-white-beaded milk-jug covers, bentwood Vienna rockers, biscuit barrels crammed with rock cakes, the chromo-lithograph of Queen Alexandra.

The customary objects, much older than fourteen, seem richer as though nearer, out-of-focus as though too near.

The swan-shaped teapot, the brass fender, the maroon silk in the harmonium front, the bronze stallion on the clock, the gipsy tables, all have some meaning he could sniff out if only . . . if only. . . .

Where his younger fingers have fondled and followed the involved stems and flat buds of the wall-paper his present eyes go uneasily hunting in the extravagant growth which appears on the point of splitting into blossom, of parting to reveal what is secreted. He watches for the miracle. Nothing happens; the orgy of foliage is stubborn; the room shuffles sideways; his face mimics his face in the glass-panelled door. He remembers that it is—that it *was*—delight to peer outside, first through a blue pane, then a red. Without peering, he grasps the door-handle of white china, opens the door, walks from the mouldering veranda onto the brick path ripe with moss. A little boy wails: behind him and inside him the little thwarted boy wails for blue fuchsia bushes, blue tanks on blue stilts, blue clouds and bluer sky, the blue stable with the plumbago-blue horse dreaming under the granite archway blue as sleep. He sees as he walks, and has no desire to skip screeching toward them, four immaculate roosters and a crowd of their women under a mulberry-tree. He is dressed still in his best suit with its corker of a waistcoat and his tight boots with the patent leather toe-caps.

Aunt Sophia appears above him at his upstairs bedroom window. She is going to call out, "Greggy, come back this minute, and change your good clothes. Put on your galatea suit. Greggy!" while she gesticulates like a beetle and he, light and cheeky, laughing, runs away to the hay-loft or behind the loganberry canes. He watches her lips separate, and is horrified at the quiet of her voice: "Are you going to change, Gregory?" In a moment he will cry; a contortion, smile of an impure orchid, mutilates his face, "Not now, aunt. Later. Not *now*." The last word is rude. He dares not look at her longer, he cannot stop moving; behind his back the window moans down and, as his feet fumble with the ground and his hands with splintery gates, he feels her face withdrawing little by little, disintegrating until nothing adorns the pane except her loitering and agonized eyes. Before him, around him, smoke ghosts about from tumuli of smouldering garden rubbish—zinnia stalks, sunflower skeletons, rose hips, loquat leaves fallen from trees which Japanesely incense the air from unseasonal blossoms on felt-covered twigs.

As he crosses the road, which once led to breath-taking

places where a little boy found skylarks' nests and snake-skins, and that now is the three-tracked way to vice and weariness, Gregory sees the grave-digger standing faceless where left a year ago, centre of sinister flashing in the cemetery: domes of glass, ginger jars, and pickle-bottles and tumblers becoming deeper and deeper mauve.

Tiny sexless lizards flicker through haulms of dead and overthrown chrysanthemums as the grave-digger goes on speaking, "Yuss, you've growed into a reel toff. Yuss! A reel Gilbert-the-filbert."

He will, Gregory knows, re-tell all he has re-told and re-told since Gregory was a gaper of seven in a sailor suit with anchor-embossed brass buttons. Year after year Gregory has seen the lips ceaselessly labouring, covered with white scum which now and then bird-limes them together so that they must be torn apart by "Yuss!" He has seen no more—under the dirty frill of the grave-digger's hat brim is the unimaginable remainder of face.

"Yuss! In the Metho's and Pressy's corner the coffins get af-flic-ted with dry rot. Yuss! When I do a re-open the shovel cuts through them like. . . ."

Gregory stares at the experienced shovel, it at him.

"Yuss! Howsumever, in the R. C. and C. of E. sections, over in the west corner, it's wet. Yuss! Pre-serves caskets fifty years or more. Get a re-open: they're like new—yuss—hard as granite."

Clashed awake, a dead boy of last century, wearing the sealing-wax of suicide on his fourteen-year-old temple, mumbles in his stony drawer.

Gregory does not want to watch the lips. He looks at lizards, the blond bricks of the Chinese altar, the hot pines fruited with parrots, while the sticky lips, all he knows of a shrouded face, go unceasingly on: ". . . as-ton-ish-ing the snakes I found when I was burning off, yuss! Hundreds! There was a seven-footer on the very grave you're sitting on. Yuss! There's a chunk out of that marble—see. Yuss! I heard him buzz. Like a blowie in a cobweb. So I up with the shovel and. . . ." The shovel winks at Gregory.

After years the mechanism of these old tales stammers to stop while the shovel nervously shuffles in the clay in attempts to divert Gregory's eyes from the lips which, inspired, wriggle lustfully toward sound. "*Yuss*!" It is a crow's cry, foul with warning. Crows themselves, in racked gums beyond the cemetery, cry out like dying sheep. Headstones, each pregnant with the essence of its night-shirted skeleton, retreat a little. The grave-digger, strangling his shovel with flaky hands, lowers his face until, at last, Gregory sees all of it, sees and smells it. Before he can wake up screaming, a new voice begins to unravel behind horror:

"Yuss! You're a big younker now. A flash townie, eh? Fifteen? Sixteen? You know what it's all about, yuss! Tell ya something. In that grave with the urn"—a ripple of shame shudders across the marble—"re-pose the mortal remains of Mrs Fairweather, died August nineteen-o-six. Yuss! Left Mr F. with four daughters and a coupla boys. Six years ago. They used to have the place down the road. Kept pigs. Yuss! About four years ago your auntie was hor-rif-ied to find the two eldest girls up the duff, in the family way. One sixteen, the other about a year younger. Your auntie, she's a Christian lady. She went to Fairweather and. . . ."

Aunt Sophia! *Family way*! Four years ago—one, two, three, four visits ago!

". . . to mind her own business. Yuss! All came out at the trial."

Gregory has torn feathers from the Guinea fowls' tails, slept with a raw carrot under his pillow, has climbed and raced and enjoyed himself while. . . . The gummy lips are losing control:

"Yuss. Yuss. The trial. Everyone there. Your auntie a reel lady. Because why? Because he ordered her off the place. Yuss! 'I *was* upset,' she said. Didn't know what to do. Didn't guess he was the one. Yuss! His own daughters. When the babies came—it was in all the papers—he fed 'em to the pigs. Yuss!"

Gregory is stumbling and slipping now as he runs on the leather-coloured pine-needles through horrible land and horrible day. He flees what he has said foolishly:

"To—the—pigs?"

"*Yuss*! *Yuss*!"

Then, quickly subject-changing above the backs of galloping pigs.

"Whose grave you digging?"

"*What?*"

"Whose grave? Who's dead?"

"*No one dead.*" The grave-digger had spat.

"But?"

"*Yuss! No one. But tomorrow. . . .*"

"How d'you know?"

"*I—just—know. Yuss!*"

There was the face he should never have seen—gnawed, crumpled, its eyes leaking like rotten mulberries. There were the babies flowering in sty-muck, small blind hands groping under the pigs' teeth for bunny-bunny.

There—there was Aunt Sophia, meagre, dried, neat, yet waterlogged with appalling knowledge.

Gregory flees, runs, slips, stumbles.

Strange and sweet, there is no one in the brickyard but a cow of black-and-white plush being nudged by a shaky calf with a glazed-pork nose. No one else. The kiln, an animal patient and untended, breeds effortlessly within itself, steam dissolving from its back, as horror dissolves from Gregory. Sorrow—is it sorrow?—presses a final drowsy chord from his heart. Sorrow and a flock of swift starlings swing down into the grass and are lost. He lies in the grass. The afternoon coils on the grass, on the plain, on the mild hills, like a great golden woman. Close to his soothed face, two ants, meeting on a stalk of grass, rub masks together and pass on, one to air and heaven, one to dirt and hell. He, Gregory, and the woman . . . he and the woman. . . . In seconds, when all is stiller, he will know. The road will lead somewhere, veil after veil will fold back, he will be less grotesque, will be able to run nimbly, bare-kneed, crying, "Auntie, auntie, I tutted me pinger." She will unlatch the hole in her where the menthol jubes live, and there will be nothing to tear his mind. In seconds . . . in one second. . . .

"*Ev'rybody's doin' it, doin' it, doin' it,*
Pickin' their nose an' chewin' it, chewin' it, chewin' it!"

Young Alec! Young Alec, shining and smelling of brown soap, blinks down at him. He will never be able to rise.

"Miss Lancaster says for you to come in and git ready for tea. She's been ringin' the bell."

Gregory crawls up from the bath of grass; he feels the feathery greenth slip from his flesh, and with it peace and strength. He has not, cannot, have slept and yet, in a flash, the afternoon, the golden woman, has glided away from him taking her secret, and leaving nothing on the land except the luminous impression of her body. This fades and fades. And the bell has faded to sleep beside the teapot, the cold pearls of sound have tinkled into eternity and he has caught none of them. The pools of grass, in which float puff-balls, wash over his patent leather and Alec's cow-red boots. They climb fences awkwardly as two wallabies. Young Alec is a sonk; he can go and eat coke with his Greg this and Greg that. He is only Aunt Sophia's odd-job-boy who snores in the room by the scullery. He has nothing to tell—not really. And yet he says, after a silence, as they are passing the piles of shorn-off boxthorn branches, "See here, Greg." He produces his hand from within his breast and, grinning, holds something out into the twilight: "What d'ya think of *those*?" They stop, they stand like two posts with wet wind streaming between. Then the wind ceases; they are closer together then, even elbows touching. The day, drunken with renewed nastiness, leers over Gregory's shoulder at the French postcards: "The buck nigger and the three women, eh!" Gregory wants to say, "You're a dirty pig. I'll tell Aunt Sophia," but his reply emerges, "Any—any more?" He hates himself and loves Young Alec; the stunning waistcoat restricts a battering heart. The little bell, waking again, scatters green pearls and, miraculously, Young Alec is gone and he, Gregory, has gone too, is standing at his window thinking. "I'll never speak to him again." Meanwhile he watches, down below, sparks springing from the angry kiss of the hammer and the long nail Young Alec is beating into the peach-tree which grits its teeth and shudders with pain. What a blob, to be beating and beating. Tea is waiting. Young Alec is off his chump. When the sparks stop and the noise, Gregory will call to him. There will be an answer. Already he sees Young Alec's voice growing up and up, a silver lily on a silver stalk, to be plucked, "See here, Greg," before it passes his window and sheds petals in the rain-gutters.

For the third time the bell sprinkles, and Aunt Sophia's

voice spills over all the world, "Alec, you young Turk, leave that tree till tomorrow. Come in to tea." And next she wears a smile no one can see but anyone can feel in her voice as it climbs the rose-padded stair-carpet: "Gregory, what *are* you doing?"

Night.

In bed Gregory recalls that, at the other end of his journey, the clinking fish-cart has long, long ago joggled away the afternoon into remoter suburbs, the chimney-sweep has trudged off with the last of light into unhappy back-lanes, the lamplighter has fed scraps of flame from his wand to lamps that wink twilight into night. Night: he has played Tit Tat Toe with his mother and brushed her sleepy hair. Her brooch with crescent of pearls and comet of rubies has exhaled the final splinter of fire and waits tomorrow and the boned collar of her blouse. She is in bed; the gas-blue fish-tail of flame throbs and purrs in the globe; the rats from her hair are curled at the base of the haughty Eau-de-Cologne flask.

He is not there, has not been there. Where is he? At Aunt Sophia's? Scarcely—for at Aunt Sophia's, at night, the joyous kettle squats black on the pink-hot bars while one presses finger-tips into the furry crimson table-cloth, and her old-fashioned voice enchants with "Casabianca" or "Down in a green and shady dell" or:

Heigh, Domini-Domicum!
Leave your Easy Degree;
Put on your Three-farthing Crackers,
Likewise your Soft Downtreaders,
And come and see . . . !
Poor old Simony White-face
With a Rackororam on his back
Has climbed to the Highest Top o' the Mountain
And, without the aid of Absolution,
We shall all be undone.

Tonight, this visit, he has not been there. Indecorous, relentlessly, the day has churned on and on, working itself out like a nightmare Euclid problem. It must be almost the conclusion.

After tea, while the bronze stallion watched from the clock,

Aunt Sophia, unasked, had given him the camphor-sacred stereoscopic views which for years he had unsuccessfully pleaded to see and tonight had no desire to see. Jaded, he arranged the double-pictured cards one by one to reveal their sharp and static world, a world too voiceless and perfect to be loved, a world of stone monsters and cathedral saints, galleries with parquet floors and looking-glass walls, market-squares sown with moveless people, the world of France, of postcards, of the buck nigger.

If only, after tea, his heart had licked its hardened lips, "Auntie, say 'Domini' for me, please." But all he or his heart could say was, "I'm tired, Aunt Sophia. I'd like to go to bed." Neither he nor his heart had ever said that before. He climbed the stairs of dead roses.

He is in bed. The wick of the candle, black and bowed, prays hidden prayers in a pale spire of flame. He sees the wall-text *The beloved of the Lord shall dwell in safety*. Once, text and flame had power to fascinate and heal. Now, they are gelded. They lend no strength to solve the Euclid problem and its imperceptible coalitions—baby and bunny-bunny, startled gleam, menthol jubes, stains beneath his eyes, blossoming autumn, stench of the grave-digger's face and story and pigs, pigs and babies, golden woman, postcards, three women, France, buck nigger—the problem darkly drips the tears he will not shed. Night and nothing; he has moved all day to do nothing and arrive nowhere. Where is all that was his? And those others—Aunt Sophia, Young Alec, the grave-digger—what has turned the tap in them from which has run to waste, to misery, all that was theirs? Something has run to waste, to misery. This is the same room, same bed, same candlestick, same safe door. On the door sounds a ghost's knock.

"May I come in, Gregory?" It is Aunt Sophia. This has never happened before; for him no one has ever before knocked on a door.

She creeps in. Why creep? He watches. She seems the same in the same grey wrapper; her hair is plaited as it has always been when she came, every year before, to kiss him good night and ask, "Greggy, do you want to do number one before you go to sleep?" He watches and waits, heavy, unoiled, bound in and pressed down by the glinting net; but he knows she is not the same. He seeks some sin on her, some physical signal of her intimacy with vile facts. Upon her are shades and a closer veil of wrinkles than he has noticed before; but these, and her stiffness, recall nothing except his mother's drawl while her finger-tips fiddle with the enamelled watch buried in her beaded belt, "Poor Sophie! As a girl she was beautiful, according to gran. Now: a hopeless old maid. A perfect duck, of course, but—an old maid." Sophie . . . Aunt Sophia . . . Miss Lancaster . . . *Miss* Lancaster . . . old maid . . . she stands, tiny and dried, in her grey wrapper. She does not advance to kiss him. He knows that she will not, but cannot think why.

Oh, kiss me, Aunt Sophia, kiss me and say, as you always have. . . .

She licks her lips. Why is she nervous? Here, at last, is her voice: "Gregory, if you . . . if you . . . during the night . . . the evening bowl is in the little cupboard."

Evening bowl?

"Goodnight, Gregory. Don't forget your prayers."

She is gone.

Evening bowl? Evening bowl?

Evening bowl!

Suddenly, like the meeting and marrying of many drops of rain, many tears, sliding sideways along a wire, all things of the day gather together in one full and blinding drop, one overwhelming drop, conclusion to the problem. He violently puffs away the minaret of candle-flame. The drowning drop falls with the darkness. As it plunges, swiftly, deeply, and for all time gone, he knows that it carries within it something never to be replaced or experienced again. He has found no answer to his formless question, has been left with no new secret. He has found only what he knew he should find, something he has not let himself know all day. Yet he has known all day, as Aunt Sophia knows and Young Alec and the grave-digger and all the world, except his mother, know, that the time for little boys' tears is past. He is no longer a little boy. That is sold, used up, over. The tears that burn from his eyes are for a child who wails for a blue world, and the taste of the tears is different, and the beating of his heart is different, and the agony that poisons his tears and inspires his heart is unique, will never be suffered again, never. (1938)

Otto Ruff

Really, this is all I know about it.

Otto Ruff and I were boys together, next-door neighbours in a country town. Together, inflexibly faithful, we collected postage-stamps, cigarette-cards, marbles, matchbox tops, everything. Of the same age, in the same social stratum, we gave each other birthday presents, which our parents paid for, as unaffectionate gestures to be duly repaid. We utilized friendship for separate though similar ends, tacitly never overlapping purchases: if I bought *The Magnet* he bought *The Gem*; our possessions were each other's. It was a selfish and satisfactory arrangement but so unemotional that I was not disturbed when in 1921, at the age of sixteen, he went to Melbourne. Besides, at sixteen, I was occupied with passions for people unaware of my existence, busy with hatred of my parents. The following year I went to Melbourne. I stayed with an aunt. Having shed the chrysalis of parent-haunted provincialism, I began to acquire amateur affectations, was conscious of my slightest gesture, felt myself under a glass cover. I saw everything with lopsided clearness, and suffered agonies waiting for my enclosure to dissolve.

My aunt, recently returned from Europe, was Modern. Her bobbed hair had a *chic* that made it startling even among other bobs then beginning to appear. Openly, with flourishes of perverted femininity, she smoked tinted and scented cigarettes. Regularly she held what she called a *thé-dansant*. They were faintly unreal these gatherings which twilight seemed always to envelop. There was a fire that wavered without warmth as though imitation; there were bowls of Frau Karl Drushki roses, every petal in place; violin and piano drawled *Smile Awhile* or *The Midnight Waltz*. The women wore cable bangles with little locks to which the keys were lost. I do not remember the men. Somewhere sat a Gaby Deslys doll. I invariably lounged, glass-encased, by the cool fire, my arm lying by the clock of *bisque* porcelain. Once, suddenly, Otto Ruff was there. Our glances crossed, uncrossed; we said, "Oh, hullo you", and no more. I had no more to say. Aware of a pimple by my nose, I watched him and the woman who had brought him. She was about twenty-six—almost middle-aged! With her facile sang-froid, her strictness of outline, the harsh black of her rigorous bob, she was the focus of veiled attention. Someone whispered, "Moira Morrisey! She drugs. That poor boy." Poor boy! The ease with which he smoked cigarettes and smelled a rose, the control he had of his body, the emptiness of his remarks, were to me miraculous. He and the woman, each holding a lighted cigarette, eyes half-shut, executed a tango, a series of passionless posturings that displayed nothing except that they had danced beyond the stage of enjoying each other's steps. There they moved and there I leant watching until he and his partner seemed to dilate, lengthen, tango with unrelenting languor across a calendar of *thé-dansants.*

For a while I tried to imitate Otto Ruff's poise while making no move towards a meeting. Gradually, I forgot him. Then, unaware of the machinery of liberation or the moment of release, I was out of my glass cage; I plunged hilariously to the year 1927 and my next encounter with Otto Ruff. Arriving late at some galloping Jazz Age party I found him Charlestoning abandonedly against a tempest of Eton-cropped and shingled women in sacks of jade-green patterned *à la* Tutankhamen. Flushed, younger-looking at twenty-two than at sixteen, he was the incarnation of the time—hideously prancing and portentous upon a volatile garbage-heap of silken legs, feathered garters, gin bottles, garish roadsters, lips unnaturally cupid-bowed. I perceived little unusual about him except that I, starting from the same year and street as he, had reached that party, that drunkenness, that night, still almost wholly my dull self, whereas he was easily imagined as the force behind this stream cascading impenitently over the precipice of time. We yelled with frantic amiability above the Prince of Wales's favourite *I wonder where my baby is tonight?* It was nine years before we met again, as accidentally as ever.

In 1936, 28 Collins Street was popular with actors, women journalists and metropolitan high school teachers; each room contained the Penguin *A Farewell to Arms*, the portable typewriter, the bottle of Scotch. One day I arrived at the bathroom at the same time as someone tall in a Japanese kimono. It was Otto Ruff. He displayed no surprise, presented me his pallid fingers as though we had met a month ago, asked me to his room ". . . but *immediately*, my dear . . . to savour an *enchanting* wine . . . yellow as a page-boy's hair . . . an elixir begged from a *creature* who had known Oscar Wilde." Windmilling Charleston-fiend and its backdrop of polyangular orange and black disintegrated as I followed white ankles upstairs, disconcerted by the opinion I had formed before reaching his door. The room, however, rather than underlining that opinion, erased it, substituting a problem. The room had irises painted on door-panels, blue-and-white ginger jars, palm-leaf fans, William Morris wallpaper, poems by Austin Dobson, beribboned olive-oil bottle—had I looked from the window I could have expected not to see the backyard plane-trees of the Melbourne Club but a rustic arbour shawled by smilax and noisette roses. In that room so obviously reconstructed, his lisping of Pater and Rossetti while brandishing a peacock feather, I began to suspect a bizarre scheme. It fascinated me, it made me encourage the re-beginning of our relationship. After that, no one but I travelled beside him, a useless portmanteau, to every station of his haunted journey; only I remained, a common factor, a brown dog of a person misplaced in a series of settings. No one knows—despite painstaking research—what I missed between 1922 and 1927, between the jazz-boy of 1927 with Rudolph Valentino hair and the aesthete of 1936. After 1936 I witnessed each metamorphosis, but even to me his *lives* remain inexplicable, the seed of such varied blooms evades classification. This life composed of lives, made so public by the literary brilliance of one life, is a mystery. Yet, accepting resentfully all contradictory evidence, I could not believe him anything more than an actor. I cannot believe it now, despite his last letter and his guile in switching characters so that one never saw him between characters or out of character. One hour he *was* this, the next he *was* that. And often—oh, the gap between, the difference! Nothing except congruent boyhood which gave me a sort of invisibility for him can explain why he sought me as a witness, to the last, of his arborizations about the wire of an idea, of his reproductions of dominant types which were so brimming with acid reality that one drop more would have meant overflow, burlesque. That never happened. Change of voice was possible—intonation, key, vocabulary, texture. The infinitely graded adjustments of gait, grimace, gesture and so on, were explicable though frightening in variety. Less explicable but still possible were more subtle physical changes. Least explicable were the apparent inner conversions, the discarding of an elaborated creed and, in a moment, the absorption of an utterly different, equally elaborate tenet. My observing these transmutations should, now, convince me most that he did not simulate but *become.* I cannot believe this, cannot, though I want to.

Two months after our renewed friendship I was absent for several weeks from 28 Collins Street. On my return a letter awaited me. I had seen his handwriting just before leaving; toying with rondeaux and triolets, he had given me some to read; the script was exquisite as Baron Corvo's. The handwriting of the letter ran in curlicues like the tracks of a lively little pest: he was at Hawthorn Cottage in the Dandenong Hills. I *must* visit him, lugging along Camembert and black olives from Franz's. The letter intimated that I had been wilting in the city while he, my affectionate Ot, had flourished like a zinnia waiting my long-proposed visit. By the time the train reached his station I was almost believing this fable; when I saw him straddling in a decrepit buggy outside the station there was nothing else to believe. He wore sandals, blue shirt, creased flannels; his plumper face was sun-browned, his hair bleached and tousled as the grass in the midday paddocks. "*Ave*, you old sod!" he shouted. "Get your chalky bones aboard before this whore of a nag bolts." I felt his strong hand, heard his "Ups-a-daisy, decadent! Whoa, you hell-horse! And how's the great grey metropolis? Gee-up, moke—to the inn!" Through the sugary crunch of wheels in gravel he chattered on: "Mind those eggs with your city feet, old brownie. Had to haggle for 'em; they must be the exact shade of tan; my trull abhors 'em white." His *trull*? *His* trull? There was the basket of eggs, lettuce, radishes. The lamp rattled in its socket. Skylarks let themselves down, spider soprani on crystal threads, from the blue ceiling. There were scents of hay-ricks, cows by creek-willows, dusty pines. The sun shone through me, and he ceaselessly talked. His succubus adored cheese. He was writing this and that; he read them to Betsy-bitch, she cried like a water-spout because she had no more grey matter than a dog-biscuit, not a thought above her navel. Soon it seemed that I had long known of Betsy-bitch and her swatches of collie-coloured hair, of the other guests—Cowley with his insecure pince-nez and T. S. Eliotian verse, Maisie Green with her Elizabethan vocabulary and unbuttoned scarlet blouses, of the farmhouse collapsing in an untended garden, bags of onions in the bathroom, cracked washstand sets, nineteenth-century copies of *Cornhill Magazine*, lamplit nights of beer-drinking, beds rattling brass knobs like cymbals to the amorous exercisings of Otto and Betsy-bitch, Cowley and Maisie, while I caught fleas. And although I enjoyed his reading them I could not guess his poems brilliant; I am no judge of such things. Tutored by critiques I now see that his *Country Poems* have genius, and are the exciting evocation of one aspect of Australian rural life.

Within four months he was nightly in the gambling rooms of Russian Jews on the top floors of old cafés in Exhibition Street, suet-faced, eyes tenantless, tunnels that struck back dark and congested with useless aces into nowhere and nothing.

For five years I tried to prevent circumstances foiling my discovery of him at Interval, in the hiatus between; it was obvious that when he had discarded one mask and not assumed the next I should glimpse the real Otto Ruff, though what, meticulously, the *real* means I cannot determine. Impelled by curiosity, and the bloodless boyhood affection which the most hateful transformation could not lessen, I trotted by the side of more than a score of creatures many of whom would have been as unpalatable as stale water had they not all been the one creature, trotted with the desperation of an exhausted spaniel, compelled to keep moving.

And then, suddenly, Otto Ruff disappeared. I did not, of course, immediately think of him as having disappeared. I momently expected a call to set me trotting again. Within a month expectancy had dissolved into anxiety. Anxiety gradually forgot itself into lacerated vanity, into forgetfulness itself. Days lapped over Otto Ruff.

Eighteen months after his disappearance, a grimed and flimsy envelope came to 28 Collins Street where I had kept my one room during the years that he had gone from room to room keeping none. I could not place the blotched handwriting . . . Otto Ruff. Would I come instantly before it was too late, please, instantly? Perhaps I was tired: the greasy scrawl, the slummy address, the *before it was too late*, seemed extravagant. I felt that, for once, he was over-acting; that the letter was a property one. However, as soon as it was possible but not instantly, I set off.

It would have pleased Otto Ruff to know that I came to him on a day and at a time of day which could not have been more fitting had I chosen deliberately, knowing what I should find and delaying my arrival until that day and that hour. I had walked through twilight streets which Pole-cold and rain-fringed wind did nothing to relieve of stench. I had knocked at last on the door of a pastry-cook's which reeked of sour cardboard and rats; there on a grey marble slab sat four little tarts each containing a consumptive's gobbet of jam. I was not shocked when a toothless monstrosity, garbed in female clothes, told me in the accent of a theatre cockney that she was 'is lan'lidy, that poo' Otty 'ad passed orn, 'ad been lide aht and looked loverly. With a stinking sob she handed me a letter, "Give it to me at the last," she said. I read it, and its words were tainted with the blue hissing of the gas-jet above my head. I read it before I went to him; the words seemed to have been known to me for a long time:

When you are beginning to read this letter I am beginning to write I shall be dead. A second ago I looked into the looking-glass. Knowing I was dying I wished to see what was coming upon my face. Then I turned down the last looking-glass I shall ever look into. The last door closed to close out everything. Last room. Last letter. Odd—I can't think why I want to write, yet there are things I desperately want to tell you. Something prevents me. Things slip away. I forget. All except this: have you ever returned to your room, late, the world running down, walls and furniture accusing you with inimical silence of something you cannot understand, have you ever stood, tired, a wafer to be crushed, not needing to talk or think or move, and then have moved to a looking-glass, looked into your own eyes, seen lips break to breathe, "Who are you?" Have you? I wanted to know what you saw behind the colour of flesh, the flesh of bones, the bones of your mind. Isn't there something of oneself no one else has ever seen? Do you understand? Listen: my name, the unseen ticket tagged to my body is Otto Ruff. I have seen Otto Ruff dying. I have seen other faces, all ticketed Otto Ruff, all different, and not one is . . . is Otto Ruff. There was a film on every face, a film that nothing removes, even dying. Listen: when I am dead I want you to look on my face. Then you will know. Surely you will know?

There, paper. Unsaid what had to be said. It eludes me, flees back and back through a thousand looking-glasses into childhood and beyond. Useless. Cold.

OTTO RUFF

I walked through Otto Ruff's last door.

Under pennants of wall-paper, on an iron bed, lay the corpse. Other hands had plugged its orifices (with old rags?), combed its hair, controlled its limbs to coffin-shape. Other hands had left a jug of arum lilies. Other hands. Yet I could not restrain the thought that lilies, jug, rain and night, were granted wishes of the dead man. As he must also have wished, I recalled "carefree, boyish adventures" with him. I might have experienced the sorrow one does had not an annihilating ray stung into my mind: when we were boys, long ago, during the Great War, was not Otto Ruff the Perfect Boy? Had he, even then, taking cues from me, the plodding adherent to boy laws, already begun his strange trek?

I looked brazenly on his face.

There was no answer.

There was only a smile, incorruptibly calm, indissolubly fixed:

Here lie the mortal remains of one who disappeared from the world while it still landed him with journalese in literary periodicals and Saturday supplements, who disappeared to seek alone, suffer alone, who sought and starved, starved and suffered, suffered and died, glad to die, glad to fling burdens off, to sleep . . . to sleep. . . .

That was the smile, the cliché smile.

I could only think that Otto Ruff—whoever he was—had played his last scene as scrupulously as any. I walked into the rain, bewildered, as unanswered as he, frightened.

And most was I frightened, and most am I still sometimes frightened when I think of him—it is surely reasonable so—merely as a wonderful actor. I am frightened to receive letters, to open them.

Do you understand what I mean, and why I am sometimes frightened . . . no, no, often frightened, always frightened?

(1941)

The Daughter of the Late Bishop

Prolonged sickness had left him too too assailable, he said. He was a long-unoccupied room, doors flung wide. However, the train journey had been soothing; he expected contentment to continue.

Yet, when he walked from the station portico, he was confounded by a feeling of nudity, as though some last layer had been ripped off: it seemed he had crossed a frontier into inimical territory, slipped through a looking-glass, taken a wrong turning. Sky of odd colour flared above the provincial city he was to spend several weeks in.

"*And, y'know, I can't really at all recall why, now*," he said, choosing words as one might fastidiously choose phials of precious essence. "*Unable to escape for weeks—why? Too long ago: I forget; eludes me—quite.*"

The only lodging obtainable was in a run-down hotel, its planks veined with bleach. Here, he had a ground-floor cell, seedily furnished, in which years and fifth-rate intransigents had brewed an odour. The window looked on a backyard of turkeys of a species he'd never seen.

Indeed, everything seemed hitherto unseen, was imperceptibly wrong—the outlines of houses, flagrant chimneys just too tall, windows minutely out of plumb, alps of blazing iron roofs too steep. If he walked, he was tormented by these houses, terraces of, with narrow liver-coloured boards harsh in texture, inconsequential verandas edged by metal crochet, by the always-down blanched window-blinds. As he limped like a faulty machine along the grilling concrete, ashy scabiosas protruded through crimped-wire fences.

"*In other cities*," he said, "*one is aware of a sort of current of predominating plants winding from garden to garden: in Adelaide, rosemary and poinsettia; in Hobart, white lilac, elder, auricula. But there, in that place, nothing but those dots of unseemly hue, stems over-long and meagre, foliage debilitated. No other plant. I recall no other. And no weeds, never a weed. That one mockery of a thing suckled on grit and mica. And,"* he continued with distaste, "*and—beeless. Yes. Not a bee, no leetle birds, not even a dried snail-shell. Among the scabiosas, hens sat in dirty stupors in nests of tobacco-coloured dust.*"

Public buildings were ungainly, of brick—a congested red like stale blood on which stirred a stealthy glaze of metallic purple.

The streets were flat, straight, too wide; each, no matter which direction he tried to escape the uproar of the pub, was blocked at its distance by hills.

Movelessly older than moving things, the hills were blunt and muscular surges of stone-sown ridges low as crab-shells, infinity on which tarnishes of hock-bright growth, like hair of the sun-smitten dead, now and then gleamed momentarily to the burnish of some immeasurable hand faltering in from the horizon.

Leather land! Old man land! No animal, no one, trod the mottlings of unendurable browns except outrider dust mopping and mowing, spiralling on feckless feet, willy-willy dodging emptiness in emptiness.

"*Several times,*" he said, "*I ventured to the end of a street. 'T may always've been the same one; the streets were so the same mica-shot concrete, the hills so the dust-frequented same. Y'know, to traipse back-streets has always delighted me; to see the clam-shells set on each side of doorsteps, the hanging baskets of Wandering Jew, the cherished tins of lachenalia or maiden-hair fern, minute picket-fences on sills, concrete kookaburras, drain-pipes covered by putty in which alluring scalenes of broken fruit-plates are preserved.*

"*'S in back-streets one catches glimpses of one's stranger-self slipping across 1920 looking-glasses behind lace curtains, hears half-forgotten tunes faltering from pianos, and sees on lit blinds the shadows of people one will never know.*

"*Not in* those *streets! Always they ceased abruptly at a surf of domestic jetsam—squashed tins, shrivels of boots, shards of earthenware maimed by the passions of slatterns. Beyond lay a* cheval de frise *of water-tanks, perambulator-wheels, barrel-hoops, wires and barbed wires—knotted, impenetrable. To keep in? Out? We-e-ell, the ghost or god of dust ceaselessly gesticulated like a smoke of snuff on the hummocks without. I remained within, I and those others. . . .*"

The streets were restless with stealthy children, mongrels that stole by with eyes like women, twine-haired women in barbaric juxtapositions of colours, men in black flashing spectacles. To him, all, as though grit had irritated to malformation the very seed of their beings, appeared imperfect—bandy, stooped, hare-lipped, blotched on lid or cheek, lopped, eyes too close or askew. And from these eyes, person after person, dog after dog, some meretricious tadpole spied unblinkingly.

The conviction became his that these passers-by were on bogus errands, had a religion of which he knew nothing, belonged to a sect possessing unutterable tenets which veined with insinuation their plangent voices. And if, still sick, too doorless, too aware, he was unable to disregard these beings, he was compelled to be revolted by the more blatantly distorted, the "characters".

One or other would coagulate in the seething air—the old man with the profile of a criminal aristocrat, powdered and beaked, his dinner-suit spangled with a pattern of flies that now and again lifted an inch from his hump and, retaining its texture, replaced itself; the woman whose tennis-ball tongue bulged from her raspberry lips; the girl whose chin was scooped into her chest by the weight of the jelly wen on her nape; the narrow youth without hands.

"*Yes,*" he said, "*these and ghastly others seemed more powerful than the pack, of an inner circle more mutilated by rites; they insolently shambled by to leer over shoulders as if to signify by a swivelling of their varnished eyeballs towards the god bound to the hills by its thong of dust, 'Wait! We'll get him yet!' In the mood I was in, they terrified me, trivialized me.*"

He sought relief at the cinema showing third-class talkies he did not wish to see. Some acoustic error frayed the actors' voices and caused a lag between sound and movement, so that the merely vulgar became grotesque and obscene. Moreover, in the fervid darkness, he shuddered to think what soft monstrosity huddled beside him.

He tried the drug of alcohol, but writhed all night in his cell; outside, the turkeys made strangled gollopings, and a drunkard clawed the bricks for hours, gabbling and vomiting.

There was nothing to do but wait—unfaltering sky, manacle of debris, blemished land—wait, with the sense of a sidling nearer, a repulsive revelation to be made, an assault on his integrity, a process of initiation to be begun.

"*Finally*," he said, with care, with confidence, "*I was directly attacked. Yes. At the pub there had been off-hand treatment, evasion, duplicity—oh, deadly irritating, deadly. Nothing that touched. All oblique, hovering sidelong and casting a half-shadow, snipping at nerve-ends—that sort of thing. Suddenly, however, one of the masks was tipped aside. And even that was the trick of a decoy, a preliminary initiation!*"

He entered the Public Library. To the left, inside, a closed door—*Public Reading Room.* To the right another closed door—*Lending Library*. He opened the left door. No one there. The room had an atmosphere of preparedness, as if, under its sprinkling of dust, it awaited him.

He moved to a table, was about to lift a magazine, when there was an appalling shout:

"Wot ya think ya doing 'ere?"

Shocked, he had the impression that, though he straightened up and turned calmly to face his attacker, another he had run in terror to crouch in a corner.

In the doorway stood a squat unwinking creature. As its voice had moulted human quality so had it moulted masculinity for asexual viciousness; a slab of upper lip lacking the central depression twitched back from fangs.

He wanted to cry out with resentment, outrage, horror—make a protest composed of his complex despairs. However (imagine his beautifully grained voice) he replied:

"I—I merely wish to read."

The other, instantly, again shouted—that was the power and savagery of the trick, the shouting in that small effulgent room peppered with dust—shouted more loudly:

"Only members in 'ere, only members!"

"*It was*," he said, "*as though the beast were nearer, though no physical move had been made. You understand? As if there'd been a tangible emanation of malice and intolerance.*

Intolerance, yes, and, oh, too too intolerable. I wanted to rush out, m' face in m' hands, but drew up enough words to say I was a visitor, that I assumed 'Public Reading Room' to mean. . . ."

That was shouted aside—"Only members in 'ere!"—by noise so beyond what human voice could be expected to produce that it shattered him like actual blows of a mechanism; malevolence pillaged the final niches of his defencelessness.

"*I was too sick*," he said. "*Felt that I might almost, as tiny man has from the Beginning, fall to m' knees, turn up m' silly seed of a face, raise m' fly's arms heavenwards to pray, plead, promise. In that place, what use?*

"*One needs a* Heaven*: some maelstrom of planets, some moon-blemished gloom, some celestial landscape freighted with Troys of cloud, even an indifferent ultramarine.* There *was no Heaven one knew: the place wore its own fake.*

"*I was beaten; found m'self believing the creature reasonable: how dared I? After all, I wasn't a member. I intended saying, 'Forgive me; really very sorry', but may not have said, merely moved past, and through the door.*

"*And then*," he continued, "*once again, as when I'd stepped from the station portico, there was a switch in quality. Initiation begun, subdued by malice, I was ready for the next illumination.*

"*The other door to the Lending Library which had been shut was now open. Behind her counter, smiling from a long face like a pallid kangaroo's, was the librarian, the daughter of the late Bishop. Great teeth gleamed as her head nodded gently on a Burne-Jones neck.*

"*'Twas not, you will understand, until m' last day that I understood the diluted vacancy of the smile. And 'twas many months later that I realized something chilling (she must have opened her door while the beast was raving): that the smile was already nodding on the stalk before I saw it, that—had I stumbled on into the street—the smile would have persisted, archaic and edulcorated as the smile of a sinful gel. But, then, drawn by the smile, I turned towards her to hear her say, in an accent I condoned, and as though expressing facts learnt:*

"*'You may become a member. We've a special rate for visitors.'*

"*No mention of the other. At any rate, he'd vanished as the wounds of his shouting had. Who was he? I never found out.*"

He became a member, and found himself daily chatting with her about formless anything.

She told him about her dead daddy the Bishop, about her dear dead mummy. He wondered how she managed to exist, apparently unsophisticated, certainly undusty, in the uncouth city.

Occasionally, he was disquieted by some minute queerness of intonation or echo of distasteful memory, but queerness and echo were untraceable. Anyway, at the time, he was a little queer himself.

One night she asked him to supper. He accepted, dubious because, though she appeared far less alien than the others, it was unimaginable that anyone who lived behind those atrocious screens of wood could be anything except—the exact word evaded him—unsavoury, perverse, something of the sort.

He walked beside her, wheeling the spinsterish bicycle, through fevered moonlight, upon slabs of concrete shining like wine, while she decorously strode, six feet tall, in bottle-green velvet with tatted cuffs and collar.

Near the city's rim, in a street he could not formerly have mooned along, they arrived at her doll's-house place. One room was lit (who? who?); from its window light spread on a lavender bush, green turf, the trunk of a monkey-puzzle which, because the house was low, relaxed low branches on the roof. He was astounded but refreshed by scents of bouvardia and rose, by the topknots of flowers thrust over the white picket fence.

The front room had a silverish ceiling, low. When she lifted her head after stooping to enter, the oaken braids of her hair seemed to attract a little sparkling powder.

The wall-paper was looped with swags of forget-me-nots, on deer-legged tables no bigger than meat-plates were set out miniature treasures: millefiori paper-weights, Bristol glass scent-bottles, ivory elephants no larger than wasps, seal-top spoons, little muffineers, Derby birds and Rockingham sheep. Aware of the collection's uniqueness in that place, her singularity, and the way she reared like giantess Alice-in-Wonderland in her pretty box, he nevertheless felt at home with her and in that box.

"*This feeling*," he said, "*was, I suppose, encouraged by inflections, civilities and objects which it had begun to seem I should never again encounter. There occurred, but far back in the last lanes of m' mind, a premonition of awakening to come when she said: 'I live alone, except for my poor invalid Jo Jo.'*

"*At this point*," he sipped words more delicately than ever from the lake of them, "*I must be scrupulous. Listen. I didn't inquire about Jo Jo. One doesn't. Nuances. Reticences. Naturally, in such cases one doesn't interrogate, even by glance. One does not, really, expect explanation.*

"*But it seemed*," he sipped more warily still, "*that she might, with a gesture of several words, have been a leetle more explicit, have flicked away the ghostly moth of question. That lighted room, y' see. Lit all day? The searing weather and she at her library. The simplest needs of the most active invalid.*

"*No gesture was made; she said merely, her upright creamy teeth and gel-ish, soap-bubble eyes graciously gleaming: 'We'll have supper first. I'll play with Jo Jo later.'* "

He shuddered, then continued: "*We had supper. The moth, wings circumspectly folded, did not move away—but did not move. We had many suppers; night after night, even after midnight had clashed from some hideous tower, I heard her say: 'I'll play with Jo Jo later.'* "

Heat persisted. The streets, as they slid towards debris and hills, reflected the capers of the trembling and shambling, halt and nodding, the lolloping or deformed.

"*But*," he said, "*I was now less tormented by these. I entertained m'self by conceiving the city to have been got up by a cheap-jack creator whose materials, measurements and colours were not orthodox though intended to appear so. It had been crammed by animated beings composed of a substance easily flawed. Unsanctified, this imitation peopled by imitations had been slapped among the hot hills, fenced by a death-trap of rubbish and lidded by a false sky.*

"*And the Bishop's daughter? Once, as I watched her inclining from near the silver ceiling towards a lisping precentor and an archdeacon with dust in his folds who were jammed with me in her front room, it seemed to me that, although rank of growth, she with her finer mechanism was perhaps no more than the* pièce de résistance *of a monstrous chicanery, a more detailed imitation in a more detailed décor, high-priestess of a temple on whose roof rested monkey-puzzle boughs.*

"*Finally, after years it felt, the day of m' departure came. Departure! What does one mean? Y'know, one can never depart, never exorcise anything made known to one by the senses, at least not until one has made one's—well—ultimate departure.*

"*Winged with the illusion of life one flaps laboriously in the vacuum of the present towards the future, the chimerical ecstasy beyond; one exerts oneself ceaselessly and is beaten ceaselessly back into the past which alone extends its frontiers as visions of the future founder. Void present, ghostless future, immutable past!*"

He paused; looked over the brink of knowledge into depths. Then he withdrew, closed his eyes, continued.

The train was to leave at five in the afternoon, he thought he remembered. There was to be a "farewell, very very special afternoon tea" with the Bishop's daughter.

As he chewed at the edges of his repugnant hotel luncheon, the air began to flush darker.

As he struggled to the station to leave suitcases, he was amazed to see draperies of cloud—ancient, so often arranged and rearranged above the futility, rancour and peevishness of the world—sagging, pressing down on the city which had sharpened its angles and ruled lengths with the arrogance of false potency confronted by power.

Panes flashed like looking-glass in which emptiness was captured. There was an impression of a drawing closer for final rape, a sense of idiot preparation behind walls; electric glances shot sidelong from person to person.

Sweat dripped from the backs of his hands and the roots of his hair.

As he returned from the station into an atmosphere accelerated towards consummation, he saw for the last time, at the end of a street, on the hills which seemed aroused and uneasy, the spectre of dust, the faceless willy-willy, darker, taller, gyrating with lunatic flourishes.

Stock-still, he watched, trying to guess what this tormented wraith, the city and its occupants, might really purpose. He was startled by a sucking gulp at his elbow; there the narrow lad fanatically gloated, about to fondle him with handless stumps.

He hurried away, and found himself turning towards the library.

"*And then*," he said, "*I stopped. I was rattled. Not the library, I thought. I pictured the shouting manikin's appearing. Oh, I was odd, quite odd. So I walked, scuttled rather, up one street, down the next. Escaping; but, y' know, in these cases there's no escape. None. What had to be, had to be: there had been something arranged—the pub had egged me to the streets, the streets to the manikin in the Reading Room, he to the daughter of the late Bishop. Now, since the ritual of afternoon tea had to be gone through, I was hurtling to her white house.*"

Meantime a preposterous searchlight of silence had been turned on the city, a silence into which his soles fleeing along the concrete shed slices of unpleasant sound. As he reached her house there was a splash of lightning. The tapestries of heaven swung with all the frankness of an elemental force across the hills; from under the very rims of mammoth wheels rolling in turmoil of darkness it began, morose vehemence, to rain.

He stood on the veranda, sheltering, waiting: it was too early for the Bishop's daughter.

Another explosion of lightning struck the rain to momentary glass. Thunder followed, violent, near, a brutal ejaculation.

"*Immediately*," he said, "*from the house came a din it's beyond m' ability to describe. It was—how shall I put it?—not intelligent, not human. It was guttural, the nightmare sound of something choking on cannibal gobbets. M' hackles rose, m' legs streamed with icy nerves. Yet, without pause, I entered the house; I plunged incautiously on the last stage. Poor Jo Jo, I thought, and entered the room.*"

He halted; looked at me clearly earnestly.

"*I know you've visited that city. You've recognized it—well, partly. You yourself have called its design and architecture moronic, or was it cretinous? It's undeniable that its inhabitants must be victims of heat, dust and ugliness. My con-*

ception's defamatory and warped: I saw through the lens of neurotic convalescence.

"I admit bias. Bien. *But you cannot deny that, stage by stage, I was cajoled, even propelled, into the room. And—about this have not one leetle doubt—what I saw there I did see.*

"By the time I'd opened the door the—the thing that had made the sickening noise was silent. It did not look at me. It went on staring at the lighted electric globe with eyes like pennies of slime. It lay still.

"It was propped by frilly pillows in its puppet's bed. The body was about two and a half feet long; arms lay dead on the quilt. From the sleeves of its dinner-coat stuck starched cuffs with sleeve-links and two blunt thick dwarf hands. Its dress-shirt was topped by a misproportionate black bow.

"The head, with a vent of white mouth, was a melon of a thing, nostril slits like a pink caret. There was no nose. Eyebrow arcs seemed to be painted blackly on. The one signal of its recent effort of din was the false moustache, which was awry.

"I could not have stood in horror at the doorway for more than seconds, but I recall too too vividly the rows of wall-pegs on which hung the doll's regalia of the—the poor invalid Jo Jo. There were school-concert Dutch costumes, male and female, a Red Indian suit, flounced dresses, baby overalls and spangled boleros.

"More grisly than all was a frothy wig of yellow curls, tangled in the luscious threads of which was the giant butterfly of a hair-ribbon. Jo Jo stared towards the globe, didn't move, didn't utter.

"Did I run through the streets, through the havoc of water?

"Behind hangings and streamers of rain, on hills I could not see, lunatic dust must surely have lain down appeased. The streets were empty, not a person, not a dog; doors were closed, blinds irrevocably drawn. Nobody could have seen me reel under the station portico to a waiting-room where I shivered, embalmed in m' saturated clothes.

"In the train, I did not dare to look from the window until it had undoubtedly passed through the zone of interlocked rubbish and the hills badged by every shade of brown.

"Not until much later, miles on, with the roulette wheel of space sedately revolving, the cicatrices of stubble raying off, sheaves leaning together on brushed cleanness, unsewn bags of wheat gaping with placid obesity, was I to be forced to think of the Bishop's daughter.

"The train was at a wayside station. There—pet of some lonely official—a sunflower, a tapering obelisk with formally arranged storeys of huge coarse leaves the conventional shape of hearts, flaunted its flat dark skull coronetted with impudent yellow.

"It was tall.

"It nodded succinctly in the kind air; it bent its head.

"I seemed then to see the Bishop's daughter, weary of waiting for me beneath the silver ceiling, bend her head to pass under the low lintel and decorously, a good leetle gel, lope to the play-room to play with her doll."

(1947)

Act One, Scene One

In my boyhood whirlpools of wind, a scum of cirrus on top, span over the flanks of the country; cyclones of light heat-logged it; recurring eczemas of frost or cape-weed slid across; within it voices of coolness were bred to soar; night repeatedly cascaded, soaking in like black champagne. Parakeets struck phosphorescent flashes from its flesh; soda-water-bubble sky-larks were spat from its pores; it was bruised often green by floggings of waters, negro by passions of fire. In its summer pelt of peroxided grasses a lice of grasshoppers perpetually itched, clicked and whirred. It had always only the power of a barbarian, this body, but all the power. Its sweat slimed clods and stones; it breathed out the willy-willy; a scurf of dust sometimes sloughed off; its juices collected in pink swamps. It flinched, stirred, swooned down, restlessly dreamed on and on and on in an unwaking dream. What was the ichor in its branches and bunches of veins?

Odours arose—pigs, creeks, brier rose, mud, smart-weed, sheep, rain and dung and waterholes and wattles and ashes—odours of all its fevers or bugs or diseases.

Upon it Lilliput scars: cicatrices of asparagus fields, ram-shoe pock-marks, the scratches of fennel-edged ditches. Gravel roads, clawed every way, twisted like sulphur tattooing from wart to navel, mole to dimple, abrasion to buttocks.

Overlaying these were the ornaments of cemetery, slaughter-houses, hop-kilns, canneries, cow-sheds, the buckles of culverts and bridges, nets of fences and telegraph poles pinned on thigh, breast, cheek, eye-hollow, nodule and whorl.

Finally, concealing the immortal but mutilated privates with a heavy, deadly, embossed, clattering life of its own, was the man-made lap-lap, the fig-leaf town.

Main Street. Water tower. Hitching posts. Advertisements for pills and polishes on post-and-rail fences. Boer War memorial.

Cattle-yards. Livery and baiting stables. Shire Hall. Emporium (1894). Mechanics' Institute. Rechabite Hall. Railway station: afternoon train snuffles among milk-cans, cabs grind gravel. Painted weatherboards. Muscle-coloured brick. Veils are lifted for unpainted women to sip in the Crystal Tea Rooms where the tulip soda-fountain adores itself in the Spider-advertising looking-glass. Gipsies enter the Terminus Hotel where brewery horses with crimped Assyrian fringes stamp petulantly. On the river flat the Hindu in pink turban strolls his alleys of maize.

Now, to last chords on anvils, sunset slithers along past the tannery into peach orchards. A coach-builder gilds a final divine line on a varnished spoke; a hand plucks a pedestal of lamingtons from a pastry-shop window; jeweller's boy fixes shutters. Finishing, the sawmill yells commonly once. Back streets smell of frying undercut among woodheaps, wild amaranth, broad beans, sunflowers and old loquat-trees.

About barns tarred with sunken New Years—1901, 1908, 1913—is heard the sly rustle of the toga of approaching night. The convent bell bleeds several cold notes; the presbytery blinds and all blinds glow with lamps. The lamplighter cycles. Inside Saint Patrick's Cathedral the Italian pea-picker climbs down from painting gaudy Purgatory; the Anglican bell-ringers practise at eight o'clock; the Fire Brigade rehearses; Saint Andrew's choir wails.

Ten o'clock—breath of baking bread.

Midnight—the electric light plant pants to stop; the street lamps' little wings blink shut.

Candles out. The beds whisper and whinge.

Far far away, upon the wooden bridge in the river valley, horse-hoofs of the last rider (who? who?) click to silence. Or is it to strangling in mists, among the rotten mushrooms on the flats? A thing bumps the water-tank. Dogs—or slobbering wolves—cough dully upon dark's precipice; roosters or witches chant behind the houses.

There were many houses designed by my architect father: mansard roofs, French-tiled turrets, bull's-eye and dormer windows, lead-lights, lightning charms, stucco cartouches, terracotta gargoyles, Gothic barge-boards, grained doors, rusticated stonework. Our house, in a Loudon *gardenesque* jumble of monkey-puzzles, oleanders, bamboo, clarkias, fuchsias and asphalted paths, was his most outrageous and admired atrocity.

Wax-moustached, dapper, humourless and still as cold gravy, he was as without taste as his second wife, my mother, who had displaced much of the interior air with Dante chairs, many-bracketed oak sideboards, biscuit barrels, celery glasses, stencilled leather cushions, pet ferns in jardinières, white vases shaped like rustic fences, teams of shoes (china, nickel, German silver, false bronze, glass—any substance), wash-stands and console tables with scagliola tops, and—especially and everywhere—photographs of herself as a young woman taken at the beginning of the century.

In these photographs I glimpse a creature of Sterne, a Greuze coquette of equivocal simplicity, who might have sidled, dubious and arch, through salons decorated by Fragonard and injected by Voltaire's acid. Above imitation ermine muffs, under rose-clotted hats *à la* Marie Studholme, is the smile of secret audacity, the flitting leer. She, corrupt lees of my grandparents' spawning marriage, was a snob, underhandedly waspish towards those maternal uncles and aunts coarse as Olympians who formed a flamboyant frieze of bodies arrogantly straining stays-busks and waistcoat-buttons, and flaunting lustiness in glossy moustaches, in mounds or torrents of rich hair. They towered vulgarly, uplifting in ruby-knobbed fingers the burning Madeira glass, the riding crop or cavalry sword, the gaboon fan heavy with ostrich plumes. They threw long shadows in which my flimsy mother hissed like a cinder. Unaware that I inherited their grossness she was happy when, denying myself, I re-hissed her spite.

One's mother is the inescapable first being one senses in detail. For years all others are blanker surfaces. It is impossible to realize that others have flaws one knows she has, that her sins and graces are, greater or weaker, also theirs. Her firstness is her power; from her: early good, early evil, but, oh, early reality.

My mother was mistress of petty deceit, I her aptest one pupil in those stale rooms, that house deceased, that town obscuring the ageless genitals of the country. She was curdled, perverted, unintelligent, silly as a bantam. I loved her passionately.

On social occasions I sat, geared like a ventriloquist's doll for every nuance of provincial etiquette, with those of her set, the wives of doctors, lawyers, bank managers. She listened, eyes enlarged with stupidity and belladonna, to *her* son, her production, making prim sentences, performing monkey-tricks from her scroll of small-town middle class duplicity. I was adept. Our breaths were Sensens or cloves. She had been glazed in the kiln of insincerity so that even the heart was stoneware; she can never have noticed how abominated I must have been. It was my impeccable superficiality she anointed with the oil of flattery; she demanded no love, no careless warmth; her pale stinging kisses were paid onto my face for the spotless finger-nail, the gleaming toe-cap, the slicked hair, the unimpeachable vowel. My cleft palate had been skilfully sewn, yet, earnest and desperate as lust itself, she taught and nagged, taught and nagged me to speak more and more correctly; her clipped voice, convent-acquired, Swiss-finishing-school-burnished, will be till I die the light behind mine.

What else did she teach me while the river knotted about the town bred its mosquitoes and sparkling flies as a putrescent python corpse breeds them, while willow braids decayed in the soupy current and cicadas seared the air, while male and female were drawn to the banks by the water odour as, at night, all lovers and the lusting in river-towns are?

With genteel gestures like the Milo girl's in the barber's, she reclined smoking cigarettes no one else in the world knew she smoked for, she said, an asthma of which I never heard a wheeze, the fringed blinds half-down, Charles Garvice yellow-backs scattered about, telling me of The End of the World, of Spring-heel Jack, of those water-spouts, earthquakes and showers of stars so popular in her nineteenth-century girlhood, of the muttering frog that she believed tenanted her, of the grape-vine growing in her belly from a pip swallowed years ago. Ash sprayed from her cigarettes as she chattered: there were three knocks on a door before death, or a clock stopped, a black moth flew in, the portrait of the dying slipped from the wall, he or she died as the sun sank, the moon set, the tide turned, the last leaf fell, as dogs howled. There was, she whispered, a dark dark street in a dark dark town, in the dark dark street was a dark dark lane, in the dark dark lane was a dark

dark house, in the dark dark house a dark dark room, in the dark dark room. . . .

She taught thus the ecstasies of night-terror, certified them as we sought with candles behind doors and under beds for namelessnesses, pinned them upon me with a ghostly good-night kiss.

Shrilly whistling she crouched, rimless pince-nez clipped on, working a huckaback something never to be finished, crocheting around a pillow-sham never to be finished—pieces to which publicly, without pince-nez, she sometimes added a symbolic stitch or so.

She never desired maternally to darn or patch for me; worn things were tossed to Cook. The constantly replenished city-made wardrobe that kept me immaculate was a suggestive revelation of her care and stitchcraft.

Although despising cookery, she sometimes attempted, like a half-wit playing mother, to decorate a trifle with blanched almonds. Invariably it arrived at table incomplete. Her one pride was a salad she too often made—a Sargasso of lettuce, onions and tomatoes in a peppery morass of Champion's malt vinegar. She distributed pear ginger or cheese straws made by Cook with, "You *must* try it, dear; I made it yesterday."

She lied, perhaps, for no reason. I imitated, my reason she.

As she sipped vinegar from her dreadful salad she said, "Don't tell your father." He would not have cared had it been ratsbane. After smoking, after gossiping with the washer-woman, she said, "Not a word now to your father."

He would scarcely have listened: he had his moustache, his slate-grey eyelids, his Masonic Lodge, his music teacher mistress, his room as insipid and still as a trunk in which nothing is kept. Once, when I was thirteen, he beckoned me there to tell me some mystery . . . about my body? I heard my mother slap aside the bead curtains in the vestibule; she moved swiftly as plague between aspidistras on pedestals; she appeared at his door like Medea, forbidding him to present the award of embarrassment. She led me to *her* room, and cut my finger-nails with a German instrument called Klip Klip. There: half-open drawers voiding camisoles, stays and petticoats; there: hat-pins, hand-bags, ring-trees, curling-tongs, bangles, hair-rats and -switches and -nets, atomizers, dyes, tangles of amber beads, fur necklets with mean noses and eyes, spirals of dusty hair wound off tortoise-shell combs, fuzz snipped from her armpits, toenail cuttings. The maid polished the rest of the house like a non-conformist church.

Several times, engaging him in a conversation poisoned by the saccharine leer of the photographs, she delayed the John Chinaman greengrocer at the back door while I, as she had suggested, robbed his cart. Empowered by her to fashionable boyish devilry, how swift and successful I was! I must wash my hands then. The spoils rotted in the pantry maybe, or Cook made off with them. Other booty was similarly abandoned—the mushrooms, blackberries, hawthorn, shivery grass, wattle, maidenhair fern, heath, birds' eggs, shrimps or yabbies she had taken me to collect. How she knew where to go God knows. Pale, muddied or grass-seeded, in agony from her corns, her veil torn, her gloves and the armpits of her dress sweat-blotched, she had tottered through the groins of the country she abhorred, high heels snicking its flesh, her fingers wrenching at it, her mechanical voice ridiculously piping in the pastoral exhalations, the gurglings, grindings of fibres, the chorus of minute billions—ants, bees, worms, beetles, wings, leaves, saps. These jaunts were the ultimate perversion: she risked self-contempt to teach what she considered no other socially fit to do. Skilfully as an Indian scout, I came through unripped and speckless.

Dutifully, but as one performing a cheap parlour trick, she tore the lower lip from the antirrhinum to reveal the Blessed Virgin who extends peace to us from the petal niche; she unveiled the scarfed midget taking his mustard foot-bath in the violet; she disdainfully threaded lilac flowers on cotton or broom-straws.

She knew, for she had designed them, every plane of my hypocrisy, mendacity and guile. She knew nothing of my passion for the earth and earthy, nothing of the ardours and sins and qualities that were earthiness's and which she had not designed. And I knew, then, in my boyhood, I thought, all about her. Now . . .? Nothing, I think, now, nothing.

I had endured boarding-school ingratiatingly and slyly for three months, and had not had time to scupper my parochial vices or acquire those modish there when, without three knocks or a black moth, the telegram *Your mother is dying* came from the man my father. Extra brilliantine on my brush-back, I moonlight travelled across the abated and listening plains to the town pasted on them, to the private hospital overlooking the river that was placidly stewing slime under the white planet and effortlessly breeding as it sucked the breathings of this planet into its own cold steams. In the cab from the station I dusted my shoes with my scarf, straightened my school tie, and combed my hair. With cap and overcoat gracefully held, I went in.

A priest was fanning her with a Fijian fan in the electric light of her last room, so much tidier, barer than her own. He went away. My father withdrew unruffled and waxed to lie down or to pitter-patter through mist to the music-teacher. The matron, her spectacles alight with miniature sliding electric bulbs, fed my mother like a pot-plant with champagne from a spouted vessel. Floated out: I think her carved red hand touched my shoulder. My mother and I were alone.

She peered through some mysterious cobweb at me. She spoke. She had waited for me, she said. She had had something removed from inside (the vine? the frog?)—a dermoid cyst; she was dying of septicaemia, she said.

Three knocks? Wailing dogs of death? In a dark dark room . . .?

No.

Silence simmered on the land's milky body; inside—stare, stare, monkey-bear—the electric light. To my astonishment I began to cry.

"Be quiet," she said. "Behave yourself. People will hear. You'll make your eyes red." Tears watered no seeds; seeds of tears fell nowhere. I obediently became silent and drought-stricken. Nevertheless, I walked near to kiss her, to kiss her before that mask—which had waited within her, that waits in all of us, the last scraped impolite face now nearing the surface—should meet the skin of life.

"Don't. Don't kiss me," she said. "Give me some more champagne."

Into the flaring room the night was gradually absorbed, once over the sill its colours were immediately annihilated.

Now and then the Matron popped her head in like Judy; snatched it back. It became green dawn; the mask strove nearer the surface; the voice said almost viciously from under the film where she lay thinking or not thinking, "Be quiet. Stop the fidgets; your shoes squeak." She slapped at my wrist, her rings now rattling faintly on depleted fingers. Then, she was *so* sorry, she said. I looked *very* nice in my school suit, she said, very charming: it was a good school. I sat down politely, careful of creases, my knees together.

"Comb your hair," she said, three times, at intervals, not looking at me. Each time I combed.

Ultimately, loud and wild, her final secret, the last words from that world: "I owe Mr Dahlensberg twenty-two pounds. You must settle for me. Don't let your father know."

Day. Electric light remained forgotten on. I refused Matron's gift of tea; it was too strong. My father and the priest returned at blatant half-past eight. Precisely enough, her eyes halved, my mother repeated religious prattle after the priest, upon the completion of which he marked a cross on the air, and departed with the red and blue design of his nose. To the lavatory? To bacon and eggs?

She wilfully murmured addle-patedly on; her eyes closed themselves (what colour had they been, those eyes?); she murmured out a creamy froth upon her lips. My father stared decorously at this misbehaving while I slobbered with care into a handkerchief, and dared not otherwise move because of squeaking shoes. The Matron, suddenly flushed and seeming somehow angry with herself, said, "Ai'm afreed she's gone." I was advised, by someone or other of others who appeared, to kiss (in all the blaze, no sun fading, no tide turning) the mask which had arrived from where it had been nurtured. I cried successfully quietly, fifteen years old, for her who had given as her one gift the information she kept from all others just as she kept the knowledge of corns, hair-dyes, vinegar-tippling, yellow-backs, lies and smoking. She had shared her pettiness with me—the one honesty.

With modest gesture the Matron indicated the rings on the shrivelled fingers. Decidedly, nodded my father decidedly. Off they were slipped. He took out his purse, and as though warily accepting change, put them carefully in—one, two three, four five six. Finished.

Finished. I, meantime, had certainly been a little gentleman to the end: charming in my school uniform, quiet sobber, courteous, and smooth of hair. For all that, for all that, the umbilical cord was irrevocably snapped.

Next, beyond the window and the river, the country stirred, the earth, savage simple female. Upon her, poured all the devices and benisons of heaven; from her furred, scarred, abraded, stained, scabby, beautiful limbs buzzed and mumbled the scents of her reality; smokes of insects roared up; her deep-set arteries thickened with the conversation of animals sensual and unrefined; shadows lunged without manners across her glory; trees fed; nightshade and saffron sucked shamelessly. There was untrammelled and unceasing suckling in her sponges and marrow, in the pus of her pits, the horniness of her wounds, the very sores of her parasites, even in the blood of her sufferings and the stench of her pain.

For some lost last moments, a curtain of tears hid this older mother . . . upon the curtain moved the other, my human mother, leaning to me in her spotted veil, handkerchief over kid-gloved finger. She licked the handkerchief. She dabbed the speck from my forehead and, with this movement of a lacy scrap, erased too the feckless town, the streets leading nowhere, the garden of asphalt paths, the ugly house, the rooms of rubbish, and herself.

The curtain of tears thus engraved with nothing then slid down for ever on Act One.

(1948)

House-Girl

At night, Tokyo, like all twentieth-century Babylons, can be seen in the sky. The city's daytime monotone—Gippsland-cow-shed-grey—has disintegrated to dazzles and blazing bars of frost and salmon, of saffron, Cape-weed, aquamarine, fuchsia and Mars-orange: colours to lure, to exaggerate, to obscure wattle-and-daub makeshift, and spangle the stench rising to the God of Poverty.

Netted miles of neons and fluorescents, hundreds of paper lanterns gross as niners, thousands of naphtha-flares, millions of sizzling bare bulbs dangling off-handedly on flex—the night-air sucks up these cheap glories and digests them to an achromatic reflection, a phosphorescent flaw in the upper dark, which can be seen for miles. It is then that the restless young, fed-up with the lightless village street, rebellious as they stumble alone along the shrine-tracks or through the camellia-groves, imagine under this distant halo a city like a vast opal, smouldering with fantastic life, and yearn to walk by its luminous walls behind which pulse the shapes of lust and all ecstasy and the future.

One by one the bravest of them, freed by their own defiance, or by domestic calamity or necessity, break the age-old village tradition, wrap all they possess in a square yard of coloured cloth, take some persimmons, and wait blank-faced by the bridge.

Jizo-san, the children's god with a dozen disease-speckled bibs about his plump stone neck, waits there too, as he has for centuries—his time-worn eyes are the only ones to see their departure. The sun is low, shines horizontally through the upreared and tattered lotus leaves, through the wing of a heron hoisting itself from an irrigation-channel. Casting a long warning shadow the bus draws near.

And so, in time, they arrive on the rim of Tokyo. Once it was called Edo, and the flames of its recurring fires the Flowers of Edo. Now the city spreads like a weed far and flat on the plain as though the fire-sprung pods had sprayed seeds farther and farther afield, as though earthquake and typhoon had scattered the multiplying tiled huts farther yet, as though cloudburst Allied bombs had splashed seeds to the very limit to infest the millet and sweet-potato fields with ramshackle factories, slums and suburban labyrinths.

Here then, to the rustic young, is the city of desires, and they can descend stiffly into it from the shabby bus and be lost for ever, make a fortune, commit suicide or finish up in the fetid beggars' subway near Ueno Park.

It was somehow thus, orphaned in some one-pig village, too ugly to engage the interest of brothel-suppliers, belonging, I suspect, to the untouchable Eta sect, but with a thick personal artery of will-to-live traversing her national indifference to death, coarse, squat and neurotic, that Ikuko-san came to Tokyo and by unguessed-at ways to me.

How near her wanderings came to suicide or the Ueno tunnel I do not know; fortune to her would certainly always be the crow flying over; but she was too much of the earth ever to be lost on it. For what reason my unforeseen arrival in Tokyo, and her movements about the city seeking rice and pickled radish to sustain her ugliness, should have intersected I am at loss to say.

All I know is that a mess-sergeant who had a nervous breakdown some days later was able to produce a house-girl for me. Why and how Ikuko-san? I should like, purely for history's sake, to question him. He handed her over with dazed relief—the conjurer who finds in his hand griffin instead of rabbit. Japanese girls are very plain; she was by many points the plainest. The sergeant walked away like Oates; I never saw him again. Ikuko-san and I faced each other; she dropped a broken-winged paper sunshade and giggled repulsively. I picked it up for her, and a year of life together began.

How shall I tell it?

From before six in the morning, before the shutters of the noodle-shops, curio-dealers and vegetable-markets are down, before even the bean-curd sellers have set out their trays, the house-girls awake on their threadbare rice-matting floors and buckwheat pillows, rise in the double-shuttered room among the still-sleeping others, crawl from under the mosquito-netting, and dress. They do this imagining jealous liquid glances at their American nylon stockings, English brogues, European tweeds, sweaters of Scotch wool, and solid leather handbags. They draw lips with magazine-famous sticks, clap at the house-god and give it some rice-seeds and a little bowl of chlorinated water, and leave their cell as though it were merely a dream.

They walk actressishly under the iced-water signs, each as if a happy secret lay in her tailored sleeve. They ignore the house-boys reeking of camellia hair-oil and mincing hand-in-hand and, proudly, handmaidens of the Conqueror, approach the artificial, official and hideous luxury of the Occupation Messes in which they work. Arrived elegant, they strip and re-dress. Now they wear the faded short work-frock that reveals too cruelly the pitiful shoulders, the flat chest, the bandy legs mottled like bamboo. On go the scrubbing-brush-grey clogs of paulownia. . . .

She slips off her clogs in the corridor where they have been making a noise like a Shetland pony, ceases to sing loudly "Samisen Boogie", opens the door with infinite care, tip-toes in barefoot as though I am dying, whispers:

"Will-come, Porter-san! Wake! Wake! Sivin-oh-clock-fifteen!"

She smiles the pure Japanese smile, radiant (but that need not mean she is happy), and sets my tomato-juice on the bedside table. She turns on the wireless and the electric fan, arranges my dressing-gown, slippers, bathing- and shaving-gear. She does it this morning silently, with an inward look as though the teeth of her mind chewed gristle. She has a slight droop and her mouth droops; she sighs; even her stubby feet contrive to appear distressed. Shall I be brisk, grab my things and hustle out taking no notice . . . or see what it is *this* time? She is doing something that seems unnecessary to two very small dahlias, one red for the male, one white for the female . . . does it mean anything?

"Ikuko-san!"

She acts a faint start as though roused from sorrow's lethargy and cannot quite look at me.

"*Hai*!" she says; a minute sound.

"What's the matter?" While waiting for her to enact reluctance-to-discuss-a-certain-topic the wireless plays "I Can't See You in My Eyes Any More", and I seem to catch my ex-wife's eye from the dressing-table photograph: what was the photographer like at whom she is thrusting that absurdly heart-piercing gaze which still, in times of half-drunken nostalgia, I imagine directed at me? And why do I cart her about the world and stand her up in foreign bedrooms? Is it because she is so beautiful and a sort of diploma of manhood?

Ikuko-san hates her even more than I pretend I do; often I fish her out of strange crannies. So far there have been no pins stuck in her well-covered heart.

"What's the matter, Ikuko-san?"

"Ver-ee not happy." Her thick-lipped pout makes her really hideous.

"Oh!" I decide to go on with it: "Why?"

"Momma-san ver-ee sick."

I do not side-track by inquiring into this loss of orphanship: Momma-san occasionally makes these Lazarus come-backs.

"I'm so sorry," I say politely.

"*Hai.*" Very flat, this.

"I hope she is better soon."

Ikuko-san mentally stamps a foot. She flashes a venomous ray at me from her seal-brown eyes. Then, with a dying fall, she accuses me: "Momma-san ver-ee, *ver-ee* poor."

Ah!

"Cocoa?" I say.

"Thank you, Porter-san." She is dignified, ladylike, but far from overjoyed, but at least I've started. I can feel her intensely directing my thoughts somewhere. However, there is, this morning, no time for the subtle rites of beggar's ping-pong.

"You tell me what you want, Ikuko-san, and I'll give you a canteen-order."

Of course, of *course*—Canteen Day. I have forgotten: she is the wife who must remind, on behalf of her own rake-off if for no lesser reason.

She flashes on like a lighthouse; immediately after becomes serious, nervous, confused by visions of what she might scrounge; hoping earnestly not to ask one thing too many and suffer the face-losing humiliation of refusal; hoping most fervently not to stop asking too soon. She watches some section of my face—the treacherous corner of the mouth?—and recites meticulously and too loudly, a trial-and-error pause between each item.

"Cocoa, oh, yiss . . . canned milk . . . cak-ee . . . Aspro . . . choclit cand-ee . . . Lux soap . . . toothpast-ee . . . salt peanut. . . ."

She falters, becomes pathetic and smaller; my assistance, assent or refusal, is needed. My expressionless face defeats her; moreover, a sleepless night of preparation for this has set the little flame of her mind flickering in exhaustion. I, too, have been watching—a sudden illumination makes me say with despicable magnanimity "Go on. Whatever you want: O.K. Go on, woman."

Woman! For the first time it has struck me that, since I neither love her nor sleep with her, this necessary begging is painful for her. Indifference makes me careless of the unwritten rules. I see her fear and her womanhood trying to veil decently what life and greed demand she must do.

Some of these delicacies may go to her own version of a Momma-san, to someone or something she, in her turn, can be magnanimous to. Some she will sell on the black market for a *presento* to me, some useless atrocity costing yen that she needs herself. Some she will arrange with antlike precision in one of the two drawers she has taken over for herself—a drawer for cosmetics, and another for supplies of food for some future drought. Alas, that her sweet tooth gnaws constantly at this future!

When I first found clothes of hers hanging beside mine in the wardrobe I was startled, irritated and had a faint feeling of repulsion: too many years of boarding-school, boarding-house life had given me that careless meticulousness that is the bachelor's. It was an intrusion and suggested an intimacy; but it was the custom. And as I looked at the small exquisitely darned kimonos, the couple of schoolgirlish pre-Occupation frocks in which the dye had run like tears, and the much finer attire that had been wheedled from me or given in maudlin pity or . . . or affection, I think I felt moved; there was certainly pathos and a sub-acid note somewhere.

Along two unbelievably different ways we had come to this temporary companionship—her broad feet had stepped for a short space from the excrement-mud of the rice-fields into a kind of film-setting; those feet would return there taking her back to the Fox Goddess, the moxa-burnings, the medicine of dried snake, the endless destructive nobility of a life of poverty. This was the one holiday between the old life and the old life she would return to with nothing to show except a hundred or so English words, some Australian slang, a taste for Aspros and Players cigarettes, a wardrobe that would wear to threads, and a collection of useless objects—a pair of old nail-scissors, shaving-cream jars, boot-polish tins, Bovril-bottles and worn-out underpants.

And, I suppose, memories of a year or so of—*de facto* motherhood? Sisterhood? Unconsummated wifehood? My room, shoes, sheets, buttons—all her special care, every day; my hangovers, tantrums, selfishness—all hers. I see her too vividly in all sorts of situations: rump in the air walking on her feet and hands to polish the floor with dark-tan shoe-polish; radiant and freshly shaved under a *permanento* one could play like a xylophone; absorbed for hours in a flower-arrangement which offends the Western eye but which one must be gracious about; filling the ash-trays with water; running across the Mess-compound in the snow—a cold-germ mask of unattractive navy-blue tied across her mouth and nose, neatly and slowly making herons, frogs, little boxes out of cunningly folded paper; teaching me the haunting age-old children's song, *Ame, ame*. . . .

My feeling for her generally is one of the deepest pity—an unwise emotion at all times; between man and woman most unwise. Yet, for all my sympathy with her lot and all my attempts to keep on emotional no-man's-land, there are times when control slips, the gears grate:

"I told you, Ikuko-san not to wash my towel every day."

"*Hai.*"

"That's all very well. You said '*Hai*'; you said yes; but you still wash. Now listen. Understand—no wash tower-u, no wash tower-u. . . . You know . . . ?"

"*Hai.*" She seems bewildered. "*Hai.* No wash Porter-san tower-u."

F

I am really irritated, almost angry. She does not flinch outwardly, and her face sets at zero; her hands tremble slightly, that is all. She goes about her tasks: I see her hanging socks under the gingko-tree; I see her picking cosmos in the Mess-garden; I see her doing this and that, but like someone reluctantly hauled back to chores from the grave.

It is not until much later that I can bear her silent comings and goings no more, for they have become huge and portentous; emanations from her distress have made her a giantess. She is polishing one of her *presentos* to me—an appalling cut-glass salad-bowl the blue of a castor-oil bottle.

"Oh, for God's sake, Ikuko-san. . . ."

There is no need for such a tone in my voice, but the situation has taken charge of us both—Australian and Japanese, boss and servant, conqueror and conquered, Church of England and Shinto, man and woman. I do not see her face, but know that a spasm of suffering cuts across it; quickly she wheels and, with a primitive animal movement, goes to the wardrobe and stands behind its half-open door, her back to me. She makes no sound, but the sounds she wrestles with disturb her body, making me aware of the strength of will which so often lends these small bodies the semblance of a physical strength they are far from possessing. I can see the hairless blotched legs quiver as her toes press into the linoleum; her body in its scanty rotten frock now and again shudders violently.

I will not look. I will not be affected. I remain sitting in the arm-chair of rhubarb-red plush and nickel like someone in Act Two; I attempt to read off-handedly, but find I am glaring at the pages. The air between is volted with misery.

Presently, from the wardrobe comes the faint rustle of a paper handkerchief—she is crying. I still make no move. The minutes float out towards the walls and moat of the Imperial Palace outside which firemen in butcher-blue Happee coats are performing marvels at the top of tall ladders.

Now that the first cruel wrestling with her pain is over she has, in the backwash of tears, begun to listen to me not taking notice of her. Human beings, East or West, know a lot of simple things about human beings. She rustles her handkerchief—and again, more loudly, and sniffs designedly. At this stage the thing could stop; she has work to do and cannot remain in the wardrobe; yet the simplicity of coming out neat, without embarrassment, is beyond her. So:

"Porter-san." Oh, a mere sliver of voice, the voice of a naughty little daughter.

"Yes."

"You *pisto*?"

"No, I'm not angry."

"True?"

"Yes, true." Pause. A Buddhist priest drives the swinging log against the temple gong. "Ikuko-san."

"*Hai*?"

"It's all right. You toddle off and get me some soda-water from the bar-boy. Everything's O.K."

In an instant she lands like a grasshopper by the chair, sobbing noisily. It is ultimate disgorgement. She grips my hand in her work-cracked paws.

"Me not happ-ee. Me bad girl."

"There, there, there—everything's O.K."

"Me bad girl."

"Come on, now. Wipe your face."

"Oh, me die . . . me die. . . ."

"Ikuko-san, soda-water, please."

"Last night me pray for Porter-san . . . today bad girl . . . me die. . . ."

"Soda-water, *please*. And you can ask the bar-boy for a bottle of lolly-water for yourself. . . ."

"*Hai?*"

"Get some lolly-water from Butch. . . ."

"*Hai*!"

She is at the dressing-table; she opens one of her drawers and powders her face, she rakes her hair with the brush with rusted wire teeth, paints her lips. She knocks over my ex-wife's photograph, but remembers not to stand it up. An accident? An expression of power over the cardboard representation of a distant woman? The smile that she turns on me has the beauty and singleness of a child's. Her eyes glitter with the ebb of tears and the dark sparkle of yet another despair hidden within, hidden deep.

"Porter-san!"

"*Hai*! . . . that is, yes, Ikuko-san."

"Lolly-water and . . . and. . . ."

"O.K. O.K. Candy, too."

She is gone. I hear her slip into her wooden clogs outside the door and run. She is gone.

She is not anything more than a human being, which is the least of reasons for pity, love, hate or tolerance. She is only a woman in a dream between war and peace. I shall never see her again, although the finger-prints she has left on the windows of my memory are far clearer than those of people I count as necessary to the life I seem to live.

It would be difficult to recognize her again . . . the blurred face in the group-picture of millions, one of those forms bowed in the stinking rice-flats, in the bath-house queue at six-o'clock, jammed in a bucking tram on the Ginza, waiting with endless patience on the benchless underground-railway platform, walking up the steep shrine steps past the dried-squid sellers, crossing the muddy midnight road in the jeep's headlight with a white pinafore and a bowl of shrimps.

Or, years hence, bowed to a semicircle under faggots, a towel tied over her almost hairless head—the old woman of fables, in the maple-mountains, the pheasant-woods, by the sandless shores where the stakes of the oyster-gardens and the cryptomerias of the off-shore island shrine are as black against the sunset as her black sleeves in one of which the pipe is concealed and the tobacco in a Players fifty-tin which someone she can't quite remember used years ago.

(1954)

On the Ridge

His death—author's resurrection from an enigma of silence—startles younger fans who have not bothered to expect it; the older have forgotten to. Gilbert Rasmussen, who years ago seemed photographically more beautiful than Rupert Brooke, is dead: his machinery already dissolves to iridescent muck. Eyes too, the fevered up-all-night ones of Old Masters. Does *City*, his one novel, shimmer, a cake of agate and emeralds, at the grave-head? Does . . . ?

Outside the run-down railway station jammed in archipelagos of pepper-cress, the lean man who has just left the train supports his face, passionless except for the Roman four above the nose, towards the country taxi: ". . . cemetery!" This is a mile off. Late hawthorns pepper the air, salt the dust of roadside dock-leaves. The wireless recording of a boxing-match, plucked from November blaze, travels with the taxi, and is the first the fly-speck lark embellishing infinity above the cemetery has ever heard. Leaving an attaché-case filled with air on the car-seat, and without interrogating the taxi-man's boil-pitted nape, the stranger wades upslope to the grave, forerunner wreath directing him. There lie seven limpnesses of ignoble flowers, hick things, beside his own city circle of white lilac edge-frizzled like fried egg.

The boxing-match continues dictatoring towards clouds heavy as pelicans while he—he removes his Homburg. The downturned bowl of a bald head flashes above eyes holding an incessant wariness to destroy kind errors of the past. Or perhaps a demon of cold control has possessed his mind: he appears unattachable, his own and final generation. He straddles as though peacefully pissing among the skippers. Then this unflinching one, this apparently chaste mind, this man covers his brain's heliographing shell, takes out a notebook and copies 477 from the cast-iron trefoil at the grave-head—final cell number. Erect, he conveys his civilized masculinity to the taxi. About to bow himself inside, he turns, he examines the cemetery as one does an astonishing painting: scurf-white double gate, post-and-rail, inferior tombstones hooped in brier. One marble angel, dishonest bird, lichen-brocaded, gestures from its nest of blackberry. He picks from his pocket a key small as a horse-stinger, looks from it to the scene several times.

Next he is driven back to an hotel.

Hernias of hills lolling across its outlets, the town surrounding the hotel pretends emptiness but, under corrugated iron, arrangements of generations are chewing, slopping and sweating in lean-tos musical with blowflies.

He eats alone, dead-centre of a quincunx of tables crowded with electroplated vases, water-jugs, cheese-covers, butter-dishes, salt-cellars, pepper-pots, toast-racks, ash-trays, bread-containers, sugar-bowls, sauce-bottle-holders. These, nearly all empty, minify, distort and multiply him. Again, once, he fingers the key as if it were being a hopsac sample, yet his face commits nothing, so carefully, as it does for the chimney-piece with varnished storeys, heater-shaped shields of looking-glass, plaster of Paris Bozos.

In the streets again, a Judas who can spy while other disciples sleep, he cleaves the heat, indicating *Farewell!* with each pace to the leopard-rusted verandas, the display of adored atrocities, the tawdry shoes, hurricane lamps, vanilla slices and magenta steaks. He turns corners to back-streets of paint-shorn human-hutches with unpinned barge-boards. Paling fences topple under mattresses of morning glory towards gardens of fat-hen. Plantain occupies drains. All and all stink of the paper-mills. How the grasses grow!—heavy with seeds the shape of adder-fangs, ferret-teeth, maggots, superstition and despair; they stand on footpath, under the water-tank, at the doorstep, in the churchyard, ugly and perfidious as people. One ex-coffee-palace uplifts three urns offering entrails of stucco to windlessness.

Now he is waiting in the bus, only passenger except a front-seat girl-friend whose profile pecks with gossip at the driver's cat-dark face, beery breath and muscular heart busy behind a cross of chest-curls and ferocity. Her nose is whitened, is edged. On the floor are morons' wet-batteries, sugar-bags of vulgar vegetables, a bundle of horror comics and a wet-the-bed child's tricycle. At the last moment a runt or jockey frisks from the hotel babying a parcel.

"Mrs Rasmussen's steam," he says, leaning in like Punch to set the four bottles of cheap muscat beside the girl-friend. The bus starts.

For awhile the stranger looks at the wine-bearing seat or through the cogs of a clock that has ticked him to the putrefying author's shire.

Later, he extracts this attention, fanning it open on a land level in a vacancy between whichever winds were and will be, and rugged with uncherished grass; weedscape into which mussel-coloured ravens occasionally flounder electrically shouting. Once occurs a black-gulleted chimney in a decadence of periwinkle, once a lost furphy rusted chrysanthemum; always the shifty grassings beneath thigh-bones of dead gums, pelvic uprootings, fractured stumps and remnants.

Finally, one unmurdered eucalypt heraldically appears. Its spilt leaves form a mica-and-milk pool at which a beaked sheep-skull appears to sip. Absolute departure is thus somehow sanctified; the bus ascends into the recesses of the range and a nearer future. The traveller can look downwards and see, over the sparkling and rank dust, thousands of killed trees—finger-bones, match-sticks, bristles. Each turn of the rising round and round thirsts higher into repetitions of undulations quilled with spikes. The vehicle reaches mid-afternoon and Strzelecki Ridge.

Descending, he must observe from under the shadow of his brain the school, the post-office outside which the bus stands, the curry-coloured road and nothing else except sky-scrapers of living trees; he must hear behind these vegetable bastions the coughing of woodcutters' axes. He must turn from the columns holding tons of pointed glistening leaves, and speak to the . . . people. Emancipated from the platitudes of mateship, he nevertheless momentarily makes his smile a revelation of Rameses-like charm: ". . . me, please, Rasmussen's . . . ah . . . place?"

The group stuck nearby and stuck together—fish, sow, two tapirs, cat and cat's bird—symbols of the ignorant and wily: the postmistress, a pregnant woman, two long-faced children, driver and driver's girl-friend raise fin trotter paw claw, and point, calling in brutal accents. "*Theer, up theer; three moiles on; no, three-four moiles on; turn left; no, turn roight at the fust turning . . . three . . . three-four moiles . . . up theer. . . .*"

They repeat, again and again, anxious to be told something. He says no more than thanks, and moves off. They watch, thwarted and foxy, wishing a thrush to shit on his Homburg. Eighty-six yards away, two hundred feet high, are the packed trees. The road is sucked there, cascades upslope perversely in reverse. He seems frailer, is about to enter gloom. The bus-driver brays. He turns. They gesticulate witlessly; one holds up the muscat—"For . . . Mis-sers . . . Ras . . . muss . . . en . . ."—and begins to follow, but Lord Muck of Turd Island, already at a great doorway, sternly yelps, "No!" and disappears to quest or task.

He walks as though expressing, "I am gall, catharsis, over-civilization and rectitude. I am the lit past appearing in the blown-out silence, the elegant goose tippity-toeing on the coffin-lid. I am to speak with clarity among the sniffling mutes. I am that Nemesis which follows the last of all other dooms."

He walks the cleft in a brain, a rift in botanic centuries. Not for man these abnormal verticalities, the solitude from which vein-paths enter the conduit he is using, the hermetic walls that have absorbed Gilbert Rasmussen's comings and goings. For the newcomer it must be a power-house of malignity; founts of loneliness lie in gullies under leaf-plated girders and cantilevers; there is no perspective; the road contracts behind, contracts in front, so that he climbs in a Fingal's Cave of darker. No signboard, no door-handle nor electric bell for this man designed to walk corridors and Rues de la Paix. Once only appears a vertical panel of heaven: some paw of weather has sliced a loop-hole through which he looks out and down on tree-tops and, far below them, the white nails of dead trees, the paddocks unrolled for miles to an ocean dado-ing the sky in which one stupefied cloud mopes on its cylinder of atmosphere. He stares also at the near slope where the elements have arranged knick-knacks of a rite either domestic and careless or sinister and significant: branches fallen to form a clause in code, logs directing shattered ends in the direction of some shocking secret, hairy boulders tossed like marbles to state an unguessable total of coming horror.

He leaves the gap, enters again the Jenolan of trunks. He

reaches the turn-off. He approaches a house in an elderly orchard of walnut, quince and cherry-plum. There are guelder roses in the unknitted garden, and . . . and, oh, white lilac. He advances through milk-thistles and fuchsias with forgotten names. Above are lichened branches and a hawk-torn sky. As he nears the door it opens.

She is a sort of woman, Mrs Rasmussen, the fastidious author's widow—example of a human, no more. She was a baby once, coarse then, and a sly coarse girl and young woman; she was coarse in the womb, now is coarser. Sinless as a she-hippopotamus, she has never travelled from the district, for years has not left the Ridge; but Content's child, and dirtied. The melon-seeds of her eyes cockroach over his decorously panting shape. They find nothing to germinate in: he exhales untouchability. She listens to him, appears to listen, yet it is only the inflamed filaments of her flesh that do so truthfully as those of one dog do to another dog's. The sticky breasts use raw eyes; the navel corkscrews in to offer giddiness above the triangle of greying hairs. Insect in the silk of her moustache, a creamy crumb is caught on the brink of parched lips. Craftily she exudes oniony food and souring wine.

". . . and although I have not seen Gilbert for about twenty years, I feel . . . I am *sure* he regarded me as his . . . as his closest friend. And . . . ah . . . of course I was his publisher . . . *City* . . . as you doubtless know. . . ."

She does not know; she does not know what a publisher is; she has never heard of him. If ever she knew of *City*, she has forgotten. Closest friend? Words on the other side of her Venus, yet this . . . this man . . . goes on with words, heartlessly wagers them with her. Still yap-yap-yapping, he reveals a key:

"He sent it to me before he. . . . You understand, Mrs Rasmussen, he wrote to me. It is the key of his . . . of a box he wishes . . . he *wished* me to. . . ."

She feels she should move and let him enter the house, so she backs. She sees him standing surrounded by daylight that stains over his outline. Then he seems to advance into her. He enters the house.

The front room contains the vigour of her sweat and privates, her loneliness, animal idleness and simplicity. She is capable of offering only what Nature eggs her to, a gift untainted by intellect, the gift of nakedness.

Fluff everywhere; windows behind curtains of decomposing lace are green-paned from a sort of alga. From walls tiled with photographs, faces statue-stare with waning stupidity. So many already dead: the unwinking unsmiling dead. A Gilbert Rasmussen photograph in Rupert Brooke vein? No: but leg-of-mutton sleeves, thick jaws, Alexandra fringes, buttonhole roses like curls of pine shaving. Though she cannot recall what she should do next and is shy, she gestures to an open door, shows him—solicitous hostess—the unmade double bed, that altar of iron and brass beside which stands the pot half-filled with its persimmon-coloured fluid. Two blowflies there, Leander-dead. A muscat bottle and a tumbler sit like a Cézanne still-life on a chair.

"Yairs. In 'ere . . ." she says.

She means, or thinks she means, that here Gilbert Rasmussen died, selfishly, decarnalized, spitting peevishly to the rattle of loose brass. She has already cried. She will not cry again. Does the man understand what she thinks she means?

"Dead," she says.

"The Doc. . . ." she says.

" 'E was reel crook," she says.

And, "Dead," she says.

He uses his eyes upon it all, seeming to see the dead moths in the soot-crumbed fireplace, silver-fish moving like thoughts out and in, Gilbert Rasmussen's braces hanging on a sea-grass chair.

"I . . . *can*-not . . . tell . . . you . . . how . . ." He does not continue; lies die of their own weight. Standing there, pot between them, can he smell the hessian under wall-paper? He puts his case and hat . . . on . . . the . . . bed, gets her husband's letter and reads some to her, "In the box you will find, all ready, manuscripts, my will, and a document which is confidential, for you alone. . . ." He reads no more, but: "The box?"

She pours muscat and drinks it; from timidity does not offer any. She is almost sure she knows what he means yet watches on, contentedly perturbed, trying lips with a flannel tongue.

"A box, Mrs Rasmussen. With his papers in. This key, you see. A box. Do you know where it is?"

Now she thinks she knows. She leads through a rancid kitchen where a sybil's fire smoulders to death also. At one end of the back-veranda is a large bathroom, surprising, enamelled, speckless still. One half, with mats, desk, chair, Tilley lamp, was the author's study. All shipshape: a carpet-beater like a caduceus stands in the corner—and Mercury dead. On the desk is a, the, cedar box.

"Always washing hisself," she says.

"The box?"

She nods, proud of her wisdom, and smiles, showing enamel decorated with decay.

He unlocks the box.

She is not interested in this, merely in admiring how skilfully she is carrying off an encounter with someone from foreign elsewhere. He sees manuscripts, will, the document on which is his own elaborate name and *To be destroyed when read*. His voice mounts to a clarity that even ear-drums anxious for nothing but a beast's strenuous snuffle must allow admittance to, "Gil wished me to have these, Mrs Rasmussen. The manuscripts we shall probably publish—a decision very soon. You can certainly rest absolutely and utterly assured that. . . ."

In another eleven minutes he has gone, still infected with purity; his case encloses the contents of the cedar box; the globe of skull is again Homburged.

Since, unwithered Ceres, she has not mind enough to kill primitive hope, has said and is not certain she has, hopefully, "Y' could stay 'ere. Y' could stay ther noight." He has said nothing except many words. Her body remains, unmoved, but realizing an intemperate and inconsiderate chastity in his.

Now, pre-sunset, not once turning to farewell by any sort of bo-peep the genius's house with its slimed panes, he returns to the Ridge, and through its darkening mind descends. At sunset he reaches the aperture; elastic shadows of the match-sticks line pains towards the ocean. The rite-hurled branches, boulders and logs are more galvanic now, their message over-written with portent. As he goes, a forest of unseen trees grows among the seen; birds gibber parsimoniously. At last he steps from the maze, perhaps hears swans creak over and momently black-out Betelgeuse, decidedly must see a lamplit window in the post-office house.

He has three hours to wait for the return bus. If he may wait inside?

Yairs, yairs, of course.

If he may sit by a fire . . . perhaps? And perhaps a lamp?

Yairs, yairs, of course.

So, in the postmistress's parlour, by lamplight, he opens the case. He reads.

In an hour and a half he has assessed the manuscripts, is obviously skilled, decisive and . . . pleased? He seems to be not displeased. He replaces the manuscripts. Outside are night's intricate limbs, night's refreshed and wicked silence. He closes his eyes as though to cleanse their paleness and then, revealing them wiped, unfolds the document addressed to him:

You will remember, when we were young together, so long ago, how I became absorbed in a search for the heart of goodness, and how I laboured to make myself pure. *My conception of* pure *I cannot define now: it is an insolence only youth dares have—or fanaticism. It was something beyond Christian: no scourging the money-lenders for example. Conceit told me I'd acquired* purity; *that it was wisdom and duty to evangelize subtly and pacifically. At this fantastic stage, you recall, I was sent to teach at the country school on the Ridge.*

Twenty-odd years ago, Gilbert Rasmussen, young, beautiful—and *pure*—is off! He reaches the town trapped in morning glory; he ascends roads floury with dust; his eyes angle in double-yous and vees of interknitted valleys. Next: the post-office, the school. His pupils, timber-cutters' children, advance on his complex simplicity, as still-eyed as puppy Minotaurs, from among the trees. Days pass. Nights pass. He is, he thinks, happy.

There was nowhere else to lodge except, four miles' walk from school, this place in which I've lived ever since. Even then it was ramshackle because the owner, who had inherited a well-run mountain-farm, was feckless, apathetic, bothering with only a few pigs and geese, a cow, a dozen Border Lei-

cesters whose dissipated masks scorned me as I athletically waded the morning mists. He grew the crops of the improvident: potatoes, swedes, broad beans. In the bathroom hung a side of bacon above the bowl in which he washed, meantime pressing his head against the bacon so that it was hair-oil-scented. The hairs in his nostrils and ears, on his cheekbones, had run wild. He was older than his wife and as lazy. She was gross and placid. They were easy-going animals; at night it was impossible not to hear the activity of their matings. An only living child, a twelve-year-old son, was the most intelligent child I have ever met. Indeed, he was perhaps a genius—or insane. But, I soon discovered, his was the genius or insanity of evil. Evil? *Now, I cannot tell. Then, I had an encyclopaedia of* evils. Evil!

Childhood is the sleep of reason; his nature was already too awake—corruptly so. He lived, as I saw it then, in the artery of evil *that flows, has flowed and always will flow across the minds of the world. That two primitives should have idly bred a cynical monstrosity frightened me but fascinated my* purity. *His* evil, *unblemished as it was by conscience, was a test for my evangelizing. Oh, how I worked! Enthusiastically, with ceaseless cunning. Time, I thought, given time I shall win.*

On the fin of Strzelecki Ridge, where thunderbolts crash-dived past very ears, and winds ground all together like rushes or exploded apart the giant trunks, dispersing the execrations from axes like chaff over unexplored defiles, Gilbert Rasmussen stood, handsome Christ, and tempted a child Satan to *purity*. Time . . . given time. . . . But the boy's genius lit his *evil* too clearly; nothing childlike remained to be appealed to. Months passed. The tempter walked to school, the boy with him. The boy padded home every day through the tunnel of trees beside him. And all day the boy sat before him in the schoolroom, ate at the same table, lay in the veranda bed outside Rasmussen's window, interminably patient, while he inside directed his delusions intolerantly outwards. Obsession! Time . . . given time. . . .

Time does not alter men—it merely unmasks them.

I thought to pave the days with such plans of pureness

the boy could not step beyond them. Useless. So, though I thought I abhorred the idea, I decided to flog him.

Time had unmasked Gilbert Rasmussen. Prepared for inferno but victory, he faced the boy and said, "I am going to flog you."

"Yes," said the boy, immediately removing shirt and trousers, all he wore, and, naked, then strutted, and looked at me, using a sidelong glance as disconcerting as that of an immortal, saying softly, "Go on. Flog me. I'll tell no one."

This last churlish challenge rioted on Gilbert Rasmussen like a waterfall from a height of horror, so that his vision was marred. Then a nausea of disappointment overcame the schoolmaster, who began to sob.

Through slobbering self-pity he heard the boy snigger charitably as a victor or . . . a saviour. When he could see again, through final tears, he must watch the boy revolve slowly, for some diabolical or kittenish reason showing the immature wafer of his body which contained so much voodoo. Outrageously the boy held up his grimy arms like a lyre to reveal the tender secrets of his armpits, saying with Cain-like sweetness, "Come on home, sir", and dressed himself.

The boy preceded him from the school as meekly as a Quaker, guiding as if along a tight-rope electric cable that must be kept to and Rasmussen had no knowledge of. The two advanced to the trees, and the road riven, an earthquake crack, between them.

The schoolroom shock still sent charge after charge of vibrations that abnormalized Rasmussen's vision: his eyes saw the trees not as before—colossi in pelts like the hairiness of brutes stirred leafed heads secretly far-off from the roots that had for centuries, fibre by fibre, equally secretly, probed the mass of the mountain. So deep, so high, so trammelled, they seemed to him the powerful emblems of sacrilege on a planet soon to be as bare as the moon. Now and again a snake lay on the scroll of road like a sick one's S or J.

Presently the boy began to speak—patience informed his words, and absolution shone there. Yet the enigma of his *evil* still remained, a web of snow concealing a crevasse into worse and worst.

"Why do you try to make me good?" he said, might even

have cried aloud. "It's useless. I can't do anything about it. I couldn't let myself." Another snake lay by the roadside, pointing straight as any arrow feverish to be at its destination. "Nobody can do anything. If you flog me it will make no difference."

Where the snake's poison-kernelled head pointed, the man could see a display of late afternoon sky through a breach struck by some vendetta of nature in the tree-wall. The boy's voice continued to fly in this direction: "Flog me as much as you like. I won't yell or telltale. I'll say you didn't . . . yes . . . yes . . . I'll swear you didn't."

Rasmussen, baring his teeth, was aware that they gave mercurial glints of his horror. The voice continued swording: "I won't telltale. I don't care if you kill me."

They had reached the gap.

At this spot Rasmussen murdered, for, as the boy finished chanting and exulting (or was it praying and forgiving?), the man plucked him like a sheaf of barley, for a second held him like a small leopard, then, in two strides reaching the edge of the slope, with strength and skill, shot the living caber head-first at the end of a trunk's crown of tusks.

How quickly the present overtakes the past!

The murderer heard nothing except the arrival of silence, saw only the boy's form which seemed to have been lying below at its bloody coronation the same long time he seemed to have watched an unofficial and improper thing just found. Nevertheless, presently, he scrambled down calmly. The boy was dead.

In the postmistress's parlour, the bald man, the first time that day, lights a cigarette and deeply inhales. The postmistress's lamp-thrown shadow slides up to her kitchen ceiling-planks, swoops, sways. Her kettle sings. Outside: blackness, the charter of stars hidden. Outnumbered by trees and miles, the mountain people herd about smoke-bruised lamps.

Gilbert Rasmussen, the body balanced in his arms, began to walk. From the broken comb a honey of blood drained away, while before the walker shuttled his shadow as perfunctorily as someone else's. The blood, of the ripeness of hare's, scattered on bracken: he could not look, did not feel entitled to, at the disarranged face, but from it rained fascinations. Blood. And *blood*, that kissable word. As he pushed through the gate, drops lashed musically into a pool of water and opened out into networks. The end of his shadow touched the house which was itself conventionally extending shadow upon the mountain. He entered, stood heroically, and tendered to the barbarous mother and father the spoiled remnants of their son. As he posed, aware of melodrama and the set tea-table, Gilbert Rasmussen's tongue assisted in releasing the criminally dated lie, "He must have fallen."

Priest now of confusion, he noted the father go dazzled, gesture hands towards his muscle-staved breast as though to repeat his late child's action and unfrock himself, next crash so heavily on the slattern's linoleum that the tin chimes of a clock began while the first dead's blood dribbled staidly on.

Five nights later, still feeling upon his arm-nerves the outline of the buried child, Gilbert Rasmussen participated in his own seduction by the murdered boy's mother, the widow. So simple and sanctionable and absolute: in this manner Nature converted deprivation and anguish to possession and ecstasy; Nature thus uselessly prepared to replace the grain of flesh lost from her illimitable silo; Nature thus attempting to preserve the incalculable power of motherhood kept in proper use one of her natural females.

Six months later the handsome Gilbert Rasmussen, who was to become famous in another ten years for *City*, married the amiable and half-witted woman. He was faithful as a madman, from then on moving only from her bed and squalid house to the school remote on the mountain-spine, and back again. That. No more.

It was, you must know, necessary to destroy the boy. Even if you do not understand as I do not now, *it was necessary then. Victim and knife are not chance acquaintances. The knife has obligations as any visitor has to any host. Especially, I had to pay for my lie, as for the truth I should also have had to pay on what it called the scaffold. Son and husband were dead,* mea culpa: *it was only on her body, of a sort I should never have chosen, which repulsion wished me to deny and selfishness to abandon, that I could prove to myself the possession of integrity and find, in myself, the heart of goodness.*

When manuscripts, will and confession are snibbed in the case, the publisher asks to send a telegram. He may listen to the feverish silence, and his eyes shine treacherously as he writes. The postmistress smokes a cigarette he has given, and takes the telegram which arrives as IN SYDNEY NEXT WEEK WITH RASMUSSEN MANUSCRIPTS AND ASTOUNDING DATA FOR BIOGRAPHY.

This business over, he sips tea with her, eats a slice of cake iced lung-pink. She tells him a new schoolie is expected next week. She says, she says. "There's the bus coming!" she says and, almost too late, asks one question which he unhesitatingly answers.

Immediately, there is a gothic crying of dogs on the map of night, and the echoes of outburst.

These rites are ended, over in a minute—over. What bush deity or who is appeased?

Gently, a speck Mrs Rasmussen farts; a snail slides, scot-free with its twenty thousand teeth, on the lilac wreath; the visitor repeats the actions of lifting his burden of words, of concealing the truth of his hairlessness; the pin-point driver, half-drunk, stops his fairy bus with a reed-like squeak outside the minute post-office.

Presently, it jerks to huge movement, descends monstrously and fashionably with its one passenger towards the paper-mill town and the railway station.

From uncouth here along the black railway line will he wearily read the successive platform names like messages inscribed on dead-beat foreheads?

No. To sleep, to sleep, to sleep like a child.

The postmistress has asked (ten . . . eighteen and a half . . . thirty-four minutes ago . . . an hour ago), "Are you a friend of Mr Rasmussen's?"

"Yes!"

His voice has rung out; the bright disease of his eyes has not lessened.

"Yes! I am a friend."

Now, his smile that has basked so long under the polar moon of his mind uncoils, and the bus-wheels, descending between black grasses thick as fur, wind this heavy anaconda of smile around, around and around the convolutions and uselessness of the foothills upon whose uppermost fin he has come upon a newer resurrection and a scurrilous and delicious nativity.

(1957)

The Cuckoo

At ten years of age, that twilight, garden spider after garden spider manufacturing her abattoir of silk, I acted playing in my country town as one who affectedly drawls, "Sorrow? But I am very happy. Death? Who *is* Death?" even though bells of some sort had rung all the summery time: school-, church-, dog-, and dinner-bells, the stationmaster's, shop-, fire-, cow-, cat- and ice-cream-cart-. Or things had made such delicate clauses of melody—gaslight chains against etched grey-pink globes, Japanese wind-bells in grannies' ferneries, Jew's harps, upright pianos, the Celtic-king brasses on carriers' horses, blind-acorns on Muranese window-panes: bells and melodies in the elm-shaded streets where we children blew down the tails of water-filled china canaries, thus bubbling away tune by tune our dread wily ruthless childhoods. The centre of the music-cirrused crystal I inhabited was Eternity: Eternal Summer through which aunt-sized whirlwinds waltzed, Eternal Happiness, Eternal Boyhood, Immortality!

However. . . .

However, what else could I do after a morning of doom, the doom of an adoration fascinating as a cemetery, except act playing, at cicada twilight, in my elmy street? What else could I do, O Time, what else?

Can you hear us, thirty years ago? . . . far, and it all mourns of anxiety as though labourer-bee wings fanned the moisture from hives. Listen! Our feet are bare and the fuming dusk veils us in the smell of roses which will fall soon to nothing as soldiers have already done, or golden-irised frogs, popes and queens, people in other houses, and told-of great-uncles. Listen! The players play; the seeker seeks; the frowner frowns and the suffering suffer; the dying die. I am the Mother Sheep with cigar-band rings on every finger and a corroboree design of Bathurst burrs hooked to my flannel shirt, and I must help advance the schemes of Time. Yearning, for I really understand that my heart is broken, I wait so that my voice runs—as murderous she-spiders do—across the road:

"She-e-e-ep, she-e-e-ep, come home!"

From the other side of the road, the gloom, from under the portal of death with its crevices, slaters and spiralling bindweed, the playing children I call friends fearfully chorus:

"A-fra-a-a-aid!"

"What of?"

In agony, while Spring-heel Jack surely shakes scorpions from his cloak behind the boxthorn hedge at the corner, while sinister adults certainly place nice enamel milk-billies spotted like Dalmatians by hydrangea bushes, and in richest tones lie forcefully to neighbours, my . . . friends (but who *really*?) shudder out:

"The Wo-o-olf!"

Knowing evil and what seems reality, yet (uncertain even then which child of my childhood crouches in the middle-road plantain) I cry, *so* wearily:

"The Wolf has gone to Jericho,
and won't . . . be-back-for-seven-years
so-o-o
run-sheep-run!"

They run. They pad-pad and thump-thump like lunatic hares, screaming, long-eyed, in their own imitation nightmares. Their screaming . . . theirs . . . and:

Someone else's? Miss Read's?

I am acting near Miss Reed's place, outside the corrugated iron fence, seven feet high, on which 1919 or 1920 larrikins have tarred *In 1904 the Scotchies went to war, they had no drums so they used their* . . . and no more of that naughty doggerel. I know, thirty years later, what Miss Reade is doing inside while Earth's little creatures begin horrifying nocturnal lives in her garden, but it is too late now as it is already too late in the Wolf-haunted twilight where the mantis devours bite by bite a throbbing husband. Gone forever the morning when all might be hoped for; love, the last barrier between two humans, is down, and reveals . . . despair, harshness, me acting playing under narrow-waisted Orion while the cicadas keen on in elms for the stupidity of their brief resurrection.

. . . Miss Reid?

Now I know.

Always Summer, of course; and her two-storeyed house, its roof-edge stucco amphorae brimming with cobwebs and fly-husks, eyes this Summer: from the shelves of consoles, Athena faces, ram's heads and two Socrateses with pigeon-whitened beards stare across her rose-stuffed garden, over the York-and-Lancaster bush in which is the thornbill's nest the cuckoo violated, over the M and jerkin roofs, the lobster-coloured tiles and rough-cast chimneys, the elms and planes, to the ring-barked gums that surround for miles, to the salted areas of noon-flowers shining like foil, to the sandinesses where the creeper Blue Love outlines a design of eternal cruelty, to the plush mountains dying of dodder and mistletoe, and the inescapable sky screening a rigorous God and angels with vials of acne, aphids and inevitability.

Why did ten-year-olds adore this woman whose name I do not know the correct spelling of, whose appearance I cannot conjure up except in one shocking vision? Did this old maid possess any of what I learned to love in other women—slenderness, wit, sympathy and a dove's voice—or was she what I later came to distrust: slender, witty, sympathetic, hoarse-throated as a dove? And what did she find in false, plump me? Now that I cannot assess anguish or love or hatred at values they once seemed to wear, now that I evade gauging the infinitesimal difference between Heaven and Hell, I can only think I thought I adored her because she appeared not to have the clearly recognizable adult vices of petulance, turncoatism, arrogance, evasion or bitter self-protectiveness. She—or was it the opium of her roses and thousands of roses?—anæsthetized me for a while to all those child lonelinesses of which I knew everything instinctively but actually nothing.

Most, however, I adored her garden as much as I seem to have loved her. It was crammed during my brief passion with roses thrown like musical comedy skirts, with burdens, vines and shapes of them like great pheasants and flamingoes, like moas, like rocs, all moulting feathers or shouldering them off to be moth-caught on the guy-wire spider-silks. I loved her ragwort and hedge-mustard tall as dukes, the wistaria, the may, the japonica, the two pear-trees under the enchanted elbows of which I hoped to meet those who obsessed me: Oenone, the Swiss Family Robinson, Rackham goblins and Dulac ranees, Titanias resembling Mary Pickfords on Painted Lady wings. I was permitted to moon in what I told myself were nooks, dells, arbours and bowers; I found a special quality in *her* sideways brick-edgings like those in fourteenth-century gardens, *her* moss, Heraldic Thistles, lilac, soldier beetles, caterpillars and grasshoppers; in *her* Apple of Sodom, the fruit and casemoths were placed like oriental ornaments. I was fascinated by the orange-tree, exactly as tall as the house and pressing so close, fitted to one wall, that I conceived half the tree to grow inside. Most I loved the roses, sorts I otherwise knew only on postcards: the moss roses, old purple ones, damask, Frau Karl Druschki studded with tan beetles—perhaps I loved them as much as she, for . . . about this I do appear certain . . . she had chosen solitude as husband and roses for children —single roses with mouths gaping to dews and bees, roses uncurling scented skins from their faces, fairy roses, striped roses, the superb and the second-rate, good and bad, but all exquisite and arm-filling.

Within the house she oil-painted them, immaculate things more glossy than any without, nobilities on whose flesh ran spherical faultless raindrops, in whose marble curves lay dew dazzling as quicksilver.

She allowed me, from vanity and loneliness or for some reason she did not know herself and I can only guess at, to stand enraptured before these idealizations, to stand as though I were prone in obeisance. We must have talked; I must have questioned and admired aloud; she must have answered and accepted. Whether her replies were wise, cynical, merely placid or politely empty-headed nothing will ever reveal to me, but never did she display that, in peering to paint present roses, she attempted to outwit futurity and lack. Yes. She permitted me to enter the front door, cross the hall whose fawn and blue tiles smelt of cold parsnips and kerosene, to a room in which she painted, though I never saw her do so. She permitted that revering intrusion and no more, no farther—the rest of the house was secret as anyone else's thought. How often, my boot-soles noisy and in danger, almost skating on the geometrical chinaness of tiles, I—who had never been upstairs anywhere—lusted under a mock-decorous mask to climb the stairs. I used to imagine myself, Michael Darling, Wee-Willie-Winkie-gowned, night-light in hand, proceeding romantically to the unimaginable ecstasy of first-floor sleep; but I lusted more to visit the room of the oranges on the chimney-shelf, the fire burning harmlessly among twigs, the wagtail singing *Sweet pretty creature* and threading the copper floridities of gas-fittings, a leafy heaven with its Eridanus of blossoms scenting the ceiling, the anointed orange that would fall like a rocket and roll on the Axminster to my princely foot. . . . Never did I and never shall I lift boots above those risers, those fateful risers.

O baneful Time, for Time is to blame, I think.

You see, Time went on adding to her collection of inferior pasts and feathery gestures shocking as earthquakes, Time continued undoing animals and people and lands, replacing hope with denial and climax by frustration; the cicadas started like engines at eleven one morning and eleven the next and eleven the next; women with maternal moustaches thought over wash-up dishes about black poplin Duchess sets, azalea plants and foxgloved cretonne, but once in best petticoats and costumes bought button-hooks, sand-soap and Gregory Powder; bakers' carts varnished with Lombardic lettering and sheaves and slopes of wheat cantered into our street and out; sometimes a flock of sheep, hoofs rustling like St Barnaby's thistle, jonquil-pale faces, swarmed in, deploring but quite unweeping, thigh-deep; how criminally St Mary's bell struck down noon after noon; the grieving grieved in the dust-seasoned air; the mockers mocked and, at its appointed moment, the cuckoo came.

Time and her cuckoo! Cuckoo and her egg!

Second by second this bird, born of generations for this purpose, had blindly contrived to live and mature, had been shaken by instinct to mating, on fate-coloured wings had been inexplicably drawn to the one garden and the one thornbill's nest, where she had committed her epidemic act and laid the greenish seed of betrayal and agony.

Miss Reede had probably sworn me to secrecy about the thornbill's nest, as though I had unconstitutionally fertilized her and she had laid the eggs: why otherwise do I almost see her hovering about the nest, a sketch of maternity and a blueprint of tenderness, fingers crocheting on the sacred air about the liver of grassy rubbish a sac of protective magic tough and permanent as happiness or sorrow? Within the nest, wadded with finer dryness and feathers, and carefully domed, lay the eggs which, with care and reverence (how well the sinful child can act!), we felt by dipping fingers into the small entrance as into an intimate vessel of holy water. O secretly in the garden ardent with the predestined and assassinating! Doubtless the spinster had somehow expressed an attitude to me for I, outside the haunted-with-roses a ruthless bird-nester, treated this one nest with artificial and extravagant gentleness. Jesuit!

How long was Summer, then?

A moon, or two, or three, pitted and pimpled by cataclysms, waxed and waned; my mother made raspberry vinegar and said, "Hell and Tommy!" every time she broke a cup on the bottom of which was sketched a gilt clover-leaf; the queen ant descended from near heaven, tore off her bride's wings and slaved like an Egyptian; while I passed diplomatically, sugar-tongued, to and fro among the surfeit of senseless roses, and guilelessly adored painted ones. Murderers murdered, female insects cracked and shattered each others' demon armours, the bunglers bungled, and the day that was the end of a world came easily alight, a well-trimmed lamp, with its engorged and detailed morning, its pellicle of dew and tiny corpses, its dew-weighted spider nets that some wheelwrights had neglected to destroy before dawn. Listen again to my leather-laced boots crushing the elm-shadows and drawing nearer and nearer and nearer to Miss Reid's front gate. They will never crush so happily again. I place my hand (the same hand with which I write this) through the latch-hole.

Instantly the hand-surface seems to sparkle like a glove of lemonade on which an expected future sprinkles pin-sharp kisses white as frost. I press the pulsating handle, open the gate on crowded-in-ecstasy, close it on a world of gaps and vistas; after dream-walking a little of the asphalt path between butlers of weeds and the imperial flowering sculptures, for no reason at all, as I do not sincerely care about the thornbill's nest and eggs, insert my fingers (same hand, same fingers) in the organ of scraps and dehydrated grasses, the roofed-in font. O liar! O sinner! O fool! there seems no holy water . . . there seem no eggs. My mind switches from *Fair* to *Change*, permitting whom I pretend to be to remember what I know as a boy-of-the-world. I remember from raids on other tomtit nests in other younger Summers that this nest is now refloored: inscrutable powers have compelled the tit to obscure her own first setting of eggs because among them lies the egg of the cuckoo.

Everything ordained; and all driven—thornbill, cuckoo and now I, for, alas! with useless knowledge, primitively tender and unwarily, I stir my finger-tips below the feathers of the new lining, stroke the concealed largest shape, then, extracting it, stand there mindlessly, a portrait—Country Boy with Cuckoo's Egg. Thus I am to be examined and mistranslated as I look at the cuckoo gift, the olive-dyed sin. Does Anything know what I might have done next, what simplest action have made that would have confused planning and led on to experiences of delight since lacked and without name? Forgive me Miss Read, Miss Reid forgive me.

Too late!

Mademoiselle for ever and ever—immediately!

As I stand, she rises like Death from among her roses and sees me and speaks. Clumsiness and innocence are restored to me, a blindness. Guilty of nothing but guilt, I drop the egg which breaks like the world. The woman goes on saying things.

What she hurries through I cannot recall, I forget, but—today—imagine constructions of anger-veined words, sentences I had heard from other adults binding together hurt, betrayal, treachery, disgust and their bitter berries. As I listen, blazing with blood like a rose, I lower my head, like a rose, and am as voiceless as a rose—no explanation or protest, no syllable of anguish. There is a pause. So Adam, the angel guard approaching, could not hide his primitive nakedness with the sophistication of truth, only with silent vegetable scraps. A spiral pillar of liver-spot fruit-flies is suddenly visible, the soul departing, in a biblical ray which probes the garden and strikes then a rose-bush so that it stands stereoscopically—Joan of Arc in a kimono of fire: doomed ratified by an intrusion of the exquisite. This is truth, this extra luxury of pain in the dewy luxury. While, heavily, the crown of childhood is screwed again upon my forehead, the garden wastes heart-beat after heart-beat on a soundproof gap between two eras.

At that moment I should have died, still rosy with guilt, before the eight words are tattooed through my senses, before sorrel leaves close at evening like pages of a book, before the thousands of miles and cigarettes, the seedy lies and lost drops, the drunkenness, stains, evasions, impotencies and torments, before she said (I almost see her face but words and roses hide it), before she said (and the breath that pumps forth these words blows out peace and blows in prophecy), before she said:

"Go away. You will never come here again."

Will she said, not *must* or *may*, but *will*.

Perfect in her power, she walks away among the vegetation . . . how mournful but light-footed, how insect-delicate this movement is in retrospect . . . she retreats weightlessly and enters the house.

Tears—mine—falling like a little swift storm? Yes, I think —for I conceive myself ringed by a burning shower and can see and hear within its privacy nothing but the surf of my mind snarling itself lost in a fearful fjord.

Then, gradually, gradually, I become aware of her voice. I next decidedly hear it, torn at the seams by thorns and jagged leaves, screeching thinly through the dusty lips of the Hippocratic countenances on the house-front—the garrulous dead. It is my name she calls again and again and anguished.

My rain immediately ceases. I am elated, and grow pitiless and plumper, but the diadem of childhood still rings my brow, so with nimble clipped steps as though I wear high heels I go to the gate, toss my forelock like a poofter and, as I press the latch, whisper, "Bugger old Reed, old Reade, the old bugger." I slam, and am in the Saturday street where elms enclosing heartshakes and starshakes stand like some sorts of heroes.

I was not old or urbane enough to manage gossip self-pityingly to others, to drink myself silly, taunt myself with wit, be magnanimous or write a picturesque apology from which uprose the penurious and poisoned fumes of righteousness. The incident did not make me older as the memory of it did when I was older, it made me wickedly younger, as war makes a tolerance-wrinkled man, as private informal lust makes a formal native, as hate makes a philosopher and jealousy a Christian—it made me younger and more animal.

That Saturday afternoon I went to the Carnival on the Friendly Society's Oval.

I moved with dusty boots among the adult towers hung with cloth, hair, necklaces and watch-chains; I saw old men, with buttonholes of asparagus-fern and Cécile Brunner roses, peeling apples with penknives; I saw poor boys in sand-shoes and richer ones in navy-blue twill knickerbockers; I saw a horrifying man who wore no hat. Hat-pins, beads, MOTHER brooches, ear-rings, pince-nez, purse-edgings and shoe-buckles of cut steel glittered between the pine-boles. In the merry-go-round looking-glasses blackies, swaggies and kilties passed and repassed while little girls with greenish teeth and velveteen dresses lost ribbon butterflies from their waterfall hair. Between the lozenge interstices of my fly-net I inserted the liquorice stems of sherbet-suckers. I picked up cigar-bands. I heard the despair of bagpipes and the dry fall of hoop-la rings. Then, Four-o'Clocks everywhere closing, I walked home through the pink smoke of buggy-wheels. A cab was filled with drunkies singing *There's a long, long trail*; one stood crimson-faced on the fish-slice back step. Sometimes I saw Carnival-dressed people sitting in dunnies, and some sunflowers saw me through their huge powdered eyes. Shadows of apricot-trees, clothes-copper tripods and bean-poles began to lengthen to weariness; how wearily hung the lace curtains; how wearily one was home.

All day one is compelled to move, to keep on moving—Something's chessman or the pawn of Custom. Night, superstition, twilight, is a game one plays oneself while Aldebaran and Sirius and all the others glitter. Perhaps, occasionally, a spider bites a moth poisoned as a Borgia pastry, vomits, wipes her mouth on a leaf of a Tree of Heaven, and I, after tea at twilight, I, I, I act playing outside Miss Reed's corrugated iron fence in a street of cockchafers and wanings.

I cannot be sure now whether I heard her calling as I had heard her in the morning, or whether I certainly heard her, under clouds like lost hair-ribbons, screaming more and more faintly as the players screamed and the bagpipe-squealing world turned into its own shadow a weight of merry-go-rounds, while I wailed bestially beneath my riveted-on coronet, "She-e-e-ep, she-e-e-ep, come home!" . . . and Saturday died.

Time, that day, thirty years ago, *then*, did I hear Miss Reede?

It was on Monday afternoon that someone, the reeking dunny-man unfitly, did hear her, although she mouthed mutilated words only and screamed much less skilfully from the urine-smelling hall as she increasingly had while drinkers drank and eaters ate, from the tiles where she had lain sleepless with broken hip and wrists while the sleepers snored and the lustful laboured towards sleep. She lay, as she had lain since scorning me by the nest, at the foot of the stairs I desired so fervently, and still perversely and hopelessly, desire, to mount to the room of the orange-tree.

Months, darkening months or years before I saw her again, so medievally grotesque that my twentieth-century eyes could accept and remember only one portion of her: the goliath boot, its foot-high block of sole thudding Gog-like and silencing the crickets, its tower heel nightmarishly grinding the gravel as she lurched like a smashed boat through the invisible waves of Life, through the elm-awninged streets where the pitying pitied, the gossiping gossiped, the whistlers whistled, gigglers giggled and the bells rang. The boot . . . all I saw.

What of the hands on broken stalks that once upon a time wove a useless spell around the nest that the cuckoo and I violated, what of those hands that painted roses more exalted than any in the Eden she had forever forbidden my body to enter, roses in whose each petal shallow as the palm of a seraph lay the spherical and perfect tear she must have thought was merely dew?

(1957)

A Double Because It's Snowing

Scene: *Saloon bar of Saint Ives, uphill from Salamanca Place, Hobart, the waterfront.*

Saint Ives: *Steep-roofed railway-station Gothic—quaint and cosy to sea-people. Ship-stewards, wireless operators, sometimes a purser or a ham-pink engineer, climb up Montpelier Retreat past the freestone Georgian cottages with their fanlights, gig-houses, area railings and plots of Dusty Miller.*

Outside: *Snow, intensifying, rice-like, rakishly thrown for some singular marriage far above which the organ-piped granite of Mount Wellington seems about to explode an eccentric voluntary.*

Time: 7 *p.m., recently enough; maybe two, maybe three, years ago.*

Inside: *A newly-arrived friend has been greeted by a man who appears older and younger. His face too controlled, he is dressed in pied neatness, furtive richness. White shirt—white face. Dark tie—dark lips. He is speaking:*

If you want to talk tonight you must listen; you see it's snowing. I listened to you last time. Didn't I now, when you were. . . . Autumn, wasn't it? "It was autumn and the golden leaves were falling"—early Hedda Hopper that from a Lonsdale play called. . . . Eh? Of course I'm drunk, of course, of course. Eyes mum as cats now but in two hours they'll be running about like mice. Yes, it's snowing again so I'm drunk and hate my mother, hate her more again.

Nonsense, why not me? Hate is thicker than water.

You know, when it began snowing, the scales of my mind tilted, I began to watch her. Obliquely and, oh, skilfully. Do you sometimes watch something, say a—a horse, un-assessing it, neutralizing associations so that presently it seems new, out-of-drawing and. . . .

You don't? You really don't?

I do. I did. A tame horse that once bit too deep. A horse one hates, and waits warily to hate more. So I left the horse, the hearse, the house. No horses here. After an hour I telephoned you, wanting your ear, a nice ear, red and kind.

A *double* brandy, you urk, you traitor, my only friend and ear. A double because it's snowing.

Let me, for God's sweet sake, get drunk.

All *right*, drunk-*er*.

I'll do and do decorously, and you drive me home when Elvie says, "Ten o'clock, gentlemen", and takes off her plastic apron, and out blink the teeny-tiny fairy-lights around the liqueur bottles, and that affected fire relaxes. My eyes are still still as two cats, eh? Two nasty moggies.

My mother.

She was a hotel chambermaid. You knew?

No?

She doesn't really look like a horse or chambermaid, more a lady teddy-bear with a Pond's Cream skin. Something from Beatrix Potter. Cuddly. Motherly.

Father's a bookmaker. *That* you knew.

I have never—I say this with conviction, from experience, without malice—met two more vulgar people. Not merely common. Vulgar. Vulgar emotionally, vulgar morally, vulgar parentally, vulgar from A to Z in triplicate. Plenty of pelf—stinking oodles of mug's money, dreamer's money—and not an aitch between them except for haitch. Don't smoke. Don't drink. Don't fritter. They garner.

They garner me. They've garnered a succession of me's from peeing babyhood to piddling manhood: the brilliant and astonishing fruit of their loins lecturing with every aitch on at that scrubby university perched on yet another foothill. Hobart and its humps and hollows! Rome is *flat*.

Indeed, Elvie, the same *sorts* of drinks, please and thank you.

Hills! Up-and-down, skew-whiff, nothing straight except the mountain shadow slicing down toward the Estuary. I daily want to run before it, be scraped off into a liner, a launch, a coracle, to escape.

What do I want to escape? You don't mean that!

You do?

Morbid, unoriented, ungrateful boy I am—I want to escape them. Vulgarity and them. I am *the* bird in *the* gilded cage.

The cage looks attractive, you say?

The proportions of that Regency cage are superb, serene, et cetera, because John Lee Archer designed it to the last valance-board for some colonial bigwig. Inside—Christ! A looney-bin of possessions, of unbelievable mines and thines. Theatre-lounge carpets, crammed china-cabinets, battalions of statuettes, of Woolworth figurincs, ebony elephants, Majolica plaques, love-birds, gold-fish, fixed cats . . . everything inside to be fondled, tallied, ranged *seriatim.* Tutankhamen's tomb by Dali! a firsthand secondhand shop!—I the central *objet d'art*, the chilli in the pickle-bottle. Even Summer, Autumn, Winter and Spring, marble statues that lived under the garden-trees and had for nearly a century, were gentled into the conservatory. Oxalic acid baths keep *those* seasons in order. Couldn't get the trees inside—so—"T-i-m-b-e-r!" Now, lawns everywhere and lousy contemporary annuals. Let the scent-less bastards but bloom, and *snip*, inside with them, water and Aspros, alum for them in some hand-painted atrocity. Chambermaid's delight! No escape from loving care, from being dusted and owned.

I'll whisper this . . . my mother has a ceaseless hand soft as a feather duster.

Your ear does not pale?

But I did escape once. Once, and for nearly a year.

Mesmerize Elvie away from the hearty shellbacks. I talk too much. I'm parched.

Thank you, Elvie, thank you, thank you and thank you.

A-a-ah!

Escape was ten years ago. Oh, I looked no younger. I look no older. What could make me look older? I am the apple of a chambermaid's eye. The core doesn't show. All spit-and-polish, me. No older. Except when it's snowing. And it's snowing. Oh, indeed, it's snowing.

It's been tabulated so often and scrupulously and with such verve, why does one never learn . . . the printed pages of other hearts, the maps of sorrow, the impeccable diagrams of anguish, the soundings, the graphs . . . why? Why never?

How I raked up courage to get a travelling lectureship despair alone knows; all was irreversibly settled before my mother knew; she had little time to do it but I was a virtual matricide by the time I stubbornly escaped to Japan to lecture to the troops, telling men, who knew more about life than I'll ever know, all about life. I, the solitary man in the Chinese café, the lone stranger peering at the name-plates on trees in Botanical Gardens, the dipper-into Gideon bibles in single bedrooms in middle-class pubs.

Land of the Rising Sun!

After a couple of months I was at Shimoda—the Townsend Harris place, the first foreign settlement after all those un-Westernized centuries of . . . well, never mind.

Shimoda.

Education-types from Tokyo had guided me there educationally with copious Suntory whisky and several million of those little salty biscuit-things with seaweed in. It was spring. It was *accidentally* spring; the Pacific was treacherously pacific outside the inn-shutters.

Your turn to buy but I'll buy. I'll buy your ear a stimulant.

How large your ears! How small your alcoholic needs!

I insist. I'm dry as a briquette.

Nonsense! Brandy dehydrates.

Fiddlededee *and* poppycock—I *insist*, and shall only lower my voice if. . . .

Ah, you resemble Marie Antoinette, Elvie. Before execution naturally. The Petit Trianon days maybe.

Decidedly a double, *altessa*. . . .

Shimoda . . . spring-time . . . Suzuki. . . .

Suzuki was one of half a dozen local almost-geisha engaged to amuse the Tokyo gents on their intellectual ran-tan. I . . . let me drink this . . . fell in love with her.

One never learns. All I'd studied, all I'd taught the descendants of ticket-of-leave men and Cockney go-getters, all those poetic accuracies and searing details . . . pouf!

The girls did their turns—the sing-song, the meticulous paper-folding, the corny fan-balancing—mysteriously boring. The education boys were as merry as grigs: giggles, hot flushes *et tout cela*. My yawns were just not showing. Then Suzuki did the dance of O-Kichi.

O-Kichi was Townsend Harris's woman, the first Foreigner's

Woman if you count out the missus of poor shipwrecked Will Adams a couple of centuries before, and give Francis Xavier and his gaunt mates the benefit of the doubt.

There we all were, half-molo or as pissed as minks, squatting on the padded floor. Night and the sea immediately outside; the night with its back turned; the sea shushing itself: "*Thalatta! Thalatta!*" One of the dolls was slicing with an outsize plectrum rather like an ivory battle-axe-head at the samisen, a hellishing long banjo with the round part square and covered with cat-skin. Distraught music; pentatonic, I fear. Convincing though. Suzuki danced the story of O-Kichi. She danced with expressionless face—the Greek theatre mask idea—the thickly-whitened face must show nothing; gesture tells the story, hands, fan, the floor-touching kimono sleeves. There was dead-pan Suzuki of the Port of Shimoda being dead O-Kichi to the life. Sleeves, fan, wrists, fractional movements of her white cloven booties illustrated everything.

She was . . . was . . . heartbreaking.

Did I really say that?

First she shuffled with her young lover along the shelly beaches of rapture, entrancing butterfly O-Kichi. Then—she danced horror at the village elder's command to be Harris's plaything. You know, I should write for Hutchinson's. She pleaded; the plectrum slashed restlessly and remorselessly at the nerves of the samisen. At the nerves; yes, at the nerves. Pleading and horror were useless, were replaced by agony as her lover was torn from her. Next came repulsion as she was pawned—get that "pawned"!—into the arms of the hairy red-skinned barbarian. Weariness now, alone with her loathsome master through odious days and obligatory nights. Yes . . . yes . . . I *should* write for the shoe-shop girls.

Don't ask how I understood it. Suzuki was O-Kichi.

I understood.

I understand more now.

Finally, Harris having been recalled to America, she danced her relief and, more movingly than anything, her elated but timid emergence into the village. And now her shuddering sleeves and hands revealed the loneliness of the tainted woman, the fruit with the blemish, the classic outcast. She ran from the thrown stones. At this point, at the crux of horror, the snow began to fall . . . blinding snow, scorching snow. She acted this, she did, she did, so that I saw snow, *saw* it. She faltered through it, up Shimoda's minor Fuji-san, to suicide.

Poor O-Kichi.

Suzuki—poor Suzuki.

The dance was ended; the party whinnied and groped and spilt on. But I could not take my eyes from. . . .

Another drink, please. My eyes steady? Look, still snowing outside. . . .

Thanks. And *grand merci mille fois.*

Brandy is handy.

Suzuki became my house-girl. During the Occupation that was too possible: a half-word there and there . . . and there we were!

The remainder months were ecstasy. God! an Honours Degree and all one does is re-state a cliché in a cliché. Of course, I'd fallen in love with O-Kichi rather than Suzuki. At first, that is . . . mother-ridden male virgin falls in love with art-form. Suzuki herself, the real one, may have been as common as my mother; she was a house-girl, a sort of personal inn-sister which is the Jap equivalent of chambermaid. And I wouldn't know if she dropped Nipponese aitches or had an accent like a Queenslander.

But not vulgar.

Never, never, never, never, never . . . Lear!

It wasn't, you understand, until we'd travelled yon and hither together for a month that I . . . well. . . .

I was lecturing around Kyoto. High summer. Suzuki had met me, and we'd walked to our hotel together through streets shaded with split-bamboo awnings—flicker-flicker the skinny zebra shadows; little fountains had gurgled in wooden tubs filled with melons and ice; glass wind-bells everywhere. . . .

We were staying in one of those inns in Kiyamachi Gojo along the Kamo River that divides Kyoto. At this spot, inns on one side, brothels on the other, between them the river like lemonade fizzing and hurdling over stones. Opposite our shutters, shabby-green electric trains shot through the mugwort, past the brothels, and now and then screeched—a perforating cry, a scalding cry, poverty-stricken, infinitely pathetic.

We had dined. Twilight. I was in the cotton kimono hotels

supply guests with. She was in the blue-and-white summer robe that all young women there wear. Cool-making designs on it . . . waves, reeds, clouds, willows. All undulant. You know? The Kamo was making the same sound the Rivulet does as it escapes through Hobart. The same: sometimes on wet nights I walk down past John Lee Archer's jail. . . . Exclamation mark! My parents' house *and* the jail . . . what an architect for posterity, tourists and cages! I walk, as poisoner Wainewright must often have walked, to the Palladio and lean there, as he must have leant, on the same balustrade, to listen. What poor little Wainewright was listening for with his convict's ears, who knows? I listened for the Kamo and—would it be happiness?

Of course, fill 'em up. I'm much more articulate full than half, much more nostalgic, happier than when reputedly happier. Moreover, notice please, I acquire the same elegant lisp Wainewright had. . . .

Paper shutters open: heat, a lantern moon floating above all the brothel lanterns and garish fluorescents, the acetylene lamps of the noodle-soup stalls: occasionally a train squalling in the very voice of twilight Japan . . . oh, sad, sad. It was then, there, that I knew I needed Suzuki for fulfilment and peace. It was there, then, that Suzuki split away like the half of a philippina from O-Kichi, and I felt for the first time like other men, like dinkum effing Aussies, like blokes.

Flourish of hautboys: I had a girl of my own!

I can remember . . . ah, Marie Antoinette, your condescension is timely. For friend and self, please. A double for self. And one for you or a chinchilla stole.

My friend ungraciously declines?

He has to pilot the motoring-cart? I don't. I dee oh en apostrophe tee.

Now Elvie's returned to her roaring porky seafarers tell me why they're all tattooed on their great ruddy hands. A ploy between bar and brothel? Bloodhouse, brothel, tattooery—the ports of the world fringed with 'em!

I'm aware my eyes resemble garnets. Next time the reds of my eyes will be white, I'll be the dull friend and listen to you.

Suzuki and manhood.

What?

I was saying, "I can remember . . ."? Was I now? Was I indeed?

I can remember a long addition sum of fascinations and delights. Before fleeing *maman* I'd imperfectly pictured Japan: eaves entangled in cherry-blossom, women lithe as irises, rococo croquet-hoops of bridges—all the floating-world colour-print stuff. Not like that. Not the design on the bread-and-butter plate at all, at all. More . . . oh, skip it. Contentment between male and female doesn't need local colour, either plate or fact, doesn't need illustration, eulogy.

Just happiness, day after day till the last day. . . .

A son, at first, doesn't estimate the omnipotence of perverted maternity, doesn't credit its additional senses. My letters must have stunk of joy, maybe I'd written with naïve cunning that I was planning a job in Tokyo University when my lecture year was up. Anyway the atom-bomb cable: *Mother gravely ill, return at once. Ill*, you see—she's the sort who says it too. She'd never been sick. Never has—physically.

I am a fool. Was a fool. Was the Pope of fools. Hadn't foreseen that lie, hadn't conceived a mother would play motherhood like an ace of bloody hearts, didn't realize how tenaciously vulgar she . . . is. Then I made my greatest mistake, I. . . .

No, my friend, not that, nothing psychic or so masterful even as hedging. Dutiful son caught the next plane from Haneda. Home in three days with a hangover head that could have been Baudelaire's to be met by a mother strong as a horse stamping expensive hooves in aitchless victory. Back to Hobart, back to the Rowlandson alley-ways, the butchers' displaying blowflies and minced kangaroo, the hilltop university, the hill with KEEN'S CURRY monstrous on it in whitewashed rocks, the streets that go uphill then down. . . .

O.K., Queen of France, I shan't sing if you replenish. Shan't lose my head if you don't lose yours.

Yes. Back to the mountain and the mountain-shadow moving like a blade towards the Estuary, back to the bucket of ashy ice hung at the bottom of a bitter world.

Eh?

My greatest mistake? Didn't I tell?

My, I must stop tippling in the next few decades.

Suzuki and I were in Yokohama when the cable arrived. I grabbed a jeep and—the mistake—drove her home to Shimoda. A lack-lustre day. All those fabled towns—Fujisawa, Oiso, Odawara. Snow began to fall on the sloping streets of Atami, kept on falling, falling along the haunted shores of the Sea of Sagami, went leaping down Suicide Cliff, fell on Ito, on the camellia orchards of Kawana, on a hundred and fifty miles of disciplined agony to Shimoda. No tears; control like a mockery of plate-glass between us and the truth. Because of snow we travelled slowly; my time was running out; the plane to obligation would start in five hours. One last kiss under the snowy pines outside Shimoda Inn—pure Hiroshige the scene. By the street-braziers men and women in snow-caked hats watched us unmovingly, unblinkingly—foreigner and foreigner's woman. We tore ourselves apart.

As the jeep leapt forward she cried out savagely, squawked like an electric train, shattering the glass of self-restraint, and began to run after the jeep, arms outstretched in the snow, screaming my name while I shouted through tears at the road ahead, "Good-bye, O-Kichi!"

O-Kichi! Dead for so long.

I shouted it for miles.

Who said *Es ist nichts auf dieser Erde so still wie der Schnee*? Nothing on this earth so still as snow—liar! The snow wailed and sobbed, cried my name and stumbled behind the jeep stretching out its hopeless arms . . . the snow . . . the lonely snow. . . .

Sir Ear, how charming of you. . . .

I *could* drink an-oth-er doub-le brand-y. Then, at your be-hest, be-*hest*, I'll come qui-et-ly oven if thoshe—*those*—two Marie An-toin-ettes are not ready yet to turn out the twinkly fairy-lights and us. My eyes are now sprucely darting about like wet mice . . . aren't they sprucely? aren't they?

It was much later when they left Saint Ives and reached the beautiful house with its hideous garden.

As the friend's car slid away, the man, older now, talked-out, crunched with stately care to the conservatory, its nineteenth-century panes replaced by plate-glass. Within stood four immaculate statues.

With a savage cry he had heard somewhere before, with

deadly power, he pushed Spring, Summer and Autumn through the glass.

There was less noise than he expected, or his sobbing drowned it.

Wantonly celebrating, the snow hissed in as he stood embracing Winter, head battering her breast as though demanding admission.

When his mother reached the conservatory from upstairs to stand sweetly saying, "Come now, Boysie, I've kep' y' dinner 'ot. Don't worry, Boysie, y' dinner's 'ot", he and the icy marble woman he was gutturally and fiercely addressing were already crusted with snow, the gritty confetti of a crippled, bygone and unavailing nuptial.

(1958)

Fiend and Friend

Perrot was young enough, at twenty-four, to be enthusiastic, energetic, sympathetic, to have all the softie bents of an inexperienced junior master in a Public School—doesn't matter where. He was hopeless; the boys off-handedly disliked him. That was the year—oh, long enough ago for *Cappuccino* to suggest a monk, Zen Buddhism to be a zealot's study rather than a fad; the Windsor Knot was just making Australia and Perrot and, while a cannery was a cannery, canned peaches were tinned peaches. Television was years off; people therefore sometimes looked at sunsets as though they were living in the nineteenth century. Perrot even, now and then, after cricket practice, blinked at Turner, Harrow-on-the-Hill sunsets from the disproportionately grandiose Italianate portico of The School which, on its last Victorian legs, nevertheless still took charge of a view that sloped down for miles, and was open to the common-cold- or hay-fever-bringing gusts from . . . from an ocean needless to name. The School prospectus, sprinkled with Hollandse Medieval initials, used *panorama* and *ozone*, and extolled as *healthful zephyrs* largely southerly and often refrigeratingly antarctic winds.

The School's heyday had been also the bicycle's, Brittania's and Beardsley's; in Perrot's time all was flaking, cracked, sutured by Virginia Creeper, down-at-heel but not seedy. The place had *cachet* though doors would not lock, windows would not open, floor-boards were so worn that knots stood up like carbuncles. Glass cases of stuffed hawks and unglittering geological samples stood in subfusc corridors. It was draughty as the Parthenon; the fly-wire screens of kitchens, sculleries and dining-hall were more ragged than the Bayeux tapestry.

The Head, the Common Room, Matron, Sister, the Housekeeper, the ex-Test-bowler cricket coach all intimated or brazenly kept on indicating that they had come from—how long ago?—somewhere better. *Somewhere better*, of course, meant *youth* and was the answer; jobs had been no better; they had been younger. While too intelligent, educated or experienced for hope, and aware they could be on their way nowhere else, they were not resigned to their own unhappiness though, the easy sagacity, they were to each other's. Fretfully they droned like senile bees; there was an atmosphere of Eventide Home. In the Common Room hung academic gowns like attire Villon might have worn. Perrot's gown alone seemed Byronic. It was new. Perrot, the one young master, alone represented the generation between boys and ageing staff. Perrot alone of the adults was on his way somewhere else. For others this was the last year because, after seventy years of lathing out judges, knights, diplomats, dipsomaniacs, professional bores and one undramatic murderer, The School was to close. Next year the desks incised with unthinkable dates, the FOO-haunted changing-rooms, The School barber like someone out of Jerome K. Jerome, the music master who affected a velvet-collared overcoat and Lisztian hair, all, everyone, would be gone, the boys doubly so.

Doubly? Gone as schoolboys of that School, gone irrevocably as boys for, turn one's back and temperamental tennis professionals took their places, quick-gnawing sub-deans, shy graziers, terse shire engineers, turners-and-fitters, tally-clerks, journalists, *divorcés*, no-hopers garnet-eyed and bender-skinny quavering, "Two bob, dig", in a Russell Drysdale town: but, fleetingly, boys. Conventional as cannibals, secretive as stool pigeons, shrewish as little girls, sensitive, six inches above the footpaths of common sense, a rabble with its own two-up school protocol, they missed nostalgia, wistfulness, the end-of-an-era atmosphere. They acted *Boys will be Boys* with *éclat*. No one, indeed, can act a boy as well as a boy.

Except for Rymill. He overacted, at least for Perrot and largely for Perrot.

Rymill seemed the scandalous boy from nowhere. He was spare as if his spirit abhorred the luxury of flesh, Murillo-eyed changeling, the unsmiling gipsy at the manor gates. He travelled south from some unimaginable part of Queensland—hinterland, borderland, Goblin Market, God knew!—by shattered buses to board other shattered buses on teeth-splintering back roads, by trains with sandpaper seats through landscapes of glaring antagonism or where impermanent rivers, momentarily mad with seeming ginger beer, flushed like lavatories. End of term—abracadabra!—he disappeared. First day of term, while others were unpacking, there he was—whoosh!—as though riding it bareback to puncture yoo-hooing about on someone else's bicycle. He was Perrot's Old Man of the Sea, his nigger in the woodpile, his *bête noire*, his. . . . "I could givc Dr Roget a hundred he hasn't thought of for *bane*," Perrot would cry. "A thousand! I'll disembowel the Rymill; I'll garotte him; I'll commit mayhem; I'll. . . ." Perrot was thus desperately facetious as people are when they imitate Cockney at sticky moments. He hated Rymill. The Common Room smiled like a waiting-room of Mona Lisas, a club of Punches, a jury ardent to pronounce, "Guilty!"

"I shall cane the next boy who . . ." Perrot cried, deliberately dramatically for the little monsters, sweeping about so that his gown was Hamlet's cloak on the swirl. Rymill was the next boy.

"Who said that?" called Perrot, spooning out rissoles at table. "Who said 'compost'? Ah, I might have known! See me after luncheon, Rymill."

Perrot, looking up in prep., impelled to look up, met the intense and shocking gaze of a little man with an enormous *papier-mâché* Jewish nose and horn-rimmed spectacles who was sitting in Rymill's desk. "Out here, Rymill!" he shouted.

"Hell!" yelled Perrot leaping like Buster Keaton from the thistle on his chair. He knew at whom to direct his outrage. Rubbing his behind, Rymill was already on his way, face bleak as a saint's.

Rymill's misdemeanours had the dreary innocence of japes and merry pranks conned from a 1913 *Boy's Own Paper*; they smelt of the lamp, of Baden-Powell and Good-natured Boyish Fun: there were crackers, treacle in the ink-well, sewn-up pyjama legs, vile stenches, tin blots on pages, lizards in desks. . . . It was persistence and repetition, impenitence and intensity that marked Rymill eccentric. Perrot was the target.

In choice of friend Rymill carried eccentricity further. He had screened The School to find an *alter ego* as like himself in appearance but as unlike in behaviour. Van der Velde, a Dutch consul's son, was the choice, a boy of his height, age, curls and colouring but bland, cautious and smilingly courteous. War and Peace, thought Perrot in distracted moments, Whisky and Water, Mad Hatter and Dormouse, Fiend and Friend. Van der Velde spent much of his time eating, an exercise Rymill seemed to like little, gorged as he was, Perrot thought, by plottings, plannings, and venom. The consul's son always ate Rymill's pudding; as left-handed as the King of Spades he was rarely seen without a bag of *éclairs* or grapes into which he south-paw dipped and dipped. He was affable and godly Rymill.

Tirelessly, sombre, with nicotine-stained fingers, skulls-and-crossbones inked on wrists, Rymill himself continued over-acting Tom Sawyer, *Triumph* and *Stalky and Co.* until The School was bored to screeching, "Ow, chuckit, Rymill!" "Pipe down, Rymill!" "Go to *buggery*, Rymill!" Only his friend, left-handedly pecking into caramel cartons, laxly indulged him. Only Perrot was beyond the shallows of boredom or forbearance; Rymill was to him the seventh wave, the deadly bumper, the slug in the salad, as ever-present as Satan, as over-shadowing as a Doré one. Rymill was thirteen.

The older masters were invigorated, as with moral penicillin, by Perrot's distress; it graced their morose last year that he was rattled by a mere whipper-snapper; young-manhood, with its imperfections of disciplinary technique, seemed less worthy of regret.

Even the Head, as classical of profile and as remote as a Carrera Olympian topping an insurance building, said with dispassion, "My dear young man, Rymill is impermanent. Boys are, you know, quite." He paused; reflection from some high-flying pigeon of thought flicked his rigid handsomeness. "He's an only son, you know. And fatherless. Perhaps this campaign of terror is disguised affection, hero-worship. However, though I can't expel him *yet*, shall I cane him for you? Brutally?"

Cynical bastard, thought Perrot but, "Heavens, no," he said. "Heavens, *no*, sir. I'll learn to cope."

"Cope?" said the Head as though Perrot had used four-letter obscenity.

"Manage . . . that is, handle the situation, sir."

"I'm certain you will. You—a vigorous, intelligent stripling.

. . ." The Head looked at his knuckles as if they were new.

Perrot flushed. "It's just, sir, that his behaviour's so incredible."

"Nothing, Perrot, is incredible until one has said it is. And saying it . . . well, untruth, eh? I *myself* find it all credible."

"Thank you, sir," said Perrot as though imparting, after losing all toe-nails, the secret the Gestapo wanted.

The Head stared an unwinking four seconds at the air agitated by Perrot's exit, then returned with detachment to what he called a railway novel, a paper-back James Hadley Chase, whose blood-house world seemed calmer much than the one he had long inhabited—bickering Board, backbiting masters, pregnant maids, parents with delusions, neurotic housekeepers, imperious Matrons, hyperbolizing tradesmen, drunken ground-keepers, domineering archbishops, conveyor belts of boys transparent and meretricious as Christmas stockings, and, above all, an ex-actress wife who felt herself gifted and young enough to retreat into the costly fantasy of fashion from the cut-rate indelicacy of having fallen, almost immediately after marriage, out of love with him.

Then came the absurd affair of the Music Room ceiling.

Perrot was on evening duty which usually, for him, resembled the French Revolution. However, prep., showers, lights-out had passed in such peace, as though another master were on duty, that he should have warned himself. Instead, he went gulled to bed to find himself stark awake at some deep hour: horizon askew, raft sinking, the moon turned over. God, he thought, resident masters are like mothers. There was a wrong weight of silence; an area of breathing and dreaming and stirring had been subtracted from the sum of boarding-house night. He switched on. Two-o'-bloody-clock, *ante meridiem*. He padded seeking with electric torch. Dormitory One—dead to the world. Dormitory Two—eight-year-old Bernstein, frail as Tiny Tim, snoring like a wart-hog. Dormitory Three—"I . . . might . . . have . . . known," said Perrot to the twelve beds and their bulges that neither twisted, snorted nor dreamed. Midnight feast! he thought. Rymill!

As though seeking Jesus's lambs, but fuming like Etna, Perrot stamped here and there. No one in the gymnasium except the vaulting horse grazing tan bark under the trapeze;

no one in the cricket pavilion except Callaghan's cricket boots, and a singlet abandoned like an after-birth in one corner; no one in the old science theatre except the memory of useless lectures; no one in any custom-sacred place. Within twenty minutes Perrot began to suggest to himself the notion of being in nightmare, himself ranging the famous slope for a dozen Jack-o'-Lantern sub-adolescents, his torch springing junior Erl Kings under olive-trees and stabbing the head-hunter rustles in canna plantations, barking, "Rymill! Rymill!" in the provoking darkness.

On the boil, he returned to his study and waited, gnawing at the smoke of cigarettes, and deciding to become a jackeroo with an English accent and a *fiancée* called Christine. What else to do except turn on the sun like an electric light?

At last he heard sibilances and grave-side shufflings that should have been theme-musicked by Grieg. These approached; it was reminiscent of *Alice in Wonderland*, something about Bill the Lizard, "Hold up his head. . . . Brandy now. . . . Don't choke him. . . ." Ahead of the tissue-paper hubbub Van der Velde appeared first at the doorway; his dressing-gown pockets bulged with Chocolate Royals. His eyes were too starry, were lunatic's "Oh, sir," he cried, "Oh, sir—Rymill's hurt!" Perrot disconcerted himself by stubbing the cigarette he had just lit.

And there, over zealously supported by *all* the Lost Boys, everyone a finger in the pie, lying in a pansyish though awkwardly sustained pose, was Rymill. One leg, on deliberate foreground display, dripped blood and stained the pyjama-leg torn like a beachcomber's at a Fancy Dress Ball. Perrot transformed himself to a competent schoolmaster. There were cuts and more dramatic blood than seemed necessary. "I'm perfectly all right, sir," said Rymill. "I'm perfectly, perfectly all right. I'm perfectly, perfectly, *perfectly*. . . ."

"Take him," said Perrot, suddenly raddled with a cut-throat's anger, "take him to the nearest bathroom. We'll see if we need disturb Sister or Matron." In a stimulating hush of doom Rymill's Caesar's body was borne to where his washed wounds were revealed as scarcely more than scrimshawing. Joy faded from the mob at this treacherous let-down. "Get to bed, all of you," said Perrot, angrier than they thought a dope could be. "Get out of my sight. Except Van der Velde. You'll tell me everything, if I have to use torture. And for God's sake stop eating," he said viciously. "Your whole life is a litter of banana peel and a trail of paper bags. Stop it." Ruthlessly, yet with a suffusion of paternal affection he had no cause to feel, did not care to harbour and certainly not to admit, Perrot iodined and sticking-plastered while Van der Velde, an un-devilled version of the patient, told of the feast.

"It was my fault, sir," said Rymill with death-bed weariness. "I planned it. I am to blame. I. . . ."

"Shut up," cried Perrot. "Do shut *up*. Don't come the noble, self-sacrificing schoolboy with me. I'm sick of you."

Planning had taken weeks. Climbing to get tennis-balls from rain-gutters Rymill had prowled the elaborate valleys and steeps of the roof, and had so loosened a sheet of corrugated iron that the caveland of rafters was opened to him. Perrot perceived the value of this to Rymill; even those fed-up with his *Schoolboy's Annual* pranks could not resist a beano in such a setting. Old mattresses were filched from the infirmary store-room, a cat-walk of planks was made across the rafters, an electric light circuit tapped. "God, you little fools!" said Perrot and, bitterly, "Then, *then*, all you waited for was a night *I* was on duty, eh?" Rymill stared with luminous fixity. Van der Velde gushed, "Well, sir, not *really*. The day after tomorrow's end of term *and*. . . ." Perrot disregarded him. "You are to blame, aren't you, Rymill?" he said. "Remember saying that? You waited until I was on duty, didn't you?" The stare, its quality untranslatable, continued. "Didn't you, Rymill?" Perrot could just control his voice. "Yes, sir," said Rymill as though he were lying to save some face or other. He closed his eyes. Van der Velde continued.

Feast over, the boys were returning when Rymill had fallen from the cat-walk; his leg had gone through the Music Room ceiling.

"How do you know it was the Music Room?"

"We flashed torches through the hole," said Van der Velde. "There's plaster all over the grand. It looks frightful, sir. Tons and tons of it."

"Get to bed," said Perrot. "Get to your wretched beds. I shouldn't like to be in your shoes tomorrow when the Head sees all that mess."

Rymill opened his eyes, said with passionate earnestness, "Sir, couldn't we clean up the mess so that it won't look so bad, and then the Head wouldn't be so mad with us? *Please*, sir?"

Perrot could hardly speak; when he did he was astounded to hear, "Rymill . . . Rymill, I hate you. Hate *you*. I have never in my life. . . . Get out!"

When the two had gone, Perrot, distressed at anger but still angry, walked to the Music Room. Tons and tons was right; the hole in the ceiling seemed too small for the wreckage below. I wonder, he thought, if there's blood up there and, remembering the torn leg which seemed younger, as though it belonged to a child, as though it had a mother and could be loved, Perrot cleaned up. It took a long time, and became a labour of fantasy for he could not tell himself why he was repaying months of torment with furtive dirty work.

He did not see Rymill until next term. At Break-up, the boy had disappeared across horrors of scarcely inhabited space, and had returned bearing a gift. The fact of the gift astounded Perrot, the nature of it electrified him: eleven feet of swamp-python's skin. Eyeing gift and what he felt was Greek with distaste, Perrot listened to Rymill attempting to consecrate the musty tribute. "Belts, sir," he chattered desperately on, "and little pouches for money. Or combs. You *know*. Maybe a wallet or a portfolio. I know a bloke . . . a *man* who has shoes." Perrot was able, just, to say, "Thank you, Rymill." This meant, "O.K., I don't know what you're up to, but leave the repulsive thing and vamoose. I don't trust you. I don't like you." Rymill got the meaning, faded-out his chattering, looked paler and shocked. Then, "Is that all, sir?" he said, was it pleadingly? Is what all? thought Perrot. Should I burst into fireworks because he's sucking up to me? Run a hand over his curls and pretend that snake-skin shoes were what I wanted most in the world? "That's *all*," said Perrot. Rymill turned and left.

The final term was given over to ritual farewell: the last Old Boy's Cricket Match, the last Swimming Carnival, the last Knight-and-Bishop-studded Garden Party; bunting flapped continually; potted palms were always being borrowed from the City Hall. It was the *Titanic* sinking with lights ablaze, ragtime and ornamental behaviour. The Head, distant behind railway novels, nevertheless conceived imperial notions, and sent the Second Master marathoning from him to Common Room like a Euripidean messenger—shields and silver cups were polished for the first time in memory; a six-fold School Magazine, gilt-embossed, and over-decorated with nineteenth-century fleurons, was distributed free and, *crescendo*, the messenger recited that *Peter Pan* was to be produced by the Head's wife who had been plucked, as it were, from the very sill of the Darling nursery for she had been being a notable Peter Pan almost till her wedding-day. Auditions happened as incontinently as nervous breakdowns. Proud seniors, acne aflame like sprays of Cartier rubies, were returned from failing Hook or Smee to their degrading skill in the elementary properties of the parabola, whey-faced boys whose voices had not broken were pincered out of German classes to try for Wendy. Van der Velde—curls, slight build, Consular-Englishy voice—was Peter Pan. Since no expense, ardour and hard work were spared, the Head's wife was able, on the second last night of the last of all terms to bring off a technical and dramatic success.

One moment seemed to Perrot to have oblique poignancy. Peter Pan cried, "Look!" and rose on his invisible wires, cleaving the air with unforeseen grace. All fake, thought Perrot, and it's only Van der Velde and his smile on wires, someone who will be a molly-duked loud-mouth with false teeth and hairy ears but, for a moment, a dream child flitted charmingly, Peter Pan, the dream no one should have. The show went on. The Indians stamped; the pirate cutlasses flashed; the show closed. The School closed. The School was pulled down and the appalling abode of a politician went up. The sloping view became sloping streets and crescents. The birds lost their Public School accents and, fidgeting in suburban bird-baths, acquired unsurer ones; the southerly "zephyrs" scattered largesse of hayfever on housewives in super-market head-scarves; the Head in retirement wrote a remaindered mystery novel containing five split infinitives, and died, and Perrot became an anodized schoolmaster no boy could faze. Rymill had taught him much, and not to let ells be taken, never to give an inch.

Eleven, twelve, thirteen years passed.

Perrot, ambitious, unlovable, cultivating loneliness, moved from school to school. As such schoolmasters are, he was often disconcerted by unplaceable men who fired at him their "Sir! Nice to see you!" These reunions with their hand-pumpings, post mortems and mediocre revelations had for him the garbled air of embraces at funerals. He did not know what to say to these strangers, but unwritten rules stated that schoolmasters were interested, and that the advancing unknown who might merely be wishing to ask where the next corner was, could not be repulsed when he cried, "Sir!"—that invocation to boyhood lost in the quicksands.

So there was Perrot mincing wine matters with his favourite Basque waiter at the Trattoria Triaca, when "Sir!" Two of them. Which school? Who? It was Rymill, they cried. It was Van der Velde, they cried. It was two men. It was two half-drunk men—one huge as Orson Welles, fleshed and flushed, the other slender and flashing smilelessly more teeth than a rajah. Perrot learnt with deep uninterest that Rymill and Van der Velde had bumped into each other, first time for years, below in Young and Jackson's Hotel. (Perrot: How did *they* recognize each other?) Now, to meet their schoolmaster (Perrot: Beloved? Revered? Respected? Disliked?) was coincidence worthy of over-drinking and unrelenting *brouhaha*. Perrot knew the grisly drill, resigned himself, drank quickly, arranged an expression and listened. It was necessary, as always, to submit to a depersonalizing and repersonalizing that made him feel that someone else had badly impersonated him years ago. Rymill and Van der Velde recalled what he knew nothing of, told an involved Perrot legend of a doing so contrary to his essential nature that he could not recognize himself. Did he remember this, and that, and the other? Oh yes, he did, he did, he did, he lied, and shocked Leo the Basque by asking twice for double Scotch in the middle of claret. Did he remember one night, when Old Nodsy (who the hell was old Nodsy?), short-cutting through the basement, caught Halliburton (and who was *he*?)—did he remember Halliburton? ("Of course, of course. Old Halliburton, eh!") —well, Halliburton was in a pretty hot clinch with one of the sewing-maids in a niche, and nearly fainted, and all Old Nodsy said was, "Goodnight, goodnight. You should be in bed!"

They roared. Perrot mimed roaring, idiot on the rack, and tossed off another drink.

Did he remember . . . ? *And* did he remember . . . ?

By the third bottle of claret Perrot had scraped together his own scant memories. Peter Pan flying in the spotlight, he thought. And the Music Room ceiling! No wonder at all that Rymill had crashed through for, within the boy who had nearly driven him bats, had hibernated this double-chinned, gutsy hearty who had just knocked over his claret. So this was what happened to naughty boys; this was justice! It warmed Perrot but he also felt old hatred like a re-awakened indigestion. He'd always hated Rymill, hadn't he? Wasn't there some old back-blocks background? And something about a snake-skin?

Van der Velde had shed boyhood more effectively, his manners were gracious (consular background, Perrot recalled) —at least he hadn't knocked over two glasses of wine. Yes, Van der Velde hadn't turned out badly though he had been smug, always chewing at bits and pieces like a pregnant woman.

And then the fat man, the uncouth, the knocker-over, suddenly blundered to his feet. "I think," he said, "I'm going to perk . . ." and walked out.

"Look after that man, please, Leo," said Perrot. He had never spoken like a schoolmaster to the Basque before. I'm drunk, he thought. I hope Rymill is sick as a dog. I hope he crashes through the lavatory floor into Young and Jackson's. I hope. . . .

"What are you thinking of, sir?"

"I don't think I was thinking. But I was before, you know, of the few things I do remember about the old School. Things you two wouldn't. The sunsets, the parklands sloping away. All gone—the big porch, the Virginia Creeper, the oak-trees. I'm drunk, you see . . . nostalgic flapdoodle. Hadn't thought of them for years. And you . . . Peter Panning away there. I'm not usually sentimental but I *am* drunk. And Rymill. I used to hate him. A fiend. I used to call you two fiend and friend, you know, war and peace. Absurd! You, of course, were peace and friend." Perrot giggled. "Rymill would plummet *right* through the ceiling now. . . ." He seemed to hear a Marx Brothers' crash into a grand piano.

"Sir?"

"For Pete's sake, don't tell me you don't remember that? I've listened to so much tonight that *I* didn't remember. . . ."

"Of course I remember, sir. I've still got scars. And I've never forgotten how kind you were."

Scars? Kind?

"I *thought* you'd got us muddled, sir. That's Van der Velde who tottered out to the dyke. I'm Rymill."

Perrot now observed that the man before him not only had a moustache like the Knave of Hearts' but that he held his wine-glass in his right hand as the Knave holds the nameless and baffling leaf. This was not the consul's left-handed son. This was the hellion who had vaccinated him against boys for ever. Here he was facing again in a restaurant smelling of *minestrone* and garlicked salad bowls, two untranslatable eyes set in luminous, unsmiling fixity. As once before, but drunkenly now, he was aware of something paternally unzippering: an *exeat* had to be given, an expiation made; words *had* to be said. Reluctantly Perrot said some, "I didn't really hate you, Rymill." These were not right; they were, indeed, a lie.

Perrot frowned, closed his eyes, thinking: here—now—are two grog-soaked men who had nearly fought out something thirteen years ago, but merely nearly. Time's inevitable simplicity being revealed, it was easy to follow the paper-chase of greasy bags that led absolutely from Peter Pan to a fat man; it was difficult to chart what unfinished business, what trail of misgivings led to this overdue confrontation in the Trattoria Triaca. He heard Rymill saying (insolently? gratefully?), "Why, sir, did you clean up the mess in the Music Room?" The question left echoes in the sound-box of Perrot's conscience; fantastically he seemed to hear a dead man, the Head, intoning, "Only son . . . fatherless . . . hero-worship. . . ."

Perrot's frown melted; he opened his eyes with conviction; he realized what should have been said years ago instead of "That's *all*." Revolted, unwilling, but as enthusiastically as possible, he therefore said it now, "Did you kill that enormous python yourself?" It was a confession of sin.

He saw Rymill smile *Yes, of course, silly sir* as he would have smiled thirteen years ago. Whether the smile was tinted sardonically or affectionately Perrot neither knew nor cared, but it was the appeased smile of one who has finished training his schoolmaster.

It was also, Perrot realized with horror, the first smile he had ever seen on Rymill's face.

(1959)

Country Town

This, you must know, is less a story of people than of a country town. Australian? Unmistakably. Plot? Life? Yes. Love? Well—y-e-e-e-s. For example, I am put out to know that, in some windy part of my mind, *I* love this home town as one might inescapably love a hypocrite uncle as boring as immortality and with the points of view of a blowfly, or a recurring sweet dream one knows too well is a dream, or a cocktail that has a terrific lift though it tastes like the inside of a coffin. Love, you think? Eh?

I left the place thirty years ago. Absence did no more than qualify me to dispassion about *Before* and *After*, make me see more clearly what happened next, the new make-up and changed lighting after Intermission. All I learnt while out smoking the cigarettes too gaudily labelled *Experience* is—a safe cynicism—that civilization makes anything no less accidental, anything at all: living, lusting, dying and so on.

I return one sunset, accidental (you see!)—accidental nice timing—the town seems, for a thin slice of time, to be not one skerrick changed. It has the *High Noon* frontier town look Australian country towns have when horizontal rays stress that two storeys is the limit and in Main Street only, that the rest of the town is on one floor and mostly weatherboard. Those ridge-and-gulch acres of corrugated iron roofs! Those chimneys!—a functioning museum of bricklayer fashions: 1873, 1885, 1902, 1919, 1926, 1938, 1959. . . .

My nostalgic, just tearless eye strains to unfade on upper-floor brick side-walls words still there from my boyhood and earlier: *Bush's Family Grocer*, *Kyle's Cash Bakery*, *Mantles and Robes*, *Horse Bazaar—Omnibus Depôt—Wedding Carriages for Hire*. The tide of falsifying plastic paint, peg-board, and plate glass canted off the vertical does not rise to the first floor; above is the past; as well, in Main Street back-yards Chic Sale privies loll spastically against tors of packing-cases.

The two poplars still domineer, dead-centre of the town, like nervous Azraels; the aluminium-painted penny-farthing sits as ever on the roof-line of the bicycle shop. Well, well! Are there, beneath these tongue-and-groove false fronts, still fruit-shops unaware of sweet-corn, canteloupes, milk-bars and juke-boxes but which display, as of old, their decay-velveted Valencias, flaccid rhubarb and firkin-sized ironbark pumpkins under fretwork arches and dusty witch-balls? Does artificial rain meander down the butcher's plate-glass in front of the parsley-eyed pig's head on its fly-corpse-curranted marble? Is the arc of enamelled letters BOURNVILLE COCOA (two letters always missing) stuck yet on grocers' shop-windows?

No; and for ever, no.

No the monumental mason's urns and scrolls poking through horehound and fennel; no the smithy, the saddler's, the doctors' red lamps, the Show Day procession, the elm avenues, the hitching-rings on shop-veranda posts; no the hickory golf clubs mashie and cleek, washerwomen, bullockies, knickerbockered boys in boots, girls in ribbed stockings, the hat on every outdoor head, the immodestly defining cotton bathers from which inky dye seeped into the white-edged sleevelets, and no no no the sound of hoofs on gravel roads. Gone cabby, rabbit-oh and fish-oh, John Chinaman green-grocer, the dago ice-cream cart and its bell, the Hindu old-iron man, the scissors-grinder, the Afghan pedlar, and all their clockwork nags which wore in midsummer their earholed equine millinery above wowserish William S. Hart faces; gone the medieval pageantry of hearse-horses, Black Prince plumes, the top-hatted undertakers in cutaway coats. Gone what was called the night-cart though it came, two-horsed, also in daylight, a zeppelin-grey tank-like machine, two storeys high, back to back terraces of dunnican cubicles that clanged shut as jails must clang. *That* was one of the town's sounds.

Early in December, one found a card on the lavatory seat:

Enjoy Christmas as best you can,
And don't forget the dunny man.

Did parents leave a Christian half-crown near the egg-shaped hole? Or, not breathing, waylay the burly untouchable with the top of his felt hat squashed so horizontal from reeking burdens that he appeared mathematically scalped, and present some gift with a gracious clause? I don't remember. One should know, but. . . .

I knew lies, carnality, happiness, despair, even viciousness and *ennui*. I had heard of Rembrandt, Bach, Pavlova, Tutankhamen and Jack-the Ripper but never of fish and chips, spaghetti or grape-fruit. Oh, a local, a yokel, a hick, a peasant, a simple boy from Woop Woop! Had I heard of wireless? There must have been crystal sets in the shire, but as I prowled back streets, criminally over-nonchalant, to steal quinces or blood-filled Satsumas, I heard only the melancholy of old-maid uprights behind fringed holland blinds. Fingers of unseen pale hands tinkling ". . . *I loved beside the Shalimar* . . ." where, indeed, are you now? Piano or pianola, just around the next picket-fence corner overhung by cassias lay—had I known it—the opening of Canberra, *The Jazz Singer*, the Depression, miniature golf, Club Sandwiches, and, for me, long pants, silk socks, Melbourne (The City!) and what I thought was Life. It took years, that last one.

So with Life dwindled to life, kings and kingdoms foundered, bombs dropped as frequently as bricks, the moon to be colonized by scientific dogs or mad Crusoes, I return, middle-aged and less *dégagé* than I thought, to another chain-store town. Fluorescent street-lights glare on the metallic venetians and desperately garish doors. Neons display their *tics* above all the pubs, the cinema, the drive-in, the ice-block automat, the auto-port, the self-service petrol bowser, the motel, the transport drivers' steak-and-egg road-houses, and the caravan park whose machicolated public lavatories like Disney castles have been built with municipal delicacy on the top of pioneer graves. Neons utter *Hamburgers*, *Fish and Chips*, *Milk Bar*, *All Night Café*, *Smokes*, *Snacks*, *Eats*—God-knows-what-else—and *Espresso*.

The shingled virgins in berets who tormented my adolescence, and Black-Bottomed or Parma-Waltzed in the Mechanics' Hall—chocolate stencilled dado, tangerine *crêpe* paper streamers looped into gas-less gasoliers under the pitch-pine ceiling—now sit beneath the Wandering Jew and other pendulant weeds of *Maxim's Espresso* smoking king-sized filter-tips, continentally rapping out, "Cappuccino!" and tempting the Providence of matronly zippers as they stretch to choose with plastic tongs another musty Jewish-Viennese cake from under the plastic cover. Forsworn the pottery teapot, the toasted ham sandwich, and cheese cakes!

Coronetted sewer-poles pierce up in every direction but hoisted high above them like the Euclid problems of ex-*avant-garde* wire-sculpture or Woolworth potato-mashers are the symbols of a sinister craze—the H.P. T.V. aerials.

Had I foreseen all these? Nearly all, for they are everywhere else, the production-belt contrumpery, the wrought-iron knick-knackery, the Yankeefied barbecue furniture, cheap-jack self-service stores, cellophaned rubbish, grubbed-out street elms, municipal vandalism, pre-fab. schoolrooms, jerry-built Commission houses, "1984" public address systems, the arc-lit pennants and tubbed privets of the used car dealers, the labour-pains of a second Industrial Revolution—how could I not have foreseen? I had not foreseen that I should spend my first night in what, to me, was Mrs Topper's bedroom.

In days when tracks in the river-bank grass or across homestead paddocks were triple, two for wheels plus one for hoofs, and are now merely car-wheel double, in days when Christmas meant eucalypt saplings glorifying every veranda post of every shop, when Jew's Harps and German transfers could be bought, and cigarette cards were silk-covered, Topper was a schoolboy friend and what I considered rich. His parents' house with slate roof, wide tiled verandas, stables, orchard, tennis court, septic tank, even its palm lawn, arbutus and monkey puzzle had, for me, then, much elegance. Lorraine Lee roses sum it up: they were just in; Toppers had them. We played Mah Jongg, listened to *Horsy, Keep Your Tail Up* and *O, Katharina* on a Victrola inside, a portable Decca outside, ate the non-alcoholic almond-porcupined trifles left over from Mrs Topper's parties and, to make the bosomy housemaid bounce about screeching like a cockatoo, chewed mouthfuls of walnuts which we regurgitated in front of her, pretending we vomited.

One Saturday a charitable bazaar called a Garden Fête was held there. All I remember is one stall, lattice hung with home-made wistaria, and run by the cinema pianist, a fluting spinster beaked as, and now as dead as, Virginia Woolf. A blue paper chrysanthemum at each temple, and hung with a kimono, she sold heart-shaped velveteen pin-cushions, shirt-flannel pen-wipers, gilded wheels made of matchbox drawers (what were they *for*?) and the first Turkish Delight I had tasted.

And once, as though destiny were showing me the other side of the medal first . . . the ornamental side, the side for romantic little boys, a side to remember . . . I was taken into Mrs Topper's bedroom when she had some *malaise* to say "Hullo", or even "Hello". Since my own bed was rather shame-makingly like the brass and enamelled iron death-bed of Pius XII at Castel Godolfo her wagon-sized one of fumed oak had a Cecil B. de Mille quality, and Mrs Topper, fragile and *eau-de-Cologned*, rather the air of Gloria Swanson. The room seemed to me enormous and was large; its lavender wallpaper was panelled with strips of what formed the terribly dainty black-and-silver frieze. Through the lace curtains of the bay window could be seen, far off behind the pergola of Dorothy Perkins roses, the morass where I waded for swans' and plovers' eggs, and learnt to smoke, having stolen three Britannia-embossed pennies for the packet from my mother's kitchen-purse, the shabby morocco one with the steel catch.

Now, here I was, more years later than seemed possible even to me who had enthusiastically used up or outrageously thrown away every hour of them, in Mrs Topper's bedroom for the second time—to sleep there for one night.

Topper's is now a boarding-house for men run as scrupulously as a hospital by Hungarians called New Australians; a hoarding under the monkey puzzle shouts Something-or-other Guest House. The property has been subdivided; women's magazine houses, architectural illiteracies of built-in plywood and man-made fibres, share out such Topper trees as remain. The house is also subdivided, partitions bisecting rooms, fibro-plaster sleep-outs lining the verandas. Some garage hand or gas-works stoker is always removing Al Jolson under the shower; ironstone china clashes in the pantry; transistor wirelesses play constantly and from every direction, and—oh, that other side of the medal—Mrs Topper's bedroom, with aseptically white walls, contains four monk-cell beds, four gents' wardrobes, four bedside cupboards and reading-lamps, four vacuumed hideous scatter rugs. Cheek by jowl the men live like well-behaved butch dolls.

Since I was to sleep once only in this room—there was some

one-day hitch about a promised bungalow outside—I was unpacking just enough to make a homing perch, and getting my eye in before going out to get anaesthetically drunk, for in no other way would I be able to sleep in this dormitory with three unknowns whose paraphernalia disposed strictly in each quarter-room advertised variously addicted men but undeniable young ones, young *blokes* and to be eluded: middle-aged men of my sort relish young men far less than old men do.

I was, however, not quickly enough unpacked to escape young men for, in acrobat vees, patently dewy from a shower, enter, *vigoroso*, on peanut-shaped toes, one of them. Say, rather, a young man made an entrance: chest out, belly in, a *pas seul* seemed imminent. Instantly, though it was impossible, I felt I knew him, had met him. He was somewhat above short, flaxen, pretty as a pretty ape with little electric-blue eyes which, in a crackle, assessed my suit and shoes and condoned his tooth-paste smile and knuckle-deforming handshake. My mind said, "Ouch!" He was pleased to meet me, man. I how-d'-y'-do'ed. He was Kurt Schmidt, man. He was now—ha, ha—a dinkum Aussie, man. He flexed.

Now he would examine *my* silver-mark.

His torso and arms were physical culture magazine, Mr Universe; he kept on wincing these upper wonders which tapered to skinny legs bandy as Rupert Brooke's and feet small as a girl's. Decidedly better kit-cat than full.

He strutted, he prattled, reluctant to obscure his top-heavy form, to enclose it in whatever usually contained it; he juggled two cut-in dimples as Sonja Henie used to—oh, he turned it on. His English was good though larded with bodgie-isms and low camp patter that were not *quite* right. Self-possessed as a musical comedy child he dealt questions like a Five Hundred hand. How long was I sojourning in this weirdsville burg, huh? What did I do for a crust? How had I got here? Did I have a car? Did I have a car, huh? When I told him that I could not drive one and had no desire to own one, it was as though I had stabbed him. "Oh, no!" he cried in agony. *So I was a weird-o! Really rat! Did I have any bread?* I saw him think that. I saw him jettison his first assessment, sensed his interest change direction; he became as busy and charming as a cat when the refrigerator is opened. But I *must* have a car, man, just for hacking round, like. For cruising, huh? He became fanatic as a missionary; his voice went off key with zeal. Daddy-O, a car was the *most*. A car had protein.

Behind the dimples, the stomach muscles like an active anatomical chart and the heliographing teeth I was aware of dead-pan evaluation: Daddy-O, oh, Daddy-O, how I could send you up! You're a double freak, a squarehead square, a fossil with your dullsville old hand-made brogues, but I dig you—I dig you, creep.

He could, he raved on, *he* could drive a car, but any, and neat-o. Cars fractured him, like. He was a car cat, yes, *man*. Drive! Z-e-e-o-o-oom! Here he unconsciously mimed, trance took him: hands and forearm on a steering-wheel, dimples flattened, he slitted eyes at some roadway flaring under at seventy, eighty, ninety. . . . Then he came to, lit up, moved in selling hard, saying that a flip . . . a *gentleman* like me *should* have a car; I was a grool not to; listen, Daddy-O, he had a gasser of an idea, like—he'd drive for me, with pleasure, but definite *pleasure*. I must must must get a car. Next, intensifying his dimples and so suddenly so very offhandedly that I heard the gears grind, "What you doing tonight, Mac? Dolls, huh?"

It was a try-out subtle as evisceration. A naughty monkey, he looked slyer than he thought he looked wistful and charming.

"No," I said, "no—er—women."

He registered. He rippled muscles at me, smiled and smiled, tacked over me again with miss-nothing eyes. I exchanged jargons, "No dolls. I'm going to get full as a State School, whittled as a penguin, cacko, blind sleeping drunk."

"A booze cat, man!" He looked at nothing on the ceiling, and "By yourself, Jim?" he said.

"By myself." He waited bridally for the unless he'd like to join me. Background hi-fi should have been doing muted dog tunes for ickies—*Moonlight and Roses*? *Shine on, Harvest Moon*?

I let him ask. I let him thrust himself on me. Since I had long ago learnt to by-pass the eccentricities of the innocent, to be beware of, to flee the naked heart, I was safe dallying here, for this was no simon-pure innocent, this was a shandy one, a pony-shandy and no trouble at all. So, I said, I'd be pleased to have a . . . but he was already at his dressing.

I waited while he got into a nylon singlet, a drip-dry non-iron nylo-poplin shirt, while he knotted in a manner new to me a lean strap of tinsel-threaded tie; I waited for the nylon-neon sockettes, the velvety royal blue shoon (they were scarcely shoes); I watched him tease his gilt pompadour with a pink plastic comb and breathe-on and polish his antiqued signet ring. Now—*now*—the suit!

Therefore, the first night back and out in the home town I had never drunk in was spent drinking in vinyl chairs on laminex table-tops with a suit of a colour and cut I had never drunk with before, sprayed by the dimples, and arch and ancient boyishness of a quarter-bodgie from a Berlin slum, a camp-fringee, New Australian railway fireman who thought that the answer at the end of the book was *The End Justifies the Means*, and that the use of a car to lure fiffies, chickies and sorts was worth Time Out from normality, was worth whatever might occur—the off-beat, the sordid, a gamut of distaste, recrimination, bitterness, any-bloody-thing. He was too young and tainted and foreign to know that my indifference to some conventions was boredom and vanity, and not the colour he thought; he mistook it for tolerance, *laisser-faire* and anything-goes. As we bumped shoulders back to the dormitory that night alternately singing *Die Dörf Musik* and wrangling patiently as father and son about cars, it came to me why he had seemed familiar—he was a later but other Otto Nowak from Isherwood's "Good-bye to Berlin". He was a boy of the Friedrichstrasse amusement-joints, corruption and simplicity pathetically balanced, his trained-animal tricks too orchidaceous for an Australian country town, his judgments impaired from a past in which he had sat nibbling sugar wafers, a *Puppenjunge* playing a pick-up in a Hallesches Tor *lokal*. Although a Beautiful Friendship blessed by a scarlet M.G.'ish sort of open-topped and souped-up car did not develop, Kurt Schmidt and I moved from Mister to Christian- to nick-names. I liked him because I did not like him enough to be moved by his desires and frustrations. There was not even a scrap-heap 1929 Chevrolet in sight for him. He could not imagine that I could see through his automobile bowings and scrapings which familiarity bred to nagging; he could not see that I might have pitied him because, to him, I was a rock-head he couldn't drive ape, I was as square as a butter-box and practically a primate. Nevertheless, from time to time, I for catharsis, he to employ doll-less desolation, we went on the scoot together. What he got from these outings except hangovers and grog-blossoms I do not know; I learnt the last verse of *Die Lorelei*.

The town is indeed more changed, or rather is changing more rapidly, than I first thought. It is also less changed, much less changeable. One hand of the clock races on, the other slackens, drags, is reluctant.

The unpainted virgins of my adolescence who handed Conversation Lollies—*Meet me at the Corner*, *Do you like kisses?*—in High School geography lessons now play the mother's part in the Drama Society's *Quiet Weekend*, rule the roost at Red Cross meetings, support hefty backsides on shooting-sticks at country race meetings, are avid Solo players, make Shepherd's Pie on Tuesday, sell for offshoot Christianity and too much on market-day street-stalls their no-egg Swiss Rolls, their sugar-bag peg-aprons, their jars of unsuccessful jams from which the mould has been skimmed, unbelievable jams—Green-Tomato-and-Passion-Fruit, Carrot-and-Grape. The Angelus rings the same pattern of threes on the same bell I heard as a boy but Pioneer buses now pull up outside St Pat's to let Protestant women holding gesture handkerchiefs on unsure heads and men stiff-legged as Don Juan's Commendatore go staring at the Heaven-and-Hell painted ceiling, while, aloft outside, the Virgin with daddies-long-legs up her marble sleeves holds dusty hands towards the neon-eiffel-scaffolding of Rash's Tyre Service. Seventy-year-old hawthorns still hedge the river-flat paddocks but the hop-kilns have gone, and it is not an Australian navvy or bank clerk who showily swallow-dives and jack-knives from the willows by the Rowing Club but a Berliner, brute-shouldered and maiden-footed, looking younger than he is, peacocking without hope in the minimum of baby-blue satin trunks, spying among the lunch-time shopgirls and Shire Hall typists for a sort, a bint, a woman, a wife, even a talkie-teener sweetheart. Changed, you see, yet unchanged: the Technical School and High School adolescents wear grey *mélange*, school-striped ties, crested caps; only a scattering of these acned androgynes become bejeaned and rug-headed Coca Cola boys when the lawn has been mowed and the morning-wood cut.

The gasometer is rustier; the water-tower is grubbier; the back-streets are blanker now the elms are torn out; but gasometer and water-tower yet, streets yet. And in those back-streets, their Coolgardies replaced by refrigerators, their outdoor coppers by washing machines, their supper-cloths embroidered with crinolined women by aboriginal *motif* ash-trays, those I knew years ago still live among saddle bag suites, music canterburies, Maxfield Parrish reproductions, Congoleum squares, and sideboards as elaborate as reredoses. They are those whose undeveloped beauties of being, whose immature cruelties, nobilities and magnanimities are scarcely used, rarely seen. All the powers of language, and pleasures of communication are nil and nix-nought-nothing. Theirs the servile but deadly gestures of animals, the slogans of popular science, the monosyllables of news-items; when it is 103° in the shade, "Hot, eh?" they tender. Much besides charm is truant. Resignation veils all, or self-abnegation reeking of conceit, or the egotism, savagery and delusions of motherhood. My once-friends, those Oxford-Bags-and-Fair-Isle-Sweater youths are R.S.L. men bewitched to Brickhill fans, Masons with ulcers, Rotarians with moustached wives and clean-shaven sons, budgerigar- or delphinium-cranks, committee-men, vestrymen, aitchless speechmakers, Rechabites, beer-goitre boys, scout-masters with the morals of Lamas, saints in an air-lock, mute inglorious Casanovas, filleted Satans, half-cold or flyblown morsels on the plate of Time. I—haunted by such important unimportances as when to write *spirt* and when *spurt*—am irrevocably one of this mob. My once-friends? Perhaps friends yet, whom death will change to nothing but the dead, who see the lost sections of their and my boyhood town shining with false but blinding seduction through the overlayings of thirty years. There, we think, was the pine avenue, *that* garage was the joss-house for the settlement of Amoy Chinese from the gold-fields, there were the pioneer vineyards, the wharves for the river-steamers, the old convent, the row of giant mulberry-trees. Cook's Corner, we say, Balmer's Hill, the Tannies, the Cut, Russo's, the School of Mines—names that will go when we all go. Now is for them and me the transparencies *Now* and *Then* superimposed one on another. We walk two streets when we walk the one.

Not so the foreigners, the New Australians walking in the very heart now of our barbarians' luxury, rubbing shoulders with those who carry like a useless breviary the magic rubbish of *How to Win Friends and Influence People*; not the black-stockinged women all in black and their podgy, sullen daughters, their Latin male-children who switch from raucous boy to raucous Tennessee Williams man between one Saturday morning's Main Street gossiping and the next; not the Sicilians or Albanians or Greeks under 1911 street verandas and the click of changing neons, short-legged, rings on their dirty fingers, womanlessly engaged in melancholy or professional carping, their eyes meantime racing about like crickets to covet in side-glances the *cinemaromanzi* breasts of paper-back platinum blondes; not the Fire Brigade Dance refusee, purple-suited, smelling of Californian Poppy hair-oil, stale sweat and Latvian loneliness; not the gangling Dutchman chewing unwanted lips before the display, like circus machinery, of orange-coloured bale loaders and rotary hoes; not the side-burned pair, in tight trousers of nameless cloth and pointed shoes polka-dotted with punctures, dawdling, as through the mazes of homesickness, among the little girls' games drawn like aboriginal totems on the footpaths. One street only these walk; they inhabit an Ionesco stage-set, a province without memories, or memories only of the day before yesterday: the hysterical misunderstanding at the employment office, the fight behind the Greek Café, the night-out with drunken aborigines under the Wy Yung Bridge, the voice crying, "You bloody dago bastard, you!" the male tears and threatening knife in the shadow of the tannery.

Until my flat was ready, and flats are still as rare in country towns as ants' holidays, I stayed on at the Something-or-other Guest House occupying what the Hungarian proprietors called a bungalow, Kurt Schmidt *die Hütte* and I my cardboard box. It was a seven-foot cube of plaster-board and masonite under a Topper loquat-tree I had often climbed as a child. I fitted into it, just, Laika in Sputnik; a visitor meant a physical relationship. Entering the back gate, near the cave of shadow under the peppercorn, to reach this toy dwelling was, night after night, like turning to yet another illustration in a work by Goya or Hogarth. It was here, outside the gate, that boarders returning home went through a kind of ritual purification. It was partly the result of the stern commercial motherlinesses of the Hungarians, partly unwritten etiquette, to complete pre-sleep dirty work under the peppercorn, to remove all make-up before bedding down; once the gate slammed behind, the night was formally over. Consequently someone was always emptying himself of too much Ruby Port or bottled beer, or maudlinly mopping up the blood-nose he had given his bubbling china, or hooking arms for a surrealistic half an hour over the fence-top to auto-suggest legs strong and biddable for the walk across the yard, up the steps and down the dangerous corridor. Presently, night after night, it was obvious that the snowy-haired one of two bodies wrestling, mumbling and mewling amorously in the cavern of shadow was Kurt Schmidt. The other was the new kitchenmaid-waitress who occupied a cell simmering with cheap scent somewhere in the hive of the boarding-house. After Football Dance, Old Time Ball or cinema, this nightly rehearsal for the activity of consummation boiled down to merely male and female, Kurt Schmidt and Vi'let Smith, saying good night at the front gate, the same gate for both, and a back gate. Vi'let Smith, indeed, may never have had a front gate. For her, the kitchenmaid who was a pantrymaid's daughter, Kurt Schmidt might well be Cinderella's handsome foreigner from a Mills and Boon romance; for the German who had been exposed to more thousands of miles, more sharpening and hardening experiences, this too ordinary relationship was possibly a treachery of his own flesh—or was he astute enough to accept that no grazier's golfing daughter in a Humber would fall for his cute fireman's face, film-star-smutted, at the railway crossing? no doctor's widow (1958 Chrysler Royal) turn her hot eye himwards some enchanted morning outside the barber's? no crumb of country town woman fall to a New Australian from any table the subtlest class higher?

How time blows by gustily as the breaths of passion!

How time blew by!—mopping and mowing like a willy-

willy past the plastic bracken in the butcher's Sunday shop-window, past the gravestone of my mother who died ten years younger than I am now, past the Gothic Boer War monument (imported marble), the towering 1914-18 Cenotaph (local granite) with its footnote for the dead of World War II (cracked cement troughs of gazanias), past all sorts of lovers who thought they loved, past Vi'let Smith and her chewed finger-nails and engagement ring of three pin-head diamonds. Kurt Schmidt no longer deepened dimples to excite me to buy an M.G., a jinker or even pawnshop roller-skates. He asked my advice, stern and dedicated, on the fundamentals of setting up house, on radiograms, wall-plaques, musical beer-steins and plastic salad-servers. He austerely dropped tailor-mades for the makings, drank porter-gaffs, put threepences in a milk-bottle, and finished mauling Vi'let good night at the first whistle of the midnight train.

Most evocative, most haunting of night noises is that cry of the late train—wearily exultant journey's-ending, a telescope of sound through which the eye in the ear sees the acres of moonlit paddocks surrounding the town, the never-ending net of post-and-rail, the golgothic slaughter-yards, the cemetery over-run with sparaxis, the rams or ghosts of rams, the mopoke-haunted wind-breaks, the windmills, the messmate hills and bell-bird gullies, the smaller towns beyond—tin and boards and silence broken only by a baby crying like a ewe, the suburbs half-country, the suburbs half-city, and, dirty as a potato, the faraway youth-luring city itself. Ah, the midnight train!—the train awash with fatigue, with abandoned magazines, crushed paper cups, lolling bodies, faces wearing eyes looped in shadows. It is bringing Auntie Ettie the common-as-dirt old age pensioner or Aunt Margaret the well-heeled whinger with her beloved papilloma, it is bringing the end-of-term school-girl boarder, grandpa with the shark's tooth on his watch-chain, Bruce from the Melbourne Show, mother and the new city-born baby, bringing Australians home again. Now it brings too the smell-of-an-oilrag escapees from tourist countries littered with the fabulous wreckage of pasts, the shrewd, the defeated, the go-getting, the horizon-chasing, the under-cutting, from Athens, Bethnal Green, Hamburg, Haarlem, Mammola and Vysoke Myto, the women in black with fate-like faces and dandruffy madonna coiffures, the runtish men reeking with garlic and grappa, the cockney with rotten teeth. Here come the sly eyes, the bare doggy eyes, the lips hemmed together, the cheeks twitching still from a life of unfulfilled ventures, the spiv hands, the beast hands with grimy knuckles, the foreign garments buttoned on savings folded as tightly in purses as fear is in the kernel of being.

In this story of a country town I must, reluctantly, imagine one scene only. One sentence, then, of invention: Kurt Schmidt sits, decorously disposed on the green leather of a second-class smoker, dimples in abeyance, suitcases Teutonically buckled, his tiny cheap-brooch eyes glinting in appraisement of the miles of rich weeds and butter-factories and timber-mills through which he is in a few years to drive a train, perhaps the very one he is now driven in. You see him? . . . blond, clean as veal, exercising those emotions that work in pairs, ambition and self-distrust, curiosity and uneasiness, hope and alarm.

Do the sleepless, the wide-awake dying, the woman in labour, the telephone girl on night-duty, the late reader, the insomniac debtor, the youth entangled in prayer, the adulterers under the river-bank horse-chestnuts, the High School teacher correcting algebra, the saxophone player limping homewards, do they all really know, when they hear the whistle that bores the night like an enchanted gimlet, what travels in with their returning flesh-and-blood, with Auntie Ettie or the fourth generation Australian baby brother? Or what else tomorrow might bring besides an aunt's coarse gossip, and new nappies on the rotary-clothes-line by the unsatisfactory lemon-tree in the backyard?

Tomorrow is still, of course, the fancy dress football match, Thatcher's Summer Sale of Men's Wear, the C.W.A. raffia-work display, the Legacy dinner, the Chess Club final, the Buffaloes' booze-up, the Library Committee meeting, the C.A.E. Mozart evening at the Prince Regent, the rock-'n'-roll in the Mechanics' . . . tomorrow is still tomorrow and a repetition of customary yesterdays. The kilties sackdoodle, the band practises *Poet and Peasant* Overture, the trout-fishing opens, the duck-shooting closes, blackberrying is on, mushrooms are everywhere, there are frost, and thunderstorms, and north winds like Magog's breath . . . why not? Tomorrow has gone on thus for years.

Thus?

Have you seen the papers on the notice-board outside the police station headed FISCHEREI UND WILDEHOERDE and UFFICIO DELLA PESCA E DELLA CACCIAGIONE? Have you looked in the delicatessens that no longer call themselves Small Goods but sometimes Delikatessen and seen the tins of olive oil, the packets of poppy-seed and noodles, the tinned Dutch strawberries and spinach, the salami, the twenty kinds of cheeses, the sauerkraut, the spaghettini, vermicellini, sopracapellini, fettucce, ziti and calzoni? Who are the once foreign, still foreign-looking, men with greased hair, *café noir* eyes, and sores on the corners of their mouths, whose photographs fill the photographer's display cases? And look!—in the cemetery where a headstone of Welsh slate under an actual yew ninety years old states *Sophia Ellen Knight, 1863*, there are now photographs behind glass cemented into the grave-edgings: this molten-eyed tot with the prissy half-smile and frizzy hair appears to have died here in 1956 somewhere in one of the streets named after pioneers, explorers or Great War brigadiers, *Mariarosa Serafina Tocchi, born 1951, Casalbuono, Italia.*

As country town people do, I know a lot about my country town in a common-or-garden way; eyes and ears get information *gratis*, one breathes in facts, lies or legends effortlessly without needing to nosey-parker—to use the jargon—writerwise.

I know that, tomorrow, if I am or you are by chance near St John's Church of England which looks over the river-willows, across the lucerne flats to the Old People's Village on the hill, it will amuse to cast a glance at the Rectory opposite. The front door will be hurled open. The Canon's fox-terrier will nimble about Grockishly, yapping like a heathen. The Canon will shoot, jet-propelled, out of the ecclesiastical front gate and come sprinting ex-athletically across the road, back just in time from blessing the fishing-fleet . . . just in time, for here comes the bridegroom's taxi containing Kurt Schmidt, the blond fireman from the gnawed core of Berlin, the up-and-coming engine-driver, in a black suit with, thank God, horizontal pockets. His face is brightly silly with nervousness. Now, just femininely late enough, here comes the bride in a nearly charming gown she can wear later at the Hospital Ball, here comes Vi'let Smith the waitress with Woolworth flowers in her hair and a Marilyn Monroe mouth painted over her mouse-trap one, the waitress-kitchenmaid whose mother was a pantrymaid and whose daughter will be, whose son will be, whose children will be . . . will be. . . .

I wrote that I knew much, but that is really all I know about my home town, a country town I am startled to discover that I love as one loves an ageing mother with dyed hair, slapdash lacquered finger-nails, and skirts too short for her varicose-veined legs. Or do I love it as one shudderingly does a cocktail tasting like the inside of a coffin but with a terrific lift? Anyway, some sort of cocktail is poured—whew!—and I, you, we, they must drink it. Not pronto, of course, for me . . . but certainly later. Oh, cer-tain-ly!

(1959)

Party Forty-Two and Mrs Brewer

I don't know Sydney very well. The daylight part of my fevered forays there are spent in an ague of traffic terror on a pedestrian-refuge I can't remember why I'm on, or soothing myself in the saloon bar of Aaron's Hotel. Otherwise, I inhabit taxi-cabs *en route* to yet another party . . . somewhere.

See me, then, about eightish on a Sunday summer evening so recent that I am surprised to be already dealcoholized enough to control a pen, sliding out a taxi-cab . . . somewhere, some suburb *somewhere*. There were three other men with me, though they seemed more because of Da-vid's banjo. We were just late. We had been lost, long enough for it to be droll, and almost long enough for it not to be, in vertically lofty streets swanking it as avenues. The house was so new that I felt paint-splashed shoes still to be in the garage; there could have been no time for corks and string to overrun kitchen-drawers; the frangipanis each side of the front door were infantile.

As we entered, I perceived, nearly not in time, that it was not a gathering to enter rather vividly with a dilly-bag of witticisms: the room—the *lounge-room*—self-consciously contemporary (one stubbornly wall-papered wall) was chock full of men and women jumbled together like general-store kitchen-ware. There was an air of bath-water . . . sub-tepid . . . gurgling down the plug-hole. On the wall-paper I could see, Belshazzar-like, intimations of the near speech-riddled future: "Ladies and gents, and others! Now, let's have a little bit of shush . . .!"

Indicatively, the hostess, a doggedly brisk secretary when normal, was called Dot. She wore, of course, a pleated skirt that could not not swish and whip about. Her husband, an s.-p. bookmaker, was—it goes without saying—called Frank.

There would be, I also instantly knew, a belt of husbands

called Frank—the sort of Franks whose wives buy their shirts and ties. Over Dot's newly-bingled hair I saw these Franks in the glimmering worsted trousers with an abundance of buttoned pockets by which Australian men can be picked in Trafalgar Square or Montmartre. It was as patent as massacre that something supremely dreadful had happened, early, so early, too early: there was a surfeit of out-of-tune gaiety. Men, and the unmarried women with finger-nails lacquered pallidly, were laughing *Ha, ha, ha!* with their eyes fixed. The married women, with finger-nails lacquered darkly, talked with earthy verve, and immodest decisiveness, of detergents. I am, I thought, going to shrivel with boredom. I deserved, of course (I also thought), no more.

You see, I had been being off-the-chain (hang the expense!) for six weeks, in *Sydney*! This was my forty-second (you get it?) and final party. The next day I would be returning to South Gippsland, behind Wilson's Promontory, to be a sobersides among the peat, the grass trees, the black cockatoos always flying north with rain at their tails, the surely false-eyelashed Jerseys, and the high-heeled Berkshire piglets.

In my visitor's guise of Simple Country Boy I had over-enjoyed the six weeks. I had, among other things, spent four hours in Darlinghurst lock-up, punched a drama critic, broken a rib, told-off an editor, conversed with a negro, four Communists and a lesbian, drunk half a bottle of South Australian whisky during a rococo performance of *Love's Labour's Lost*, and been turfed with skill and taste out of the Journalists' Club.

I was staying in Elizabeth Bay, downstairs from King's Cross, in a sort of underground palace coated with *Ficus stipulata*. It contained chandeliers from Murano, a bathroom bigger than a kitchen, a kitchen smaller than a bathroom, and seeming acres of entertainment-inducing parquet like a shot-silk chess-board. Sky-high camphor-laurels, which once edged the drive of Elizabeth Bay House, fastidiously dropped an odd leaf or two to impel perfectly circular ripples, *à la* Disney, on the surface of the swimming-pool. One of my forbearing hosts was a psychic A.B.C. producer with the mien of an intellectual koala, a Whistleresque tongue, all the Belafonte recordings, a cat called Mrs Woffington, and a 24-carat heart. The other host was a well-heeled, middle-aged playboy called Da-vid who twangled his little banjo in the only room I've known subdue a television-set. Life-sized Goddesses of Mercy closed their golden eyes with repulsion on the top of vast carved, lacquered and gilded chests and tallboys.

We three, *plus* Laurence, an actor awash with a Sunday of gin-and-milk, were all discreetly middle-aged, two bachelors and two *divorcés*, and as disenchanted and potentially sparkling as a quartet of Bemelmanses. We had been driven to this forty-second party by a Singapore Chinese university student, driven to wherever the party was . . . Cammeray, Collaroy . . . some fairly perpendicular suburb with a view of other vertical suburbs' electric lights, and their reflections in an area of liquid —a lake, or harbour, or something.

This Oriental taxi-driver, with whom I had been coincidentally lost for an hour the night before (the forty-first) on similar perpendicularities near Beauty Point, was called Peng Chin.

Until we entered the house, I considered Peng Chin a surefire entrance topic. This topic, burgeoning like a Jacobean tapestry as we climbed a million concrete steps to the house, died its sudden death in the open door. Half a visual sniff, and one thought—I repeat—I am going to shrivel with boredom.

However and however, one had not foreseen—how could one?—Mrs Brewer, the hired help.

Hi-Jinx's Melbourne Cup win a week over, Dot was doing the grand on Frank's rake-off. A buffet meal, eighty-guest-sized for the forty in the living-room was set out more heart-rendingly and lavishly than in women's magazine illustrations. There was more than a touch of Mrs Beeton in the cairns of prawns and oysters, in the ham, the chickens, the turkey, and the subsidiary delicacies.

Mrs Brewer had been engaged, I later learned, to help prepare and arrange these succulences, to pass out plates and forks and, more brutally, to wash-up and clear away. She was *cachet*. After the cleaning-up she would put on a browbeaten hat of navy-blue felt and (surely) speed off on an old bicycle.

Not so.

By the time Peng, after consulting his map often on the brinks of precipices, had nosed out Dot and Frank's aerie, Mrs

Brewer had, as it were, dramatically rocketed from the sink to the height of Nazidom.

"God!" said Dot, wild-eyed parlourmaid at what she had considered her own door. "Oh, God, thank God, you've got here! I'll kill her; I'll *kill* her!"

We imagined she spoke thus impatiently of some time-honoured murderee: a mother-in-law or a busybody aunt.

"That woman. My *char*. She's drunk as a wheelbarrow. She's *let* us have two—*two*—drinks each before we eat. And no more. She's taken charge of the bar. *We can't move her*."

She seemed to feel her neck scorching. She raised her voice, and swished her pleats as though she still possessed rights.

"Here they are, Mrs Brewer. They're *terribly* sorry to be so late. Their taxi-man got lost."

We had said not a word. Da-vid dropped his banjo and said, "Witch!"

"Shut *up*," hissed Dot. " 'Fyou want a snort, for God's sake, charm, charm, charm."

Then, "Come on, boys," she trilled with the most bogus jubilation, "and meet our Mrs Brewer."

She led us, like a cinema usherette, through and past the standing Franks, and the sitting wives and women, who gave us, long-entombed miners at sight of rescuers, glances of positive love.

We reached Mrs Brewer.

The long, Laminexed counter which cut off the kitchen from the living-room cut her off from the world of capricious mortals. Klytemnestra her very self, she was alone, fiercely imperious, sacrosanct. She and her domestic sanctuary were beyond rape of any kind.

In the manner of one sponsoring gormless serfs to a Celtic warrior-queen, Dot began a spirited, near-hysteric litany of introductions.

Mrs Brewer closed her eyes as against a silly willy-willy. I had a blood-curdling impression of inner eyelids moving horizontally across the eyeballs as the outer eyelids contemptuously descended.

Dot faltered.

Mrs Brewer spoke.

"One at a toime, love," she said nasally, malcontentedly, but with eyeless power. "One . . . at . . . a . . . toime. *Please.*" Oh, the perfect lady. She vouchsafed her eyes. "Do you moind?"

The *Do you moind?*, despite its irrefutable Queensland accent, was delivered as offensively as the English deliver it, attended by a smile as false as her teeth. Mrs Brewer was drunk. Not wheelbarrow-drunk; but firmly drunk, at the *idée-fixe*, no-shenanigans stage where life was real, life was earnest, and administration was all.

She, Mrs Brewer, was logic's king-pin, and alone could save.

She was short, stocky-short—nuggety—and swart. All this suggested the fortune-telling gipsy, but she really resembled nothing so much, particularly about the eyes, as a middle-aged cocker-spaniel with an obsession. It was easy to suspect her face of, at that moment, much unused mobility.

Without delving, I can remember seeing only two other women with her cast of unhaggling directness. One was an Italian matron in a little bar in Cremona where an American millionaire's alcoholic son and I, doing Italy in a Fiat 500, were drinking grappa and avoiding buying veesky-sodah for a German prostitute in a dress of a houndstooth pattern so large that it blinked blackly and whitely as one looked.

The matron, who was perhaps the owner's passing-by sister or sister-in-law, was feeding one of those Belgian milk-cart dogs with ice-cream to amuse us into spending more *lire* on more grappa, when a brawl began between two nasty little Italian men.

Nasty little eyes appeared—four.

Nasty little knives appeared—two.

Everyone scattered, jabbering operatically, knocking over chairs unnecessarily, for effect. The prostitute screamed with Teutonic verisimilitude.

Handing me the ice-cream and, so to speak, the dog, the matron reached a Michael Angelo arm over the counter for a broom. With the *handle* she chopped, she hacked—*crack! crack! crack-crack-crack!* (*da capo*): Punch killing Judy.

The two men knifeless, she picked up and chucked the knives through the door, replaced the broom, and returned to dog and ice-cream with no more than a draughty brief smile which said, in effect, "Thank you for looking after Toto while I was busy."

The other woman, I remember, was called Bunny Something and, dressed in cheese-cloth and beads as Cleopatra at an Artists' Ball in the St Kilda Town Hall, some summer in the 'thirties, lifted a helmet from a policeman's head, sauntered the length of the hall with it, and disappeared, and for ever.

The third was Mrs Brewer, to whose leery and alarming façade Laurence, the actor, was the first of us to be (the word is hand-picked) presented.

She absorbed Laurence's status, and him, with a damp and dampening gaze. He gave her, steadily, a famous look. The suspense was killing. No one would have been surprised if she had barked—or bitten.

After three years: "Wotillut be, love?" she said, unsmiling, but mollified to melting-point.

"Gin-and-tonic. If I *may*. If you will be so kind. *Please*. My *dear*," said Laurence, as on carnal knowledge bent, throbbing like a motor-launch, and unleashing a smile of some brilliance. "May I beg a fairly *strong* one?"

He augmented the smile from sufficiently to quite brilliant. "My ticker . . . a little dicky," he improvised, setting his fingers (slender, sensitive, *et cetera*) on his dove-grey waistcoat, and releasing a light cough.

"Wotchew want, love, is a noice great big brandy," said Mrs Brewer, her spaniel eyes having appraised and estimated. She had put her right hand on the Laminex, and was judicially tapping on this member's glazed and toad-back mottlings with stubby left-hand fingers, in the proper one of which was embedded a time-smoothed wedding-ring, vintage 1921.

"Brandy!" Laurence's voice sounded as if it wore a muzzle, and the pouches beneath his eyes momentarily sagged in dismay.

"Laurence, *honey*," said Dot, toothily, showing strain and an inclination towards hysteria even though in a model lacy blouse and too much mascara. "Do listen to Mrs Brewer. She *knows*. Have a brandy."

For God's sake, let's get it over! was understood.

"Huh!" said Mrs Brewer instantly scuppering the idea of brandy. "Huh! Women! Stuck-up! Ear-rings too toight. *And* nag, nag, nag."

As abstractedly and confidently as a blindfold knife-thrower she whizzed a curare-dart glance, bull's-eye, at Dot, and reached for the gin-bottle, meantime tossing sidelong, "You better get those ear-rings off, my girl."

No one, but no one, had ever called Laurence anything except Laurence, yet: "Oi seenya on the telly, Laurie, love," said Mrs Brewer sloshing out three-quarters of a goblet of gin. "Oi seenya. You're a gennulmun."

She poured, negligently competent, about a teaspoon of lemonade on the surface of the gin.

"Drinkitup, love. It'll warm the cockles. But don't . . ." She began to act conspiratorially, leaning forward to give the impression of whispering, but declaiming loudly: ". . . don't give none to that thing in the green. Him all mockered-up in his corjaroy pants!"

The mild young man, with his green cumbering pullover and medievally-pointed shoes, simulated deafness but went paeony-pink under his organized fringe of bull's-wool, sipped in a poised way at his empty tumbler, and dropped a sophisticated *mot* into the grassy coiffure of the skittish widow perched like an imp on a Port Said pouffe.

"Corjaroy, but! A tonk, that's what. If me hubby was aloive . . ."

"Mrs Brewer," said Dot, just able to keep to the social rails, and schismlessly gracious, "please excuse. I'd like you to meet Mr Jack, of the A.B.C. who . . ."

"Some people, Laurie," said Mrs Brewer, sparing no more than an oblique though envenomed dart, "some people are prolly so drunk that they don't know no better. Manners! Interrupting, but! *And* won't take advice about ear-rings and *im*flamed lobes and cancer. Drinkitup, Laurie, love."

"Mrs Brewer," said Laurence, perceiving his duty, and smiling back as far as wisdom-teeth. It was the best acting or, at least, the most magnetic I've seen him do. It approached the classic. A second before, he had started from his devil's nostrum of gin as from a bowl of hemlock. Now, his eyes were melting with ardour in the direction of Mrs Brewer's three-haired mole, and his voice was saccharine as a chocolate laxative: "*Dear* Mrs Brewer . . ."

"Reet," said Mrs Brewer, licking a finger to wipe along one tousled eyebrow. "Call me Reet. Rita Jessica's me full name.

But friends call me Reet, but. You call me Reet, Laurie love. Me late mister useta call me Reet."

She licked an opposite forefinger, and spittled the other and higher eyebrow.

"The old basket, me late," she said ruminatively, with a tincture of dislike.

"Reet," said Laurence in the tone of one deeply purring, *Do-lor-es, my be-lov-ed*, "Reet, *ducks*."

Was he getting too far into character?

"My *friend* Mr Jack—of the A.B.C.—is dying to meet you. Reet." And he added, for better measure, "But!"

Mrs Brewer emitted a clear and involuntary hiccough. It surprised her.

"Beg yours, love," she said. "Gherkins!"

Brandy, being gherkins, revealed her unfaltering grasp of the situation, and: "Any friend of yours, love," she said and turned her mole, her dog-eyed gipsy face and groomed eyebrows towards her waiting subject.

"Pleastameetcha," she said. "Oi lissen to 'Green Paddocks' on the woireless. It's . . ."

She considered.

She admitted.

". . . It's very true to loife. You're a gennulmun. Wotillut be, Jacko, love?"

It was in this manner that the four of us—Laurie (love), Jacko (love), Davie (boy) and Hal (-pal)—received each our ration of two terrifying drinks. As we got them down (mine was a quadruple whisky with an accidental addition of gin) we could not have fawned more on wicked duchesses than on Mrs Brewer.

The world awaited us and its buffet meal.

The women had dropped detergents for children drinking kerosene.

The men seemed to have got into a stalag-prisoners' huddle, perhaps planning a tunnel under the counter, perhaps lynching.

Dot had gone, with brave straight back and subdued skirt-pleats, to the lavatory, to forestall cancerous lobes, to cry, to restore cried-off mascara, and purge herself of filthy language.

"And don't, moind you," we were warned, "give nothing to that thing in the green. Or"—her eyes became small as sweet-pea seeds as they sighted another enemy—"to that bit he's earbashing. Deliquids! Lairs!"

That Bit wore a quantity of black hair arranged like a busby from beneath which a diminished, floury poker-face confronted humanity with unmoving Japanese eyes.

"If me late hubby was aloive, he'd *do* him, but, the little tonk."

"What," I said (oh, brightly, subject-changing) "was your husband's name, Mrs Br . . . Reet?"

I hoped for *Frank*, to prove something my second drink was making me think I thought.

She didn't quite turn on me.

"*Mist-er* Brewer," she said, non-committal, with sinister flatness. Her eyes performed some female insincerity, a side-glance mentally and visibly: she hadn't *liked* Mr Brewer.

"He's passed on. Old basket. Trouble with his tubes."

Tubes?

We put our brows into furrows.

Jacko, love, told me later that he saw a very involved ants'-nest in section. I favoured the disembowelment of a dead horse I'd witnessed as a boy at Seaspray in Easter, 1928.

"Oh, nod t' worry, nod t' worry," said Mrs Brewer as one saying, "Hiroshima! A bagatelle!" and as though we looked, we and our furrows, as if we *were* unduly, unnecessarily and neurotically worrying.

The widow of the late *Mis-ter* Brewer stimulated herself: her inner clock had struck a serious hour.

"Drinkitup!" she said, addressing us each severally and with maternal severity. "Drinkitup! Drinkitup! And you, too, bozo, drinkitup. Quick-smart! That woman's left it all to Reet. Cancer of the lobes, that's what the poor liddle thing'll finish up with."

To our fascination she began to pound on the Laminex with a soda-siphon. The hubbub of factitious joy faded. Into this abatement she shouted, as from a far-off hilltop, "Come and get it!"

They came to get it, shuffling rather, laughing somewhat and somewhat showily and with much ease, and mingling in a sort of factory-canteen queue.

Mrs Brewer regarded this immoral pattern with deep distaste.

She bided her time.

She struck.

"Ladies first!" she cried. "Think you're Russians, eh? Ladies first! Do you moind . . . *gennulmun*?"

The brutes, the roughnecks, the animals, the bronzed Anzacs who'd forgotten their courting-days, side-stepped, sincerely abashed though wishing not to show it; the women became unnecessarily elated and decidedly showed it.

Mrs Brewer took up a handful of forks, and then remembered that she was, after all, a general.

"Me heart," she said, attempting faintness, and placing the handful of forks on her Roman matron bosom. "Davie, boy . . . Jacko, love . . . Hal-pal. . . . You come around here with me. You're gennulmen. The plates and forks. Me heart! Where's me brandy? A noice quiet liddle brandy'll set me to roights."

She began, the ghost of Hamlet's father, to drift off. She sat on a low stool by the refrigerator, screening her goddessliness from the common gaze with an open cupboard door. As we turned to our task of handing over plates and forks, there was the sound of fluid descending from bottle to tumbler, and the voice of the all-knowing and ever-watchful: "One plate per person. One fork per person. Oyster-shells to go in the . . ." Brandy washed that one out of hearing.

While we handed over plates and forks, as it were from the altar, we and the guests exchanged many a merry quip. But how censored! How underlined with winkings and shruggings and smiles of a certain sort! How censored even these voiceless gestures!

Dot appeared again, bereft of tears and with cold-cream-shiny lobes, having learned of life, as her guests had, that no matter how closely they had electric-shaved, or how constricting their new girdles were, no matter how heedfully they walked on social eggs, they were, right there and then, no more than visitors in a world of runaway pantechnicons bulldozing into the bird's-eye maple bedroom, a world of burning toast, enamel bed-pans, hangnails, influenza, and unsuccessful permanent waves.

Mrs Brewer, heart or no heart, brandy or no brandy, was the objectification of this intrusive world, the bitch goddess, the schoolmistress with sour stomach, the rude salesgirl, the malicious mother-in-law, the tram-conductress handing on her headache, the one who hamstrung you when you were about to caper to *The Spring Song*. Even in her retirement Mrs Brewer was a force; gurglings and glassy clinkings from behind the cupboard-door testified to her reality.

She was, moreover, resurrectible.

Indeed, just as the young man in the green jumper was about to take his plate, Mrs Brewer slammed the cupboard-door shut, and revealed herself.

She was now immortally shicker.

She swayed like a more squat foxglove, sadder and swarthier.

She doubtless saw more of each of us than each was.

The young man, disposed too centrally, retracted the guilty leprous hand that had been about to tarnish the rim of a plate.

"You!" croaked Mrs Brewer.

Facing the Angel of Death the young man was courageously steady, but his pullover seemed suddenly bluer than green.

"You!" She appeared to wish to have the refrigerator-handle let go her hand. Tears suddenly flowed down her cheeks. She was understood to say, "Shorry, love . . . shorry. . . . Call me Reet. Odly a boy. Odly a chuvenile deliquid. Reetie's been rude. Oh, Oi been thinking . . . Laurie, love . . ." she said, uprooting herself to take, like a toddler, a few bow-legged steps towards Mr Jack, producer, A.B.C., and laying hands upon his Harris-tweed sleeves, to implore: "Laurie, love, givim a noice liddle brandy, the poor boy. Letum allhava noice . . . lid-dle . . ."

In a manner gymnastic and stylized, with some flexibility, no noise, a bottle clasped to her diaphragm, Mrs Brewer descended towards, sank to, the highly-coloured floor, and passed out.

As in a republic founded on the assassination of a despot, there were immediate and disgraceful confusions, there was undisciplined and pointless drama. There were cries, bumpings-into-others, orders and counter-orders, even some immediately-rebuked incivilities of gloating.

"Oh, poor old *dear*!" cried Dot and a number of women with chicken-greasy mouth-corners, and they entered the temple where the priestess lay, the brandy-bottle welded to her hands, curled up like a crayfish.

With conscious tenderness, and a clattering display of warm

humanity, and a sense of burying and praising Caesar in one, she and the undetachable bottle were carried to the bedroom, laid on the candlewick quilt and, when her worn little bunion-moulded shoes were removed, concealed beneath an eider-down. The bobble-edged bedside-lamp was turned out. The queen was dead. The war was over. The drought had broken.

The party now adopted shapelessness.

We four were thrown out of the kitchen.

Frank recaptured manliness, and poured drinks competently as though that were the thing.

Owners of orchid-coloured finger-nails began asking for drinks that needed slices of things in them.

Owners of ox-blood finger-nails washed plates or one-upped each other's tales of hepatitis, fibrositis, tonsilitis, appendicitis.

Dot, renewed into hostess, showed guests who lived in *old* houses how doors opened (and shut), how drawers slid out and slid back, how cupboards worked, and what shelves were for.

Presently, a young man who could have been Ern, for people called him so, a man young enough to wear a bandeau of blackheads on his inch-and-a-quarter of brow, professionally remotely exercised a concertina below his dreamy but disdainful grimace. One felt that, should the listeners' wariness have faltered, he would have executed, masterfully and brilliantly, *The Warsaw Concerto* and, to astounded and oceanic applause, torn off his lubricated wig and unsatisfactory Ern-mask.

The mood was, however, otherwise. Voices implored for sadder music. And sadder. The yearning melodies of thirty years before were wailed with much attention to melancholy. Loneliness, broken dreams and hearts and vows, depressed their spirits and discouraged drinking.

Two reckless creatures, man and wife, who had won a Charleston competition in 1927, shamelessly called for madder music. His bald head and glossy, huge, silver-grey behind, and her legs of sinew and bone spastically flailing, did nothing except recall *I Wonder Who's Kissing Her Now?* and *All Alone* and *Melancholy Baby*.

Everyone was well on the way to asking Ern for *Won't You Buy My Pretty Flowers?*, *The Letter Edged in Black*, and *It's Only a Beautiful Picture in a Beautiful Golden Frame.*

"All passion spent," said Da-vid from a corner of his mouth.

"All dreaming done," said Mr Jack from a corner of his.

"Let us telephone for a taxi-cab," said Laurence, ventriloquistically not moving a muscle.

"Peng Chin!" I said. "The ball is over. Let's get shot outside rather than here."

I knew that, somewhere in the cigarette smoke and melodious dirgest lurked the man with more eyebrows than hair who was aching to spring into prominence through the merest second's gap and . . .

He sprang.

Little Grey Home in the West had sadly guttered out; there was a pause; *there* was the tiny sandy man like a football-club secretary.

"Hey!" he roared. "Hey, ladies and gents. And *others*." No one did anything. "Now, let's have a little bit of shush. I would like . . ."

We had our hands on the telephone.

"Aw, don't be auntie," crowed a hoarse and heavenly voice. "No bloody speeches but. Do you moind?"

I seemed to hear *High School Cadets* being played, masterfully and brilliantly *and* loudly, by six angelic brass bands.

It was Madame Lazarus. It was dat ol' devil She. It was life. It was Mrs Brewer.

She blinked at the door. She surveyed disorganization. Her geiger worked. She licked two forefingers and burnished her eyebrows.

"Gawd, you're a broight lot of so-and-so's," she said.

Slowly, very slowly, she crossed her eyes and said, "Poor Old Reet can't get her shoes on, but."

It was royalty proclaiming, "Our crown has shrunk. So sorry. Nevertheless, on with the *levée*."

She uncrossed her eyes, cried out, "Drinks on the house!" raised her skirts above the knees of her lady-harrier's legs with hairs flattened like scales beneath the nylon, and began a delirious witch-doctor's prancing while she shrilly sang "Knees-up, Mother Brown! Kneesup, Mother Brown . . .!"

Her face, as it bounced, was radiant rubber with enough permutations and combinations of expression to outlast anyone anywhere. I'll swear her ears moved contrapuntally but wittily.

Da-vid grabbed his banjo.

Mrs Brewer's warped suspenders were more exhilarating than skiing.

We forgot telephones and Peng Chins.

At last, with a roar, the party began.

Ern dropped his disdain; his brow shot up an inch.

That Bit opened her eyes, which flashed like . . . like stars! She smiled! She had teeth! White!

The thing, the tonk, the mild young man in the green pullover, advanced at a canter towards Mrs Brewer.

"Knees Up, Mothah Brahoon!" he sang. "Knees Up, Mothah Brahoon . . .!"

It was a gaudy, a lively, an orgy, a bawdy, a rort. It was far and away the best of forty-two.

I cannot clearly understand how Reet (bull) and Hal-pal (toreador) and Hal-pal (terrified spinster) and Reet (bottom-pinching Latin) managed to break three Noritake bread-and-butter plates by 4.16 a.m., when one would have been more than enough. Since I've had to buy six to replace the three, Dot and Frank are three plates, two hangovers and a successful party up.

That's only natural.

It was Mrs Brewer's party.

(1960)

The Cats of Venice

Venice, late May, eleven *ante meridiem*, the weather divine, the canals already a little whiffy, and abob with rotten oranges, and chucked-out bunches of carnations spreading like broken fans, and early-tourist droppings: Chianti bottles and blobs of Kotex. Along the Grand Canal, gondola mooring-poles were yet being varnished, gilded, or painted in barber-shop stripes, but the orchestras of the Quadri and Lavena Cafés in St Mark's Square—the reception-room of Europe—purposed playing outside from noon, as though the season had already begun.

Six canals and six bridges away from the Square along the Schiavoni Esplanade, a grubby white liner *Thalatta* had released on the Esplanade and the City three hundred yards of Spaniards ceremoniously carrying gentian-blue plastic satchels with *SBARRA* in advertising white letters on them. Led, but not appearing to admit this, by two smart-alecs in berets who had been there before or were brazen, the two-by-two queue of new shoes, and dark eyes busy sucking in their money's worth, advanced towards the Square, St Mark's Canal on their left.

Just beyond the Arsenal ferry-landing, maddened gondoliers came at them like revolutionaries, harshly barking, many-armed and flailing, flashing teeth white as garlic and golden as brass. It was not a sight to soothe or to be relished. So she waited inside the glass door of the *Pensione Bucintoro* until the final Spanish back had passed, and opened the door, and came out.

Striking? Beautiful? She had the appearance of one sort of beauty: straight-nosed, bright- and pale-eyed, subtle but forthright make-up, heavenly modern legs.

She was better dressed than an Englishwoman, though in a manner somewhat English: she had too much discretion and far too much taste, it was obvious, to dress as badly as an American woman. Her shoes, for example. Her handbag. She had no bits and pieces of glitter. She could have been . . . twenty-six? Twenty-nine? Thirty-three?

She began to walk. She did not slap five-to-one-o'clock feet on the paving-stones like a Teutonic or Nordic woman; she did not enact progression trot-trot-trot like a Gallic one; she walked.

She decisively took the opposite direction to the Spaniards, she passed the liner on her right; in a haze, also to the right, the Lido and the horizon and the Adriatic pursued their purposes. Within five minutes she was in the Public Gardens, never tourist-ridden, designed, it seemed, not to attract.

The Gardens were Monte Carlo-ish, early twentieth century. Curly paths were hung over by unsightly trees and edged by unsightly shrubs and led to unsightly rockeries or reeking lavatories. Under the trees, writhing from the shrubs, gesturing atop of the rockeries, contorted outside the lavatories, were old statues of deities, classic heroes, amazonian seasons, whose bulging eyes of grime expressed unutterable anguishes for snapped-off hands, noseless faces, scarred draperies, lichened swords and cornucopias of sooty fruit. Neither frantic gesticulations in marble nor bold fronts of marble muscles and breasts had protected them from the vandalizings of silken air and velvet time. Above their marble moustaches, newer busts of opera-composers and nineteenth-century patriotic fire-brands glared Lido-wards.

There were more eyes, however, many more, than the many marble eyes.

Seated on branch and rockery and plinth and bust-shoulder and chipped pedestal and broken-toed goddess's foot, silent and still, were cats.

They watched her reach, watched her dust with her handkerchief, watched her sit on, as if she were quite and composedly alone, a cast-iron bench that could have been in any public garden in the world.

As she lit a cigarette the cats watched.

From where she sat she must have—she could have—seen thirty, maybe forty, immobile cats. Their faces, larger pansies, were bold, quietly ravenous, and deceitfully at rest, for one knew that they brewed restlessly within. They digested intentions. They electrically conveyed a shaping purpose each to each, and to all. They were as hard-boiled as immortals; they sat, claws concealed, like immortals, to watch her.

They were under a compulsion. They seemed, all of them, and even she, at her second cigarette, to abide some moment. This future moment's arrival was not to be impeded—how could trite and unforeseeable fate be?—by the senseless and fairly furtive chasing and ducking about and throaty chirping of children so very cheaply well-decked-out that they seemed on the point of being ragged.

She sat on, self-possessed, and for long enough to light a third cigarette, and be touched on her unwrinkled elbow by the shadow of Verdi's marble chin . . . or was it Garibaldi's? Then, as though chosen by an undercurrent of voting, as though destined, as though permitted, one of the cats rose and began to pick its way towards her with a calm ferocity of hunger and a noiseless delicacy.

Her eyes got deeper in tint, and yet wonderfully clearer. She could be sensed to ripple, within—one drenching, colourless ripple. Her smooth throat arched, stretched itself as she raised her chin to breathe smoke towards the sky to which she said, clear and soft, and unpassionately, "I hear you coming with your clattering boots."

Silently the cat came nearer. It stopped thirty-four inches away. She leaned fractionally forward, and spoke, "Perhaps yes; perhaps *no*!" Then she said, "How stupid of me! You are not cat but *gatto. Forse che si; forse che*—no!" and threw the cigarette in the cat's beautifully decorated, beautiful, hard little face.

Not bothering to observe the result of this wilful yet seemingly required action, she got up; she walked out of the Gardens, St Mark's Canal now to her left.

She passed the liner with its name in Greek letters, passed the *Pensione Bucintoro*, she hurried decisively over the six bridges on two of the stairways of which she passed priests in descent, handling their skirts like Edwardian matrons, she disregarded the whinnying gondoliers, the stalls selling maps of Venice and views of Venice and destructible toys and miniature plastic gondolas and the dangled expensive rubbish of Muranese bead necklaces, she gave the Bridge of Sighs no look, and Adam and Eve no look as she rounded the Ducal Palace, and came to St Mark's Square, and sat at a Quadri Café table.

She ordered, as though it were an affectation she condoned without absolutely approving, a Fernet Branca. She put her handbag on the table. While it was thus horizontal she opened it to withdraw, adroitly, a packet of cigarettes and a lighter. Each calm move had purpose. As in the Gardens she exhaled the mood of dispassionately waiting, of readiness.

Soon, very soon, he subtracted himself from his friends, and came, and no one could have heard him come with the Quadri orchestra playing *Santa Lucia* and the Lavena orchestra men yapping and gabbling as they waited to outdo with *Arrivederci, Roma*, and the pigeons whirring in hundreds, and photographers bleating at the tourists, yet her eyes became deeper in tint, and clearer, and she arched her smooth throat as she tilted her head to breathe smoke towards the zenith in an echo: I hear you coming with your clattering boots.

He sat at the next table.

No more than thirty-four inches separated them.

She was now looking, doubtless with interest, towards—oh, the Bell Tower, the pigeons, Florian's Café opposite—anywhere but himwards while he ordered his rhubarb-scented muck: "Rabarbaro!" in a voice, tenor rather, to be heard. Otherwise, why so loud?

Then in English, very, very careful, and humble, but seductively certain:

"Do . . . you . . . moind . . . if . . . Oi . . . smoke?"

She took a sip of her Fernet Branca.

Scarcely less loudly, more seductively, his horrible lighter out, his horrible cigarette between fingers as preparedly scrubbed as a surgeon's, he said again:

"Please, excusa me. Do you moind if Oi smoke?"

"Yes," she said.

"But you are smoking."

"Yes," she said, not having looked at him. "A cigarette." She added, informatively, towards the Bell Tower, "Tobacco, Virginian. Benson and Hedges. Terete in shape."

"Excusa me," he said, not yet lighting his cigarette. "Oi think so, you are English. Oi am clever at knowing this. Oi am roight?"

"No."

"May Oi ask then?"

"No."

Pigeons, or Florian's, or something engrossed her. She sipped idly, idly. Her profile, although engrossed and at the sip, was perfect.

"But you have the English voice. The English cigarettes. The English beautiful flesh."

"*An* English voice. *English* cigarettes. *A* beautiful . . . thank you . . . English *skin*."

She spoke towards a Japanese woman being very Japanese in kimono and obi and, of course, camera. She spoke abstractedly, a gentle indifferent governess.

Then, as one taking a first pawn, he lit his cigarette. Its smoke could not, to her, have smelt like tobacco-smoke. The exhalation was accompanied by the sound, which she must have recognized, of a self-satisfied Italian crossing his legs: there is no sound like it.

"Oi think you *are* English, and joke me."

"I am Australian. *South* Australian. Which is a quite different kettle of fish from South Italian. Married. Educated. Mother's name Elizabeth. I abhor turnips. I am expensive to run."

"Ah! It is your first toime in Venezia, Oi think."

"I like to think it's my fourth time in Venice. I said I was expensive to run."

"You like to come to visit? You have noice husband who leaves you alone?"

"My husband is—of course, of course—ninety-four years old and a crashing bore. You will readily understand that. You would *like* him. When he comes off duty—he's first violin in the Lavena orchestra—you must meet him."

"You loike . . . Venice?"

"I like *Venice*. The *place*."

"Can you seek your way about alone, a beautiful lonely woman?"

Did she pause to contemplate a governessy *find*?

"Certainly," she said.

"Will you not lose yourself?"

"No. Oh, no."

She drank, as though privately. A fraction of smile slid on to the side of her profile farther from him. She waited, as though secretly waiting in all the hubbub and circling about, for something obvious, destined, platitudinous . . . not to be impeded . . . how could tepid and foretellable fate be?

"Oi should loike to lose-a moiself in your beautiful arms. You are most beautiful. You make-a moi blood boiling."

She smiled at those pigeons not crawling along tourist arms, and not beating the air, but milling and mincing madly in currents as if they had buses to catch.

"*Boil*," she said, and, "Really? I feel like the faggots under a witch's cauldron."

Had she not been the sort of woman who was cool as a bread-knife one would have said that, suddenly, at this point, she became a shade radiant, illuminated with the first symptoms of an excitement.

"Shall Oi come with you where you are living, and you shall correct moi English, and we shall make love?"

"No."

It was off-hand refusal; she was scrupulously taking a long time to stub a cigarette as though utterly grinding out a spider.

"Why no?"

She drank her heel-tap. She cleared her white throat. She spoke towards the . . . well, she had not once turned in his direction.

"Unaccustomed," she said, "*absolutely* unaccustomed as I am, you Latin galah, to public speaking and, Jehovah knows, one could be no more public than here and now—and yet how private and cosy we lucky twain are!—I emphatically give you another, No! For why? First, because I do not like thee, Dr Fell. Secondly, because I am not a tart who has reduced her fees. Thirdly, because, like your concupiscient brothel-trained brethren, you are an amorous confidence man seeking a sop to vanity, *and* because you have a hysterical preoccupation with what you call love."

Having, at least, heard the last word, he became unfazed in reality though he had not deigned to reveal fazement. He uncrossed his legs and recrossed them the other way; he jetted out a lot of smoke; his voice prepared deepness to dictate truth to a half-witted stenographer.

"Love," he stated, "is loife." Many metal-stuffed teeth came in sight to adorn this revelation.

"Go *hon*," she said and, lighting a cigarette. "Do you maind *terribly* if Ai smoke? Ai just know some gents dislike it in a gel."

"Oi have planty love."

"*Of* love, student of our fair English tongue. Well, *well*! Indeed, and fancy that now. One could not have guessed. Planty love, eh? Let me, as an old wedded hag, give you—for free, you understand—a little advice. Give it to women of your own race. There are planty, planty love-loving chicks in Venice . . . pardon, Venezia. Italian, too. The clip-joints are chockablock."

"No."

"*That* is my word."

"No, Oi give moi specialty love to you . . . only to you."

"I knew," she said, "I should have worn a hessian jibbah. Only to little me! Call me ingrate, call me looker in the mouths of gift horses."

"Yes, yes," he said, "Oi give-a gift of love because you are beautiful foreigner."

For the first time she turned to look at him, and directly, and blandly, unsmiling although almost not so. The Lavena orchestra had soared into *One Fine Day*. What eye saw, what ear heard . . . veal cutlet drenched in chocolate sauce?

"Foreigner? You are no more Venetian than I am. Sicilian? You mean you think I have more money than I have. And fewer morals."

He gave her, directly enough into her directness, his Mona Lisa look. Doubtless expected to have effect in ratio to length of existence, it lingered on and on, and she meticulously examined it, entitled to, for, though hundred-hand, it was hers. Italian men are conceited bitches as Mona Lisa obviously was: was that what she arrived at—again, anew? She arrived at somewhere that caused her to gesture the waiter into the café for another drink, while the Mona Lisa expression was put into words.

"It is not money. Oi have planty *lire*." He smacked at his chest. "Planty. You are most beautiful. Oi am crazy of you."

"*About*, Croesus. Planty *lire*, eh?"

"Yes, yes. Oi need-a practice for English. Oi needa you. Oi come with you. We practise together. Oi make-a the joy for you and the happiness. Oi needa too the exercise of love."

"Heigh-ho!" she said, and " 'No,' she said wearily, 'no, no, *no*!' But he is not, you foolish girl, an intelligent subject; he understands not 'No!' "

"Why no? How always no? How is it you say no? Oi speak-a English. Oi am good a-looking. You think so? And well-dressed in very beautiful fashion-wear."

Apparently she could not resist a second turning to him, a second survey.

She could not not have seen the arrow-pointed orange shoes with tasselled laces, the sockettes stripe-encircled like Alice in Wonderland's stockings, the . . . She turned her eyes politely away, and farther away to where, on the other side of the square, something or someone caused them to become still as if, at last, at long long last, they decidedly saw someone or something.

"Anent your fashion-wear, Giorgio," she said much more brightly than hitherto, "I must say I've scarcely, in Australia, Down Under, seen gayer on any—but *any*—of your compatriots, those espresso-bar-boys *par excellence*. And many have I seen for, believe or believe not a chatterbox foreigner, they are Australia's largest import."

"You see!" he said, making, unseen by her, a presumably Continental gesture of both hands, each two-ringed. "Oi am very good lover. Very strong. Very man. Very *gooda* lover. You know? Troi me."

For the third time she turned to him, vivaciously, very. The waiter put down her drink. Even though radiant she observed this.

"Oh," she said, and her eyes shone, and her smile was glittering, and she took up her drink with a flourish, "oh, *do* excuse me. I must drink this. You have undone me. You have upset me, now. Oh yes you have, you *fas*cinating creature. It's a dream Venice! Southern skies! And you—your warmth, your childlike charm, your carefree spirit, your quickness of perception, your *humanity*! But I bore you. Everyone says this to you. Oh, how utterly you fascinate me! But . . ."

Here her smile fled into the sunlight. She seemed distressed almost to tears.

"But . . . oh, saddest of words . . . too late! Alas, too late!

I feel I can confide in you. I am waiting for my lover."

He spoke, for the last time. Even though his lighter would not work, and his last cigarette he held was bent, he spoke with thinned conviction, and she watched him with *her* Mona Lisa expression.

"Oi am better than your lover. You do not troi me. Troi me."

"Oh, *no*!" she said. "No, little man. He is taller than you. He is handsome. No gold in the toothie-pegs. No need for built-up heels. A wonderful lover. I a-*dore* him. Name—Lyle."

She watched him, he mute as a haddock, in his bile-green mock-suède jacket, fumbling his broken-down lighter out of sight and his bent cigarette and his lost face.

"You!" she said. "*Gatto! Forse che si? Forse che no, gatto!*" and flicked her cigarette towards his beautiful, hard little face.

Not bothering to observe the result of this wilful yet seemingly required action, she swung away from him, and raised her shapely arm straight aloft, and gently stirred the hand with its wedding ring and large solitaire engagement ring at the other woman wading out of the surf of pigeons.

"My dear," said the other, pseudo-breathless and sparkling, "I've been trying to get across the square for *days*. That frightful Mamie. Pigeons all *over* her. Little claws caught in the blue rinse. Photographers three deep. I must have a dirty big beer."

She sat at right angles to her friend, so that had she wanted to look at him, the man in the bile-green, and the stove-pipe black trousers, she had only to look at him. She seemed to have no need to. He was anyway everywhere, and certainly not out of the box.

"My dear, I had to be rude *twice*. Where's that bloody waiter? Mamie Whatever told me, in American, that she came from Pasadena, California. You Ass Ay. Which, I suppose, is *in* America. I said, my dear, I was *terribly*, terribly sorry. Ah, he arrives—what are you drinking? I'll have a beer."

"A double Scotch. Water."

"My dear, then I'll have *two* beers. Two beers, Giorgio. And you heard what madam said. *Vite*, boy, *vite*. You look *radiant*, my dear."

"Yes," she said, again draining a Fernet Branca heel-tap. She turned farther aside from the persisting man.

"Yes. You know," she raised her voice, "Italy would be quite enchanting were it not for the Italians."

"I *see*, my dear. I *saw*. I could hardly not," said the other, and leaned confidentially on the table, and interlocked dark eyes with her friend's bright pale ones, and also raised her voice, "My dear, do you think he sets his own hair? I can always tell from the nape. When he goes away . . . *if* he goes away . . . I'll look. Unless, of course, he backs away. Is he, my dear, already standing or still sitting? *So* hard to tell."

She swept her eyes blindly across him like a stroke of ink, across the face harder now in the mould of one who came from the north of Italy, preferably Turin, and spoke faultless Tuscan, and understood not a word of English, and had a lighter that worked.

"My dear, even that didn't get rid of Mamie Pasadena, You Ass Ay. I had to insult her mink. Is ubiquitous the word? Anyway it goes everywhere like a plastic mac. My dear, I said to her, 'My dear, if one has enough money to buy mink one has no need to buy mink, my dear.' She could have pushed me in the Canal. My dear, don't look now, you're not being followed. Lover-boy leaves us. His dear little tapering legs take him away."

They watched.

Still watching, the rims of drinks resting on their lips, they saw him reach his group of friends. Without gesticulation, he told them something. For a second, twenty eyes turned, across the distance, at the two Australian women, and unflickeringly regarded them, and for that analysing second only. Then the legs in tight-fitting cloth balletically disposed themselves subtly differently, and the eyes slipped elsewhere.

Presently, another of the young men ran a comb through his curls and, as though chosen by an under-current of voting, as though destined, as though permitted, picked his way towards a braceleted young woman . . . German? . . . dressed with uneasy boldness who had settled herself, uncertainly at ease, by herself, at a table.

"Oh, I hear you coming," said the woman who had ordered double whisky, "with your clattering boots."

She said this softly, wearily, a shade regretfully. Her mouth winced. She could be sensed to ripple, within—one drenching colourless ripple, almost a shudder.

She quickly lifted her drink.

Before it reached her lips, she did lightly shudder.

"Darling," she said to her beer-drinking friend, as she put down the whisky, and nibbled at her wedding ring, "do you hear the cats at night? Hundreds of them?"

"My dear, *cats*?"

"Cats. Hundreds. Making love. The breeze blows the . . . the din from the Gardens. All day long they wait. Then, night-time—hundreds and hundreds of screaming cats."

"My dear, *nothing* wakes this one once it's closed its little tipsy eyes. But *nothing*."

"Cats. I can't sleep."

She looked towards the graceful pretty young men.

"I wish to God Lyle would come back from Milan. Today. To*night*. Another week of this! *God!*"

Her eyes grew darker; she drank deep; this time she really shuddered.

(1961)

Princess Jasmine Flower

My father, to mention two things about him that indicate nothing except that he earned his living at the bawling top of his voice, and spent his leisure with his larynx hanging in silent shreds, was an auctioneer and a chess player. In those days, 1930, the Chess Club met every Tuesday night.

My mother, who smoked mentholated cigarettes semi-secretly and had an affected cityish accent ("Bah-ee, dulling!", her constant cry as she darted off somewhere else and odd, sums it up), was the worst cook between the Tropic of Capricorn and the South Pole. She was for ever up to something new: making raffia hats, barbola brooches, poker-work tobacco-jars, stencilled night-dress cases and *papier mâché* bowls the shape of poes. Everything she made was askew, unwearable, unusable, ungivable-away, and of a hideousness about which no more need be said than that she had a genius for making a pickle-bottle look even worse than the worst souvenir in a Belgian commercial-traveller's front parlour. In 1930, she had abandoned Art for Culture. The Play-reading Group met every Tuesday night.

We had a maid-of-all-work, Florrie. She and my mother had a wonderful, gossipy, slap-dash time dropping jugs and sauce-boats, and burning things. Just as I shall always remember my mother's "Bah-ee, dulling!"—they were also her dying last words to me—so I shall always remember Florrie's, "Sugar! The milk's caught a-*gane*!"

Florrie's eyebrows were plucked to single lines on sore-looking baldnesses; under eyelids lustrous with vaseline her eyes rolled happily and inconsequentially hither and thither like ball-bearings. She had many satin blouses, tangerine, cerise, royal blue and primrose. From every blouse two or three buttons were always missing—doubtless lost behind the boxthorns on the cliff-top where my salacious friend Wock and salacious I sometimes eaves-dropped on her squealing and wrestling joyously with a footballer-butcher. Florrie's day-off, and night-off, was every Tuesday.

In retrospect, Tuesday night seems to have been Mardi Gras in that late-Victorian, decayed, port-cum-seaside-town composedly coming unstuck between the Marine Parade tamarisks aslant from the Southern Ocean, and the dairy farms covering the plains and mounting the lower slopes of the Big Dipper hills, for Tuesday night was also the night of the Junior Rechabite Lodge meeting. To my parents I appeared to appear a dedicated Rechabite.

In truth, I'd not tapped on the blistered tongue-and-groove door ("Guardian, open the *door*!" is all I now remember of the mystery) of the Temperance Hall for two or three months. I was bent on *sin.* Wock and I, both sniggering, two-faced, sewer-minded fourteen-year-olds, used to go smoking, lover-tracking and sex-talking along the beach or the cliff-top. I doubt if, to us, the word *sex* was in. To us, our exchange of ideas was plain, enjoyable filth enriched with more exhilarating misinformation than a mediaeval bestiary. It took years to unlearn what I didn't learn on those far-off Tuesday nights.

On Tuesday nights my two little sisters were bedded-down by a Miss Singh. *A* Miss Singh! By *the* Miss Singh.

In those days she was not called a baby-sitter nor paid in cash, although I don't really know, for my parents were off-handedly lavish—there was always a pineapple going rotten in the fruit-stand, sandy-bristled tramps (they seemed always sandy) were shooed off with five shillings, my father would not wear darned socks.

I know that Miss Singh had a sort of four-course supper when my sisters went to sleep. I know that my mother, who was skilled in their manufacture, gave her flat sponge-cakes, pallid scones, botched biscuits, as well as Collins Street hats worn once or twice, evening-dresses fringed and embroidered with seed-like beads, shoes she had taken a dislike to after a week, once even an old coat of some unidentifiable fur somewhat resembling a marmalade cat's.

Miss Singh, who lived in a cottage held together by dolichos, with a rickety, ancient, turbaned father, was some sort of Indian . . . Afghan? Parsee? Cingalese? . . . and worked in a little shop on the Marine Parade. This shop was next to the

Crystal Palace, where the names of sundaes and spiders were misspelt on the looking-glasses behind the marble counter under a perpetual greeting:

A MERRY XMAS AND A HAPPY NEW YEAR
TO ALL OUR FREIND'S.

Next door to this Versailles glamour, Miss Singh sold—or did not sell, for the revolving stand of them was changeless—postcards of enormous wives (or mothers-in-law), all semi-circular curves, in red bathing-togs, being nipped on the biggest curves by crabs. These assaulted females all wore coin-dotted bathing-caps, just as the postcard mashers all wore boaters, striped blazers and co-respondent shoes as they rolled goo-goo eyes at the jazz-garters a breeze from the briny had revealed by tossing up the insufficient skirts of flappers. As well, she sold, or was there to sell, shell-covered handkerchief-boxes, kewpies wearing the district football colours, crystal scent-sprays, and trays under whose glass lay flashy landscapes in which were incorporated iridescent-blue butterfly-wings.

Miss Singh was small in a conspicuous manner; she seemed deliberately diminished; she could have appeared larger had she not withdrawn to some wary inner fastness. She was mediocre in an exotic but *declassée* way, and *declassée* to the point of a shyness so pat as to be obviously fake, and designed to fit her slender hands flexible as seaweed in water, her strained-open treacly eyes with whites yellow as elderly knife-handles and underlined by bruise-coloured arcs. Her ears were always on show; their lobes were pierced by circles of gold. She smelt of stale sweat with an extra quality that may merely have been extra staleness. I thought her sly, but kept that to my sly self.

One Tuesday night Wock did not turn up at the Crystal Palace where we always met, sophisticatedly, to get rid of our Rechabite money and any more we'd been able to steal from our mothers. I dallied, raising one eyebrow villainously at myself in the looking-glass in a Lew Cody manner, until three raspberry spiders made me feel sick.

I walked the beach to the cliff-base where rocks taller than I sucked the cream of the surf—it was full moonlight in autumn—between their fangs. I toiled up the path to the cliff-top. No lovers in sight. Not that I cared to spy on lovers without Wock reeking of liquorice at my shoulder. I gave a monarch-of-all-I-survey glance at the ocean. Alone, it seemed a longer way down and not at all water.

The head-bowed rollers wore flakes of nickel across their mile-long humpbacks. Remorse, autumnal weariness, anguish at the thought of cold closing in, and an ominous rebelliousness, rose from the ocean almost like sentence-forming words. The lovers' boxthorns moved several feet nearer behind my back; I turned to catch them just as they pretended movelessness. I went home—quickly, not looking back, whistling *Bye, bye, Blackbird* in a key so high as to be bat-like.

At the back door I heard a keen monotone going on with unsettling choir-boy sexlessness. It was Miss Singh and a bedtime story. As the fly-wire door banged her voice ceased.

"Who's that? Who's there?" she cried, as if she were a mere broom-handle away from Lon Chaney in *The Phantom of the Opera*.

" 'Sme, Miss Singh. Back early," I said, contemptuous of fear. Then, evil-mindedly thinking she might depart, even supperless, and leave me to my sisters who meant nothing to me, though I assumed and felt that I loved them, I adeptly constructed and most clearly delivered a lie: "I've got some studying to do. Some reading. *Books*."

To indicate poise to the unseen and unseeing I tugged a dirty comb through my stale-brilliantine-dirty hair.

Miss Singh made no reply. I poked out my tongue in her direction. I walked up the passage to my bedroom, which was opposite my sisters'. I heard them implore, at the same time anxious, sincere and cheeky, "*Please*, Miss Sing-song, go on with the new story."

"Miss Singh, if yew don't mind," said Miss Singh, less than graciously, but immediately slipping, as into a dull and comforting macintosh, into her story-telling monotone.

With a sufficient display of drawer-opening noises and damn-and-blasting ejaculations as if to myself, but primarily to convince Miss Singh that I was study-mad, I got out my copy of *The Awful Disclosures of Maria Monk*. It fell open at titillating pages I knew as well as the Apostle's Creed. I sat on my bed to perve over them.

However, Miss Singh's deadly and elaborately static account of the adventures of some Princess Jasmine Flower was more overpowering than goings-on in a nunnery. I was considering going to Wock's place when, suddenly, I realized what Miss Singh was talking about. It was another of those fissures which, in my adolescence, used to appear, unheralded, in the walls of the adult citadel, to reveal something blinding and new, though often incomprehensible, about the adult.

"*Now*," Miss Singh was saying, "poor Princess Jasmine Flower was forced to go to work in a shop. Not an *ord*inary shop. As yew shall see. It was a very high-class establishment. It was right next to a reely high-class, a very, *very* high-class palace called the Palace of Crystal, which had lots of lovely mirrows."

"Florrie says mirrors," said Janice sternly—or was it Irma?

"Put yewr feet under the bed-clothes, Irma. Quick now!" said Miss Singh, tartly enough.

Ah, I thought, Irma!

"And," said Miss Singh, really tartly, almost sinister, "if yew interrupt *again*, Jan-ice, *Miss* . . ."

So it was Janice! Sly, oh, sly, sly, sly Miss Singh, I thought, for some obscure and insulting reason silently gibbering like an orang-outang while scratching exaggeratedly under one armpit.

"Lots of reely very, very lovely mirrows," she proceeded flatly. "There were some in Jasmine Flower's shop, too. What do yew think she sold? She sold pretty postcards of many varieties, and sea-gulls made of mussel-shells, and dainty cups and saucers with vi'lets on, and tasteful crystal perfume-atomizers. . . ."

Ah! The fissure in the citadel brickwork!

Princess Jasmine Flower who sold tasteful crystal perfume-atomizers was Miss Singh who tried to sell machine-cut scent-sprays.

Immediately—*Abracadabra!*—she became as fascinating, almost, to me as the silent film actresses and actors I was allowed to spend sixpence to adore, each Saturday night, at the School of Arts Hall. I became, in short, a Singh fan. Peremptorily, though with guile, I banished the pretence of being Rechabited towards wowserism, for the pretence of being, to my parents' confounding and their cynical delight, a scholarly bookworm, a Tuesday-night-only one. With an "Algebra" or

"British History" open, I listened avidly to Miss Singh's pastiche of fact and fantasy.

I considered inviting Wock as a co-listener, but decided him too insensitive, too uncouth. Hurt at my withdrawal, he continued to hunt on the cliff-top every Tuesday night with a handsome though flat-footed boy called Lionel whom I loathed with an unreasonably jealous loathing. Meanwhile, chewing Milk Kisses, I pieced together, from her repeated and often maddening retracings of old ground, the tale of Princess Jasmine Flower.

The beautiful Princess Jasmine Flower with her lustrous almond eyes, her jet-black lashes ("Very, very long and upcurving," said Miss Singh. "Irma, little *ladies* don't pick their noses.") and blue-black hair she could sit on, had been brought-up on the best of everything . . . salmon sandwiches, roast lamb on golden plates, cream-puffs, kola tonic in tasteful cut-glass goblets . . . in a far-off country where the sun glittered from morn till eve. Princess Jasmine Flower spent a joyful girlhood picnicking in flowery glades under the jasmine trees, served by slaves with dainty salmon sandwiches and kola tonic. She grew into a very beautiful young woman.

("About how old is Miss Singh?" I asked my mother, with loudly creaking off-handedness, the day after Miss Singh had called Princess Jasmine Flower young.)

("Rilly, dulling!" said my mother buffing at her fingernails. "Rilly, mothah doesn't *know*. But she'd hazard a tiny guess at thirteh to thirteh-three. At *least*, dulling!")

By the time Princess Jasmine Flower was a very, very shapely young woman, S.W. in evening-gowns, there were cruel plots against her and her kindly father, the Grand-Emperor Ranjit.

(No one called old Mr Singh Mr Singh: he was known to the town as Old Ranjit Singh, or less kindly, Old Monkey Singh.)

Wicked thieves broke into their lovely high-class palaces. Chests of rubies were stolen, emeralds, sapphires and very many other precious gems. Bales of crêpe-de-Chine and fuji silk. The Princess's two thousand dresses. Yards of diamond necklaces. Glass slippers. Fur coats. Tins of salmon. Chocolate sticks. Hundreds of packets of jelly-crystals.

Bereft of all their priceless valuable treasures, of everything except the clothes they stood up in, the Grand-Emperor and Jasmine Flower were forced to flee the country on a very, very high-class ocean-liner owned by a kind neighbouring emperor. They were set ashore (after an elaborate but dull three-day storm, the description of which occupied one whole agonizing Tuesday night, and nearly turned my hair white with frustration) on the sea-coast of a far-off land where they retired to a very comfortable humble cottage.

"The cottage," recited Miss Singh, "was a thatched one,
"The outside old and mean,
"Yet everything within that cot
"Was wondrous neat and clean."

Thatch apart, I knew the outside of the humble cottage well enough: shattered and gateless picket fence, privet hedge run amuck with buffalo-grass run amuck in it, a back-yard of horehound, a dead cherry-tree, a shoal of salmon tins. I took Miss Singh's word on a neat and clean within with many reservations.

The Princess, because the Grand-Emperor grew old and feeble from disappointment, very, very nobly went to work in a shop, a reely high-class establishment, with mirrors. How lonely she was as she watched the waves of the sea through the shop window!

She suffered all this very, very patiently for she knew that, one day, a prince would arrive to save her.

He arrived.

Handsome as Richard Barthlemess. Blue eyes. Reddish hair, reddish-*gold* hair. Jasmine Flower knew that he was only buying the packet of *on*velopes so he could gaze into her lustrous eyes and . . .

Miss Singh's relentless monotone cut out: my sisters had obviously fallen to sleep.

I could have cried.

As Miss Singh, softly singing *Mary Lou* just out of tune, tucked in my abominable sisters, I switched out the light.

Miss Singh, loudly attempting to tiptoe quietly, next whispered at my door, "I'm going to make myself a little supper."

Little! Huh!

"Would yew like a cup of cocoa?"

I snored.

"Are yew asleep?"

I snored more loudly.

Miss Singh crept with ear-splitting inaudibility to sack the kitchen while I undressed in the dark. I did not know how I would live through the week that separated me from the Somethingth Episode of the serial.

Next Sunday was windy; not a veering, thrust-and-parry wind but an endless, streaming one as though it poured through an immense keyhole on the horizon.

Since I affected solitary walks in wind, muttering, "The teeth of the gale!" I strode in knickerbockers along the empty beach to the pier. No sooner had I set foot on its planks than, to my intertwisted embarrassment and excitement, I found myself compelled to pass . . . oh, those lustrous, almond eyes, I see them still! . . . and be greeted by Miss Singh dressed to kill in a red hat, a red coat, red shoes, all once my mother's, and all of different reds.

She hung, doting and brazen, on the arm of a stocky young man, slightly pigeon-toed in light-tan shoes, with a pig-pale face under a nut-brown deeply dented felt hat.

From the pier I watched them walk on the wet sand. Once he executed some show-off cart-wheels. His hat fell off. How quickly she picked it up. How ginger, how reddish-*gold*, his hair was!

Linked once more, they laboured up the cliff-path, seeming to fuse together, to kiss, to melt into a tremulous red unity. As he melted thus, so he melted from my vision. I never with actual eyes saw him again, or saw them together again. Never. With the eyes of my mind—oh, yes. Often. To this day.

On Tuesday, I learned that the Prince, whose name was Prince Larry, was in disguise. He had heard of the Princess Jasmine Flower's very, very tragical life, and had come to save her. To be near her, and to prove how much he loved the dainty young princess, he had taken a position in a high-class pastry-cook's where he made cream puffs, Victoria sponges, *de*-licious Boston buns, and wedding cakes.

Miss Singh's voice across the corridor ran riot like the dolichos over Monkey Singh's shack-like cottage. She described wedding cakes in a choosy, questing fashion. They grew taller than cathedrals and more embellished than Dresden shepherdesses.

I was just going mad when she returned, with less dreamy dreariness, to Prince Larry. He had very white refined hands, strong and very, very manly hands. He could stand on his hands. He could turn very, very circular cart-wheels.

"Pooh!" said one of my evil sisters. "I can turn cart-wheels."

"Yew must *not* get out of bed," said Miss Singh, unavailingly.

"Ooh, I can see your bottie," squealed the other diabolic sister just before the crash. There were screams; there were sobs.

By the time order was restored I was so exhausted by murderous inclinations and their suppression that I went to bed while Miss Singh was lullabying:

"Mary Lou, Mary Lou, cross my heart, I love yew;
"All the bells in the steeple
"Are ready to ring
"And all the people
"Are planning pretty presents, all for yew, Mary Lou."

I fell asleep, probably as soon as my sisters, to the fourth or fifth singing:

"For miles around they're waiting
"To start in celebrating,
"When yew say, 'I do,' Mary Lou."

The next two Tuesday nights gave me glimpses of the external adventures of Princess Jasmine Flower and Prince Larry. Miss Singh sounded so gay that she could have been as radiant as Princess Jasmine Flower certainly was. The disguised royalties saw Charles Farrell and Janet Gaynor in *Seventh Heaven.* They ate high-class sundaes at the Palace of Crystal: the King of the Palace was very, very gentlemanly and refined.

The Prince gave the Princess a sweetly pretty scarab brooch bought in the Princess's shop. They climbed a picturesque hill to look at the moonlight on the sea. The moonlight was also very, very picturesque.

My ears pricked up. I lasciviously wondered if Jasmine Flower had blouse-buttons missing. I attempted, still somehow keeping in the frame of the story, to imagine *a* Prince and *a* Princess wrestling as Wock and I had dimly seen, but largely heard, others less royal wrestling behind the boxthorn clumps, while the tusked rocks below chewed and spat back the soapy ocean-edge.

On the next Tuesday night no pretence of study was necessary: I was lumpily in bed with a throat which seemed raw as far as my navel, and a headache that Aspros had reduced to a burring: a steadily rotating knife-grinder's wheel.

My skull reverberated, spacious and muggy as a crypt. My pillow and I were soaked with eucalyptus. Death would scarcely have been incommoding; I almost hoped Miss Singh would not heighten my forlornness by a gaily rippling account of Princess Jasmine Flower and her ding-dong love-affair with Prince Larry.

Indeed, my father having departed to chess, and my mother ("Bah-ee, dulling . . . and no more Aspro-things till mothah's back!") to play-read *Nothing but the Truth*, Miss Singh seemed reluctant to utter a sentence.

My sisters, however, nagged in a fashion so relentless and somehow threatening while being cunningly sweet and pathetic that, presently, Miss Singh gave way.

My ailment having put me in a sort of other dimension the strange quality of Miss Singh's voice was blameable on my expatriate senses. Her voice was thickened, slower, burdened with a mud of despairs. It seemed as though folded smaller.

Princess Jasmine Flower was having a hell of a time. I cannot recall all. . . . The Grand-Emperor Ranjit had been sick; the Princess had knocked a crystal butter-dish from a shop shelf; its price was docked from her wages; she had cut her thumb opening a tin of salmon . . . there were perverse and bitter winds tugging at the Princess's tattered garments. It was cold, cold . . . Miss Singh said something acid about old fathers and firewood.

Her voice began to speed up, to become gritty and, in some unexplicable way, unhealthy. Prince Larry, it revealed, was not of royal heritage at all! Far from it. Jasmine Flower should have known. He was very, very false. A bad man. A deceiver. He betrayed the Princess with others who were not high class. There were a barmaid, and the daughter of the town's pound-keeper. Princess Jasmine Flower's heart was broken.

"What," said Miss Singh, "was the deceived Princess to do? What *could* a woman do? What would yew do?" she seemed to be asking my sisters aged six and eight. "Poor Princess Jasmine Flower!"

Silence fell. Silence persisted for minutes. Amazingly, my sisters did not broach it. Perhaps they had long ago fled into sleep from the drizzling climate of aristocratic griefs. I shall never know; they may have lain comfortably half-awake, warmed, as women are, even so young, by the thought of another woman's anguish, and contemplated it, sleepily blinking. Silence continued so long that the knife-grinding wheel in the crypt began to lull me; my eyelids began to descend.

Suddenly, I was wide awake.

Miss Singh had abruptly tossed a laugh into the silence, a short throaty laugh as if she were a chunkier, more muscular woman.

I was certain, now, that my sisters were asleep. Miss Singh began again, her voice guttural and pitched nowhere.

"What was the Princess to do? What could she do? Very, very proud. Intelligent. She promised to meet . . . to meet the Prince. . . . On the hill. . . . Above the sea. . . . Waiting. . . . A red hat, red shoes, the red dress. . . . Waiting in the cold. He comes. He takes her in his arms. He kisses her. He says 'I'm going away tomorrow morning. But I'll come back.' Lies! Lies! All lies!"

It was difficult to hear Miss Singh.

"A pack of lies! The Princess says, 'Light a match. I dropped my purse near the edge, while I was waiting.' He lights four matches, looking and looking nearer the edge. She pushes him. His hat on. 'Oh,' he says, 'Oh!' "

Miss Singh stopped.

I was disappointed by Miss Singh, and bored. I restrained myself from croaking out, "Shut *up*!"

In a few moments I heard her go to the kitchen. I fell asleep to her furtive but almost visible din. I saw kettle hit stove, drawers open and shut, dropped cake-tin lid strike linoleum.

On Wednesday the doctor said I had influenza.

Next Tuesday, Miss Singh did not turn up. My mother said she'd have been madly livid but she was, anyway, giving the play-reading the go-by to ministah to her poor feverish 'ickie dulling.

Miss Singh, my mother went on, had left on Monday to go to a wardsmaid's job in a Melbourne hospital. "Rilly," she said, "I expect it's a gay change for the poor little thing. Awkward-making for me, though. I'll have to chivvy out another old maid for Tuesdays."

She fussed high-heeledly about making my room untidier. She put scent on my pillow. She made a hot lemon drink with lots of pips in. Although puffing a cigarette she undoubtedly felt like a Sister of Mercy, and was inspired to offer to read to me.

I was having hot and then cold flushings. I refused, so ungraciously, that she snapped.

All this came from traipsing about in the wind and rain on the beach. *And*, while on the subject, dulling, I was to be madly careful on that giddy-making cliff. Yesterday they'd found a bodeh that had been stuck between the rocks for nearleh a week. Some little pastreh-cook from Rule's had fallen ovah. The crabs . . . wasn't it shudder-making? . . . had been eating him.

I could not tell if the hotter and colder waves that surged through and through the length of my body were from influenza or the fact that I had learned something I did not want to, and could never impart.

(1961)

Great-Aunt Fanny's Picnic

On and off through the years, by Otterwells alive and kicking as well as by Otterwells tucked away in the family graveyard, the scandal of Great-Aunt Fanny had been mulled over with conscious dispassion, and repeatedly put aside like a tricky crossword. There was, anyway, always happening, in this or that Otterwell-dominated part of Tasmania, another Otterwell wedding, birth, or birthday. Or Lent began or school holidays or shearing or a vice-regal visit or the racing season or war or . . . well, tedious external things. No one alive seemed sure how Fanny's prolonged sojourn in foreign territory had started: she herself divulged nothing, but a tattered rumour inclined to some necessary patriotic gesture during the 1914-1918 War. Aunt Ann, being Aunt Ann, had other ideas—unpleasant ones, suggestive of hanky-panky, and diplomatically disregarded. Great-Aunt's legendary predicament was a subject as engaging as a pet tortoise; it often came out, like a snail, at night. It withdrew, pronto, at the merest squeak of new christenings, courtships, or tonsillectomies. Finally, however, explosively out of the blue, Uncle Eustace pronounced a decision: he himself would fetch her back.

In the family, Uncle Eustace was famed and feared for this nineteenth-century forcefulness, this taking-the-bull-by-the-horns Chinese Gordon resolution, as much as he was renowned for being the one Otterwell bachelor, not only for his period but for as far back as records were known. The probity of his bachelordom, with no heart-of-gold barmaid kept in a Battery Point love nest, and certainly no one or nothing else more dubious kept anywhere, added a dignifying halo to the eccentricity of wifelessness. Who knew what forces galore, untapped by wife, child, hidden sorrow, poverty, or unmentionable vice, still occupied him? For example, at seventy-three, he had just given up Royal Tennis.

On Christmas Eve 1960, after performing a Father Christmas

as terrifying as Lear, and while reviving himself with Courvoisier, he czarishly shouted them all . . . even Uncle Hereward who always fidgeted whether to take an umbrella or not, blazing or pouring . . . into believing that they had inclemently abandoned Great-Aunt Fanny "among who knows whom," Eustace blared Ezekielly, "among tradespeople, shepherds, mercer's counter-jumpers, journalists! And *exactly* where, who knows, eh? Forty years! A disgrace to us all. While Fergus was alive it was wise to keep mum, eh? But he's been dead for twelve years. Best leave it to me, eh? Pour me another, Varley. Leave't to me, eh?"

"Yes, oh yes, Eustace," they heard themselves cravenly pipe, and would have crossed themselves had they been one of *those*. Eustace was an alarming not-to-be-denied Pied Piper once he got going. They all quickly had another drink. After all, it was Christmas too.

By Candlemas, Uncle Eustace, in Isle of Butte tweeds, point-to-point cap, and pelargonium buttonhole, face pink as sporting paper or baby's, had dominated, sniffling rather and headachy, Fanny's uprooting. It was a chilly day, miles from anywhere respectable. Trees dripped on him as though he were a postman. Her nearest neighbour was a politician with a scruffy Socialist past. She should never, of course, have spent all those years there. She should have been with the family. With the family she would be. Reluctantly, he had to leave her, at the railway station, to travel on, poor lady, in the care of a man with a suspect accent, to Campbell Town where Uncle Eustace proposed to catch up with her next day.

The next day he was unable to keep his appointment because of what he savagely called a summer cold. This so swiftly galloped into danger that on St Valentine's Day he nearly died.

"Completely dying would, in the circumstances, have been absolutely killing," said Gwendoline, young Mrs Ian Otterwell, who concealed a marshmallow heart under a shocker's exterior.

"And *needlessly* ironic," said Aunt Ann, fingering her cameo as though she'd said nothing at all.

Not until Whitsunday was he finally out of bath chairs, and his knees out from under afghans, and he fit and pink and loud enough to ask about Great-Aunt Fanny. Silence fell. Time dropped a number of stitches. He asked again, more loudly.

Evasion was tried: Hereward offered a cigar. Evasion and cigar were roared at. "But . . ." they all began chattering at the same time, disobedient children botching justification, "but Eustace *dear*, but old boy, but Uncle, while you were so very, *very* . . ."

In listening to the dangerous wind keening around Eustace, in listening to the wind that never stopped flowing through the garden of Otterwells, tugging off a leaf, a branch, a heart, a life, they had, one and all, utterly forgotten to keep an eye on Great-Aunt Fanny's move.

Not saying they were but unmistakably considering them ninnies, he next day drove fifty-odd miles to see if Fanny were settled in her proper place.

While everybody was telephoning everybody else, there he was, in the family graveyard with its own century-old chapel, peering and poking about, getting cemetery mud on his brogues, trouser cuffs and knees. He returned to the car with the ominous stride of Alexander the Great. He drove back as recklessly as a joy-riding hot-rodder, and held the floor.

The billiard-table-sized Welsh slate slabs roofing the vault, in which Fanny should long ago have circumspectly been, seemed not, he thought, to have been recently moved. She'd certainly—he'd seen to that, eh?—been got out of that other wretched cemetery. Perhaps . . . per-*h-a-p-s* . . . he further thought . . . moss in the crevices *could* have been recently disturbed, could indeed have been replaced with a species of commercial piety. But he'd forgotten to take his spectacles; autumn leaves and a Scotch mist had made pure decision difficult. Curse that summer cold!

A telephone call to the undertaker's revealed that he of odd accent, who had been in charge of Fanny's digging-up, train trip and reinterment, had been a short-time employee since returned to Australia. A Mainlander! Eustace gave a terrible shout, and crashed down the receiver. The earth, that great globe, winced. Varley dropped a sugar bowl, fortunately silver. A Mainlander! . . . someone from . . . Carlton was it, eh? Woolloomooloo?

Swiftly as a Terrytoon vegetable, suspicion put on buds, leaves, dire flowers. Uncle Eustace became taller than Abraham Lincoln, and noisier: "The fellow's a jackanapes. Mortician he calls himself. An employer of criminals. Dabbling in cremation like a blasted Hindu, the silly ass. Phonograph music and foam-rubber lilies! Coffins of xylonite . . . plastic . . . whatever the muck is, I suppose, eh? Mortician! Right from the jump I was against his joining the Club. He's like the barber's cat: all . . ."

"Eustace!" snapped Aunt Ann. "There are gentlemen present." She had been a maidenly suffragette with, nevertheless, ears.

In the next few days Eustace occupied himself Napoleonically, very much head-of-the-family, with the minutiae of a grandiose plan. He wrote fiats to everyone, each succinct sentence brutally clear, too specific, too personal to be misunderstood or fobbed off. Intimations of excommunication glittered so ferociously between the lines of his old man's virile copperplate that newer Otterwell wives, the just-read command on Spicer's Deckle still between their finger-tips, switched off spin driers or forsook semi-built Constance Spry flower arrangements, and sped in M.G.s to buy trowels or whatever they were. Otterwell telephones were rung, and rang, constantly. Who, my God, last had the crow-bar from the potting shed of the old Sandy Bay place? What the hell *was* a mattock? Listen, dear, Varley says we'll be expected to picnic, so if you do a double lot of your divine little scones with Gentlemen's Relish, I'll do a double of my special Madeleines and we'll interfeed . . .

No one cared to let the side down; no one dared scamp Uncle Eustace's mandates.

On the selected Sunday, from every part of Tasmania, cars packed with tools, food, wicker-clad thermos flasks, children, and their Otterwell parents and relations, moved towards the graveyard. Wound up like a clock, generations ago, the family ethos was so well-oiled, had ticked so surely and sturdily for so long, that it would have been useless as well as traitorous for any member to suggest *I should like to be otherwise, someone else*, or *elsewhere today*, as useless as saying *I should like to be an echidna* or *called Marco Polo*. From faith and habit, non-Otterwells seemed to them as eels must to eagles, however glossy and silver-plated the eel, however like fractured sunshade the eagle. Sheer lunacy this plan of Eustace's, they might think, but ratifiable Otterwell lunacy. We're all in it.

So, by ten o'clock, everyone punctual, from Melton Mowbray, St Helen's, Westbury, Huonville, Oatlands, New Norfolk, everywhere, everyone had arrived. It was an autumn day, exquisite for any outing, perfection for one of this nature: nowhere are sunshine, birds, breezes, weeds, more subtly exhilarating to the senses and conceit of the living than in a graveyard.

Fecundity was the first impression—children everywhere; their knowingly uninhabited ink-blue, dead-still Otterwell eyes spotted the air. There seemed double the actual children, for each child had accompanied its own Sunday-go-graveyard self as one extra child simmering unseen to be barbaric and crazed, to flash diabolically aflame past the corner of adult consciousnesses; but, the time early and the occasion touchy, they discreetly simulated severe charm and, speechlessly as nursery rhyme characters on kindergarten friezes, carried buckets, rakes and Dutch hoes. With their tweedy aunts, with wavering aunts, champagne-bottle-legged golfing aunts, tittuping aunts and Burne-Jones aunts, they advanced towards and grouped themselves below Uncle Eustace who had mounted, civic-statue-like, the top of the vault to which, in an orderliness obscured by gorse, periwinkle and pre-Raphaelite Austrian Copper briers, other Otterwell graves lined up.

Even Aunt Ann, inclined to perpetual fractiousness, was momentarily halcyon in the group which, standing mutely as waxworks, chins uplifted, listened to Uncle Eustace. Only the oldest aunt, Aunt Beatrice, sat. She sat in a camp chair, centrally front, her bone fingers burdened with diamonds and rubies. The crowd, accidentally dramatic, of overlapping generations had the impermanent coherence of a combination in whose each mind, as much as in the corporate one, lay no mental reservation like a segment of decaying trevally. At least, on this occasion. First of all, beneath their soles lay the boxed scraps of their own dead. Second, many of their houses had once been these dead's, or contained objects wherein the grimaces or half-smiles of the dead still lingered—in Wainewright portraits, darkening looking-glasses, on the bumlike curves of silver rose-bowls, in photograph albums containing pressed pansies picked last century by fingers that, then, could write *Otterwell* on a will or a love letter. Third, Great-Aunt Fanny, so long a sherry-party joke, now claimed by right of blood this protective picnic, this family prying into her gothic contretemps. Was she here, *now*, below, in her destined niche, filed for reference on the Last Day? That is what the family, through Uncle Eustace, hoped and had jolly well paid for. Or had the Mainland ghoul, obviously with a face caddish as a monkey's, done something too nasty to think of but nevertheless thought of . . . a council rubbish-tip? a lake bed? a stinky fire in a Midlands' gully once lair for convict bushrangers?

As they listened to Uncle Eustace avoid putting these outraging possibilities into words, they stared remorselessly at him, their thoughts sprinkling salty glints of anger in their eyes. He, too, began to glint—but he was rebuking *them*. "Moreover," he was saying, "moreover, the graveyard, our graveyard, the *Otterwell* graveyard . . ." He was rubbing it in. ". . . is in a shocking state. Eh? As you can see." As they could see. "Our own people! We are to blame. We! *We*!" They were to blame. "That's why I wrote you all to come prepared to clean up while the vault is investigated. Except, of course, Aunt Beatrice." Aunt Beatrice lifted an ancient jewel-knobbed hand with queenly deprecation. Everyone looked at her as at an unbelievable idol but with sufficient affectionate respect. "There are," continued Uncle Eustace, "enough of us, God knows—eh? In my letters you were each allotted a certain task in a certain section. It took some planning." He paused. He stopped pausing, and made a dangerous remark: "Any questions?"

Before Aunt Ann could uncurl—he knew his danger—he side-stepped quickly, side-stepped imperatively: "*Good*—no questions. Charles, you have the crow-bars? Mattock, Greg? Pickaxe? Bill-hook? Mallet? Bamboo rakes . . . Grace? Varley? Ah, I see you've a trowel, Young Christopher!" Everyone had brought everything asked for, and held them up: *sans-culottes* preparing to march on the Tuileries. Everyone except . . . and Uncle Eustace's eyes narrowed . . . "Your secateurs, Ann?" Aunt Ann's German secateurs were famous. She had not brought them. She tossed her head; no angel, she did not fear treading. *Her* little indigo eyes also narrowed, and flashed wickedly. Level-toned yet sharp, she said, "I have brought Fanny's own silver teapot. I felt it fitting."

To everyone's surprise, Aunt Beatrice said, almost cried as loudly as someone younger, "*No*!" What could she mean? Her old mind wandering, off and away?

Aunt Ann stuck out her chin, whiskery as an as-yet-unshaved youth's, at Eustace. It was a mutinous gesture. Uncle Eustace clenched a fist.

"An unseemly disturbance is imminent," whispered twelve-year-old Young Christopher who was wicked, sophisticated, and far too handsome. His cousins sycophantically giggled. "Fie! So early in the day. And before us innocent innocents. Oh, *fie*!"

Then Grace, lanky gentle Grace, said gently, "Aunt Ann asked me to bring *our* secateurs, Eustace," and she held them up, high, at the end of her long long long arm, like a symbolic Communist. There secateurs were. Uncle Eustace laughed—oh, quickly and fruitily as a prime minister. "To work!" he shouted, semaphoring meaninglessly. "To your posts! To work!"

In a geyser of released conversation, of greetings, of hullabaloo and movement, children bursting like grenades from between adults, the group milled and crumbled and scattered. To work all the women went except old Aunt Beatrice whose lilac-coloured chiffon scarf was rearranged, one after another, by five women. To work all the children seemed to go except the youngest twins with silkworm silk hair who ran about clutching their flies, and squealing, "*We* are to blame. We! We! Wee-wee. Pee-wee. Wee-pee. We pee. We poo. We poo-poo!" Their stately Labrador, its severe head like an heraldic profile or one from an old walking-stick handle, lumbered woodenly as a rocking horse between them. A surfeit of forbidden things to do had lashed them to exaltation.

While the women, garden-gloved or gloveless, worked on paths, headstones, urns, broken columns, sandstone scrolls, granite tombs and cast-iron railings, their unfettered, faultless voices called in the sunlight above the buried, tongueless skulls.

"My dear, how very kind of Eustace to put me on Digby's grave—I shouldn't admit it with his age so clearly stated, but we were childhood sweethearts. Though he once stole my agate marbles."

"This rose bush must be a cutting from the big Maman Cochet at The Grange."

"Shall I scrape all this moss away? It looks so fitting and darling. Or just leave aesthetic enough, like the Japanese?"

"I wish I'd brought my old steel kitchen knife. Men don't *know* about steel kitchen knives."

"What *did* James Frederick *really* die of?"

"I," said Aunt Ann, "shall not pretend that I am at all surprised, but Eustace has allotted me the prickliest grave."

Although these statements seemed merely the trite ones of feckless humans, and utterable by anyone with a tongue, they revealed that the speakers had preserved, throughout their own vicissitudes and those of the world they had been born into, viewpoints and moralities as much of their class as their accents were, and their children. These creatures, in constant motion, had seemingly much multiplied, separating themselves from themselves as amoebae do. They mafficked about with the alacrity of vandals to whom no vandalism was that day permissible. Some, for a while, browbeatenly scratched lichen from headstones, or permitted themselves to be hectored into carrying off pruned brier suckers and Great Mullein stalks. Otherwise they roamed restlessly outside the cage of adult duty, hampered by miles of undulating paddocks and the obvious infinity of a cloudless sky. Aunt Ann kept on capturing some of them with her fish-hook eye and, as other aunts did, mistaking them for their siblings or cousins. Were they, she asked, street arabs or swineherd's waifs crept in through the may hedge? This was surely cryptic humour on her part. Yet, even to aunts and uncles less whimsical than Aunt Ann, there appeared more of these youngsters, who no longer wore sailor suits and knew of *The Windsor Magazine*, than seemed reasonable. The gold-mopped twins, for example, had become a sextuplet, banshee-shrieking by with attendant Cerberus.

Meantime, ponderously and sonorously and warily, the men confronted the paramount mystery of Great-Aunt Fanny. Dedicated and daylight Burkes and Hares, they assessed the vault covering. Under their off-hand dandyism and leather-patched sports coats was the muscular and maternal brutishness of those who worked with animals and their neuroses and needs, and who fought into submission, just as their women in labour fought necessary pain into submission, the seasons and the earth. These Otterwell males, or males chosen as sires by Otterwell women, had weathered youth, injudicious passions, disillusion, the whims of weather, scandals, and boils on the backside, with concealed and tenderized arrogance. Their manners were perfect, and would have remained so while they killed an enemy or stopped a crucifixion. Tenderly their huge hands and shrewd eyes examined the tomb; tenderly they prodded crevices with crow-bars and pick-axes, inviting each other's suggestions to poo-hoo them, before attacking like convinced burglars the vault slabs. With vigour and precision they made the first attempts at prising. These failed. Swearing began. Those who did not smoke pipes offered each other cigarettes, saying, "Christ, eh! She's going to be bloody tougher than we thought. Christ!"

Young Christopher was, of course, in earshot. He possessed a special sense.

"They are blaspheming," he said to his entourage of underling cousins.

"They are blaspheming," echoed the myrmidons and, giggling from trying not to giggle, held hands over mouths, and stuck out their round bellies farther, and rolled inky eyes.

"They are corrupting influences," Young Christopher continued. "They are immoral fiends and wick-ed monsters. We must inform the sheriff! Yippee!" And he galloped off, being, centaurlike, horse and rider; and the smaller centaurs galloped at his pace after him, caracoling like a posse of goodies behind him, and shrilling like Comanches around the church.

The men made a scarecrow of a marble angel with their coats and, thus coatlessly defiant, attacked the slabs again.

Presently, for Otterwell women were deft, most of them had fulfilled Uncle Eustace's behests. On the other side of a raffish rosemary hedge was a handful of humbler graves, not Otterwell. Gwendoline, forthrightly why-notting and dammit-all-let's-do-the-decent-thinging, persuaded others less forthright and more dubious, but amenable to sentimental platitude disguised as decisiveness, to work with her on these alien plots.

With less intensity of feeling they idly toiled, as at an inferior charity, and were so toiling, and placidly deep in obstetrical legend, when a shadow they immediately knew was monitory fell upon their bowed backs, and a fluting astounded voice said:

"Those graves are not *ours*!"

It was Varley, intellectual and perfectionist (her rose garden was a miracle, so were her potted shrimps; she read Elizabeth Bowen), who had just restored Edwin Otterwell's grave almost to the condition it was in 1863 when he had died under a runaway barouche.

"What the hell does it matter, Varley?" said Gwendoline in a contemporary way, softish but boldish, from her kneeling pad. She pushed back a lock of hair to stress barefacedness. "Dammit, let's be decent!"

"Need you swear?" said Varley, who really didn't mind a scrap. "I don't think we should interfere."

"With the *dead*?" said Gwendoline, lighting a suave cigarette.

Varley was not to be caught. She too lit a cigarette—slowly—and blew out—slowly—a vampish cone of smoke.

"With the dead of others. The dead do not belong to themselves. Graves belong to *others*. Those others should tend them with love. They are not *ours*. Your work, however worthy, is . . . is municipal. There is no love."

"Bosh!" said Gwendoline and, to show unabashment, "*Dammit*, Varley!" Young Christopher would have cherished this but was being immaculately vile elsewhere. All the children were. The twins and their dog, because they had been forbidden the road, were on the road terrifying a rustic bodgie passer-by who had intended terrifying them.

Gwendoline spoke again: "Oh, *double* bosh, Varley!" for Varley, towering, had fixed her with a navy-blue look.

Varley said, "Be that as it may. Gwendoline, you've laddered your stocking—left leg."

Gwendoline said, "Damn and *blast*!"

Women said, "Spit, dear."

Who said, "Surely Varley," yanking out a thistle belonging to an unloved non-Otterwell, "*surely* it's easy to love humanity when it isn't there?"

It sounded a Brontë-ish remark but came, naturally, from Aunt Ann whose magnanimities even had always a dash of vinegar. Varley, who had once published at her own expense a book of poems (*Roses of Silence and Solitude*), looked away, mysteriously as a poetess vouchsafing nothing, and walked away thinking something nicer.

Nearby aunts, older, some, finding it time to suggest to themselves starting a headache as reason for luncheon but mainly cups of tea, drew from their pockets noon-showing enamelled watches they had had since black *moiré* butterfly bows tied back their then-thick-and-coloured hair.

Varley, drifting, saw in the distance, frailly royal under the big Cedar of Lebanon, Aunt Beatrice. Old old aunt, time-shrivelled aunt, had long ago, restless and fretful, left her camp chair. With a trailing totter, she had moved from group to group in her Queen Alexandra manner—the painted and thickly powdered face also; the gracious word dropped vaguely here and there. Yet she seemed touched by the wind of an intangible bitterness, to be seeking wearily, seeking and seeking. Now that the vault was full—or would soon, they hoped, be proved to be, for Great-Aunt Fanny had been destined for the last unoccupied niche—perhaps Aunt Beatrice, long the widow of a husband buried at sea, sought a place for herself. She tacked; she contemplated spaces; she tacked again. Certainly, certainly, when next the family gathered she would be underground, bereft of her far too many wonderful old-fashioned rings, of her paint, of her Arabian nimbus of scent, even of her scant flesh. Underground where? Oh, where? She had entered the blue shadows of the cedar, uninterested in the housewifely kneeling, the trowelling and grating and hacking and snipping, the chattering, the bonfire the children were prodding into smoke a paler blue than the cedar shadows. "Joffre Blue," she whispered. It was a colour of her middle years. Tears suggested themselves to her. "Joffre Blue," she was whispering when Varley arrived. "Fanny spilt Indian ink on my Joffre Blue blouse with the pearl buttons."

Using a handkerchief almost all lace she blotted a shallow tear before it furrowed her powder.

"Why, Aunt *Be*atrice . . ." said Varley, coming into the shadow. "Darling, why not come and sit down again? Or should you like to be in the car? Luncheon'll be soon."

Old Aunt Beatrice looked haggard above her chiffon pussy-cat bow of scarf. She spoke with querulous wildness:

"I don't want to be buried *outside*. It's too noisy. Grasshoppers. Omnibuses going past to Hobart. And too much light." Varley knew that she sat always with her back to it, the blinds three-quarter-down. "I want to be in the *vault*. With grandmother and mama and Alexander and Galamiel. Fanny always grabbed everything. She spilt ink on my blouse. She gave my lovely scrap-book to the Orphans' Home. *Without* permission. She's in the vault. It's not fair. She doesn't care. Look where she got herself buried the first time . . ."

Varley was becoming horrified when there was a great calling-out and waving from the men: "It's open! It's open! We've opened the vault!"

Varley looked *Come on, Aunt Beatrice* and held out a hand.

"Leave me here," said the ravaged old woman in the cold shadow. "Leave me. I don't want to see . . ." She did not say *Fanny* but grew infinitely fragile.

Varley did not know what to do, and felt larger than a land-girl.

"Go away," said Aunt Beatrice, waspish. "Go away and leave me, mean selfish Fanny," said the old woman to Varley.

Within minutes, all of them, husbands, wives, aunts, uncles, children, twins and dog, cynical Young Christopher, flushed Varley, were at the vault.

What ultimately and most and for years impressed the adults was that the name-plates on the coffins were completely untarnished, as though they'd been done with Goddard's Plate Powder the day before; this despite the fact that six inches of strange still water that seemed depthless covered the floor.

What impressed the children first was a frog sitting on Galamiel Otterwell's coffin. That was explicable: water, frog, place for frog to sit when not in water.

What impressed the children most, and nightmarishly until they themselves approached death, were the metallic-green blowflies, fat and important, sulkily muttering as though drunk. Why? Whence? The boys scratched their necks, and did not want to ask questions.

Great-Aunt Fanny was not at home.

As, they all said, they had all along all known.

The last niche was empty.

Rage (quite savage) and horror (sickening) overtook the

Otterwells, and they edged more closely together. The rage was clear-cut at good money paid for what amounted to profanation, at being gypped—the *Otterwells*!—by a Mainland spiv. The horror was an atavistic and family horror that, somewhere—and they were responsible, which increased the horror—a section of their heritage and own lives had been lost as carelessly as a tennis racquet. Otterwells had been sunk in oceans, blown to bits in currently fashionable wars, buried in China, in *Père Lachaise* Cemetery near Sarah Bernhardt, in dozens of places, and even Ireland. Those were seemly enough; there was evidence; if tears were to fall they knew which quarter to splash towards. The losing of Great-Aunt Fanny was . . . was . . .

The men swore vilely, even Uncle Hereward who could rarely make up his mind. Uncle Eustace seemed to be planning something in the nature of a Royal Commission. The sun grew hotter. One aunt, foreseeing endlessness without tea, considered a fake half-faint on a suitably low tomb.

Meantime, where *was* Great-Aunt Fanny?

Varley, as always, came first to her senses. Precise and romantic and fervid, with her Otterwell-ink-dark but un-Otterwell-protruding eyes, she twined among them and conspiratorially revealed another truth to them. Presently, in silence, they had all turned their eyes towards the Cedar of Lebanon.

Without a word to each other the women started to move, to subtract themselves from the mingled group, to begin walking towards the cedar.

The men, dividing themselves from the children, moved a few paces after the women, and then stopped. The path to the cedar was not for them. They lit pipes and cigarettes, and turned inwards to each other, backs to the women, backs to the children. Life is not for men.

The children looked down their noses: they had been made to feel like children. They got smaller, starved-looking, even world-weary Young Christopher; they drew together and retreated. There was an impression of walking backwards from an insane world.

The women now began, young and old, to hasten, almost to run stumbling, towards Old Aunt. They had no manly or childish embarrassments; they were female, and of earth. Some began to weep as they hurried but without wiping away the great sweet tears, the soft soft tears, the tears coloured with life and death.

Old Aunt saw them coming, a pack with some appalling information to reveal, and some outrageous deed to do—it must have seemed so to her faded eyes. Yet, for she had been a woman too, she touched her scarf, and moved into the sunlight that was less kind to her painted wrinkles, and advanced towards them, fantastic and beautifully hideous. They were upon her; they surrounded her.

"Oh, Beatrice!" they cried, tears streaming down their smiles. "Oh, Aunt Beatrice, Great-Aunt isn't there! She's not there! Fanny isn't there! Oh, Aunt Beatrice, where *is* Aunt Fanny? Lost! Gone! Not there! Empty, the niche is *empty*!"

Aunt Beatrice knew what they were telling, what gift they had run to bring her in their hands stained with graves. She closed her eyes happily against their happiness for her, yet two old tears, and two more, and another two, ran refreshingly as creeks through the drought of powder.

"*Poor* Fanny!" she said in her ecstasy.

(1961)

Vulgar's the Word

At that time of the year, late autumn, the seaside town, empty of tents, caravans, merry-go-rounds, and indiscreetly unclothed and too-well-heeled working-class tourists, seemed larger as though to balance the unpeopled and wasteful plain of waves that rustled like tissue-paper on the pockless sands.

Nature! How ultimately vulgar, boring, old-fashioned and non-air-conditioned! Autumnally *démodé* tides of salt water waxed saltier, medium only for fishes and kelp. Houses and creepers, both fifty years old, in summer unobservable and many more than one would think, were conspicuous among closed shops in the windows of which dehydrated blowflies sprinkled the crêpe-papered display-stairs. No poetry in beaches, or anything, for middle-aged, lower-middle-class women: they are paper-backs to each other, as gaudy and as untrue and titillating and time-filling.

Thus the widow and the deserted wife, the two women and the bottle of gin and eleven o'clock that Sunday morning.

They were certainly women who prodded holes in the foil tops of milk bottles. Jugs were for ice cubes. They had not seen each other for . . .

"Actually, how long's it been since, Rube?" said Mrs Fender hostessishly peahenning about in sleeveless black with white lapels wider and pointier than a television ephemerid's, but at rest within, harmless. Women are most harmful when their bodies think they are at rest and they think they are thinking. She was the widow, the *Hair Styliste and Beautician* with hair dyed the colour of, and a voice like, apricot jam. She was sloshing over-frank gins into tumblers that had once held gherkins, or cocktail onions the size and colour of adenoids.

"Squash, Rube, or bitter lemon?"

"Matter'f embuggerance, Vi," forcefully said Rube, deserted wife, muscular false missus of a creature, and zealously conscious of it for years. She had yanked her girdle straight, and slapped the Volkswagen driving-seat out of the sat-in seat of her sale-price skirt of a fake tweed nubblier than tweed. Any minute she'd try to get her spike-heel shoes off.

"No, *squash*, Vi, love. Something long and wet. Now, lemme see when since. Gert's op. . . . yes, just before Gert's op. Just after poor old ma passed on."

Her hair looked as though a sheep-dog had lent it. Desertion was a mere segment of her life. Had she been weak enough, or a man, she'd have long ago forgotten the deserter she'd already forgotten. The rest of her life was colourful with anger, envy, jealousy, laddered new nylons, stout spilled on dry-cleaned laps, ox-blood fingernails breaking on the very night of the Fire Brigade Ball.

She was a Corset Adviser in a country town emporium. Since women are the only ones who understand the coarseness and savagery of women she called herself a meat-packer.

"I remember now," said Mrs Fender handing a streaming glass. "Jew say squash or lemon, love? Reely, the mind is going what with this and that and the other, and getting Gran off the premises for a day."

"Embuggerance," said Rube, domestically wiping the tumbler-bottom with a pink handkerchief before putting the tumbler on the arm of the Genoa velvet settee, and lighting a king-size filter-tip.

"Yes, I remember lividly. I haven't laid eyes on you since the night I and Bubba and you and Maurie Gold went to that Publican's Ball where you lost your diamenty clip. You had on your royal blue with sequins. Bubba had on his new dinner suit. Very chick Bubba thought your blue," she said, apparently somehow convincing herself, yet faintly cross-eyed and far-off staring across the top of her drink.

"Oh, *Vi*!" said Rube, politely interrupting slaking for she had caught the look in profile. "Oh, Vi, I'm sorry, love. I mean to say to bring up Bubba. However in innocence. Especially in connection with that Jew-boy Maurie. Him and his hands. I'm not a one for that type of caper. Not with a casual acquaintance. As I very quick-smart said so."

Mrs Fender lowered her sheeny green satin eyelids very slowly bravely: the foam-rubber floralities in the white china trough on the wireless became funeral-parlourish. Next, less slowly but more bravely, the eyelids ascended, and Mrs Fender —how many times bereaved?—drank daintily and deep.

"Now, don't you go getting put out over it, Rube," she said, pasteurized cream on her voice. She attempted a world-weary gesture. "I've got over it. My cross. It took time. It was a blow. The old heart's broken, that I know. But 'laugh and the world laughs with you,' I say. Actually, death comes to us all. Though I frankly never thought I never ever would actually get over it. But reely and truly I have, Rube. Oh, I'm hard now." Her face got as bland as it could. "Cynical, that's Vi'let!" And she sophisticatedly tapped ash north, nor'-nor'-east and north-east.

"Never you, Vi," said Rube, sonorous and unnecessarily salutary. She had forced her knobbed heels out of her champagne-coloured shoes. "Never you. A warm heart."

"But hard now. You have to be," said Mrs Fender to some distant appreciative ear. She lingered to listen to it listening. She brightened at a clever thought. "Life," she said, she revealed to Rube at her tumbler, "life goes on. And"—recalling further proof she further brightened—"it's not as if it was my first experience of sorrow. I'm a real Jonah. You see, Rube, the hubby passed away. Before I met you. Not in the same way as poor Bubba, of course. He was a different class of a chap, the hubby. Quite la-di-dah in his way. Had four hats. Very fussy. A sales-*manager*. In typewriters. Cancer of the throat, his was," she said with a pinch of pride. "Poor bloody old Bubba was only a rep."

She rallied against herself and her treachery, and, assuming the manner of one forced no longer to believe that her husband had had the convincing and passionate core of a man, said authoritatively, "But *confectionery*. There's no nicer or cleaner line. Bubba had his reputation in the confectionery."

Did the dead man—men—relax? Both women watched, as women watch men, even dead ones, for plans they've never intended to have. Then: "You're a brave woman, for sure, Vi," said Rube, her shoes completely shed and lying like weapons on the wall-to-wall while she ground her heels together.

Mrs Fender knew and was used to that one. "A woman's lot," she said, an absolute nun. And, "Hand's your glass, love," and, "One lives and learns," she said. As she poured, "It's a man's world," she said—would it be mockingly from a cellar of pretended resignation? Otherwise, what could she mean?

"That's for bloody sure. You can say that again. A man's bloody world," said Rube almost spruiking. What did *she* mean? Witches' irony? Or did they both mean that men will respond to certain expressions in the eyes of animals but not in the eyes of women?

"Hard you may say, but you're the tender-hearted one, Vi'let Fender," said Rube, arranging herself convalescently, tumbler on the floor beside, with her lathe-turned legs dead-straight along the settee-cushions, back upright against one arm-rest, as propped up as one props up a failing but yet stalwart doll. "And always were," she continued, clawing down for the tumbler. "Always will be, no matter what! It's your naycher." And her miniature port-wine-coloured eyes glimmered wetly and defensively between countable lashes. "Too soft, if you ask me."

"Oh, but I *loved* Bubba," said Mrs Fender, mincing carefully about on her green spikes though with a waggle. She and her brimming tumbler were on some sort of display. "As you know. None better. I'm too open, frankly. Even with her ladyship."

She said ladyship utterly without inverted commas. Her eyes suddenly spiced her face, and she had to sit down and genteelly gulp.

"As I know for sure," said Rube. And drank. "Judas Christ, you've got a heavy hand, Vi," she cried raucously but not rebukingly. "This is a bobby-dazzler! Strong!"

"Strong," said Vi, very female and secret. "Talk of strong to me! A man, Bubba was. In every sense of the word. *And* a perfect gentleman. A *man*. Every sense, Rube. *You* know. I remember everything lividly."

"I'm sure you do, dear. You were a damn' lucky woman, Vi. Some," she said darkly, "have all the luck. Some," she became as full of anger as a farm-cat of rabbit, "don't have hardly none at all." With a hot gusty sigh she relieved herself to be subtler in her anger with her own betrayals, stumbles and failures: "Anyway, you're still a young woman."

Neither of them questioned this although Rube averted her

eyes, as it were to watch closely only herself drinking, and Mrs Fender half-inadvertently released a faintly peppery skidding glance at her friend.

Although forty-eight, make-up and hair-do made Mrs Fender look no older than fifty, acrobatic little body notwithstanding. She could still insist on doing the Black Bottom at foretellable stages, even in unappreciative company, even before midnight, and invariably four gins before being sick and causing trouble, as she always did, by ejecting her gold-speckled false teeth among roadside bracken or in private mint-beds.

"Young or not, whatever, dear," she said, stroking her back hair as though it were a darling kitten and she a prissy sickly girl "—and I must frankly say actually that I don't feel no more than a day over twenty-three—it was all a wonderful dream. I could write a book. A love yarn. Oh, I see it all lividly. There'll never be no one to come up to Bubba. Always on the go. He had what it takes. Personality plus. Life and soul of the party."

Rube was disturbed by what could have been a chuckle. " 'Member how he used to say he was the life and death of the party? Little did the poor b. know how soon . . ." She stopped. She had astonished herself with horror.

Placidly, they let the mules of disaster gallop over their hearts. They heard the disgusting sea unwrapping cold parcels far enough off but too near. Then Mrs Fender felt obliged to rearrange her countenance, and deliberately perceptibly glitter like cut tin.

"Now, now, now, Rube, come off it. Don't you go going morbid on me. Bubba would *want* us to be happy. Every cloud has a silver lining and blah blah blah. Service with a smile, he'd say. Hand's your glass."

Rube swiftly relinquished her tumbler with ill-acted indifference. Abstraction of that sort did not make her lose sight of her guestly responsibilities. She had her manners.

"I can hear him now, Vi, clear as day, saying, 'Pawdon me, is your name Marilyn Monroe? Do take a pew, you lush drop. Park it there, the lovely thing it is!' "

They both smiled at nowhere. Mrs Fender's backside moved

elegantly of its own volition, and tingled in a hand-shaped area.

"Actually," she said, "he was a very special person, Rube. And witty—my God! Quick as a flash."

She poured illustratively, with sluttish speed.

Their tumblers again clasped, their cigarettes fuming as before idols, they unlocked all over. Their toes were at peace for there was not a book in the flat, not a man or a poem or any work of art, nothing except their own peaceful unravelling. They were so at peace that the house smelt like that of another and friendly woman.

Heads tilted back like caterpillars they not-saw the cobwebs on the mock-marble electric light bowl, and perhaps saw the late Bubba and his too pressed revolver-coloured suit, his what-the-hell pot-belly, his slimy rosy fingers, his hat with the parrot feather in the band, his brocade bow-tie. Where, after all, *was* Today?

"And such a delicate skin, Rube, you can't imagine."

From a dream Mrs Fender achieved a wistful misshapen smoke-ring. "Like a baby's bee-tee-em. All over, Rube. I'm open, Rube. Frankly. Us two girls know each other well enough to face the truth. All over. Angel's skin satin."

"The truth," murmured Rube faithfully into her tumbler.

"I'll let you in on something, Rube. One night we had a flea. Poor Bubba was bit all over. Bites the size of two-bobs. Reel welts. 'Don't scratch, Bubba,' I said. 'I bet that's a girl flea,' he said. Witty, you see. Finish that off, love, you're dragging the chain. A skin like a babe's, and yet she . . ."

Mrs Fender perceivably turned the colour of ageratum; her eyes stung the soiled air like wicked bees. She almost snatched Rube's tumbler from the centre of a final gulp. As she tottered crossly to the fictitious stained-oak Jacobean sideboard, for the room was certainly bigger than it need have been for Sunday morning, her guest squintingly watched the miracle of brisknesses and hospitality, and Mrs Fender's vaccination marks which a ray of light escaped from outside made seem as deep as beer-bottle tops.

"Oh, a skin like an innocent babe's. And yet she couldn't bear him. I never saw the like. Reel hate."

"Who couldn't bear him, Vi? Gran?" Her tone suggested a buffeting for Gran *if*.

"Don't be sill., Rube. Her Ladyship. Miss High-an'-Mighty couldn't. Who else? Gran *idalized* him. Shit!" she said as she bottle-openered a fractious bitter lemon that swamped the stains and cigarette-burns on the sideboard top. "Pardon my French! *Gran*! You getting shicker, Rube? No, Gran idalized Bubba. She was a bit cagey at first. But he never said a word out of place in front of the old lady. Well, he brought me some black nylon scanties. Seconds they were. But the thought's the thing. Like cobweb they were. Gossamer. Little inset hearts. And only Easter last year. Little did we dream."

She sighed. She licked spillings from her fingers. She licked at the lips that were under lipsticked other lips. "Well, joking-like, Bubba pretended he'd bought them for Gran. I was in fits. You know what a broad beam Gran's got! Here, grab your snort, Rube!"

They occupied themselves with their tumblers, one refreshing her sense of hearing, the other the machinery of anecdote.

"Gran takes an O.S. in fleecy-lined bloomers. You could camp in them, Rube, honest to God. Well, Bubba held up the scanties in front of her. I was in stitches. 'Now, modom,' says Bubba, 'let me fit you for size. No extra charge. Money back if not satisfied.' You know yourself actually how touchy Gran is about anything sexual. Flares up. Gets real niggly and hostile. I think she must have had an inferior complex when she was a teenager. After all, frankly, Gran's nearly eighty. She's not contemporary and broadminded like we girls. But she laughed and giggled and carried on. Couldn't stop! I thought she'd wet herself. Oh, he was a one out of the box. Get away with murder. His manner, see? Personality.

"No, Gran idalized Bubba. It's Her Ladyship couldn't stummick him. My own dar-ling daugh-ter. My own flesh and blood however as she is, and I'm telling you straight, Rube, but frankly she's actually a bitch. That might seem a hard thing for a mother to say, Rube, and I certainly wouldn't say it outside these four walls to every Tom, Dick and Harry, or even to Gran. But I say it. And mean it. After all I've done for her. All I been through. Sorrow and grief. Work and slave. Every-damn-thing. Day in and day out. . . ."

"Work and slave. You don't have to tell me," intoned Rube, bubbling towards the boil. "Work and slave. Morning, noon and night." Her Adam's apple made enchanting but ominous subsidences and reappearances. Her dim moustache grew less dim.

"Over those so-and-so hair-driers," said Mrs Fender with an eye to the concrete horrid.

Aroused, Rube suddenly, and not spilling a drop, swung her chunky nylon feet decisively to the floor. Straining, leash-tight and brand-new, her suspenders showed. Her legs opened like cupboard doors. She drank abruptly, underlining force. A severe *tilde* on her bull brow, she directed a look at Mrs Fender. Portentously, "Vi," she said slowly and deeply as a Presbyterian clergyman, "what I'm going to say to you, you mustn't take offence at."

Once again, oh dear, they could hear the sea furtively rustling litter at the edge of the beach. Ugh! They looked at each other as seriously as tigresses. Rube drank again for Dutch courage or . . . drank again. She pronounced, with defiance, and an air of being as practical as Robinson Crusoe, "Too bloody much education!"

Mrs Fender was relieved to elation. She wasn't going to be walled in alive after all. She expended the lightest of light laughs. Her vaccination marks somehow shone.

"Jew know you had me worried for the minute, Rube. Though funny you should say just that. You're psycho, Rube. Like Nostradamus. Frankly, that's exactly what Her Ladyship actually said to me. Blamed me, mind you. 'You shouldn't of had me educated in that sort of school,' she said. And me scrimp and save for the four years she was in that posh school. 'It wasn't fair to me,' she said. 'And, pray, why not?' I said. 'It lets me see what you really are,' she said.

" 'What exactly do you mean by that, miss?' I said. 'To see that you're a commercial traveller's sweetheart,' she said. I slapped her face good and hard. Such a pretty little thing as she was as a tottie. Four years. It cost the earth, Rube, for Cash's name-tapes alone. Frankly, not that I minded, mind you, actually. The reps from the various places got things wholesale for little Vi. But, a mother's duty . . ."

Rube made a brutal denigratory noise which surprised both

but which both, with tact inconspicuously lowering their shot-up eyebrows, refinedly disregarded. Both were, after all, not only mothers but women of the world.

"And then the hospital training," Mrs Fender continued with vainglory and an air of assimilated martyrdom. "Now, that touched the pocket, too. Jew know she's now Sister-in-charge at the districk hospital? Young with it. Everyone speaks very highly. 'Your daughter's so-o-o charming, Mrs Fender,' they say.

" 'Says you,' say I to myself, 'but not to her own flesh and blood she isn't.' But—softie me all over—I don't *say* anything. No dirty linen in public. Fed up to the back teeth I might be and have been, but I'd never crack a boo. Pride I've got. 'Oh, yes,' I say to her with her nose always stuck in some great damn' book, 'oh, yes, a street angel. But, miss, what about . . .' "

Rube burst. She interrupted like a hand-grenade. She shouted like a convict whose stew was tepid: "Ungrateful, that's what! That's the truth of it! Wants her backside tanning! A razor-strop!" she shouted, forgetting that it was 1961 and Sunday.

Mrs Fender surprisingly set up a merely mean little tolerant special face with a more than *retroussé* nose in the centre of her meaner stonier daily face. "Oh, girl-like!" she maternally tossed off as if it had been a question of chastity, and sprinkled ash kindly enough on what appeared to be her cone-shaped breasts. "Girl-like, I suppose."

She pecked with efficient vagueness to the sideboard and the gin bottle. "Forgive and forget. But, actually, she'll never know how much she's wrung the heart of her own mother that bore her and washed her dirty nappies."

"The day will come," foretold Rube, glaring up from glaring with surprise in her mysteriously emptied tumbler.

"The day will come, that's for sure," said Mrs Fender, delightedly inspired to more: "Yes, the day when I'm lying there in my coffin. Hand's your glass, Rube."

Rube was in trouble with matches. Heads flew off. "Judas Christ!" she howled, pounding her feet like fists on the floor, and flushing dark as rhubarb.

The hostess persisted sweetly and sloppily busy, scrawny and inconsequential as a bantam of fifty. Not for her the terrors of the subjective world that haunt intelligent neurotics. Indeed, she had things to reveal. Why hide humanity? Why foster the affectation of civilization? Hand out the drinks, and tell a truth.

"Actually, looking back, I know damn' well she frankly actually didn't cotton on to Bubba right from the go-off. He knew, too, she didn't take a shine to him. 'Florence McNightingale can't stummick yours truly,' he said to me. In private. That's what he called her. Florence McNightingale. Because of the nursing, you see. She looked at him like dirt. 'Excuse me, countess,' he said, 'do excuse me if my slip is showing.' After he'd *bought* her a nice bottle of sweet sherry!

"And poor old Bubba set himself out to make her laugh. But no go. She wouldn't even laugh at that trick with the cigarette-tin. You know the scream of a one where you poke your finger through a hole in the bottom of the tin, and there's cotton-wool with red ink on like blood, and you lift the lid and there's the finger laying like a cut-off one. And Her Highness didn't even smile. Just walked off to her bedroom. Vulgar! So Bubba and I went out. I knew he was heart-broken.

"So, when I came home, I tackled her. Switched on the light in her room. 'See here, you,' I said, 'Lady Muck of Turd Island you might be, but I won't have you humilating my gentleman callers.' 'Hum-il-*ee*-ating, mother,' she said. 'Will you please put out my light, and go to bed. It's two o'clock in the morning. And you're drunk.' I nearly done the block. 'Educated you may be, miss,' I said. 'But when a gentleman friend'— '*Gentleman!*' she said. Just like that. She *hated* poor harmless Bubba, hated his guts."

The room had long ago acquired the air of a glove-box in a family car despite the never-used coffee service in the china-cabinet, the plaster-of-Paris cocker spaniel, and Gran's upright piano. Cigarette smoke became it; fluff and dust and stains were at home.

"Her Ladyship was always yipping about him in a sarcky way. About him being witty. Pick, pick, pick she used to about him saying 'See you Samoa,' and 'See you later, alligator,' and 'Who's robbing this coach?' 'I'll scream,' she said, 'if he says, "Excuse my wet glove," again.' Poor Bubba used to perspire something chronic in the hands. Sensitive, you see. But not his fault. And witty about it. But not her. No sense of humour. None at all."

"Stuck-up, that's what. If my Essie was to . . ."

Mrs Fender quickly clapped her hand over that musket. "O-o-oh, mothah," she trilled in mimicry, "hah-oo ken ye-ew be so-o-o coarse! If she actually knew some of the places she went to after I'd started her . . . woops! Oh, blood's thicker than water, Rube, and I wouldn't see her in want, the bitch, whatever, actually. But, let's face it, love, she's got a nasty vulgar streak, milady has."

Rube stirred from some neolithic brown-study. "They've all got a nasty streak," she shouted. "My bloody Essie now. . . ."

"Rube!" cried Mrs Fender as though at a nice cow. "Did I actually tell you what she did about Bubba when he was smashed up and in the districk hospital? Road tragedy, the papers said, and were they right! Frankly, I happen to actually know poor Bubba had had a few. But he could take it. It wasn't him to blame: grog never ever made no difference to his driving. I blame the one in the other car. Young Howard that got himself killed outright. A wishy-washy type. Never over thirty. As Bubba used to say, 'Those careful boys are the dangerous ones on the road.' A sawn-off little wowser. No confidence.

"*He* was lucky enough to be killed instantly, while poor Bubba lingered on in agony for three days. I can hardly speak to Mrs Howard when she comes in for a rinse. Murderer's mother, is what I feel like saying. But I'm too much of a lady, Rube. She has the cheek to say to me, 'A pleasant day for the time of the year, Mrs Fender.' 'Oh,' I say, cold as charity, 'oh, is it in-*deed*!'

"Anyway, Bubba's wife came rushing up from Melbourne to the hospital so, of course, I couldn't see him. I tell you straight, Rube, frankly I nearly went out of the mind. And when milady had the hide to say what a nice little thing his wife was I sort of had hysterics. I begged her to take Bubba a message. She refused. Refused her own mum! And what do you think the vulgar little bitch said when I asked how he looked? What do you think?"

Rube did not attempt not to give up. Her face shimmied slowly and heavily in a passion of expectation.

"Her Ladyship says, 'He looks even more ree-volting than

usual.' I raised my voice at her, I can tell you. 'Is that a way for a Sister-in-charge to talk about a patient? I ought to report you to the authorities,' I said. 'Common,' I said. 'Cold-hearted,' I said, 'cold-hearted and unhuman.' 'You asked for the real truth,' she said. 'You're unhuman,' I said, 'and no daughter of mine. You're not human.' She laughed. 'Human enough,' she said. 'Daughter enough and human enough.'

"Then I started to screech and carry-on I was that upset. 'I want to see my Bubba,' I kept on moaning. It must have been pitiful. You see, actually, my heart was broken. So she came over very ladylike and quiet, and said, 'Mother, I'm terribly sorry about all this. Terribly. I'll do what I can: don't you worry, I'll do what I can.'

"So, the next day, the day he died with that woman his wife snivelling over him, and me home here seeing everything lividly, Her Ladyship turned up.

"I hadn't been able to go to the salon, but Amy carried on. And jew know what? You can't trust any of them the moment the back is turned. Well, she gave shampoo appointments to two—not one, mind you, but two—of the abo. women. Dirty gins. I took some strips off that Amy, I can tell you. Told her off good and proper. 'Who jew think you are?' I said.

"Where was I? Oh, yes, Her *Lady*ship! In she comes looking like the cat that eight the canary. 'Are you sober, Mother?' she said. 'How dare you speak to your mother like that!' I said. 'Sorry,' she said, 'but the whole place looks like and smells like a bar.'

"Naturally, Rube, I'd had a few in a medical way to drown the sorrows. I said, 'I may have had a couple of small brandies for my nerves,' I said. That put her in her place the way I said it. But she's a nasty bit of work. 'Nerves calmed?' she said. 'Frankly, madam,' I said, 'they *are*.' 'Good show, Mother,' she said. 'Well,' she said, 'he's dead. But I told you I'd do what I can for you. I've brought you something of his that his wife won't want. I'm reely very kind to you,' she said. And she put this little cardboard box on the table, and away she went. There's no doubt her dad would have turned in his grave. Unhuman. Vulgar. In the box was one of Bubba's fingers."

The two women, with simplicity, and decorously, gave each other a noiseless, barred look. It could have indicated that, truth aside, they purposed staying out with men, that night, as late as cats, and that past shock, past animal fear, were used up. There were quicksands all around to soak away blood, tears, dropped flames, quicksands deeper than theatre-lounge carpets. Happenings, however terrible, led nowhere. Climax and crisis were illusions. Howsoever large and blazing are the cinders exploding from the spirit with volcanic reality, they fall, they sputter, they die, they die. *Forgotten* is pasted, like the label of the terminal and inevitable railway station, on every mind.

"Common and vulgar," said Rube with gracious weightiness, tugging down her skirt suitably over her cubic knees. "I mean, as you yourself formerly told me."

"Vulgar, spoiled little bitch," said Mrs Fender.

"Though girl-like," said the mother.

"Could you do another snort, Rube, before Max and Tex get here?" said the hostess.

"Just one more, love, and then I'll have to go and spend a penny, and get back into these bloody shoes," said Rube, forcing a plastic comb, which still had two-thirds of its teeth, through her hair. It crackled. " 'Lectricity," said Rube. "Static. Bloody rain."

"Vulgar's the word," said the hostess, agitating the squash bottle with elaborate confidence, and as a special gesture of gratitude. "I don't know, frankly, where she actually gets it from. Where she gets it from I reely and truly actually can't imagine."

(1961)

Say to Me Ronald!

Good God! thought Perrot, my nose *twitched*. The golf-bag was the biggest he had ever seen. The biggest in the world? Or perhaps it seemed so because it was three o'clock on a Sunday afternoon in 1942, and there was a war on.

In his Adelaide housemaster's study, more oakishly panelled than Sir Jasper's stage library, the golf-bag totemically stood, its effect admonitory. It had, too, the quality of a menhir, albeit composed of a circus-red species of leather, and *fleur-de-lis*-ed, gusseted, gored and belted with whitest white. Buckles and nodules of nickel ratified its Maya-like power. From its well protruded uncountable . . . weapons? . . . virile insignia? . . . surely not golf-clubs? . . . of some surely Venusian alloy.

It seemed less to have been lugged upstairs by Wee Soon Wat than to have, like an Aztec archpriest bent on sacrificial mayhem, lugged upstairs Wee Soon Wat. Nevertheless, lugee, or lugger, Wee Soon Wat was lotus-immaculate and smooth as sesame-oil.

"My dear Wee!" said Perrot, who felt that he, all over, as well as the nose he felt he had felt twitch, had changed colour. Pinker or paler he could not tell.

"Say to me Ronald, sah," mildly although rebukingly said Wee Soon Wat, seventeen, Sixth Form, Chinese, dressed to kill, and odorous of *Soir de Paris*.

"My dear *Wee*," said Perrot, affecting firmness, feeling older and smaller and unwashed, and—oh, God—changing colour again. "I can't possibly accept this . . . ah . . ." He squinted at the bag as though it were the sort of woman American G.I.'s took out, and he his own Seventh Day Adventist Aunt Edith. The bag merely got bigger than Elsa Maxwell. "Wee, I can't *possibly*. It's . . . it's too much."

Wee Soon Wat's face, usually as unmarked as if it were simply portable heredity rather than a private growth capable of illustrating character and emotion, thereupon revealed some sort of character and emotion. It began, moreover, to emit high-pitched sound, courtesan-like, an arpeggio of it. Oriental merriment? It certainly required a fan before it. It ran its course. It petered out. At peace again, its executant seemed purged, and became charming enough to charm a porcupine: "Too *much*, sah! Whai, mai old man are a millionaire, sah!" Upon this Wee Soon Wat's face got rounder than the moon above the autumn bamboos.

"*Is*," schoolmasterishly said Perrot, schoolmaster, Senior English, Middle School French, *divorcé*, and in love with someone he had no right to be in love with.

"Sah?" said Wee Soon Wat from above the bamboos, most delicately inquiring of the low-born.

"*Is*, Wee. Singular. Is. *Is* a millionaire, Wee."

"Oh, sah, s-u-r-r-r-e thing *is*. Yiss, *sah*! Singapore millionaire, as you are knowing to date."

Wee glimmered with gladness that Perrot understood. His smile was mother-of-pearl itself. Then, less glimmeringly, for life was really serious, and he insisted on being permitted to live on his own kindness to himself, "Pliss, say to me *Ronald*, sah."

Say?

Say!

Perrot recognized "speechless" as his adjective but, "Ah—Ronald—ah—*Wee*," he said in a voice nearly resembling his own. "I am—ah—I am grateful for your kind thought. But *not* necessary. Those few extra lessons in English were . . . I thought you—ah—*quite* understood that I was happy to give them. There was no thought of . . ." Payment? Reward? *Pourboire*? Rake-off? No word fitted the overwhelming receptacle and its protrusions. "No thought at all, Wee . . . *Ron-ald* . . . ab-so-lute-ly none."

Slitting his eyes like an adolescent Fu Manchu at the golf-bag, and also in the manner of one who examines another's point of view to disregard it, "To date you are thinking, sah," said Wee Soon Wat, "she are definitely beauteous?"

"*It* and *is*, Wee. I think *it is*," said Perrot, governess-like. Then stopped dead. What the governess was saying was indubitably not what Perrot wanted said.

"Theah are Scotch within her and Great British cigarettes,"

said Wee Soon Wat stroking the nickel-barnacled white-and-crimson pockets, his manicured nails and delicate fingers aquiver on their pregnancies, an inward smile suggesting one about to feast on human frailty. "To date theah are this whiskeh and Playah's Please Cigarettes, sah. Oh, gratitude, sah!"

"There *is* . . ." began Perrot.

"No!" cried Perrot. "The plural, Wee. There *are*. Yes, yes."

He resisted tearing hairs or beating breasts. He forebore to wail. Using every effort he manipulated the wires of his nature to stimulate forcefulness.

"Wee, I can*not* accept it. You must take it back to wherever—to whoever—to *whom*ever—to the shop—to the man—to . . ."

He ceased, apparently made mad and dumb.

The Oriental moon rose fuller and *blander* above . . . well, the bamboo, the rice-fields, the Forbidden City.

"It is impossible, im*poss*ible," suddenly squeaked and gibbered Perrot, dragon-fly bamboozled in bamboo, peasant yak-like in rice-fields, witless leper at the city gates. "It is *utterly* impossible, Wee."

"Say to me Ronald, mai *deah* sah," said Wee Soon Wat in his angel-white sharkskin coat, one of his Singapore twenty. It was still only a little after three o'clock, Sunday, 1942, and a war decidedly on.

Perrot knew about the war because the School Matron and the Housekeeper had got crisper and leaner than *grissini*, and wore ration-card-snipping scissors on chains in the manner of 1912 shop-girls. The gymnasium was sandbagged. Lavatory paper was thinner; underwear got more raggedy. Charcoal-burners appeared on cars, and tan shoes on boys. All jam had become raspberry. In short, eccentricity was the mode: in becoming more unreal life had become more lifelike.

Of course, vestiges of peace-time past recurred or persisted as no more eccentric than usual: summer, winter, morning hymns, examinations. The Headmaster, ever Zeus-like behind rimless spectacles blinding with reflected light, remained correct-weight Olympian without wane. The leather-aproned school-carpenter, the tuckshop Scotswoman, the nag that pulled the groundsman's roller, the cook floury as a cook, all remained, except for time's imperceivably stealthy subtractions and additions, the same.

Elsewhere in the school, the needs and lures of war also effected subtractions and additions, but outrageously, quite without stealth, and in the comic tradition. Maids who had moused about mutchless, yet with the air of wearing mutches, were now elsewhere, pert and jimp as soubrettes, in one or other war-time uniform. They were constantly being replaced and re-replaced by a rout of mock maids with bigger or springier busts, finger-nails like dowager Manchu empresses', more make-up, more crystal necklaces, tinier eyes, hairier legs and voices like tawny frogmouths'.

On the same conveyer-belt, stop-gap schoolmasters incredible as creatures from Dostoiëvski also moved into and out of view, the probability of their having habits or hobbies that could shock trailing them like a reek of burnt stew. The School got noisier than a zoo. Above all this, that and the other, searchlights slid about at night finding clouds, no Japanese war-planes and not even a Zeppelin. However, there were compensating fascinations.

War had side-channelled a number of foreign schoolboys into the School. Not only were they foreign in tint, profile and accent: glamour flickered about them like St Elmo's Fire from the fact that they had been considered sacred enough or costly enough to be packed up like *objets d'art*, and whisked away from danger. They were less, it seemed, to be educated than put in storage until the war whimpered out.

Most fascinating of the many was a selection of princelings: Batavian, Malayan, Siamese, Balinese—it was impossible to work out which was which. They gazed with deerlike animal intensity, as though fevered with sad love, from the bodies of classes. These gazers were young, yet seemed as ancient as highly-finished statuary of a remote era in which delicacy was the keynote: their wrists, too fine for the coarse activities of schoolboys, suggested poetry and immorality of a jaded kind.

Of the exotics Wee was the most eye-catching. More than his wealth his own nature made him conspicuous, unless it was that wealth had made him flashier, kinder, more imaginative, fantastically overflowing with an excess of *noblesse oblige*, and unsittable-on. Perrot was victim of this florid misconception of the shape of gratitude. Perrot led usually a nicely edited life; his mind usually had all its lights blazing. Wee Soon Wat and the golf-bag, however, had caused a dimming and flickering: a fuse could soon be blown.

Perrot cleared his throat as does a character in a short story. "Wee," he implored brutally, "take the . . . take the bag away, *please*."

For the first time an expression approaching human stirred the Chinese moon, and yet it was no more than a look of butterfly distress, misty and unattached.

"Oh, sir!" cried Wee, fervently cracking the finger-joints of each hand with the other. "You have falsed me! To date you are telling me she are definitely beauteous. And now, 'Take away, pliss!' Oh, horror! Oh, badly! What shall poor Ronald Wee believing?"

There was a quarter-second of tragic gloom. Then, victim of a thought of more splendour, Wee Soon Wat became incandescent in worldly and enlightened fashion. After all, his father was rich enough to buy the school, and convert it into a coolie-ridden College-Tudor godown packed with cloud-ear fungus and tinned water-chestnuts.

"Ah *ha*, sah!" he continued. "You are thinking to date she are definitely beauteous. You have said. But you are thinking she are bad form. Horror and alas! How Ai see! The Awstralian fellohs will be jealousy. Mai sisters have said bad form. How raight Ai see! Su-r-r-re thing: bad form! Ai must thinking. Ai think. To date Ai am thinking raptly."

A Buddha, he put on thought. He cracked anew his finger-joints.

"A golden wrist-watch!" he cried.

"No, Wee—*no*. Nothing."

Perrot might not have spoken.

"A watch *not* for the wrist? A chain-watch of Swissland. But *golden*."

"No, Wee—no."

"A desk for wraiting? A desk of fashion."

"No, Wee."

"Arm-chairs with lamps?"

"No."

"Silken shirts!"

Perrot considered screaming. Perrot did not even sigh. He gazed at his pupil as into a crystal turbulent with some lamentable destiny.

A year-long hour later, he heard himself promise to allow himself (in lieu of accepting wireless-sets, crocodile-skin suitcases, concertinas, an aquarium of goldfish, and a variety of pets) to be entertained by his adamantly grateful pupil, in a fortnight's time, at the flat of the Misses Wee.

At the School Swimming Carnival, Perrot had already glimpsed Wee's two sisters. They had been revealingly enclosed in gowns of un-Australian materials and colours. These shape-gripping *cheong sams* had slendered them to elegance. The skirts, ankle-length, but slit to above the knee on each side, had tempered the old-ivory bandiness of their naked high-heeled legs. Their coiffures had been liquorice moulded into convolutions no hand or wind would dare or could playfully budge. On each black miracle a fragile artificial flower had quivered like something recording a delicious feminine undercurrent.

Distinguished and apart as angel-fish, they had each luminously occupied like enchanted growths the luminous and scented area under their sunshades. The Indian-ink-black of their brush-stroke eyebrows, and the lacquer-red of their lipstick, had caused mothers and aunts, even Botticellian schoolgirls, to feel barbaric and pimpled, to pant like dogs, and wish they had pumiced their legs. Sophisticated agelessness varnished the Misses Wee.

Their apparent fragility had been exported from Singapore to employ safety from war in acquiring a domestic and social extra at an Edwardianly ladylike finishing school. They lived in a flat in one of St Peter's kurrajong-lined streets towards which, a fortnight later, a taxi-cab—no, no, not a taxi-cab, a vice-regal hire-car without a charcoal-burner—conveyed Perrot and his host.

It was, in the saner world, 106 in the shade, even at four in the afternoon. Wee had not a pore, follicle or gesture betraying consciousness of heat: he was so buffed, so blindingly coated and crisply trousered that Perrot, praying to sweat inconspicuously, felt cumbered and furry as an Eskimo. As the hire-car stopped, Wee leapt from it with the grace and elasticity of

Lifar, then, in the manner of one tending a lunatic invalid, his curved hand an inch from Perrot's elbow, almost assisted him from the car. Next, he paid off and over-tipped the driver with a note conceivably minted that noon.

Perrot, stroking hopefully over his hair which felt like Struwwelpeter's with a hand that felt like Struwwelpeter's, was encouraged with dove-like murmurs and infinite tenderness through the gate and along the smooth path as over the skulls and rocks of the Valley of the Shadow of Death.

At the door the brother rang, masculinely, as one expressing unequivocally: Sisters, I am without! *Women*, open!

Soundlessness ensued.

There was no brazen gong, no struck zither, no scuttle, slither, squeak, murmur or breath.

No pin was dropped to be heard.

Silence and time continued.

Then, suddenly, swiftly, silently, the door retreated and "Good af-ter-noon, Mis-ter Pel-lot," melodiously and pentatonically in duet chanted the Misses Wee, gorgeous as concubines and, in duet, extended lily hands cold as goldfish although the hallway was hotter than outside, infernal, marbled with almost visible blastings of incense, of the Misses Wee's disparate scents, of garlic, gas, and some more disturbing smell like charred mice.

The living-room was small, but the Wees and money had taken every advantage of the spaces left between the landlord's unpleasant furniture. All overhead lights blazed, and four standard-lamps and two large table-lamps suckling current through perilous lianas of flex. Each lamp was of a different design, boudoir jostling military club; each lamp endlessly repeated its image in a mound of many-coloured witch-balls on a fumed-oak refectory table. Vases, containing jammed-in bundles of artificial and tinselled flowers, prevented every flat surface from practical misuse. Fuming incense-burners abounded.

A cocktail-cabinet, so new that a price-ticket string still hung from a knob, displayed its cut-glass vessels and Saturnalian burden of bottles in a white-hot dazzle. Competently, as though he had often rehearsed this important move, Wee approached the shrine, took up station, shot his cuffs, and the formalities began.

"Would you caring, sah, for whisky-sodah, sah?" said Wee, prepared for no nonsense, and stripping the foil from a bottle-top with the decision of a head-surgeon. The Misses Wee flanked him in attitudes of willowy effacement, as though in a cool iris-garden, but with the air of inwardly abiding a moment, every wire tuned, to be played like musical instruments.

"Thank you, Wee," said Perrot thinly as a beggar, blinded with blaze, dizzy with heat and odours and the obligations of ritual.

With the social aplomb of an undertaker, and in blood-curdling quantity, Wee poured two whisky-sodas. The moment the second crystal goblet was abrim the Misses Wee abandoned the iris-pool, and flexuously undulated to their appointed duties. Beneath their brother's unwatchingly watchful eye, one placed the drink on a silver tray, one indicated a great hairy arm-chair, and piped sweetly, "Pliss to sit with-in arm-chair, Mis-ter Pel-lot."

As Perrot sank sleep-walkerishly into this hot enclosure she disposed several hotter chenille cushions about and behind him, packing him in like a T'ang statuette, while the other sister presented the drink.

Perrot observed that Wee now held *his* whisky in a position that could only be pre-salutation. First, however: "Sit!" said Wee Soon Wat with some sternness.

Perrot started as much as he was able. The order was not at him. Sinuously the handmaidens sat, one on each arm of another shaggy chair. They were like things dreamed. Their postures were divine. The stage was set. All eyes slid Wee-wards. Wee elevated his goblet a gentlemanly fraction.

"Cheer-*ho*!" he said. "Cheer-*ho*, mai deah sah!"

"Cheers, Wee," said Perrot meekly, commending his sanity and sobriety to any gods.

"Say to me Ronald, kaindly, sah, in mai own abode," said Wee Soon Wat, tossing off his giant whisky as though he were a dipsomaniac collier. This done, he shot an invisible message to his sisters. Their eyes became still. They smiled like leading ladies. They spoke.

"Hah-oo kaind you have said to Lon-ald," said the Miss Wee

in gold and red, perhaps the elder. She had more and larger teeth.

"Lon-ald is glate-ful," recited the Miss Wee in silver and green who had the less bowed legs, and smaller but brighter eyes.

"Lon-ald is sad and tlag-ic because goffing-bags are bad form."

"We have said Lon-ald that goffing-bags are bad form."

"Lon-ald admires Mis-ter Pel-lot and not admires bad form."

"Goffing-bags are bad form," intoned the Misses Wee together.

Then, "Bad form," they again said together as though delicately saying "Incest."

Upon that, abruptly, the record ran down.

"Pliss, sah," took up Wee Soon Wat, moderately sternly, hand on bottle. "Pliss, sah, to drink. To date theah are plenty more wheah that are coming from."

As under hypnosis Perrot drank to the ruinous dregs with a sense of Gorki-ing through *Lower Depths*. The goblet empty, the Misses Wee unfolded like exquisite serpents. Gold-and-red, agitating a fan, disarranged the heated air uselessly through Perrot's mop while packing the cushions tighter; Silver-and-green brought on her silver tray Perrot's refilled goblet.

The Misses Wee then replaced themselves as before, each holding this time in fingers curved like chrysanthemum petals a claret glass enriched to the brim with liqueur. Miss Gold-and-red held *Cherry Heering*, Miss Silver-and-green *Crème de Menthe*.

"Cheer-*ho*, mai deah sah," said Wee Soon Wat heartily. "And sisters," he added with some distaste.

"Cheer-*ho*, Mis-ter Pel-lot and Lon-ald," said the Misses Wee in duet.

"Cheers—cheer-*ho*!" said Perrot.

Perrot was never sure at which moment, at which drink, the ship, as it were, left the firm shores of formality, but certainly some solid safety was sometime wantonly abandoned: there was a feeling of mural dipping and ducking, of undulations and fireworks, the floor became perverse, noise took on extra intonations and ran about like bediamonded cats.

It was at this stage, early in the storm, that Wee cried out, quite loudly and un-Orientally, "Food! Melting Moments! Fastly!"

The Misses Wee, also crying out but in flutelike voices, "Melt-ing Mom-ents, Melt-ing Mom-ents!" arose like flames, and disappeared apparently into the banks of tinselled flowers.

"Mai sisters have cooking Melting Moments," said Wee.

Melting moments? Ah, Melting Moments! Perrot remembered these delicacies of his boyhood Sunday suppers: half-spheres of crunchy, pale, sweet biscuit clamped together with icing. They scarcely went with Scotch, but the notion of any sort of food now had its interest. He proposed devouring many of these saccharine spheres which the Misses Wee, chirruping like many birds of paradise behind the lamps or flowers or cocktail-cabinet, were doubtless arranging—for he heard plate-like clinkings—on Ming.

Wee poured another drink. Perrot made a pointless gesture of refusal. Wee, who was turning *eau-de-nil*, scorned the gesture. Perrot accepted the drink just as the Misses Wee re-formed, elated with accomplishment and liqueurs, in the spinning and coruscating prison. "Melting Moments," they cried. "We learn to cooking Melting Moments."

"I," gushed Perrot before he could stop himself, before he saw what they tendered on non-Ming plates, "I love Melting Moments!" Then, sustaining a smile for each Miss Wee, and removing an object from each Miss Wee's plate—how could he dare favour one above the other?—Perrot ate each object in a simulation of relish.

The Misses Wee's Melting Moments were flat, greyish circles gummed together by a pale ooze, and flaccid as Dali watches. That smell of charred mice! The sugar (or was it ground glass?) infesting their plasticine-like texture tasted of garlic—oh, a mere connoisseur's whiff!

The Misses Wee closely watched him eat six. Then, once again arranged on their arm-chair, holding their gown-matching liqueurs in the petal fingers that had constructed and conveyed to him the Satanic sweetmeats, they continued to watch him as though he were an accident.

Where, meantime, was Wee?

"Where," said Perrot, "is Wee Soon Wat?" It suddenly seemed important to know.

The Misses Wee instantly removed their gaze from Perrot as from obscenity, and began to giggle, and continued giggling. Their manner suggested that an impenetrable wall of humour separated ladies from fact. They began to talk with melodious speed at each other in a language Perrot presumed to be Chinese. Miss Silver-and-green downed her *Crème de Menthe* like an amateur actress playing Anna Christie, and lit a cigarette in an involved way.

The Misses Wee's legs were now being carelessly revealed. As they wildly chattered, vouchsafing nothing, they shot many hyphenated glances at Perrot. He had the impression of such a number of these jet glances *dit-dit-dit-dit* from each that, between the two of them and their four assessing eyes, one solid scrutiny was composed. This and the Chinese hullabaloo were becoming disconcerting, and he blushed. He took vulgar steps: he removed two of the cushions and dropped them callously on the floor; he flicked ash on the science-fiction Melting Moments; he smiled like a fox, and spoke again, more loudly than he intended.

"Where is Wee? Where?"

The schoolmasterliness momentarily terrified the Misses Wee to silence and paralysis. Their eyes raced about like crickets but could not resist, finally, all four of them, moving in one direction towards a door which Perrot now perceived for the first time.

It was a door terribly closed.

It was a bathroom door.

From behind it came the rooster-like sounds of Wee making efforts to avoid being heard being sick. Having faltered in their sisterly camouflage of chatter and false joy the Misses Wee returned their eyes to nowhere, and began more vivaciously and noisily their exchange of . . . of what?

Perrot, in an embarrassment, lowered his lips to his drink. Meeting people unlike oneself does not widen one's vision; it confirms one's notion that one is unique.

He understood now the clamorous smoke-screen of the sisters, but could not fully applaud it for he was certain that they were not discussing the weather or hair-ornaments. No, Perrot thought, they are discussing me, Perrot. Is my hair too mad? Have I Melting Moments surrounding my mouth like a screamingly funny leprosy? Is my fly undone? He could do nothing but drink again. The bathroom door shot open.

"Bad form! Bad form!" cried Wee Soon Wat, paler than the heart of a lettuce but immaculate and unchastened. His sisters stopped as though their throats had been cut. "Bad form to talking Chainese for mai deah sah. Pliss, sah, to drink. To date theah are plenty more wheah that are coming from."

And once more, like a record one hoped would not be played again, the formalities began. Wee poured. Miss Silver-and-green circumspectly took up her tray. Miss Gold-and-red plugged cushions about her victim.

Their duties done, the Misses Wee replaced themselves like mobile waxworks.

"Cheer-*ho*, mai deah sah," said Wee restraining a shudder to drink without a shudder.

"Hah-oo kaind you have said to Lon-ald," intoned a Miss Wee, her eyes still as bullet-holes through which blew a glacial wind.

"Lon-ald admires Mis-ter Pel-lot and not admires bad form," said the other, without conviction, and smiling by numbers.

"Lon-ald is sad and tlag-ic because goffing-bags are bad form."

God!

Perrot made an effort. He called up his most dazzling party manners in an attempt to halt the cultured-pearl remarks.

"Too kind, too kind," he said like the dying Florence Nightingale. "You are all *very* kind. I cannot tell you how heart-warming to meet and to . . ."

What *am* I saying? he thought. And what the hell shall I say next? His audience impassively confronted him.

"Wee, do ask your charming sisters what they were saying before in Chinese. It really sounded fascinating," he said.

God is listening to you, you bloody liar, he thought.

"Tell! Tell Mr Perrot!" said Wee, whose face was becoming dewy, in the voice of one about to enter a tunnel.

The Misses Wee imperceptibly stiffened. Their faces stopped at ivory; one could tell that, although their eyes were discreetly directed away from each other's and on some dot in outer space, they were really staring at each other in dismay.

Their souls blinked; their spirits winced; their hearts said, "Barbarians!"

Wee, too, stiffened; the dew on his forehead increased and shone in gems above his pistachio-green face. He was visibly wrestling with some inner demon.

"Tell, pliss," he said in a voice attempting severity but in the tones of one already somewhere else.

"Not to worry, oh, not to worry, Wee," said Perrot. The Misses Wee had, however, dutifully begun to translate themselves.

"We say," said Miss Silver-and-green, "that we not understand-ing Mis-ter Pel-lot, pliss."

"We say," continued Miss Gold-and-red, "we say are Mister Pel-lot laike all Aws-tlalian boy? Are Mis-ter Pel-lot?"

They both stared fixedly and callously at Perrot.

"Yiss, yiss," said Miss Silver-and-green, suddenly very animated, but in a deadly way. "Are Mis-ter Pel-lot laike all Aws-tlalian boy? *Are* Mis-ter Pel-lot?"

There seemed nothing to do but try answering.

"Well," said Perrot, "well, Miss Wee and . . . and Miss Wee, I think I may say I'm typical. That is typical enough. Well, *fairly* typical."

The Misses Wee looked at him as if he were a flower arrangement they would like to tinker with. They uttered not a word.

"Tell, tell, tell!" cried Wee, quite strongly. He was less pallid, the will having successfully wrestled the flesh. "Tell! You cannot clap with one hand."

"We say we thinking Aws-tlalian boy . . ." and here Miss Silver-and-green made an insulting shrug of great beauty, and an exquisite denigratory hand movement.

Miss Gold-and-red imitated these sending-up movements to perfection.

Then both averted their eyes from Perrot in a commenting way and, in the next instant, began to giggle. Their giggles multiplied. They clutched each other. They writhed divinely in each other's slender arms.

"Bad form! To date most bad form!" shouted Wee, restored to full voice. "Tell and tell! Fastly tell!"

Entwined and sinuous as salamanders, the Misses Wee gave broken and hysterically bubbling speech:

"Aws-tlalian boy . . ."

"Aws-tlalian boy not . . ."

"Not . . ."

"Mis-ter Pel-lot not . . ."

"Mis-ter Pel-lot . . ."

"Not . . ."

"Not hot stuff!"

"Singapore boy," sang the Misses Wee, "oh, Singapore boy hot stuff, hot stuff!"

They screeched, supporting each other on memory's ecstatic behalf.

From whatever plane of banishment he occupied Perrot heard the voice of his host, as suave as though the party were just about to begin and there were no shame in the world.

"Would you caring, sah," said the voice of one expecting no denial, "for whiskeh-sodah, sah?"

"Oh, no, Wee," said Perrot, attempting to stir, to rise. "Oh, please, *no*."

Wee Soon Wat was already pouring.

"Not to worrying to date, sah," he said. "Theah are plenty more wheah that are coming from."

As Miss Silver-and-green unwound herself from her sister to carry the silver tray, and Miss Gold-and-red prodded the cushions to embed Perrot more hotly and firmly, "No, Wee, no. No, Wee, no," he said.

"Say to me Ronald, mai deah sah," said Wee Soon Wat, and went on pouring.

(1961)

Francis Silver

One grows relievedly older and less an amateur: the high noon of middle age is free of the eccentricities of the innocent, one's senses are correctly disposed, one does not permit oneself the pleasure of discreditable actions; altogether, reality has no frayed ends. One can, at worst, fortify oneself with memories. Nevertheless, there is one disconcerting, even disenchanting, thing: what one oneself remembers is not what others remember. In this, women as annalists are terrifying. One expects them to get their recollections as exact as the amount of salt in Scotch Broth. Beyond the practical area, of course, one has no illusions: if a woman talk about democracy or eternal peace or disarmament one sees instantly and with the most telling clarity that these things are pure nonsense. One does not, however, expect a handful of salt or no salt at all in either Scotch Broth or memories, but what one expects, and what one gets—oh, dear. Take my mother for example.

As eldest son of a family of seven I got the best of her memories, partly because mothers of that period had time to make their special offerings to first-born sons, partly because her enthusiasm and salesmanship were fresh. Among her recollections the most recurrent were of Francis Silver.

Right here, I must indicate that mother was multi-loquous, gay and romantic. Whatever else a large family tore from her, it was not her vivacity. She sang all the time, particularly, I think I remember, on ironing day. The pattern of this day was that of a holy day; there was an inevitability, a feeling of religious ritual. It was always Tuesday, always Shepherd's Pie day. To mother's heightened singing the kitchen-range was stoked with red-gum until a mirage almost formed above its black-leaded surface on which the flat-irons had been clashed down. The piled-up clothes-baskets and the kauri clothes-horse were brought into the kitchen; the bees-wax in its piece of scorched cloth was placed ready. These preparations over, and while the irons were heating, a tranquil overture began. Mother and the washerwoman took each bed-sheet separately and, one gripping the bottom edge, one the top, retreated backwards, straining the sheet taut in a domestic tug-o'-war, inclining their heads to scan it for signs of wear then, this done, advancing towards each other with uplifted arms to begin the folding. These retreatings, advancings, inclinations and deft gestures, repeated sheet after sheet, had the air of an endless figure of a pavane in which, sometimes, I attempted to represent the absent washerwoman. It was while thus engaged, and later, while mother was ironing, and between her ironing-songs which were more poignantly yearning than, say, her friskier carpet-sweeping- or cake-mixing-songs, that I recall hearing much about Francis Silver.

As a young woman mother lived in a middle-class seaside suburb of Melbourne. Plane-trees lined the three-chain-wide streets from which cast-iron railings and gates, and paths of encaustic tiles of Pompeian design, separated two-storeyed brick houses overtopped by Norfolk Island Pines exuding sap like candle-grease. These houses had such names as *Grevillea*, *Emmaville*, *Dagmar* and *Buckingham*. Stucco faces of gravely Grecian cast stared in the direction of the beach on to which oranges thrown from P. and O. liners rolled in with sea-lettuce, bladderwrack and mussel-shells. A bathing enclosure advertised HOT SEA-BATHS and TOWELS AND BATHING-DRESS FOR HIRE. Mother strolled the Esplanade, tamarisk by tamarisk, or sipped Lemon Squash Spiders in the Jubilee Café with the apparently numerous young men who were courting her. Of these beaux, two young men, one from the country, one from another suburb, were favoured most. In marrying the country wooer, my father, and darning his socks and bearing his children and darning their socks, mother left the suburb for a country town set smack-flat on the wind-combed plains of Gippsland. She also left behind Francis Silver, whom she never saw again, at least not physically. He lived on, remarkably visible, in a special display-case of her memories.

Since the time of mother's young womanhood was pre-Great War there had been a conventional and profuse to-and-fro of postcards. She had garnered several bulging albums of them. The most elaborate cards, in an album of their own, were from Francis Silver. These had a sacred quality. In my eyes they belonged to Sunday. My parents were pagan enough to regard the church merely as a setting for wedding, baptism and funeral services, but, largely for us children, I suspect, though also because of what had been dyed into the texture of their late-Victorian childhoods, they were firm about the sanctity of Sunday. On this day mother played on the piano, or sang, hymns only. We were forbidden to whistle or go barefoot. Reading was restricted to *The Child's Bible*, *Sunday at Home* or *Christie's Old Organ*. Apart from meals of great size and gorgeousness the only permissible secular pleasures were to look through the stereoscope at Boer War photographs or at Francis Silver's postcards.

Hypocritically careful, we resisted licking our fingers to turn the interleaves of tissue-paper because mother hovered wrestling with herself. Invariably, at last, she could resist herself no longer. Perhaps a postcard of stiffened lace, *moiré* rosettes and spangles would set her off. Her eyes and her voice would detach themselves in focus and tone from the present.

"Yes," she would say in this unique, entranced voice, "Francis Silver sent me that after we'd had a tiny tiff near the Williamstown Time-ball Tower. We had gone for a stroll to St Kilda to listen to the German Band. When we got there the ferry-boat to Williamstown was at the pier—the dear old *Rosny*. It was such a perfect day we decided to go across to Williamstown. There was a little man on board playing a concertina. I had on—oh, I remember it so well—a white *broderie anglaise* dress, and a hat with enormous peach-coloured silk roses on it. And a parasol of the same peach with a picot-edged triple flounce. I'd made Francis Silver a buttonhole of Cécile Brunner roses. And when we were on our way back, he threw it from the *Rosny* into Port Phillip Bay because I wouldn't talk to him. It was all because I refused to give him my lace handkerchief as a keepsake. How silly it all was! I'd have given him the hanky if he hadn't said he was going to sleep with it under his pillow. And the next day he sent me this card. But I was quite firm, and didn't send the hanky. It was mean of me, I suppose, but I was terribly well-brought-up."

All mother's memories of Francis Silver were of this vague, passionless kind. The time seemed eternally three o'clock in the afternoon of a deliciously sunny day, band-music drifted cloudily in the background, no one hurried or raised voices, there were no inflamed rages or cutting malices. It was a delicate game of teasing played in Sunday clothes and while wearing mignonette. It had its fragile rules no one would be untamed enough to break. As people walking on the fresh boards of a new floor soil it in gingerly and gentle fashion, so did mother and Francis Silver serenely walk the floor of their affection.

From accounts as lame as this, of incidents as small, flat and pointless as this, it amazes me, now, that so vivid and important an image of Francis Silver became mine.

As I saw it, Francis Silver was extraordinarily handsome in a certain way. He had a shortish, straight nose, a little black moustache with curled-up ends, lips clearly cut as a statue's, white teeth, small ears with lobes, definite but not untidy eyebrows, tightly packed black wavy hair, and an olive skin. His hands were hairless and supple; the half-moons showed even at the roots of his little finger-nails. He had a light tenor voice he exhibited in such songs as *Only a Leaf*, *After the Ball*, *'Neath the Shade of the Old Apple Tree*, and *She Lives in a Mansion of Aching Hearts*—songs laced with misunderstanding, regret and tears. He was a picture-framer go-ahead enough to have his own business. In the sense of handling Christmas supplement oleographs and "art photographs" of Grecian-robed women holding water-lilies or bunches of grapes he was artistic and sensitive. He smoked Turkish cigarettes, did not drink, was popular with other sensitive young men, wore a gold ring with a ruby in it, was very proud of his small feet, and loved the theatre.

Throughout the years, mother had provided these and many more details, partly by anecdote, partly by a system of odious comparisons ("Mr Willoughby's eyebrows are much untidier than Francis Silver's"), partly by setting a standard we fell far short of ("You must press back the quicks of your fingernails each time you dry your hands: the half-moons on Francis Silver's nails, even on the little fingers, showed clearly"). It was incredible what we children knew of him: he disliked mushrooms, tomatoes and ripe apricots, he had cut his hand at a Fern Tree Gully picnic, lost his father's gold watch in Flinders Lane, had four sisters, used Wright's Coal Tar Soap, and was double-jointed.

During all the years of talk not once did mother call him anything else but Francis Silver, never Mr Silver, and certainly never Francis, despite the fact that, seemingly to us, she had given him every consideration as a possible husband. This possibility was never directly expressed. We presumed from constant obliquities. At one stage of my early adolescence, when I was sullenly inclined to regard father as the malice-riddled offspring of parents like Simon Legree and the Witch of Endor, I yearned to be the son of a merrier, more handsome and talented father. I knew exactly whom, and spent much time practising in various ornate handwritings names I greatly preferred to my own . . . Hereward Silver, Montmorency Silver, Shem Silver, Fluellen Silver.

My placid actual father (it was his placidity I regarded as a sinister malice) was as aware as he was of anything of mother's indestructible interest in Francis Silver. It was a sort of joke with him which, as children, we loved: Francis Silver was so often a bore.

"Woman, dear," father would, for example, say, seeing mother and some of us off at the railway station when we were going for a few days to Melbourne, "if you are not back by Friday, I'll assume you've put the children in a comfortable orphanage, and have run off with Francis Silver. I shall, therefore, set up house with Mrs Tinsley." This, to us, was hilariously funny: Mrs Tinsley was a gushing woman who irritated father so much that he went and talked to the pigs when she appeared. If mother displayed herself in a new hat or dress, badgering father for an opinion, he would say, "Now, woman, dear, you know you look very nice. You must have a photograph taken for Francis Silver."

"Jealous beast," mother would say.

This light-hearted chyacking about Francis Silver made him appear for ever twenty-four, for ever dashing, for ever harmless. He was the legendary Gentleman first to his feet when Ladies entered; he daily cleaned his shoes, and the *backs* of his shoes.

Once only did this image of him take on sootier colours, and throw a disturbing shadow. This happened the one time I ever heard my parents really quarrel. What the quarrel was about I shall never know. To my alarm I was trapped in its orbit without the nous to consider flight let alone perform the act of flight. There mother and father were, upbraiding each other ferociously, in the glare of kitchen daylight, she songless and shrill and stripped of her vivacity, he loud-mouthed and stripped of his dry-tongued placidity. At the height of heat mother dashed a colander of French beans to the linoleum and, crying out, "I wish I'd married Francis Silver!" rushed from the kitchen, slamming its door, then the vestibule door, next her bedroom door. Horrified as I was at the quarrel itself which seemed the disreputable sort of thing poor people, common people or drunk people did, I was more horrified at this vision of Francis Silver as a mother-stealer. I had the impression father was startled; the framework of his being somehow showed; he seemed much less a father, nuder of face, younger, like nothing so much as a bewildered man. I began to pick up the beans so as not to look at him directly, but I absorbed him foxily. He was, as it were, reassembling himself and dressing his face again, when the kitchen-door opened quietly. The slam of the bedroom door had scarcely died but mother had done something neatening to her hair.

"I have," she said, "just caught a glimpse of myself in the glass." It was a girl's voice. She tried a smile. It was too weighed out of balance with uncertainty and rising tears to succeed. "I was quite hideous with temper. I'm sorry, Henry. Of course I didn't mean . . . honestly . . ."

"Woman, dear," said father, "Francis Silver would have been a lucky man if you had married him. Out to play, boy, out to play," he said, crossing to mother who began to cry. I knew he was going to sit her on his knee. That night we had festive jelly with bananas and a dash of port wine in for pudding: a sure indication that, although he wasn't mentioned, Francis Silver was still in the house. Nevertheless, it was several months before I forgot him as a peril and could see him again as the eternal charmer.

When mother died at the age of forty-one I was eighteen.

Several hours before she died, her singing foregone for ever, her gaiety tampered with by the demands of dying, I was alone with her for a while. After saying what, I suppose, all dying mothers say to eldest sons, most of it trite, she asked me to take Francis Silver the album of postcards he'd sent her twenty-odd years ago.

"I know what the girls are like," she said of my sisters. "They'll marry and have children, and let the children tear them up. I'm sure he'd like to have them. He's still alive, and still in the same place, I think. I've looked in the obituary notices every day for years."

I began to cry.

"Stop that," she said, as though I were breaking some death-bed rule, "and listen. There's something else. In my little handkerchief-drawer there's a pink envelope with his name on it. It's got a lock of my hair in it. Before I married your father I was going to give it to Francis Silver. But I decided against it. Burn it, throw it away, anything. Don't tell your father. About the album doesn't matter. Not about the envelope. Be a good boy, and promise."

In agony I promised.

It was not until several months after the funeral that I told father of mother's wish about the postcards.

"Yes," he said, "your mother told me she'd spoken to you. Women," he said, giving me that two-coloured look which at one and the same time questioned my knowledge and informed my ignorance, "are strange, strange mortals, and this is a strange gesture. He was very devoted to your mother, and may like to have them as a memento."

"Would *you* like to take them? It might be better if you took them—more—more suitable." I was trying a man-to-man briskness.

Father looked me over, and came to his decision about what I was up to.

"Why?" he said. "Why on earth would it be more suitable? I've never met Francis Silver in my life. Anyway, you promised your mother, didn't you? Which issue are you trying to avoid?"

That my father did not know Francis Silver astonished me. Reading between the lines of mother's tales I had pictured Francis Silver and father, stiff-collared, in pointed button boots, carrying heart-shaped boxes of chocolates in their hands, and arriving (often) at the same moment on the basalt doorstep of mother's front door.

"I'm not avoiding anything," I lied. "Are you sure . . . are you absolutely sure you've never met him?"

"I am absolutely sure." He looked me over again. "I'll be looking forward to hearing about him. And, although I've never met him, I think, in the circumstances, it could not be considered too much if you conveyed my kind regards."

Despite my death-bed promise, I had had hopes of finding father willing to return the postcards to Francis Silver. I'd justified these hopes by telling myself that Francis Silver would be more touched by receiving the album from his widower rival than from the son of the woman he had hoped to marry, from the son he might have had himself. My father's defection meant I should have to keep my promise. About this I was not really happy. At eighteen I conceived myself cynical; disillusionment was daily bread.

The next time I travelled to Melbourne the album went with me. As well, I took the pink envelope which I had not destroyed—there had been no moral pause, no sense of treachery in the betrayal. On her death-bed, I told myself, mother had tangled her values, her judgement had been marred. I . . . *I* . . . considered that the anguished man I would be meeting would be doubly consoled by this more personal memento.

I had no sooner arrived at the Coffee Palace in which I was staying in the city than it became imperative to set about handing over the album and the envelope: mother had been dead for four months; the cards with their velveteen forget-me-nots, their sequins, and intricately folded and embossed layers, the envelope scented from its long secret life in the handkerchief-drawer, were too precious and unfitting to lie about for even an hour on the public furniture of a room that had been occupied by unknown, impermanent, maybe sinful people. As though preparing to meet God or have an accident, I had a shower, and cleaned my teeth, for the second time that day, put on all my best clothes, my new shoes and tie, and took much trouble with my hair. With the envelope in a pocket, and carrying the album as though it were frangible time, and dreams of finest glass, I set out for Francis Silver's.

Since all this happened before World War II and post-war

vandalism, the picture-framing shop had not been contemporarized: it was still turn-of-the-century elegant in a slightly abraded way. Three etchings with the enormously wide creamy mounts and narrow black frames fashionable at the period were disposed behind the plate-glass on which, in Gothic gold-leaf, was the name I had heard all my life, the name in my mother's handwriting on the pink envelope containing the piece of her hair she'd called a lock. I went into the shop. There was no one behind the counter. The sound of elfin-cobbler hammering came from behind plush curtains, black, on which were *appliquéd* pale gold lyres, and which obviously concealed a work-room. When I rang the small brass bell attached to the counter by a chain the tiny tap-tapping continued for a few moments, and then ceased. I heard no footsteps, but the curtains were parted. A short, fat man stood behind the counter.

"And what," he said in a light and somehow wheedling voice, "can I do for *you*?" His small eyes (Beady, I said to myself) stitched over me in an assessing way. He was the most strikingly clean-looking man I had ever seen, composed of the blackest black (his suit and tie and eyes and semicircular eyebrows) and the whitest white (his shirt, the handkerchief protruding from one sleeve, the white slices of hair curving back from his temples).

"I should like to speak to Fr . . . to Mr Francis Silver, please."

He lowered his lids while pretending to pick something languidly from his sleeve, and to flick delicately with fingertips at the spot nothing had been picked from.

"You are," he said, interested in the fact, "thpeaking to that very perthon."

I was not prepared for this, a disillusion not cut to my template. My face must have run empty.

"I athure you," he said, "I *am* Franthith Thilver. Have I been recommended? You *mutht* tell me by whom. You want thomething framed?"

"My . . . my mother . . ." I said, and placed the album on the counter. "My mother sent this. Postcards."

"To be framed?"

He opened the album.

He turned over several pages. "My dear," he said. "My dear, how thcrumptious!"

I saw on his hand the ring with the ruby mother had told us about. I saw the finger-nails with each half-moon, even on the little fingers, unmistakably revealed.

"Jutht look! I've theen nothing like thethe for . . ." He pushed out his lips in a deprecating smile, ". . . for more yearth than I care to thtate publicly. I uthed to have a pothitive mania for them."

"They are yours," I said. "They *were* yours. You sent them to my mother. Years ago," I finished uncertainly.

"I did? Gay, reckleth boy I wath! May one have little lookieth?" He took one of the cards and examined its back. "Tho I did! My handwriting hathn't changed a bit. How ekthordinary, how very ekthordinary! And now they are to be framed?"

"No," I said. "No, not framed. Mother thought you'd like to have them back."

I knew I was expressing mother's wish very badly, but could do nothing else: the situation had become bewildering not only to me but also to Francis Silver who said, "Oh!" There was, moreover, something beyond the bewilderment of a clumsy social situation; there was something wrong. Francis Silver had not asked me who had sent the postcards. Some film clogging natural curiosity, even polite enquiry, some flaw in his humanity, made him seem careless and carelessly cruel.

I did not want to say it but I said it: I told him my mother's maiden name.

He became fretful: the past was not for him. Nevertheless he acted good manners of a sort. "Now, let me thee," he said, and he put the tip of his forefinger on his forehead in an absurd thinking posture. He pouted.

"My dear," he presently said, "the mind ith blank. Abtholutely! Nothing thtirs in my little addled brain. I'm very, very naughty. But you muthtn't tell your mother. I thhould be *tho* humiliated. You mutht tell her I loved *theeing* them but I couldn't *deprive* her of them. It'th a wonderful collection and in *faultleth* condition. Oh, if only my friend Rekth were here . . . he *adorth* pothcardiana, if I may coin a phrathe, abtholutely adorth."

Scraps of the past were blowing about my brain like the litter at the end of a perfect picnic.

"And you don't remember my mother?"

He could have smacked me.

He tossed his eyes heavenwards but not too high.

"Be reathonable, *pleathe*! More than twenty yearth! One would adore to remember, of courthe. But too much water under the bridge. There've been too many people, too many, many people. I *thaid* I wath terribly humiliated. I couldn't akthept them now, could I? You take them back. And thank your mother very, very much." He smiled a conspirator's smile, grasped my wrist and squeezed it boldly yet furtively. "I know you'll keep my ghathtly thecret, just *know*. You've got a nithe kind fathe, haven't you? But there've really been too many people. I'm thure your mother ith ath charming ath you. But I don't remember her at all."

I detached myself. Without a word I left the shop.

The album of cards remained with whom I'd promised to give it.

By the time I had returned to the Coffee Palace through the sort of exquisite day I used to imagine a pretty mother and a jaunty Francis Silver flirting through along the seafront, I had made up an outline of lies to satisfy and comfort my father for whom I felt the truth, as I saw it, to be of the wrong shape. By the time, days later, I was home with him, I hoped to have filled in that outline with unassailable detail: I dared not shock him. As my first adult chore, my initiation task, I would make a fitting Francis Silver for him, one that matched the Francis Silver of mother's recollections.

In the room at the Coffee Palace I looked at the pink envelope older than I. For one weak moment I felt like making a film-actor's gesture and kissing it. I remembered in time it was not mine to kiss. It was no one's. In that room with its Gideon Bible on the glass-topped bedside cabinet, its ecru net curtains, its oatmeal wall-paper and petty frieze of autumn Virginia Creeper, I burned the envelope. In its first resistance to flame it gave up its ingrained scent. It twisted, fighting the flame and itself. It emitted a stench of burning hair. It writhed and writhed in an agony I could not bear to watch.

(1962)

The Letter Writer

Any time, anywhere, to anyone she can pin down to a simulation of hearing if not listening, "Believe you me," Mum says, perhaps digging out ear-wax with a bobby-pin and looking at it, "I'm a great one for letter-writing. Got a gift for it. They all look forward to Mum's newsy letters."

For this announcement she arranges her mouth in a special way that indicates confidence in her power thus to enchant people.

At times, no more honestly or dishonestly, but in more rarefied mood, "I'm a great one for cor-res-pond-ence," she says, perhaps clearing phlegm from her throat with high-toned secrecy and, equally secretly, swallowing it.

It's one of the remarks she's always making: "Believe you me, kiddies are tops. They're delightful little scamps. And kiddies *know*. They know Mum's personally very inter-*est*-ed in them. They always take a shine to Mum." Or, to reveal that she has a domestically genteel as well as a cultured and lovable side: "I do quite a fair bit of fancy-work and cetera myself," she says.

Truth is that the only and last grimed bit of fancy-work she didn't finish in 1933 was a tray-cloth on which a noseless crinolined woman with an embroidered hare-lip held up a parasol under a trellised arch sparsely dotted with . . . could it have been measles?

As for children . . . *kiddies* . . . she has had four herself: Horrie, Dot, Val and Marlene, who all left her in ungrateful huffs before their storms-of-puberty pimples were ripe, and while her back was turned to say, "Believe you me, it's the mum keeps the home together. I'm a mum, and I know."

Letter-writing?

Dear Val,

You owe me a letter but none yet so here goes. Been a proper stinker today and my back playing up like billy-oh.

Tell young Ern he wrote a nice letter although v. short (1 page). He sure gave me some news (no mucking about) so have gathered up some stamps for his album (real good ones). That's what comes of writing me a nice letter. Tell him my 60th birthday (no kidding) and still kicking on Feb. 12th. Tell Mabel someone pinched my Scottie Xmas card she sent me. Did I see red and still see it. I think I know the one. Have been in bed with Bronchitis and Germ in the throat but am on the mend and am going gay (whack-oh) on my 60th birthday (Feb. 12th) all being well. Stan, Hilda Freeble's Stan that is, had a v. nice funeral. A lot of the cousins there. A nasty lot. Saw an awful case of nerves the other day. Tell Dot and Chooka that Frank is in hospital, the gas from the war. Don't think he's long for this world. You better let old Mrs Pither know that on Feb. 12th . . .

She is one of those women who collect misfortune, accident, disease and death. News of cancer exhilarates her for several days; death is fodder for a fortnight. Her own connection with eternity has never entered her head from which drifts a perpetual mulch of scurf. She lives for cheap and useless time.

Take getting up in the morning—take a Thursday morning, Country Women's Association day, seven o'clock.

No alarm goes off, but she decides to stop pretending to herself she's still asleep, and ungums her eyes to look at the clock which has been knitting away at her shroud all night. A big woman, with the bony scaffolding of a Neanderthal ruckman embedded deep in stones of coarse flesh no one wants to take, she first levers her Rodin bulk half-out of its warren, and drops her legs heavy as duffle-bags over the edge of the bed. Two disconcertingly small feet she washed a fortnight ago make a single convinced declaration on the bedside mat. It is, after all, their mat. Eight toes wear eight perfected and perfectly circular corns which she has cherished for thirty-five years. She has been married to them longer than she was to her husband who, alive, had been a slaughterman with fingernails edged all round with blackened blood. He, winkled by death out of her bed and life after thirty years of them, was a corpse with an archaic smile on its face.

"Dear old dad and I were helpmates," she says, looking unseeingly at the liver-spots on the backs of her hands.

"I gave dear old dad the best years of my life," she says, dipping ginger-nuts in tea dark as a Tamil.

She perceives no coalition between these statements and the corpse's smile which, though a mere muscular quirk, was an unanswerable comment. Before death manufactured this underhand criticism for him, he had had to limp in, morning after morning, with a large MOTHER cup of the Tamil-coloured tea, and two slabs of singed bread wringing wet with margarine, and cry ironically, even bitterly:

"Wakey, wakey! Rithe and thhine!"

Then she would grind the sugary, honey-coloured granules from her eyes, and insert her false teeth, and shed her first fall of dandruff for the day, and say, "The toast's too thin," or "The toast's too thick," or "Can't you ever serve a cup of tea without slopping it?"

Now, these flesh-and-blood pleasures denied her, now, C.W.A. day, a tealess widow, she sits with the shiny rind of her soles on their mat, and stares towards the Niles and Mississippis of cracks in the plaster wall, and reaches with practised blindness to the bedside cabinet which contains a po and a pair of crippled stays, and on top of which her false teeth, magnified by refraction, seem to occupy fully a tumbler of oyster-coloured liquid. She hooks them out. She plugs them into her face which becomes brutally public. She is beginning to resemble herself. She reaches for her bloomers.

Let us draw a veil.

Let us lift a veil: it is nine o'clock.

She is dressed. She resembles, to the last subtlety of odour, her C.W.A. self in the maroon marocain only partly rotted under the armpits, her nylons nubbled with varicose veins, and her white shoes. She has taken her Epsom salts. Her stays hem in a light Thursday breakfast: two fried eggs, two sausages, four slices of toast and dark plum jam, four cups of tea.

The day, too, is beginning to resemble itself.

It properly begins when she sees the postman go by without stopping. Upon this her jaw becomes quilted with muscles, and her eyes get smaller. If it were not C.W.A. day, and she due on the street-stall with Mrs Stein at ten o'clock she would get her indelible pencil, and lick it, and write:

Dear Rube,

Must say I was v. upset when no letter from the postie today, it's been well over three weeks. Have you had your asthma again? Doc Stafford says what with the Bronchitis and all I'm lucky to be having my 60th (Feb. 12th). You remember Stan Freeble, well he passed on (cancer of the bowels) and a v. nice funeral. I made an anchor wreath of those pink climber geraniums. Tell Bella they all said the best there and couldn't believe it wasn't bought (whack-oh). Ollie Green had a nasty ringworm. Tell Peg and Nobbie I'm 60 on Feb. 12th, and not to forget. If you want backs of Xmas cards for the Guild Quiz just drop a line and postage (1/3d.). Lot of summer colds about this year. Don't think old Mrs Dean will be with us much longer, she had a nasty turn (her insides). Tell Flossie she owes me three letters now and to drop a card (Scottie dog or roses) on 12th. Weather a real scorcher. Tell . . .

However, she cannot spare time to be entertaining and fascinating on paper this morning; the world eagerly awaits her.

"They couldn't get along without Mum," she tells herself, and pins on the MOTHER brooch she bought herself, and goes to the cupboard of jams she made herself.

It takes some time to find a jar of jam small enough, and with the special quality making it suitable for the C.W.A. street-stall, but she finds it. She removes the cellophane covering, she spoons off the plush of mould, she replaces the cellophane, she puts the jar in her basket with her plastic apron and her purse. She goes into the back-yard overrun with Cape weed, sorrel and mint. She picks and puts in the basket six bunches of mint.

The moment has arrived to complete her disguise. She rubs a grey powder-puff over her chimpanzee nose, her faded moustache and her wattles. She forces down a hat over the powerful aluminium-coloured crenellations of her hair, and chalks out some marks on her shoes.

Then, sure, but not absolutely, that her neighbour has gone out, she goes next door.

Secure in the validity of her *toilette* which says Respectability, and her bulk which says Salt of the Earth, and her brooch saying Decency, and her juggernaut advance implying Probity, she reaches her neighbour's back-door. She calls through the fly-wire with a voice louder than the size of the house requires, with the complex accent and tone of one who expects nothing to answer but is catering for ears accidentally listening elsewhere:

"Mrs D., are you there, dear? It's only Mum."

Nothing answers.

She increases volume:

"I was wondering if you wanted anything down the street. . . ."

Nothing answers, not even a budgerigar.

Directly as fate, and majestically as chancellors of universities, she goes to Mrs D.'s vegetable garden. It takes little time, and far less power than she grossly has, to pull up and throw twelve carrots over the fence into her own back-yard, to screw back into the ground carrots too small for her purpose and vanity, and to obscure the signs of her visit. Furrily humming *The Old Hundredth*, she returns to her own house. She washes the carrots. She puts them in the basket. She is ready.

She locks her house, she locks away the unmade bed, the unwashed dishes, indelible pencil, jam-cupboard, blowflies alive and dead, her husband's framed Odd-fellows certificate, and the photograph of herself and the children, she rearing up with her expression of monopoly above the simpers of Horrie with a cow-lick, and Dot, Val and Marlene cheaply overdressed and empty-eyed.

When she arrives at the street-stall she is forced to abandon an attitude, to still herself to wariness, to shroud certain powers, for, instead of her usual helper, Mrs Stein, who has a crippled foot and is bossable, she finds Mrs Radford, who is shaped and coloured too much like a mother from a magazine, and is inclined not so much to downright bossiness as to an unawareness of others' capabilities. Mrs Stein has, Mum knows, accomplished migraine. Mrs Radford, fool of a woman, obviously believes the attack is not deliberate.

"Yes, the poor old trout," says Mrs Radford, lip-sticking away in the full glare of Main Street, "when she telephoned for help her poor little voice was dim with pain. I was still *en robe de nuit*, and Radford's was a whirl of indolence. But the Stein is a lambie-pie. So I hurled myself under showers, and drove here like M. Campbell himself. Hon, is there any lippy on the snowy tats?" And she bares her brilliant teeth at Mum like a poster Polynesian. "Now, hon, what mullock has been unloaded on us this fair morn? My God, look at this!" And she lifts from among the donations of plum sauce, silver beet, broad beans, and no-egg sponges the texture and colour of bath-sponges, a framed oleograph of two children in velvet, one of whom holds a dead canary which they are sorrowing over.

"Shades of my girlhood!" says Mrs Radford. " 'The Little Mourners' it is. My mamma doted on the thing. It seemed to cheer her up no ruddy end."

"I thought it wasn't a modren photo," says Mum, unpacking her basket in a Lady Bountiful manner. "I could pick it first off. Myself, I like a more modren photo."

"Really, hon? Do you really? I think I go along with you there. Poor mamma was crazy about all this old Christmas Supplement stuff. Much more better, like, than the tripe turned out by Rembrandt and Leonardo and those upstart boys—so thought me old mum. But she'd have given me a backhander if she'd found me moping over a dead canary instead of being virtuously cross-eyed over homey."

Then she says, lighting a cigarette, "Hell, hon, you *have* gone crazy mit the mint. But the whole southern hemisphere's lush with it: the yokels'll have a hellish sales-resistance. Bet we don't sell a bloody leaf."

Mum would like to say, "If you please, Mrs Radford, I don't approve of swearing in a lady," but, faithful to a legend she has made ("Mum's always the same," she says of herself, "nothing puts her out, for sure"), she begins an oath-free and unstintedly detailed account of the bus she missed because the bus-driver was early, of the bus she caught after waiting hours because the bus-driver was late, of the bus-driver's rudeness when she told him off, and the dustiness of the bus-seats, and of the superior grain of her son-in-law Chooka who is a bus-driver on the Yarraville run. She tells Mrs Radford that, among the five letters she got that morning, was one from Chooka who writes once a week.

"Oh, Mum comes first with the son-in-laws," she says. "They appreciate what well-trained wives they've got."

Mrs Radford could scream. Yet all she says, and in front of Canon Wake's wife, who has picked up a bottle of sulphur-yellow pickles and is assessing them in a religious way, is: "Hell, hon, if my son-in-law wrote to me I'd go straight to a lawyer."

Not much later, while Mum is sharing a minute account of her costiveness with Mrs Radford, Mrs Radford coarsely—she has no manners at all—interrupts, "Look, hon, I adore being guide-toured through your fascinating bowels, but the truth is your dipso old palsy-walsy Radford is the tiniest mite overhung. You see, my ouija-board neglected to reveal that *Mère* Stein was to be in the throes, and your humble on the bridge, or I'd have been as pure as the driven, last night. But you know how it is, hon. Filthy beasts of husbands with their filthy friends with filthy bottles—lovely! Be a doll, and hold the tiller while I scarper to the Pig and Whistle for a hair of."

Mum cannot translate this until Mrs Radford is across the road, and into the Commercial Hotel.

Mum's wattles stiffen.

Depravity, however, has its silver lining. Gently grunting *Rock of Ages*, she wraps the mint bunches in newspaper. Then, choosing her time, and with the over-nonchalance of someone publicly concealing the fruits of infanticide, she jams the parcel deep into a municipal rubbish-basket on the nearby lamp-post.

Presently, Mrs Radford returns with lipstick on her teeth. This pleases Mum, who says nothing of it.

"Hell, hon," says Mrs Radford, "you should be in insurance. Or did someone steal them?"

Mum puts on the expression of someone who has never heard of mint. It wasn't mint, however.

"That eggless horror with the off-white icing? And the *dernier cri* hessian oven-mitts? No one would *steal* 'em. You must have given them away."

Mum inflates.

"I sold them. Of course," she says, large and regal and eyeless as a civic statue, but ladylike, and putting Mrs Radford in her place, and keeping her distance from the dangerous smell of brandy as Mrs Radford keeps her distance from the smell of Mum, who is biding her time.

She bides it until the noon Angelus is ringing, and their morning watch on the stall is over.

"Oh, by the way, Mrs Radford," she says, "the mint. I sold it. While you were away in the . . ." She refuses to utter the word.

"Pub, hon. Local. Boozer. Gin-crib. Rubbity. Rum-shack. I have no shame."

"The mint. I'm sorry to say you were sadly mistaken. I could of sold it several times over."

"Garn!" says Mrs Radford, who never says the right thing. "I'll bet—just to make a false prophet of me—that you ate it yourself, you old monster."

Mum's face, defying this sort of mockery too near the truth, takes on the unarresting personality of a stopped clock.

Volumnia-like, despite her abraded profile, Mum now proceeds, with the inexorable pace of foreseen doom, to the kitchen of the Mechanics' Hall, where other C.W.A. women are at work on the catering for a wedding breakfast later in the afternoon.

Already, twenty trifles are lined up, high-class slum food that the plastic-aproned and tea-drunk women have constructed from a pastry-cook's stale throw-outs soaked in the liquid of tinned peaches, thick-skinned skim-milk custard, and mean curls of mock cream. If men live too large with their diabolically uncharitable designing for another world, women live too meanly with their penny-pinching imitation of charity for this one.

Mum tells them it is a hot day. She hangs up her hat to indicate that she is about to put on her apron; puts on her apron to indicate that she is about to drink tea; makes it clear that it is a hot day; and that yesterday was a hot day; and that tomorrow will probably be. . . .

They could scream.

Mum, selflessly repeating an adorned description of her morning's experiences with criminal bus-drivers, has five cups of tea.

Silence she sees as deep interest. The poor things like a get-together, she thinks, and a bit of entertainment. Believe you me, Mum's the one, always bright and breezy.

She picks delicately as a starved dingo at the wedding food, and talks.

She scrapes Woolworth fish-paste on to the margarine someone has scraped on bread, and talks.

She chops up lettuce, and talks.

Now, to these other women, all married, all deft in the manufacture of rubbish from rubbish, all occupied in the preparation of a sickening meal to celebrate the marriage of a woman, tea takes on the nature of an anodyne for, until their money-making chicanery is at an end, they are trapped between two symbols: Mum and the wedding table.

The wedding table, composed of trestles hired from the Fire Brigade, covered with cloths hired from the Red Cross, is set with steel-handled cutlery and grey tumblers hired from St John's Church of England Women's Guild. Central among the neon-coloured bottles of gassy liquids, and the soup-plates of water in which snipped-off hollyhock flowers float, stands the wedding-cake topped by a plastic groom in a 1930 dinner-suit, and a square-shouldered bride. Above all hang the limp loopings of green and black streamers left over from the Anglers' Ball.

Before leaving with a pound of margarine, a Swiss roll, four tomatoes, a jar of anchovy paste and a packet of custard powder concealed in her basket beneath the plastic apron, Mum describes Dot's wedding-cake, and Val's, and Marlene's. They tower, higher and whiter than icebergs, above the semicircles of red beet, the tinned ham, the potato salad, on plates hired from the Main Hotel. Nobody shuts her up. Nobody screams.

Ultimately, Mum goes home.

The letter-box is empty.

She unlocks the house in which has been locked nothing to steal.

She takes off her stays.

The sun sets.

As she is cooking noisily, eating noisily, washing up noisily, the night rises into the twilight to flood it out, to refresh her back-yard of weeds. It refreshes the din of crickets, it refreshes to life the little noises of night, it refreshes most her other inner voice now that space and time have struck away the audience for her physical one. She supports impatiently the necessary interval of barrenness that eating and slovenly domesticity require; and the night is fully risen when she takes up her indelible pencil, and licks it, and writes:

Dear Marlene,

Have had no news so am dropping a line. Will be 60 on Feb. 12th and still going strong (whack-oh). Had a bout of Bronchitis but on the improve. Stan Freeble, don't know if you know him, passed away of cancer (the bowels). A happy release but v. nice funeral. Tell Cora she owes me a letter, two if I remember rightly. Remind her of my 60th. Busy day today in charge of C.W.A. stall and wedding breakfast at Mechs. Inst. All hands to pump. Had them all in fits. The lady on the stall with me (supposed to be) spent all the morning in the hotel. You know what. Could hardly stand. Did I see red and no mistake. Gave her a piece of my mind (no mucking about). Ollie Green had a nasty ringworm. Tell . . .

The dandruff sifts down. Again and again she licks her pencil; the grey of her tongue becomes suffused with violet.

Dear Gwen, she writes. *Surprised no news from you as yet. . . .*

Dear Peg, she writes. *Have been expecting to hear . . .*

Dear Dot, she writes. *No letter from you since . . .*

Warmth gradually suspires from the earth as it does from a dead body. The clock knits on. The blowflies drone themselves to movelessness. All elbows and decorously darting speed, the spiders spin in the smashed springs of the settee, between the dusty vases, along the tops of curtains.

Now, pale with effort, colossal and noisome, she finishes the last of her pencilled letters.

Now, as in the trance of a bestial priestess moving towards the consummation of a final rite, she rises, she moves to get a pen and a bottle of green ink, she sits again.

Now, with laborious care, a mammoth schoolgirl, she addresses an envelope:

"*Mandy,*"
C/o Country Women's Page,
Weekly Advertiser,
Melbourne.

Now, the day gathered in, the day solved, she writes:

Dear Mandy,

I thought I would correspond and bring Christian comfort to the lonely people in your column for advice. I am a popular widow with four lovely mites. Their dear father has passed on. The four little elves are tucked away in their nests. I am tired but happy, but couldn't drop off without a message to lonely souls of your column. The message is, you have a full life like I and no time for worry and that. The alarm went off at five. I sprang up and had a shower. The postie came and there were letters from relations and many more. What a wonderful thing to be sure. Mrs Next-door donated me eight bunches of carrots for my stall. My garden is better than hers, but you can't hurt another's feelings. Then a wealthy friend called to take me to the stall in style. They are always calling for me for just rides, or picnics and cetera, so you see there is no need to be lonely. What do your readers consider of about ladies who go smoking and drinking? I am very broadminded and popular but don't agree with it. And dirty filthy language too. She brought mint along. No good at this stage with everyone with mint to burn, I said to her. I took a lovely lot of flowers to the cemetery. It was Chris's (my late hubby) tenth celebration of his passing. Some bus-drivers are rude you find but will meet their match and ought to be reported. Do you know a photo called "The Little Mourners"? It is depicting two lovely tots holding a sad little dead canary. Whilst my late mother was alive she kept the picture and it came to me when she passed on. I prize it as it is real to life although the dressing of the children is nothing like you see today. My mother would never slap me for dead birds instead of my home work. I know a prayer for the lonely people to protect a home from fire and flood and that. My late sister proved it when an electric storm struck the town she lived in. I baked a lovely wedding-cake and decoration. So tell them what with one thing and another you haven't got the time to be lonely.

Late—it grows late.

The spiders have spun themselves empty and their numberless eyes to sleep.

From the crude branches of her bones the rank foliage of

her flesh sags down, weighs down, towards the dirty floor, the dirty earth, the dirty grave. With a thirsting movement her empurpled tongue seeks and circles finally about her lips and the last sentences.

I wish you could see my lovely home and garden. Everyone says so and are always in and out. Must now sign off with a cheerioh.

She fights her thickening fingers; she compels her bulk to answer her; she has reached the end.

Thanking you in anticipation, she writes, *Yours truly, Elfin Maid.*

(1962)

Gretel

My mother, empty-headed as a ghost, always left everything to the last minute. She persisted faithful to this pattern of behaviour even in the matter of dying. The cablegram of omen, the invitation to her final performance, could therefore do nothing but catch me with my eyes elsewhere, and my heart nowhere. When it came, I was, in fact, at my sixth glass of Samos wine, while Ionysseus, the two-sexed drink-waiter of the tatty marble bar of the Alpha Hotel in Athens, was dealing the age-thickened cards for our enth game of agonaea. We were playing for nothing, for less than nothing: one cannot outwit boredom with boredom. Distress is, however, stimulating. Charged with emotions not to be revealed, I crumpled the cablegram, and instantly left the flaccid wine and the grimy cards. At midnight, I was buckled in my seat on a plane to Melbourne. It ripped itself away from arid and aching Greece, with me and my obligations, and my sorrow too shallow to be published. The hours passed, the extravagant exhibitions of planets and clouds, the airway transit lounges humid as Turkish baths, the ugly wreckage of civilizations, and the uglier wreckings of progress.

At my age, forty-five, one should not dream of disavowing one's personality. I had long-time been *dégagé*, and smug in being so. This sparer diet nourished me more than one spiced with convictions and passions and tolerances. I knew to a pinch how little I loved, how little I hated. The skull with its long teeth clipped together in the ultimate and only true smile not only waits at the end of life's chess-board, but is there on any and every square. Events are no more than advents. Why then exert oneself in rich antics and decorated trickery? My mother, for example, could have been side-tracked by chance into dying selfishly while I was young and useless; she could, equally, have by-passed hazard to cumber—a scatter-brained centenarian capricious and fractious as a broken umbrella. Instead, she had frolicked, entertaining and well-beloved, for nearly seventy years. Enough, surely?

I was too late, of course, for her death-bed scene. The train from Melbourne got me over the mountains, and down through the foothills, to the provincial town, an old gold-mining one, just in time for the funeral. It was suitably raining. The tree-frogs were rejoicing through the canon's fruity rendition of the burial service. The cemetery, as the town was, was up hill and down dale. It seemed as vast and overgrown, no more, no less, as when I used to go there, a boy, shooting rabbits, picking wild strawberries, or pilfering from the swallows' nests under the curled-up eaves of the oven-altar that towered centrally above the graves of Chinese miners. The horizontal granite door of my father's grave had been opened to admit mother, late as ever. About this entrance to nowhere stood my three little sisters and my brother. They were all convincingly disguised as middle-aged, middle-class, married adults. They and I stood with the unrestful earnestness of mourners. It was as though, beyond the canon's elocuting, we cocked an ear to a trite lecture from fate. How different we all were. Yet we had had the same two parents, four grandparents, eight great-grandparents, sixteen great-great-grandparents, and so on. These calculations, carried to the utmost, imply an ancestral Eden so jam-packed with billions of anthropoidal Adams and Eves that it must have been a zoo-like hell. It seems to me that these sumless matings, funnelled down to us, a mere five, should have found us more alike than we were.

When mother in her pretty box was, at last, lowered towards father, my sisters made revelations of grief of a controlled kind: mother had taught them good manners. There was also an almost animal outcry from one of the other women. Although I had not seen her for over thirty years, I knew who she was. One of mother's flapper friends of the 'twenties, she had lapped over into mother's matronhood and our childhoods. Not related by blood or marriage, she was nevertheless Aunt Willy to us: Wilhelmina was her name. As she sobbed too rowdily, undone by heaven-knows-what memories of mother in the days of golliwogs, tin lizzies, banjo-mandolins, and coats with collars and cuffs of monkey fur, I too was suddenly the victim of recollection. My heart, so long locked, so aseptically polished free of finger-prints, creaked with an old forgotten pain. A forgottten voice seemed to cry through the meek rain, "I am here! I am here!" It was the voice of Aunt Willy's daughter, the girl I fell in love with when I was twelve.

At twelve, in 1929, I was at the height of my boyhood, and the family at the height of its family-hood. It seemed unthinkable that my flibbertigibbet mother and my lawyer father, who was *distrait* to the point of not being earthed, could have had the concentration to compose even one child, let alone five. Father played chess, drove his motor-car as gently as a perambulator, spoke winding sentences that drawled out of sight without reaching a full-stop, and was always mislaying a meerschaum he affected rather than, I *think*, smoked with relish and assurance. Mother, who had four Lenci dolls, and more bangles and beads than a maharanee, must have been the giddiest housekeeper this side of Jericho. Fortunately, she had authentic assistance from a tiny, toothless creature who much resembled Pop-eye the Sailorman, and who appeared each Friday as charwoman to amend what had been done to sully the house since her last week's visit. Little had been done by father, much by us children, but most of the domestic damage had been done by mother and the maid-of-all-work.

The house had been built in the town's boom period, before the gold fizzled out. Its solidity was late-nineteenth century, as the town's was. Surrounded by wide, tiled verandas, the house was of brick and granite, and was set in two acres of garden and orchard. Snowdrops and larkspur proliferated under the lichened fruit-trees of old-fashioned apples and pears; seedling nectarines grew cheek-by-jowl with islands of irises and tiger lilies, and uncorralled bushes of striped roses. All this was half-way down a valley slope on the edge of the town, the streets of which, like a flexible grid-iron, criss-crossed the bulges and depressions of the foothills. Each street was a tunnel of elms or oaks.

From our front veranda, we could see the hills gutted of gold, the spindly poppet-heads, and the mullock-heaps in their pelts of paspalum and chocolate lilies. Opposite us, just below the crest of the other side of the valley, was the lunatic asylum. It seemed tilted for our better viewing: we could see inside its high walls a sort of Cape Dutch Colonial barracks of beige stone scribbled on by Virginia creeper, and mathematical garden beds solid as mattresses with civic flowers like lobelia and salvia. As did the inhabitants of a medieval painting with its scrupulous perspective, minute people—loonies?—strolled, or bent to work, or merely stood like miniature scarecrows among the flower-beds.

Mother's familiar, the skivvy Mavis, was the woodman's daughter, one of nine. Her legs, knock-kneed walking-sticks, suggested a being of some fragility. Not so. Mavis was strong as a nanny-goat, and had untrammelled breasts, large as canteloupes, that lolloped about under her black dress, and a weighty face resembling that of Toulouse-Lautrec's Oscar Wilde, the Mae Murray lip-sticked cupid's-bow included. She and mother, busy as light-minded sorceresses, gossiped and sang as they singed batches of scones, rolled out leather pastry, and endlessly rearranged the Mary Gregories and flat-backs. In the proper season they worked with passionate incompetence to brew jams which either remained liquid for ever, or set like jasper. Their housekeeping can be summed up in the turn-of-the-screw fact that from a Sea Pie we once fished out Mavis's rolled gold brooch *and* one of mother's bridge-score pencils with a sealing-wax rosebud on the end.

Years later, Mavis was found raped and strangled under the river-bank plane trees. I was home during a university holiday, and was in the room when mother heard the news. She did not scream or break down as I expected. Before my eyes she rapidly shrivelled and abated, as though blood and frivolity had gushed to immediate waste. After a while, she uttered the thought, as women do, that lay at the back of the thought she wished to utter: "Now I'll have no one to give my old clothes to." She shed no tears, and remained older and dejected until the murderer, an Italian pea-picker, was hanged. On this day she treated herself to a bottle of champagne, drunk solo, and a volcanic eruption of tears from which she reappeared as though nothing had tampered with her gaiety, or spilt blood on her rose-coloured spectacles.

This excess and intensity of feeling had always to be burned away, and got mother into involvements with many a suspect charity. More often it swept her into eccentric enterprises with a number of other women whom she called, in her city accent, The Gels. These fads had, usually, one common factor—the products were *hand*-made or *hand*-painted or *hand*-stitched or *hand*-whatever. *Hand* seemed to bestow aesthetic dignity. It is impossible to recall all these bygone enthusiasms now, but their strange fruits were always turning up—lopsided cane baskets; uncircular "pottery" ash-trays; silk flowers of quite sinister designs—royal blue chrysanthemums were the nadir; felt *boutonnières*; stuffed toys whose intention to archness was impaired by cretinous distortions or a criminal squint. Once, The Gels took to culture and play-reading. They started on Tchekhov and Ibsen, but came to their senses and their own level in *The Patsy* and *The Cat and the Canary*.

Neither mother nor The Gels, thank God, made a fad or cult of their children. We were loved and smacked, fed and ordered out of the house to play, made to wash ourselves and go to bed early, learned the wisdom of seen-but-not-heard. The point was that we remained children until it was time for us to be made adults.

At the age of twelve it was too early for nature to start selling me down the river; another year, another spring, another summer, and nature would gash and tangle the strings of my voice, sprinkle hairs on me where there had been none, lubricate my eyes so that they would swivel in the direction of flesh, steam over the clear glass of my mind with the breath of lust, and tempt me to trace on this mist the first letters in the alphabet of profane love. Another spring!—but even then, already, the snake's shadow was in the cup.

From time to time, friends of mother's shingled and short-skirted maidenhood came to stay, often accompanied by their children. Sometimes there would be a more dashing, Eton-cropped, bachelor-woman who brought her own whisky. At least one night, invariably, of her stay one would hear from one's bed the Victrola playing *My Sweetie's Due at Two to Two!*, and guess that she and mother, panting and giggling, were reviving the Charleston. The most constantly recurring of these visitors was Aunt Willy who, in retrospect, seems to have been most like mother: chatterbox, rattle-pated but insolently cocksure, loving yet mocking, with a heart of gold guarded by the tongue of a wasp.

In the spring school-holidays of 1929, Aunt Willy was

expected. Looking back, it is today easy to see that mother had worked out a plan. This included making Mavis take a fortnight's leave at an unusual time of the year, and bundling all of us children off to stay with honest-to-God or designated aunts. The day before this exodus, I was pig-rooted from a horse, and broke my wrist. Tears and implorings notwithstanding, I had to stay home. Mother was perfectly able to accept a broken wrist, like bee-stings, cut knees, thorns in bare soles, and fallings in the river, as among the conventional hazards of country childhood. Not for all the bangles in Bombay, however, would she let the maimed child one centimetre beyond the maternal radius. So, there I was, my arm in splints, an unnecessary rug over my knees, sitting before an unnecessary fire. The house seemed hollowly enormous, full of the ticking of clocks, and drugged with the scent from bowls of jonquils and daffodils, of which there were archipelagos in garden and orchard. Enter mother, with a plate of cracknels which, at that stage, I doted on. I was reading *A Tale of Two Cities*. Mother began plumping cushions like someone at the opening of a saucy comedy-drama.

"Aunt Willy," she said, "will be here in a couple of hours."

I knew this. I was not really listening to mother who was, the years had taught me, inclined to prattle on. It is very early in life that the male learns to cast his eyes to heaven, and resignedly think, "Women!" in a particular tone.

"She is bringing," said mother, placing her hot hand on my cool forehead to find if it were hot, "her little girl with her, little Gretel."

I didn't know, neither did I care, that Aunt Willy had a daughter. If anything it was a black mark. I was not up to daughters.

"You won't be able to play with her. She's not—she's not very strong."

I went on dropping cracknel crumbs on Miss Pross and Madame Defarge, and wishing mother in Timbuctoo. How much more satisfactory than she were the women of fiction!

"She must have absolute rest and quiet. I'm putting her in Richard's room."

My fourteen-year-old brother Richard's room was at the back of the house, beyond the moth-eaten green baize door that vilely squawked each time it was swung, and separated the kitchen, the breakfast-room, the pantry and the laundry from the front of the house. It had no fire-place, as all the other bedrooms did, and must once have been a store-room. Its only window was a barred skylight.

"You must not go down there while Gretel is here. You must keep right away from the room. Never go down there. Never. Not on any account. Do you hear me, Marcus?"

Oh yes, now I heard her. Mother had gone too far. We occupy, all of us, our own five-walled tower of senses. The throne in the central chamber is the throne of intuition, so often the snoozing one. Now the slug-a-bed was as wide awake as a fish. Did I hear mother?

"Yes," I said, pseudo-laconic. Next, choosing my time, and adopting an over-the-hills-and-far-away expression, I raised my eyes. Mother was indubitably up to something.

"What did I say, Marcus?" Mother being off-hand was patently underhand.

Not only was I more fly than mother, my intuition was less mossy. "That I was not to disturb the little girl," I said with perfectly pitched vagueness. For better measure in guile, "I *love* cracknels," I gushed, and lowered my false eyes to eighteenth-century Paris. Mother left the room with the air of one who has thrown the cover over the canary's cage.

By the time the cab arrived from the station I was well into my act of decorous invalid engrossed in good book, but my body was as open-pored as a sponge, with every pore an eye, every nerve an ear. I heard mother run along the corridor to the front door, and her high heels on the veranda tiles, on the slate of the veranda steps, on the asphalt path. I heard voices in a blurred zigzag of greetings, and attended to the last details of the indifference I was preparing to display to the apparently sacred Gretel I was now feverish to examine. Time passed. Time passed. Suddenly, I was shocked to realize that I was listening to nothing. I tried to convince myself that they were still in the garden, or that mother was pointing out the blossoming fruit trees in the orchard. This was too unlikely; plants and trees were not a thing with mother. Then, it became obvious that they were in the house without having passed my glass-panelled door. I think I gritted and ground my teeth.

After ever, I heard the baize door squawking, and the female tinkle of a congested tea-tray, and a lucid—too lucid—conversation, like a rehearsed duologue, being perpetrated by mother and Aunt Willy. When they came in, the two only of them, talking and stepping as though avoiding the ears and toes of an irritable deity, it was clear that I had been—my mind mouthed the word within me—outwitted.

Aunt Willy kissed me, told me how I had grown, made the right remarks about my wrist, and fiddled with the *chou* of ninon under her chin as though it concealed a cut throat. Mother poured tea full of grouts, for she had not brought the strainer. I watched them, more through the staring eyes of the enthroned one in the innermost chamber than through my actual ones. Aunt Willy had been in tears. Her eyelashes were still moistened into spikes. She and mother bartered remarks in a way-up-yonder manner clearer than crystal, yet informed with wariness. They seemed, too, as women do when supporting a secret and painful burden, to level out their gaze, and to tilt their heads backwards with a nobility that suggested males were shell-less amateurs who, at one and the same time, were to be protected from earthy truths, and wearily despised. It was not until I had fully absorbed the nature of these social gymnastics, and had decided them deceitful, that mother handed a last-minute lie to me, "Gretel was very, *very* tired. Aunt Willy put her straight to bed."

The more reckless and impertinent I wished to say, "If she were so very, *very* tired, why didn't you come down the corridor? Why didn't you come in the short and easy way, instead of the long, awkward way around by the back door?"

This, I knew, would get me nowhere, so, instead: "I'm sorry. I hope she's soon better, Aunt Willy."

"Oh, yes," she said. "Thank you, Marcus. Yes. Yes, soon."

She put down her cup and saucer, and walked to the window. I gammoned not to see her dab at her eyes. I reached for another cracknel, and returned to Paris. Mother was too charming and honest not to tell lies. Only the careless and cruel, the inhuman and dishonest, will not lie. I had been pig-rooted from the horse, and stranded on what mother had planned as a private beach. For some reason Gretel was as forbidden as murder. This had been unmistakably borne in on me.

I was, therefore, determined to see her.

I did not have a leper's chance. Did I get beyond the baize door, Aunt Willy or mother was always a sword's length away, suddenly materialized, finger on lips, with the opaque admonishing glare of a statue. Belonging, as I did, to a more civilized generation, I asked no questions and was told, therefore, none of the lies children should be told. I was compelled out of the house. I would hear mother at the telephone, and, immediately after, would be told that one of The Gels had asked me to dinner with little Johnny, or that another was sending her twins to take me for a walk. Mother's machinations, indubitably.

If I did not see the mysterious stranger, I did, at last, after four days, hear her.

It was a night of such unblemished moonlight that the air seemed volted, as though some arctic dynamo fed it with electrical fluid. On the opposite slope of the valley the lunatic asylum was more mathematically three-dimensional, more toylike and enlivened with detail than ever in daylight. At some nameless hour I was awakened by a high sweet wailing that lifted and sank, lifted and sank, with such regularity that the eye in my ear saw the sound as an undulating line of incandescence. The moon! I thought. It is the moon calling out. Yet I knew it was Gretel. I heard the thump and patter of the bare feet of the two women, the sound of doors, and fervent murmurings, and of a spoon stirring liquid in a tumbler. Presently, the line of sound faltered, thinned, faded from the air. The house pulsed and purred, seemed almost to simmer under the vibrations from the moon. Before I fell asleep to this soothing sensation, I was more determined than ever to glimpse, at least, the girl lying in the moonlight that rippled through the skylight of the last room in the secret-hidden house.

The opportunity came next afternoon. Mother telephoned the cab for Aunt Willy who was dressed more sternly than I had ever seen her. No ninon, no transparent sleeves, no vaporous dress alive with a design of smudged and outsize roses. Her silver fox furs and eye-veil did little to feminize her outfit of sombre metallic cloth and her metallic casque of hat. Even her scent had a steely sharpness. She was going "out": I expected to be told no more, and was told no more. She walked down the path as though sleep-walking, as though drugged for some sinister assignation with High Powers in dark spectacles. I watched mother walk with her to the gate at the end of the garden, and talk with her by the cab-step while the horse tugged at the grass on the edge of the footpath. The cab drove off.

As mother was closing the gate, old Miss Stanway appeared, hobbling and hoo-hoo-ing. Miss Stanway was inescapable. Mother was trapped. I did not hesitate. With the speed of a death-adder I moved between the oak hall-chairs and serene trysts by Marcus Stone down the long passage leading to knowledge. The baize door uttered, and swung to behind me. I came to the last room. I stopped. The training of years, which forbade one to assault a privacy, disobey one's mother, or pry behind the manifest affliction of another, stayed me. Memory is more brutal than will: I remembered the moon's voice soaring through the high-ceilinged rooms of night. I saw my sinful hand float upwards, crook its knuckles, and knock. Immediately, the silence behind the painted panels changed its quality, thickened to a silence one could listen to, and which listened back at one. The hand knocked again, more loudly and sinfully.

"I am here. I am here. I am here." It was a voice that lifted a little, and sank a little, like shallow water.

I was astounded to hear my own voice saying, "I am here. I am Marcus. May I come in?"

"I am here," said the voice within.

I turned the handle. The door was locked. This horrified me. Doors in the country were not locked except in the most unorthodox circumstances. Inside doors were never locked. The handle of a large iron key I had never seen before protruded from the brass-rimmed keyhole. I turned it. I opened the door. I fell in love.

Seated with upright but graceful decorum on a low armless cedar chair was the most exquisite being I had, or have since, seen. It was a girl of my age. Her dress was of yellow velvet, the immediate yellow of a sunflower. Her long straight hair, in an era when all hair seemed clipped or cropped, curled or marcelled, was to me the miracle of the miracle. It fell like a shawl of light over her shoulders. It was the hair of Rapunzel, of all immolated princesses, of all the children lost in the snow or woods of ballads. Her hands and arms and face were whiteness without name. Above her head, on the barred skylight, lay fallen petals of almond blossom. How grey their white. On the girl's lap sat a large doll dressed as she was. It wore a necklace of white beads.

With dark eyes, behind the surface of which were extra shadows, she watched me watching her. She did not move. Then, at last, her lips moved.

"I am Gretel," she said.

I told her again that I was Marcus.

"I am Gretel. She is Gretel." She touched the doll's flaxen poll.

"A good idea," I said. "And dressed like you! But she has beads." I remembered my manners. "I'm sorry you've been sick. How soon will you be better?"

She did not answer, but continued to look at me, as I did at her. My love could find no words. Then inspiration came. I remembered that, among a handful of necklaces tossed to my sisters by mother, there was a white china one. "I have a present for you," I said. How else express love, at twelve? How else at ninety, or ever? "I'll get it. I'll be back." Although blinded, I was wide awake to the need for chicanery. I locked the door. If mother should escape Miss Stanway before I had decorated my idol with stolen gewgaws, the sin of disobedience would not be discovered. I ran to the front veranda. Mother was still enmeshed in Miss Stanway's tough net of scandal. I stole the white necklace. I returned to the last room.

Gretel and Gretel sat as when I had first seen them, beneath the skylight ruled across by bars, and littered with the petals of spring. I held up the necklace, and smiled and smiled like a dog.

And she smiled.

There are no words to describe how this addition of beauty to a beauty already overwhelming affected me. From that ridge higher than paradise, from that moment, began my journey down through seedy and seedier elsewheres. For a moment only I walked the dazzling tightrope. Slipping my hand from its sling, I advanced, and slid both hands under the cool streams of hair. I fumbled with the clasp. It took an eternity during which I imagined my mother's heels coming to the baize door. At last, the clasp snibbed. I stepped back. During my clumsy work the loop of the necklace had slipped behind the front of the yellow dress. For a moment longer her smile remained. Then she arched her neck to see her gift. Before I could speak, her face writhed and darkened. The doll fell as her hands rose to cover her eyes.

"It's under the dress!" I cried. "Under the dress!"

It meant nothing. She was wailing as I had heard her wail in the night. No longer did the sound seem to me ravishing and luminous. I spoke in anguish against its inexorable regularity so much stronger than my fractured words. I backed from it. I locked the door. I hurried from the house, terrified. Mother was still at the front gate. When I had fought my public mask into place, I walked, with the right seasoning of calm, towards her. As one performing a tiresome duty, I said, "Mother, I think that little girl wants something. She's calling out."

Mother ran.

I stayed in the garden expecting . . . expecting what? I could still hear the unfaltering wordless chant in the hollow house. I went for a long walk, mindlessly and slowly, under the trees of the switchback streets. At twilight, I returned. Several of The Gels and mother were, it was immediately apparent, merry. The Victrola was playing *The Naughty Waltz.* All the lights in the house were on.

"Where *have* you been?" cried mother in her fly-away sherry voice. "Aunt Willy wanted to say goodbye to you." No mention of Gretel. I walked down the corridor. The door of the final room was open; the low armless chair was empty.

Mother's funeral over, my obligations to the womb are fulfilled: the last, the very last of all obligations. I have none now, to anyone, least of all to myself. Tomorrow, I shall catch the train out of this town, these foothills, over the mountains, and down to Melbourne, down to the terminus. After the terminus, where next, Marcus? I do not know. Here, now, in the old house, my sisters' "common sense" importunities to return in one of their cars prevent me from thinking a decision. If they and my brother Richard, the bores and the bore, do not stop trying to "reason" with me, I shall be forced to come up with the truth rather than the facts.

"No," I keep on saying. "You are all terribly kind, but no. I don't want a lift. I'd rather go by train. Really. I prefer the train. Thank you, no."

The facts are that I do prefer train travel, and that I am going by train. The truth is that my tastes are stronger than flesh and blood: I should rather be bored by my own self-sufficiency than by them. While I do not cavil, ever, at events, I can be made peevish to the point of mayhem by the aftermath of events. *This* aftermath is treacherous. The brothers and sisters I parted from as young people are not the people I am with now; they usurp the names of phantoms.

Here we are in the drawing-room with its french windows open on to the tiled veranda. The horizontal granite door has closed. The rain has been removed like a device that has served its purpose.

Here we all are, the children, middle-aged, yet bickering and needling like children. Here are some of The Gels, touched by their own winters; three or four authentic uncles and aunts with the frost on them; several of those adopted aunts who were always popping skittishly in and out of our childhoods.

"Where," I say to shut up my most persistently "common sense" sister, "is Aunt Willy?"

"She's gone to see Gretel." She says it as though saying nothing much of no one much, and sips at her brandy. "Aunt Willy's an absurd old thing. No self-control. But she might as well grab the opportunity to see Gretel while she's here for the funeral."

"Yes, of course," I say, without knowing what it means. I now arrange a sentence with some care: "Aunt Willy's seeing Gretel right now?"

"Why not? She drives up to see her every week. Done it for years and years. She used to spend the night here with mother."

Once again I have to think out a sentence: "So Gretel's still here?"

"Still here. There was talk of her going to Melbourne about eight or nine years ago. But it fell through. When I was up here last time Aunt Willy was too. So I went with her to see Gretel. She must be touching fifty now. . . ."

"Forty-four or forty-five," I say.

"Perhaps. She looks eighty. Long grey hair hanging down.

You can see her window from here. The top one in the tower on the right."

She points through the french windows, across the valley, to the Cape Dutch barracks, and the sharp-cut garden beds, and the high wall, exposed like a medieval painting on the opposite slope.

My sister drains her glass. "Get me another brandy, will you? I do wish you'd be sensible, and come down in the car with us tonight."

"What does she look like?"

"Who look like? Oh, Gretel. Really, Marcus, you're a ghoul. Just like any loony. Sits there year after year with a grubby old doll on her lap. Quite harmless, unless they try to take the doll. Or Gretel's necklace. She keeps on stroking these white china beads, and grinning like a . . . like a . . ."

(1963)

The House on the Hill

When, after twenty years, Perrot returned to Japan on a six months' sketching tour, he was braced for its transformation, for near-skyscrapers instead of *après-guerre* ruins, for near-arrogance rather than *après-guerre* mock-humility. He had thoroughly warned himself to expect to have to put up with more than much. Having arrived, he was put out to find that not only were his own warnings too mild but that, although he had been also warned by others about the high cost of living, he had been neither trenchantly nor precisely enough warned.

Some of his advisers had been too young and piratical to understand his old-fashioned idea of what was comfort and civilization to a Perrot pickled half a century in the sweet-and-sour vinegar of the world. Not a Roman, he was unwilling, utterly, except when cornered, to do as Rome does. Other advisers had been gadabout expense-account men with a taste for strip-tease, Châteaubriand fillets, and black label Johnny Walker, and had little feeling for the lesser banknotes, none at all for mere silver. Still other know-alls had been exiles of such long standing that their points of view could be nothing but suspect. Their palates, for example, had undergone a sea-change so extravagant that they pined for wafers of raw fish sliced from the living creature, for squid, laver, shell-ligament, and seaweed, and had become orientalized to the point where they were content, even when not forced to, to sleep between eider-downs on the floor rather than in a quadruped bed.

If none of the advice had been insincere it had been, nevertheless, insouciant, vaporous, coreless, and curiously unrelated to his special requirements. No one, for example, had pointed out that a bottle of Scotch cost as much as the cosmetic surgery to aquilinize a button nose, that a pound of steak cost more than an abortion, or that the *pied-à-terre* he hoped easily to get at a moderate rental was impossible to get at even a lunatically immoderate one. During the first three weeks in Tokyo, therefore, he paid through the nose for hotel accommodation at one and the same time copy-cat American and irritatingly Japanese, on the one hand for inescapable Muzak, suffocating central-heating, and slices of orange with his poached egg, on the other for lilac-tinted plastic baths too short to lie down in, bath-sandals someone else had worn, and door-handles, electric-light switches, and taps which, as though subject to the natural law governing the corkscrew of tendrils north of the equator, all worked the other way.

Throughout these three weeks he came to see that he could ultimately be in a financial plight as well as uncomfortable without a base to work in and from, a place to leave gear and clothing in when he travelled with sketch-book and toothbrush into the hinterland, a place to put his feet inexpensively up in when the rigours of hydroplanes, mountain trains, rustic buses, and whiffy hostelries in remote villages became too wearing. Consequently, at the embassy cocktail parties and expatriate get-togethers, which his mild fame laid him open to being bidden to, he employed guile. As he was handed about like a dish of asparagus rolls, he lavishly dropped, right and left, self-mocking hints of his possible downfall.

In just which mood these calculated and strategic communiqués were talked over and passed on he could not guess, and did not care, but talked over and passed on they must have been. One night, at yet another of the continual semi-embassy gatherings, and while its polyglot guests—Russians, Pakistanis, Swedes, New Zealanders, Arabs, Iranians, Canadians—were tipsily playing charades, he was offered what sounded like the *pied-à-terre* he could have dreamed of. The offer was made by the wife of a public-relations man, Australian. They and their children were going to Australia for four months. Their house, and its three Japanese *au pair* girls, university students living in as part-time maid-servants, were, the wife hypnotically insisted, at Perrot's disposal.

Since, after an acquaintance of only three or four encounters, he had come to look on her as the sort of affected and garrulous crank not to be trapped in a corner by at a party, a woman with a glittering eye who was always dressed like an actress who had slept in her finery, who was a mistress of forcefully presented platitude and, like a child, preferred myths and objects to all persons except herself, he could scarcely believe his ears. He suffered no illusion that it was the husband, a kindly bear of a toper, who had conceived the invitation. The wife indubitably had, and for some cryptic, fey, even underhand reason of her own. To have Perrot keep an eye, however intermittent, on the servant-students? To have him pay the household bills for four months? To boast in after days that the fashionable artist, one of her myths or objects, had used her guest-room and electric blankets and steam-heated bathroom? Wary though he was of one whose bite he suspected of being worse than her bark, Perrot disregarded his instinct's almost occult but none the less visible *Beware—Stop, Look, Listen*, and accepted with an alacrity which, howsoever unseemly, appeared to multiply on the instant the woman's flattering reflections of herself in the looking-glass of her own opinion. When, several days later, she and her husband and children flew southward, Perrot was already installed in a large upstairs bedroom with heavily barred windows, a strange note of iron and prison.

The house was a quasi-folly, Western, *circa* 1912, brick, in an ex-fashionable but still far from unfashionable suburb of Tokyo, a hilltop suburb which was given a nearly countrified air by the nearby presence of Meiji Garden with its valley of irises, its turf as brilliantly green as window-dresser's grass, and its ceaselessly complaining ravens, by the Tokyo Riding Club, by the groves of gingko trees and camphor laurels, leading to the ubiquitous temples of Hachiman the War God, and by the demi-Western outbursts of April-green oaks and elms in the grounds of minor legations—Uruguay, Vietnam, Portugal, Turkey, Israel. This relatively bucolic area was ringed about by a mesa-and-butte horizon of office blocks, department stores, glassy factories, and scores of Meccano-like towers. At each day's end chemically gorgeous sunsets flared up beyond them to be replaced, each night, by the topless coal-blue cliffs of night and the hideous splendour of twitching and feverish neon advertisements.

That all upstairs windows were barred, and no ground-floor ones, exercised Perrot's curiosity, and seemed to him mysteriously captious, a whim deliberately illogical. All the rooms were large, exaggeratedly Western, panelled high in oakish timber like Pinero stage settings, and from plaster-of-Paris cartwheels of pomegranates and acanthus in the centre of remote ceilings *art nouveau* copper electroliers grew downward toward the parquet with their burden of opalescent glass shades as fluted and frilled as jungle lilies. Those Japanese, wealthy and upstart, who had, thirty and forty and fifty years before, sat disloyally on imitation Queen Anne chairs to nibble Huntley and Palmer biscuits and sip Twining's tea from cups with handles, had left the miasmata of their queerness and nullness to thicken slightly the colours of the ingle-nook lead-lights, to blur the crab-shaped designs on the brocaded wallpaper above the panellings, to tarnish the pelmets over the embrasures of bow-windows through the sea-green diamond panes of which European shrubs, local hybrid roses, and smudges of Korean grass had once attempted to reproduce a St John's Wood garden and lawn.

The place was a vault of other Aprils, false and foreign ones, other Februaries stranger than February, other November rains, other forms of snow and jealousy and gentility, other tones of life. On windy evenings the drain-pipes and rain-gutters wailed Japanese-English and Japanese-French clauses filched from the trifling soirées of decades ago, soirées at which seal-eyed and silly women sat on settees of Utrecht velvet, the hems of their chiffon skirts just touching, and exchanged glances charged with mortality and deadly silence, even though their plump lips emitted a trivial din of liquid twitterings and electrocuting gossip to fill in the unfillable hours. They guessed and acted out what they dared not attempt to prove while, in the grates of chimney-pieces crowded with abominable occidental *bibelots*, fluttered fires that, feeding on the wrong wood and un-English coals, could never ever have been Western.

To Perrot, all these now-fireless fireplaces, not one correctly baptized by *European-Labour-Only* flames, revealed their startling falsity. So did the rest of the house. It had been designed and built less to live in than to act out a borrowed life in. The swastika-form corridors attaching room to room were darkling with incorrect answers and errors of comprehension, and lined with deep and lofty presses where, once upon a time, the garments of another civilization—whalebone stays, camisoles, sixteen-button kid gloves, petticoats of *broderie anglaise*, tea gowns, osprey-feathered toques, afternoon gowns of Swiss voile—had been unjustly imprisoned before and after being unjustly paraded like fancy dress on unsuitable bodies.

The pre-World-War-I nursery, still used as such by the absent public-relations man's also-absent boys and girls, was neatly littered with their playthings: Pandas with nylon hides, plastic dolls simpering away in plastic perambulators, a rocking-horse streamlined as a gazelle, gaudy death-ray and space guns of a Venusian cast. On the upper wall of this Darling-family nursery built for Japanese children with contusion-blue Mongolian spots at the bases of their spines, there remained a mural of ghost-pale Kate Greenaway children, all wearing the chicory-azure and circular eyes of imbeciles, all occupied in acts of spoliation or unintellectuality: ravishing plots of bluebells and buttercups, harrying fairies and dragon-flies, manhandling beribboned lambs, goading frogs with bulrushes, decherrying cherry-trees, and depetalling daisies.

The house, despite its amenities, could never, with its overwhelming atmosphere of miscarried intention, succeed in making even the happy-go-lucky think of nothing, and wholly relax. Not only were the solid Anglo-alien rooms permeated by misconceptions and old mischiefs but, every now and then, teacups vibrated like larger ear-rings on their hooks, pale dust as fine as talcum powder sifted down from cornices, or a heavy six-panelled door opened of itself to admit the guest no one could deny when the suburban hill gave one of its galvanic earthquake shudders as though a Belial turned in his subterrane sleep. For the rest, no matter who went out of or into it however many times, the house behind its high granite walls and burly maples was hermetic in quality. The inner wills of dead ex-owners, and the mindless knowledge locked up in brick and stone and tiles and lath-and-plaster, seemed to intimate that nothing of value lay outside the ponderous wooden gate, quite as high as a stockade one, with a smaller gate set in it; that the world came to an end just there; that there were no tideways of cars on the soaring over-passes, no fleets of ambulances ceaselessly keening as they tore doomward, no flesh-and-blood lava flow of crop-eared or long-haired millions, no arteries of crowds pushing forward with the psychic oneness of animals.

The house was both empty and haunted. It would never be filled if filled to the ridge-piece. No crowd could crowd out its phantoms, and certainly not Perrot and the three servant-students.

Their quarters lay, with kitchen and scullery, pantry and laundry, sewing-room and boiler-room, in a wing beyond the two-storey Western part of the house. As though the entrances to the one-storey wing were for a socially stunted, troglodyte breed, the lintels of the doors were a couple of feet lower, the doors themselves narrower and flimsier than elsewhere in the building. No aspect of the house was not part of some subtle calculation, some expression of eccentricity and caste difference.

Behind these specifying doors the three young women, the disease of adolescence still in their bones, lived or made a pretence of living like conventional natives. They used a hole-in-the-floor lavatory, poached themselves nightly in a barrel-like wooden bath, slept on floors of padded matting with the rice-paper shutters slid air-proof together and, although schoolgirlishly addicted to wolfing the ersatz bread, caramels, condensed milk, and apricot-laden and sickly *gâteaux* of the Harajuku Foodliner Supermarket, mainly sustained their imperfections on what appeared to Perrot to be the diet of an albatross, on food that smelt like a fishing cove at low tide.

To his irritation he immediately found the three students, and particularly the dominating one called Yukiko, distasteful. He was irritated because his interest in the natives was less than little, and he had proposed that it was to remain so. He had not come back to Japan to mingle with the inhabitants, but merely to sketch its grotesque native buildings, its sorry attempts at the Architecture of the Future, and what was left of its landscapes. Last of all things did he wish to have ruffled his indifference to the beings infesting the scene.

At the first meeting with Yukiko, however, he knew that indifference was not going to be permitted. She would demand to be experienced, to be always seen. To her, no doubt whatever, not to be seen was not to be.

Called by his hostess in a fictitiously forthright voice, Yukiko had appeared in the frame of a shorter door leading to the region of shorter doors and lower ceilings. As she stopped, the two others, gliding along after her like a servant's servants, one behind each of her shoulders, stopped too.

"Yukiko-san," said the hostess, being very much the mistress of the house, "I have spoken to you of Mr Perrot, our well-known Australian artist. He will be coming and going while we are away, but will nevertheless be in charge as well as being an honoured guest. I know that I can trust you girls to show him that . . ."

As she went on and on with what sounded like a planned homily Perrot watched the three, and an ether rose from his bottom mind. The yapping mistress was, he saw, no more to them than a refugee from a boorish tribe, a rich savage to be suffered only because she served a purpose. Her uncouth insolence was being recorded behind the untenanted masks the trio presented to her.

Yukiko, not at all tall, was taller than the other two as the central figure of a chiselled triumvirate is taller than its supporters. Hers was the central head of a triple-headed deity: she regarded the two fly-by-night Australians with the inhuman tact and dark patience of an arbiter. Her boldness had the thick bloom of non-innocence, and stood more nakedly and imperially out against the dependent boldness of the others, which was a little veiled by dulcified slyness: had her eyes under their waxen hoods been pale instead of inky, the look she directed assessingly at him would have been ice-clear, ice-cold.

In it he thought to see that his decades of living had not been a preparation only for the reward and relaxation of a decline toward death, but for some tiresome and, maybe, terrible lesson. He was not just a barbarian from the unmentionable. He was a nuisance, a spy, an alien deputy to quell the hi-jinks of mice playing while the cat's away. He was to be Yukiko's hateful immediate future. It was at him she looked, as though she knew what happened to women who looked back at flaming cities, at Sodoms and Gomorrahs, or Hiroshimas and Nagasakis, instead of toward her religion's Third Civilization and One-Worldism. The portals to less fanatic futures were wide open, but she turned a Jesuit's nape on them just as, being ugly, not having the ingredients for comeliness, she turned her back on any thought of attempting to subdue homeliness.

She was fat, but not pneumatically or succulently so. The sleeveless dress she wore, an eye-mortifying shift of man-made fibres, left on display, like an advertisement for shamelessness or defiance, great bare arms and legs, which, although rounded and smooth as if muscleless, yet had the undentable solidity of muscles, of time-jaundiced ivory. The moon of her face, flat, gibbously lop-sided, masked every shade of will from paltry contrariness to arrant ruthlessness, and over this mask the fibres of her hair hung like a shredded black caul. The general effect was, however, moral, rebuking. She stood with her blunt feet planted apart like those of the wardress of an asylum for boobs, dupes, and simpletons.

Because of earlier experiences in Japan, it was easy for Perrot, on his first meeting with Yukiko, not only to sense but absolutely, he thought, to recognize the intelligent wickedness and inexorability which her tediously didactic mistress, a woman herself wicked and inexorable enough, albeit unintelligently, seemed not to notice at all. Twenty years back he had lived the institution life of an Occupation Army officer, each officer quartered in a commodious cell crammed with appalling and luxurious furniture, each officer tended by his own house-girl, who regarded her charge alternately with the absent-minded sorrow of a begging monkey and the contempt of one who knows that she is not a mere post-war diversion, a skivvy and a sock-darner, but a creature of divine descent who has floated down on a different and superior tributary of the current of time from the impure streamlet which has rolled the hairy barbarian into her orbit. Outside her special gifts for mendacity and double-dealing, and the unknown quality of them, Yukiko was no news to Perrot. His eyes had been opened long ago.

Left alone with Yukiko and her minions, he kept his eyes open. He would much have preferred a situation where he did not, so consistently and consciously, have to keep them open, skinned for social contretemps to side-step, always on the watch for menial touchiness to be delicately skirted. He would have relished not having to consider Yukiko's claustrophobic ego any longer or ever again. He realized, however, that the farce of polite deceit, the daily walking on asp's eggs was, in such a house and household, the particular over-and-above price due for the convenience of an out-of-the-blue *pied-à-terre.*

Whenever he stayed in to tinker with sketches in the upstairs study, his activity or mild sloth was, from down below, from other rooms, tuned into with an exclusiveness of attention so finely pitched that, no matter the domestic din echoing hollowly in stairwell and hallway and vestibule, it could pick up the minutest move or blankest silence from only one direction: his. Awake or asleep, busy or still, present or absent, it was always as if he sinned against the harmony of the universe: his very absences in other cities, at temples mouldering away deep in the clefts of mist-drowned alps, at fishermen's shrines strung along the rim of greasy seas cumbered with kelp and Lalique-coloured jellyfish were nothing to Yukiko but preludes to his undesirable reappearances.

To keep some sort of faith with the absent hostess and his own idea of fit behaviour he always sent a warning telegram before turning up after one of his sketching forays, and arrived to find everything invariably ship-shape: fresh sprays of leaves and meagre buds surgically clipped and wired to rigidity in china troughs; the encaustic tiles of the porch floor scoured; Australian butter in the refrigerator; the soda siphon newly charged; the grandfather clock in the drawing-room enthusiastically mincing time away as if just resurrected, just wound. All was as it would be when the mistress returned; he imagined that none of it was for him as himself but for him as the mistress's spy. No one greeted him at an open front door yet, when he opened it with his own key, there, under the archway out of the hall, in the green dusk, stood the trinity, Yukiko in the van, with something stealthy and disdainful on its faces—a smile—not a smile—an equivocal expression of barely polite resignation. She—for the three were always, to him, she—she stared towards him rather than at him, as toward an ectoplasmic nastiness lacking outline or humanity.

He fancied that some part, at least, of the adolescent and old-hat attempt to make him feel like a gormless tourist who has missed the last train was because to have to keep the house trimmed for an unforeseen interloper interfered with the study of Henry James's qualified qualifications and Guy de Maupassant's idiomatic cynicism. It also hampered the vehemence, the concentrations of an entire being, needed to fulfil their obligations as germ-sowers of the Value-Creating Religion they were obsessed by. Perrot, therefore, attempted self-effacement. Pretending not to notice their moodiness, he remained outwardly amiable, made a minimum of demands, and was, all in all, no bother at all. Nothing worked.

He knew he would have to jettison at least one sense, some moral perception, to get anywhere, to meet them in a sort of collusion of the blind. He saw them as creatures who had limped out of the tangles and shadows of a history gaudy with treacheries, and who preserved in their blood-stream the tangles and shadows, the menacing glow of treachery. Although they looked solely to the future, past phases of behaviour larded their daydream. What had been committed by their ancestors, by emperors as depraved as Nero, by warrior heroes with the morals of Nelson, by bloodthirsty Buddhist abbots as mad as Nebuchadnezzar, was only a shade of what they, and millions as young as they, were in training to commit. The scale of their desires was colossal, and insane.

Perrot could do nothing, and did nothing, but feign to notice nothing. Above all he was, as the weeks passed, careful not to jab a careless finger through the flimsy fabric of sham tranquillity behind which he sensed a watchful Nemesis, fangs bare and ready. He came and went, circumspectly placid, noticing sidelong how, after each absence, everything more and more had the air of objects in Tutankhamen's tomb—the rows of too-fashionable American shoes in his hostess's dressing-room; the racks of the host's loud suits run up by escapee tailors from Red China; the inherited silver-backed brushes rearing up on their desiccated bristles on the tops of tallboys and dressing-tables; the shelves of books seemingly glued together by some secretion of disuse; the glass-fronted drink-cupboard with extraordinary liqueurs arranged like a parvenu-tempting display in a wine merchant's. The total of rooms, like a total of chambers crammed with mortuary offerings and deadman's furniture, increasingly had the atmosphere of an actual tomb.

One evening, a couple of weeks before the family was expected back, he returned from sketching a series of fake mediaeval castles to find the atmosphere far otherwise. The stockade gate was thrown open; several small cars and motor-cycles stood in the drive; the house was as lit up as a casino. He was unaware that he was unannounced: the postman brought his belated telegram the next day. By then the damage had been done; he had made, so near the finishing-tape, the kind of social blunder that any Japanese would find humiliating enough but which Yukiko, exposed in the midst of an unsanctioned spree with her co-religionists, would find so devastating that nothing less than suicide or revenge could restore her lost face.

As Perrot walked up the drive he thought, at first, that his host and hostess were already back from Australia: a Mantovani record he knew they were addicted to poured out its treacle. He saw through the mullioned bay-windows, however, that the score of young people who vivaciously milled about under the electroliers, gabbling, laughing, drinking, were all Japanese, and that Yukiko, more than preposterous in a dress of pulsating tangerine, was pouring herself with the lavishness of ignorance a tumbler of some liqueur—Danziger Goldwasser? —at the buffet.

He stopped in his tracks. The situation had become a touchy one. Should he trail back to the beer-hall near the railway station and, filling in time there until the party must have ended, thus avoid being known to know that these mice were at play? Or should he try slipping like an invisible man across the hall and upstairs to the shower and early night in bed he needed? Fatigue made the decision. He advanced discreetly as a criminal into the house which was, in every respect, and more than he had stopped to think to bargain for, an open one. The baronial double doors from hallway to drawing-room were, alas, flung wide. Any chance of crossing the hall unseen was minute; hope of invisibility there was none. Whoever it was saw him first—was it Yukiko as she turned away from the buffet with her downfall-brimmed tumbler?—communicated the shock by a telepathy so instant that even those with their backs to him stiffened in mid-gesture, were struck silent in mid-word. The shock of his presence seemed also to gorgonize the radiogram: Mantovani's syrup of melody dried abruptly out of the air, leaving a silence into which Perrot, himself transfixed in the light-brimmed hall, heard his voice dealing out, as best it could, hearty snippets of courtesy:

"Hel*lo*, there, Yukiko-san! I'm off up to bed. *Ter*ribly tired. But not to worry. Go on having a good time. *Nothing's* going to keep me awake."

He was indicating that he was not a family pimp or a spoil-sport, nor discomposed by the revelry of adherents to the Value-Creating Religion. Next, with an extra try at paternal jocularity, he said ha-ha-ha-ishly, "You'd better not drink all that liqueur, young woman, or you'll be a very sick young woman."

He knew, just not in time, that he was uttering the sentence too many. Born to evangelize for the Third Civilization of her religion, born to repulse any form of foreigner's behaviour smacking of forbearance, Yukiko directed venom at him through the black strings of her hair, executed a sudden up-the-scale laugh of derision, and, like a movie actress portraying Defiant Wantonness, raised the tumbler to her lips and gulped it empty.

Je-e-e-sus! All that Danziger Goldwasser! Good *night!* he thought, and nearly said.

"Good night," he said, and moved towards the stairs.

Halfway up them he heard the unmistakable and unmusical sound of her being sick, and knew that this over-punctuality in the fulfilment of his prediction would intensify Yukiko's loss of face. A careless warning had taken on the nature of an effective curse, and, as a curse, it would boomerang back to him.

Under the shower, cut off by its world-erasing noise and soothing caress from the complexities of downstairs, he was none the less aware of a subsidence of life in the house. By the time he had finished showering the house was again a tomb. Music, vivacity, laughter, all were gone, and gone, too, all the fanatic and youthful visitors dressed as Westerners, almost behaving as Westerners, but thinking like Japanese. Through the bars of the bedroom window he looked down on an empty drive-way, the closed stockade gate. All lights but his own seemed to be doused. The house was awash with darkness, and its tide seethed with underwater emotions.

Perrot took two sleeping-tablets: it promised to be an ugly-coloured tomorrow.

When he came downstairs next morning, carefully prepared to behave as though nothing had happened, he saw through one of the shorter and narrower doors into the board-floored corridor of the servants' quarters. Yukiko and the other two were, in the normal way, at work on it, walking on all fours, rumps in the air, pads of tea-soaked cloth in their paws, polishing as they progressed dog-like along.

"Good morning, good morning, good morning!" he cried. He might not have cried anything. There was no answer. Bowed over their deep and bitter wounds, molly-coddling their self-pity, their downfalling hair veiling their profiles, they showed no sign that he existed. The drawing-room, the hall, everywhere downstairs, was restored to a luxury sepulchre in which everything was just so, and in which it was unimaginable that, twelve hours before, anyone had been blasphemous enough to play Mantovani, munch dried shrimps, talk One-Worldism, or vomit Danziger Goldwasser. The only stayer-on from what he and the immaculate rooms were gammoning had never taken place was the heavily grained silence of the trinity. Of this triple silence Yukiko's was darkest. In her own time she would reveal what it hid, what dirk had been honed or what garotter's cord woven in the extinct and hallucinatory small hours.

It turned out to be yet another month before the family came back. During this time Perrot remained in Coventry. Otherwise all was as before: he continued to come and go, alternately to stay for a few days and to travel about for a few days sketching abraded idols or semi-circular bridges or the tombs of scoundrelly heroes and infamous courtesans; the trinity continued to keep the house as burnished as a funeral parlour and, he assumed, to strive with the preciosities and indelicacies of Henry James and T. S. Eliot, Maupassant and Cocteau. Now and then, as he worked in the study, he heard them, out of sight but acoustically near, declaiming in French to each other, or practising on each other the stilted and refined English they spoke most of the time. They were always out of sight, or to be glimpsed, their backs only, hastening pointedly away to an obviously desirable distance from him. When he was about they went into purdah behind the hirelings' lesser doorways. No longer, although still telegram-informed, were they to be discovered, like a piece of municipal statuary, sullenly simulating welcome when he returned jaded with stone lanterns and sacred crags and avant-garde prefectural office buildings.

The more wars, tooth-and-nail or Pole-cold, the more one acquires of the art of the survivor.

Perrot survived the domestic cold war by forgetting, most of the time, how or why it had begun. Only sometimes, in the few minutes between waking and sleeping, it came to him that mere avoidance, unmeeting eyes, and trap-shut lips could surely not be all the retaliation to expect from Yukiko. Unbelievable that she was content with no more than schoolgirlish blackballing, that *she* could for a moment think that it made him suffer or pine: Clytemnestra and Medea were her sisters. He entertained the idea of drawing a Chad on the wall above his bed, and the inscription "Wot, no death-adders!"

Then, at last, the family returned. Perrot had arranged to make one final trip before flying on to London and the agent who was to arrange an exhibition of his work. The hostess said that she would not, simply would *not*, hear of his moving to a hotel for his last ten days in Japan. He was more than welcome to the guest-room. She was honoured to have been able to offer her humble home, and she was grateful that he had kept an eye on it, and on the three girls. Weren't they darlings, so hard-working and clever, so refreshing and sweet? Weren't they? Hadn't he found them willing and sweet?

What else to reply except that, oh yes, of course they were, of *course* he had, oh yes, but definitely.

With tooth-brush and sketch-book, he went away again for four days.

He returned at the fag-end of a superb autumn day, which had just plumped down into a sort of sensuous languor. Nothing is quite trite in autumn. The sky, plum-coloured, had a mature, fleshy texture, the peak of ripeness. Horizontal shafts of light from the setting sun glamorized the chimneys and gables of the house, the fiery summits of the maples, the stockade gate pinned invitingly open like portals to a glowing caravanserai. Something could have sighed tenderly but did not. The mood matched his: day's end, work's end, accomplishment. The front door was also invitingly open.

Invitingly?

He called out, "The wanderer returns! Anyone home?" before he saw, arranged just inside the front door, the barrier of his own suitcases, his golf-bag, umbrella, travelling rug, Burberry. Without hesitation, with certainty, his mind stated, *Yukiko! The death-adders! At last, the death-adders!* Within their deceptive, sunset-bloomed rind the rooms stretched before him and over him, jam-packed with silence, a silence contrived and lying in wait, alert to be broken.

Before he could move again—for he had stopped at the threshold—his hostess stepped from the wings where she had loitered carefully made up and scent-sprinkled and not distraught and, pausing on the other side of the hall, spoke.

Later, when it was all over, he saw that he had not been shocked at all by her accusations. He had found, rather, something disgusting, as one does in another's love-making, in the fact that she was the dupe of a fat Japanese servant. Her opening sentences did strip him as naked as a horse, but after one brief sentence of his own he found himself in a chain-mail of calm, and fascinated by the woman's whispering, for instead of her usual plangent voice she affected a much-diminished one as though unwilling to have it sully the corridors opened all around her.

"Stay just there," she whispered, "just there, Mister Perrot. There is no need for you to come in, because you are leaving this house immediately. Yukiko-san and the girls have packed everything. Everything. I can assure you that we want no mementoes of you left in this house. I've always thought of myself as a broad-minded person, but there are limits. I'll ring for a taxi and you can get out. You know why."

"I don't know why," he said, and that was all he did say.

"Don't know why! You know perfectly well why. I'm certainly not going to soil my lips by telling you why. I'm a woman of the world, but your vile behaviour has certainly sickened me. It's not just that you've abused our hospitality. About that I don't care. It's my own fault for trying to be decent to another Australian. But I do care about Yukiko-san. She's not just a university trollop. She comes from a good samurai family, and is a well-brought-up and sensitive girl with a brilliant career in front of her. Your behaviour was a terrible shock to her, and might well give her some awful trauma. You're beyond contempt. I can see by the expression on your face that you're not a scrap ashamed of what . . ."

As she whispered and hissed, Perrot found himself glancing backward into his own head, into the blaze of darkness the whispering and hissing filled it with, to see if he could find some reason for pity rather than indifference. In the glaring blackness there was none to find. One cannot interrogate or assess another's notion of one's turpitude without knowing, at the very least, how the tarring and feathering has been done. Why it had been done Perrot did think to know but, out of simple curiosity, he would have liked to taste the full flavour, all the flavours of the plot, even in his hostess's clichés. It was not to be.

Presently, regretting that she had to, but pleased with her performance, she came to the end of her tirade and, in the manner of a maharanee ordering a cheap coffin, sibilantly telephoned for a taxi-cab, and retired into the wings. In the twilight Perrot made two trips with his belongings down to the stockade gate, and leaned there, outside it, against the post of the sizzling street-lamp. The earth, circling like a quoit, span second by second deeper into a Nubian and nigger immensity measled by the flicker-flicker of planets unfamiliar to him.

He waited, unwounded though sacrificed, unhumiliated though hounded out, drowsily becalmed in the knowledge that Yukiko's revenge, to her a reality, was in reality no more than an idea, an elaborate sketch in invisible ink. Waiting, back to the house, he felt lights go on behind the mullioned windows, the barred windows, the lead-lights of flamingoes and water-lilies, the slaveys' paper panes, and the whole building to rear up luminous and hollow as Hamlet's father. Next could be heard the piping and squealing of children freed from a cage of silence. The hostess's children? The chicory-blue-eyed vandals of the nursery frieze? Then, finally, just as the taxi-cab came mounting the steep street toward him, the restored voice of the hostess—the ex-hostess—began to call "Yukiko-san! Yukiko-san!" as a guilty pilgrim might over-clearly and too cajolingly call to a goddess sulking equally guilty in the recesses of a shrine.

Who to blame?

The beef-witted pilgrim in her actressy get-up and Helena Rubinstein paints and powders and scents?

The fat goddess with her heavy metallic personality fibred through and through with dangerous nerves?

Perrot and his faux pas?

Or was it the house itself, an influence of haunted masonry, an imitation Hazeldene or Craigholme perched on its hill, from the time of the assassination- and earthquake-riddled reign of the insane Emperor Taisho, like an exotic granary of phantoms, malformed dreams, alien affectations, and the uneasy ardours of expatriates?

Downhill, ahead, far enough off, on a latitude poisoned with envies, a meridian pulsing with guile, lay the city like a jaw full of false teeth. Its breath was loaded day and night with music that those loose from their moorings would not want to hear, molten advertisements and looks they would not want to read, with importunities, malaises, germs, treachery, propaganda, crackpots' visions, with hair-trigger lunacies and primitive immoralities, with everything that affected and infected.

None of this could touch Perrot, not him.

Unscarred by the kiss like a branding-iron that she, Yukiko, hoped to have ground into the very axis of his nerves, Perrot got into the taxi-cab. It started instantly and violently to descend towards the city, towards this magnification of the house he regarded as an island too small to explore. Whatever off-hand exploration he had made he had made blindfolded or swivel-eyed, seeing himself in the outsize and anachronistic pier-glasses only as he ever saw himself—reversed, untouchable behind the cold and crystal surface.

Upstairs, a pallid zoo-beast at the bars of the nursery-window, Yukiko watched the red lights of the coffin disappear. Then only did she let herself hear her mistress calling from the catacombs below.

Pariah always recognizes pariah. She knew the mistress had been as fruitlessly taken with Perrot as she, as perversely avid to punish him as she. Crying out, "I come! I come!" she padded down the stairs. Meeting at its foot, the two women presented to each other the faces they had separately lost but together regained. Each wore a brand-new archaic smile.

Brass would no more have melted in their mouths than it

would have in the fuming mouth of the city which Perrot was, at that moment, entering with an expression of fatigued disdain on the face he could never lose.

(1969)